A DECISION TO REMEMBER

BY
SUE MacKAY

A FATHER THIS CHRISTMAS?

BY
LOUISA HEATON

MILLS &
BOON

With a background of working in medical laboratories, and a love of the romance genre, it is no surprise that **Sue MacKay** writes Mills & Boon Medical Romance stories. An avid reader all her life, she wrote her first story at age eight—about a prince, of course. She lives with her own hero in the beautiful Marlborough Sounds, at the top of New Zealand's South Island, where she indulges her passions for the outdoors, the sea and cycling.

Louisa Heaton first started writing romance at school, and would take her stories in to show her friends, scrawled in a big red binder, with plenty of crossing out. She dreamt of romance herself, and after knowing her husband-to-be for only three weeks shocked her parents by accepting his marriage proposal. After four children—including a set of twins—and fifteen years of trying to get published, she finally received 'The Call'! Now she lives on Hayling Island, and when she's not busy as a First Responder creates her stories wandering along the wonderful Hampshire coastline with her two dogs, muttering to herself and scaring the locals.

Visit Louisa on twitter @louisaheaton, on Facebook Louisaheatonauthor or on her website: louisaheaton.com.

A DECEMBER
TO REMEMBER

BY
SUE MacKAY

MILLS
BOON®

Published in Great Britain 2015
by Mills & Boon, an imprint of Harlequin (UK) Limited,
Eton House, 18-24 Paradise Road, Richmond, Surrey, TW9 1SR

© 2015 Sue MacKay

ISBN: 978-0-263-24745-9

Harlequin (UK) Limited's policy is to use papers that are natural,
renewable and recyclable products and made from wood grown in
sustainable forests. The logging and manufacturing processes conform
to the legal environmental regulations of the country of origin.

Printed and bound in Spain
by CPI, Barcelona

Dear Reader,

Do best friends change into lovers gradually or with a resounding thump? I went with the thump theory! Luca and Ellie haven't seen each other for four years when they meet up by chance at an amputee clinic for children in Vientiane, Laos, and immediately both know their relationship has changed. Is it because of what's gone on in their personal lives over the past years? Or have they woken up to something that might always have been simmering behind their friendship?

Laos is a beautiful country, which I had the opportunity to visit a few years back, and Vientiane is a busy but compact city full of colour and noise that made me smile all the time. The market where Luca and Ellie go shopping also kept *me* busy, buying leather bags and earrings. Then I visited Luang Prabang, where the night market is fabulous and the earrings… Well, I have quite a collection. So I had to send Ellie and Luca there, which is a defining moment in their relationship. They visit the bear sanctuary and ride the elephants—and fall further in love.

I hope you enjoy their journey—the emotional one, that is.

Feel free to drop by and tell me your thoughts on sue.mackay56@yahoo.com or cruise by my site at suemackay.co.nz.

Cheers!

Sue

This one's for Daphne Priest and Diane Passau—
two women I've known most of my life and
with whom I shared many experiences as we grew up.

Thanks for the catch-up lunch
and may we share many more.

Hugs, Sue.

Books by Sue MacKay

Mills & Boon Medical Romance

Doctors to Daddies
A Father for Her Baby
The Midwife's Son

From Duty to Daddy
The Gift of a Child
You, Me and a Family
Christmas with Dr Delicious
Every Boy's Dream Dad
The Dangers of Dating Your Boss
Surgeon in a Wedding Dress
Midwife…to Mum!
Reunited…in Paris!

Visit the Author Profile page
at millsandboon.co.uk for more titles.

CHAPTER ONE

'PHA THAT LUANG,' the jumbo driver said over his shoulder, pointing to a stunning white temple behind high gates with two guards standing to attention outside. On elegantly crafted pillars gold gleamed in the bright sunlight. 'Stupa.'

'Wow, it's beautiful,' Ellie Thompson whispered. She even hadn't noticed they'd driven into the centre of Vientiane, her brain being half–shut down with sleep deprivation. *Wake up and smell the roses. You're in Laos*, she admonished herself. But she was shattered. *Too bad. New start to life, remember?* Probably no roses in Laos. Definitely no ex.

Right. Forget tiredness. Forget the humiliation of everyone from the CEO right down to the laundry junior at Wellington Hospital knowing her husband had left her for her sister. Forget the pain and anger. Start enjoying every day for what it could bring. There'd be no nasty surprises for the next four weeks while in Laos. She could relax.

Holding up her phone, Ellie leaned over the side to click away continuously until the temple was out of sight. Slumping back against the hard seat, she thought longingly of the air-conditioned taxis that had been waiting outside the border crossing at Nong Khai railway station. With the sweat trickling down between her shoulder blades adding to her unkempt appearance, this window-less mode of transport open to the air, dust and insects kind of said she'd had a brain fade when she'd chosen the jumbo over a taxi. But taxis were old hat, jumbos were not. Except right now a shower and bed were look-ing more and more tempting, and sightseeing a distant second.

Leaning forward, she asked the driver, 'How far?'

'Not long.' He shrugged.

Guess that could mean anything from five minutes to an hour. Shuffling her backside to try to get comfort-able, she watched the spectacular sights they passed, nothing like New Zealand at all. Vientiane might be small and compact but there were people everywhere. Locals moved slowly with an air of having all day to accomplish whatever it was they had to do, while jos-tling tourists were snapping photos of everything from temples to bugs crawling on the pavement as if their lives depended on it.

After a twelve-hour flight from Wellington to Bang-kok, followed by a thirteen-hour turned into sixteen-hour train trip to Laos, Ellie's exhaustion overshadowed the excitement only days ago she'd struggled to keep under control. Yep, she'd had a few days after she'd fin-ished at the hospital for good when she'd begun to look forward to her trip instead of constantly looking over her shoulder to see who was talking about her. That excite-ment was still there; it just needed a kick in the backside to come out of hiding.

This was her first visit to Indochina and her driver was taking her to the amputee centre and hospital where she'd signed on until the second week of December. Ellie pinched herself. This was real. She'd finally taken the first step towards moving beyond the mess that had become her life and recharging the batteries so she could make some decisions about her future. 'Where to from here?' had been the question nagging her relentlessly for months. Laos was only a stopgap. But it was a start. Then there was the six-month stint to come in Auckland. It was the gap of nearly four weeks between jobs that worried her. Those weeks included Christmas and had her stomach twisting in knots. She was not going to her parents' place to play happy families when her sister would be there.

As the jumbo bumped down a road that had lost most of its seal the yawns were rolling out of her. Damn, but the air was thick with heat. Her make-up was barely sticking to her face and where her sunglasses touched her cheeks they slid up and down, no doubt making a right royal mess. So not the look she wanted to present to her new colleagues, but trying to fix the problem with more make-up would only exacerbate her untidy appearance. Nor did she carry an iron in her handbag to tidy up the rumpled look sported by her cotton trousers and sleeveless T-shirt. Today a fashion statement she was not. Hopefully everyone would see past that and accept her for her doctoring skills, if nothing else. That was all that was required of her anyway, besides being all she had to give these days.

Taking that train instead of flying from Bangkok hadn't been her wisest decision but back home it had sounded wonderful when the travel agent showed her the photos—highly enhanced pictures, she now realised. Face it, even riding all the way here on an elephant would've been tempting compared to living in the shadow of her ex and the woman he now lived with. Caitlin. Her sister. Her ex-sister. Her supposedly close and loving sister. Pain lanced her. The really awful thing was she still missed Caitlin, missed their closeness, the talks— Huh, the talks that obviously hadn't mentioned anything about both of them loving the same man. *Her* husband.

Sounding bitter, Ellie. Damn right she was bitter. Freddy had slept with Caitlin—while still married to *her.* She shook her head. The self-pity was back in New Zealand, as was the humiliation from having people knowing what happened. Putting up with everyone's apparent sympathy when most of those so-called concerned friends enjoyed keeping the hospital gossip mill rolling along had been gross.

But no more. Her contract was at an end, and nothing the CEO had said or offered had tempted her in the slightest to stay on. From now on she'd look the world in the eye, and make plans for Ellie Thompson. Taking back her maiden name had only been the first step. She liked her brand-new passport with its first stamps for a journey she was taking alone, in a place no one knew her or her history. It was a sign of things to come.

She patted her stomach. *Down, butterflies, down.*

Then they turned the corner and at the end of the street a muddy river flowed past and she leaned forward again.

'Is that the Mekong?' When the driver didn't answer she raised her voice and enunciated clearly, 'The river? The Mekong?'

He turned to nod and smile his toothless smile. 'Yes. Mekong.'

The mighty Mekong. She'd always wanted to see the

famous river and now it was less than a kilometre away. 'Wow,' she repeated. She knew where she'd be going for her first walk in this delightful place. Another yawn stretched her mouth. That would have to be after she'd slept round the clock.

'I show you.' A sharp turn and they were heading straight for the river. Their stop was abrupt, with Ellie putting her hands out to prevent slamming against the seat in front of her.

'Out, out.' Her new friend smiled. 'See Mekong.'

He was so enthusiastic she couldn't find it in her to say she really wanted to get to her destination. Anyway, wasn't she supposed to be grabbing this adventure with both hands? Climbing down, she went to stand on the edge of the river beside the driver. It looked like running mud, nothing like the clear waters of New Zealand rivers. But it *was* the Mekong. 'It's real. I'm here right by the river my dad used to talk about.' Except he'd seen it in Vietnam. 'Hard to imagine all the countries this water flows through.'

The driver stared at her blankly. Her English obviously beyond his comprehension. Or too fast. She tried again, a lot slower this time, and was rewarded with a glower at the mention of Vietnam.

'Go now.'

Okay, lesson learned. Avoid mentioning the neighbours. After a few quick photos she climbed back into the jumbo, fingers crossed they were nearly at the clinic.

The next thing Ellie knew she was jerking forward and sliding to the edge of her seat.

'Here centre,' her driver told her. He must've braked hard.

She'd fallen asleep with all those amazing sights

going by? Idiot. Looking around, she noted the rutted dirt road they'd stopped on. Beyond was a long, low building made of concrete blocks, painted drab grey. A few trees that she didn't recognise grew in the sparsely grassed front yard. Nothing like home—which was exactly what she wanted, needed.

Out of the jumbo she stretched her back, then rubbed her neck where a sharp ache had set in. No doubt her head had been bobbing up and down like one of those toy dog things some people put in the back window of their cars. Great. Heat pounded at her while dust settled over her feet. What was a bit more grime? It'd wash off easily—as she hoped the past year would now she'd arrived in Laos, a place so far from her previous life it had to be good for her.

'Come.' The driver hoisted her bag and headed towards a wide door at the top of a concrete step, where a group of men and women sat looking as if they'd been there all day and would be there a lot longer. It had to be the main entrance.

She followed him, pausing to nod at the lethargic folk whose soft chatter had stopped as she approached. When she smiled and said, 'Hello,' they all smiled back, making her feel unbelievably good.

Inside it was not a lot cooler, and as she handed the man his fare and a huge tip she was greeted by a kind-looking woman who had to be about twenty years older than her. She came up and gripped Ellie in a tight hug. 'Sandra Winter? Welcome to the amputee centre.'

As Ellie tried to pull out of this lovely welcome that wasn't for her the woman continued, 'We've been looking forward to your arrival all week. The doctor you're replacing had to leave early. Oh, I'm Louise Warner, one of the permanent staff here. I'm the anaesthetist while my husband, Aaron, is a general surgeon. He's gone to the market. You'll meet him later, along with the rest of the staff.'

Ellie smiled, trying to keep her exhaustion at bay for just a little longer. 'I'm not Sandra Winter. I'm—'

'You're not?' Louise looked beyond her. 'That explains the jumbo.' Louise returned her gaze to Ellie, a huge query in her eyes. 'I'm sorry. It's just that we were expecting someone and I saw you and made a mistake.'

Ellie let her bag drop to the floor and held out her hand. 'I am Ellie Thompson, your replacement doctor. Did you not receive an email from headquarters explaining there'd been a change? Sandra has had a family crisis and couldn't come.'

Louise slowly took her proffered hand, but instead of shaking it wrapped her fingers around Ellie's. 'No email, no message at all. Nothing.'

Yeah, she was getting the picture. 'It was a spur-of-the-moment thing. I used to work with Sandra and when I heard how she couldn't come I put my hand up. My contract with Wellington Hospital literally ran out the same week. It was manic for a few days.' Hard to believe everything she'd got done to be ready in that time. Getting a passport and visas had had her running around town like a demented flea. She'd booked flights, bought appropriate clothes for the climate and job and had dinner with Renee and two friends. No wonder her head was spinning.

Louise still held her hand. 'Forgive me for not knowing and thinking you were someone else. I am very grateful you could come over at such short notice. It can't have been easy.'

No, but it had already begun to act like a balm to the wounds left by her husband and sister. 'Believe me, I'm the grateful one here.'

'We'll debate that later. I'd better text Noi. He went to the airport to meet Sandra.' She gave Ellie another quick hug.

When was the last time she'd been hugged so much? She wouldn't count the tight grasp the head of A and E had given her at her farewell. A fish had more warmth, whereas this woman exuded the sort of kindness that would make anyone feel comfortable.

'I'm very glad to be here.' *Where's my bed? And the shower?* All of a sudden her eyes felt heavy and gritty, her head full of candy floss and her legs were struggling to hold her upright.

'The children are busting to meet you. And the staff.' Louise finished her text and set off in the direction of a door, leaving Ellie no choice but to follow.

Of course she wanted to meet the kids she'd be working with, but right this minute? 'How many children are here at the moment?'

'Fourteen. But that number fluctuates almost daily depending on new casualties. Then there are the families who can't leave their children here, or can't get to see them at all so that we go out to their villages for follow-up care. I'm only talking about the amputees. The hospital annex sees to a lot of other casualties, too.' Louise sighed. 'It's hard. For the patients and their families. And us. In here.'

They entered what appeared to be a classroom. Ellie must've looked surprised because Louise explained, 'We have teachers working with the children who stay on after their surgeries. Some are with us for months so we try to keep the education going during their stay.'

Chairs scraped on the wooden floor as kids stood up, some not easily, and the reason quickly became apparent. Three had lost a leg or a foot. Looking closer, Ellie noted other major injuries on all the children.

Her heart rolled. What was tiredness compared to everything these youngsters were coping with? She dug deep, found a big smile and tried to eyeball each and every kid in front of her. 'Hi, everyone. I am Ellie.' She stepped up to the first boy. 'What's your name?'

'Ng.' The lad put out his left hand, his right one not there.

Ellie wound her fingers around the small hand and squeezed gently. 'Hello, Ng. How old are you?' Then she nearly slapped her forehead. These kids wouldn't understand English, would they?

'Six.'

Six and he'd lost an arm. *And* he understood her language. A well of tears threatened, which was so unprofessional. Do that and Louise would be putting her back on that train. Gulping hard, she turned to the next child. But seriously? She really had nothing to complain about.

The next half hour sped by with Ellie sitting and chatting with each child. Not all of them understood her words but they must've picked up on her empathy and her teasing because soon they all crowded around touching her, pointing at themselves and laughing a lot. Over the next few days she'd get to know them better as she changed dressings and helped with rehab, but this first meeting was unbelievable. She filed away each name and face so that she'd never have to ask them again.

They deserved her utmost respect and she'd make sure they got it.

'Ellie? Ellie Baldwin, is that really you?' The male voice coming from across the room was filled with surprise and pleasure.

She snapped her head up and stared into a familiar pair of grey eyes she hadn't seen in four years. Mind you, they'd been angry grey then, like deep, wild ocean grey. 'Luca?' Her heart pounded loud in her ears. 'Luca, I don't believe this.'

'It's me, El.' No one else dared call her that. Ever.

As she stepped forward Louise was prattling an explanation about why she was here, but Ellie cut her out and concentrated on her old friend and housemate. Concentrated hard to make sure she wasn't hallucinating. Checking this truly was Luca Chirsky, even when she knew it was the man she'd shared notes and rosters with at med school, and more than a few beers at the pub or in the house they'd lived in with Renee and another trainee doctor. Time hadn't altered his good looks. Though he did appear more muscular than she remembered, which only enhanced the package. Bet the ladies still plagued him. Some plagues were okay, he'd once joked.

Finally she said, 'I haven't seen you in forever.' Wow, this was a fantastic bonus to her trip. A surprise. She shivered. A *good* surprise, she told herself. 'Who'd have believed we'd meet up here of all places?'

Then she was being swung up in strong arms and spun in a circle. 'It's been a while, hasn't it?' Those eyes were twinkling at her as they used to before she'd gone off to marry Freddy. This was Luca. He had never hesitated with telling her what he thought of her fiancé, none of it good. The thrill of seeing him again dipped.

If only there were some way of keeping her marriage bust-up from Luca.

Not a chance. 'Didn't you say your name was Thompson?' Louise asked from somewhere beside them. 'I'm not going deaf as well as forgetful, am I?'

Luca almost dropped Ellie to her feet. His finger lifted her chin so he could eyeball her. 'You've gone back to Thompson, eh?' Then he deliberately looked at her left hand, which was still gripping his arm, her ring finger bare of a wedding band, and then back to lock his gaze on hers. 'So you're single again.' He didn't need to say, 'I warned you.' It was there in the slow burn of his eyes, changing his pleasure at seeing her to caution.

Ice-like fingers of disappointment skittered across her arms. So much for being excited to see Luca. She'd had a momentary brain fade. *Having a few of them today.* After all this time without any contact between them he'd gone for the jugular straight up. Guess that put their friendship where it belonged—in the past. She didn't understand why. They'd been so close nothing should've affected their friendship. The last person on the planet she'd expected to find here was Luca, and he knew too much about her for these weeks to now be a quiet time. She could do without playing catch-up, or the shake of his head every time he said her surname. Luca would cloud her thinking and bring back memories of where she'd planned on being by now if she hadn't gone and got married. Plans she'd sat up late at night discussing endlessly with him until she'd started dating Freddy.

Even now Luca's head moved from side to side as he said, 'Seems you're right, Louise. Ellie Thompson she is.'

Fatigue combined with annoyance and a sense of

let-down to come out as anger. 'Are Mrs Chirsky and your child here? Or are they back in New Zealand awaiting your return?'

The expression on his face instantly became unreadable as he took a step back from her. 'Don't go there, Ellie,' he warned.

So he could give her a hard time and she should remain all sweetness and light. Too bad she'd forgotten how to do that since that fateful morning she'd found Freddy in bed with more than a pillow. 'Or what?' she snapped. Last time they'd talked he'd been gearing up for his wedding. More like girding up. There'd been a pregnancy involved that he definitely hadn't been happy about. Nor would he talk to her about it, or anything going on in his life then. He'd clammed up tighter than a rock oyster. Kind of said where their friendship had got to.

Louise tapped her arm. 'Come on, I'll show you to your room so you can unpack and take a shower.'

It was the worried look Louise kept flicking between her and Luca that dampened down Ellie's temper; nothing that Luca had said. 'I'm sorry. I must sound very ungrateful. I'd really like to see where I'm staying.' She didn't want Louise thinking her and Luca couldn't work together, because they could. It would just be a matter of remaining professional and ignoring the past. Easy as.

Luca picked up her bag before she could make a move. 'I'll take that.'

Louise scowled. 'Maybe you could catch up with Ellie later when she's had some sleep.'

To lighten the atmosphere that she'd created just by being here, Ellie forced a laugh. 'Trust me, there won't be any talking about anything past, present or future for the next twenty-four hours. I'm all but comatose on my feet. The sooner I can lie down, the better. I got no sleep at all on the train from Bangkok. The carriage was too noisy and stuffy.'

Luca draped an arm over her shoulders. 'That's what planes are for, El. They're comfortable and fast, and the cabin crew even feeds you.' Back to being less antagonistic, then. His use of El was a clue.

'Remind me of that later when I come up with some other hare-brained scheme for getting home.' She'd left booking flights as she had no idea what she might want to do next, where she might go to fill in the weeks between this job and the position she was taking up early in January. Following Louise, Luca's arm still on her shoulders and feeling heavy, yet strong and familiar, she sucked in on her confusion. Maybe she did need familiar right now. Maybe her old friend could help her by going back over that time when she'd made the monumental error of thinking she loved Freddy more than her future and wanted to spend the rest of her life with him. Now she wanted to reroute her life and, if she stopped being so defensive, talking to Luca might turn out to be the fix she needed. If he didn't rub her nose in what had happened, they should be able to get along just fine. Surely their past friendship counted for something?

Then heat prickled Ellie's skin. Damn, but she needed a shower. She probably smelled worse than roadkill that had been left in the sun for days. Except this heat felt different from what she'd been experiencing all morning.

She shrugged away from Luca's arm and straightened up the sags in her body. 'I'm looking forward to catching up.' She smiled at Luca. The heat intensified when he smiled back. Most unusual. Had to be excitement over seeing him again, despite the shaky start. 'But not today.'

Might as well go for friendly; after all they used to be very good at it. There'd been a time, when they were sharing that house, that there was little they didn't know about each other. At one point just before they'd finished their first year as junior doctors she'd wondered if they might've had a fling. They'd seemed attracted to each other in a way they'd never been before, and then she'd met Freddy and that had been that. Eventually she'd moved to Wellington and lost contact with Luca and the others she'd lived with for so long, until the beginning of the year when she'd caught up with Renee and now shared an apartment with her. Ellie had presumed Luca had married and become a father. Seemed she'd been wrong.

Thankfully today she could categorically state she felt no attraction for Luca at all. Not a drop. That heat had been something out of the blue. Hell, today she was struggling with the friendship thing after the way he'd looked at her with that 'I told you so' in his sharp eyes. It made her want to grind her teeth and kick him in the shin. It reminded her how he used to be so positive about diagnoses when they were junior doctors. That was 'the look' he'd become known for. Unfortunately he was more often right than wrong about everything.

Just like his prediction about her ex. Except not even Luca had got it as bad or humiliating as the demise of her marriage had turned out to be.

CHAPTER TWO

'KNOCK ME OVER,' Luca muttered as he stood back for Ellie and Louise to enter the small room that would be El's home for the next month. Ellie Thompson had popped up out of nowhere in full splendour, if a little bedraggled around the edges. All that thick, dark blonde hair still long and gleaming, while her eyes watched everything and everyone, though now there was a wariness he'd never seen before. 'Your smile's missing.' Did he really say that out loud?

Ellie lifted those eyes to him and he saw her weariness. 'It's probably back in the third carriage of the overnight train I was on.'

Somehow Luca didn't believe her exhaustion was all to do with her trip. It appeared ingrained in her bones and muscles as well as deep in those hazel eyes, even in her soul. So not the Ellie he used to know and had had a lot of fun with. What had Baldwin done to her? Played around behind her back? That had always been on the cards. The guy had never been able to keep his pants zipped, even when he'd first started dating Ellie. It had broken Luca's heart when Ellie had told him the guy loved her and was over being the playboy since he'd asked her to marry him. The old 'leopard and its spots' story. But she hadn't wanted to hear what he could've told her. Then his own problems had exploded in his face and he'd been too caught up dealing with Gaylene's lies and conniving to notice Ellie's departure.

Placing her bag on the desk, he turned for the door. 'We'll catch up when you've had forty winks.'

'Make that a thousand and forty.'

'You okay, El? Like, really deep down okay?' he asked, worry latching on to him. They might've been out of touch but she used to be his closest friend. He'd never replaced her and would still do anything for her— if only she ever asked.

Her eyes were slits as that hazel shade glittered at him. 'Never been better,' she growled. 'Now, can you leave me to settle in?'

'On my way. Or do you want me to show you where the showers are?'

'I'll do that.' Louise stepped between them. Putting a hand on his arm, she pushed lightly. 'Go check up on little Hoppy.' Then her phone rang and she stepped away. After listening for a few seconds she said, 'Hang on. Sorry, Ellie, I'll be a couple of minutes. Aaron left the shopping list in the kitchen.'

Ellie's shoulders slumped as she watched Louise bustle away. 'All I want is a shower and some sleep.'

Luca's heart rolled over for her so he reached out for her hand and gently tugged her close. 'Come on, grab your toiletries and that towel and I'll show you where to go.'

She did as he said, silently. What had that man done? Or was this truly just jet lag and a sleepless night on the train making her like this? 'El, while you're showering

I'll make you a sandwich and grab a bottle of water. You must be starving.'

'You still call me El.' Now there was a glimmer of a smile touching her lips. 'I'm fractionally shorter and nowhere near as beautiful as the model you wanted to compare me with. I'm fatter too.'

'The hell you are. You're thinner than I've ever seen you.' And he didn't like it.

The smile fell away, and she shivered. 'I needed to lose weight.'

'I'll have to start calling you stick insect.' He grinned to show he was teasing, something he'd never had to do before when they'd spent a lot of time together. But he needed to know what was going on. Something had happened to her. He'd swear it.

'I've been called worse.' Distress blinked out at him.

He opened his mouth without thinking about what he'd say. 'Who by?' When she winced he draped an arm over her shoulders to hold her in against him as they walked along the path to the ablutions block. 'What did that scumbag do to you?' he asked next, struggling to hold onto a rare anger.

Just like that, crabby Ellie returned. Her back straightened as she yanked her shoulders free of his arm. The face she turned on his was red and tight, her eyes sparking like a live wire. A dangerous live wire. 'You haven't told me if your wife's living over here with you.'

She fought dirty, he'd give her that. Her being Ellie, that meant she was hiding something. Stepping farther away from her, he waved along the path. 'Third door down are the showers. I'll get one of the kids to put that sandwich and water in your room.' He spun away to stride towards the clinic, where he could bury himself in patients' problems and not worry about what might've happened to Ellie. Strange, but for a long time he hadn't thought about what Gaylene had tried to do to him all those years ago, certainly not since he'd arrived here. It wasn't as though Ellie and Gaylene went hand in hand, but the friendship he'd had with El had gone belly up at that time.

'Luca.' A soft hand touched his biceps. 'Luca, stop, please.'

He turned midstride to face Ellie, and instantly his anger dissipated. It wasn't her fault that he'd been made a fool of way back then. 'I'm sorry.'

'Me, too.' Ellie huffed a long sigh. 'I got such a shock seeing you across the room, and I don't seem to have returned to normal since. I don't want to fight with you. We were never very good at that, and starting now doesn't make a lot of sense.'

'I guess four years is a long time, with many things having gone down for each of us. Let's go back to when we were happy being pals and downing beers as if it was going out of fashion on our days off.' He'd like that more than anything right about now. A cold beer—with his pal. They had a lot of catching up to do. And not just the bad stuff.

Ellie nodded slowly. 'That'd be great. A friend is what I really need more than anything.'

Don't ask. 'Done.' He followed through on his previous thought. 'Get some shut-eye and tonight we'll go to a bar in town for a reunion beer or two. Then you can catch up on some more sleep before you start to get to know your way around here. How does that sound?' He held his breath.

At last. A full-blown Ellie smile came his way, like

warm hands around his heart. 'Perfect.' She started to move past him.

Luca suddenly felt the need to tell her. To get it out of the way, because it would hang between them like an unsolved puzzle if he avoided the issue, and he didn't want that. 'I never married her.'

She nearly lost her balance, and when she raised her face to him her eyes were wide. But she kept quiet, waiting for him to finish his story.

As if that could be told in thirty seconds, but he supposed he could give her the bones of it. 'She terminated the baby. Said she'd met someone else and didn't want to take my child into that relationship.' If it had been his child. She hadn't exactly been monogamous with him. He would've insisted on a DNA test being done but he'd been trying to trust her and accept what had happened.

He'd always been supercareful about using condoms during every liaison. But no child of his would ever grow up without his father at his side, and that edict had taken him straight into Gaylene's hands—until she'd found a richer man. Luca's hands fisted on his hips, as they always did when he thought about that selfish woman. The only good thing she had done was remind him exactly why he had no intention of ever, ever getting married or having children.

'You always said you weren't going to marry or have children. I was surprised when I heard about the circumstances of your wedding, but so many people get caught out by an unplanned pregnancy.' Ellie leaned against him. 'I should've phoned then.'

But by then he'd told her what he thought of her marrying Baldwin. He got it. She'd still been angry with him. 'We were both tied up with our careers and finishing exams, not to mention other things. There was a lot going on.' *I wouldn't have told you anyway. Like I've never told you about my father and my grandfather and how they let down those nearest and dearest big time. How my father took his would-be father-in-law's propensity for deserting his wife and children to a whole new level.* Some things were best kept in the family.

Ellie nodded. 'Our friendship was under a fair bit of strain, if I remember rightly.'

'You do.' But he wouldn't raise the subject that had come between them again. Not today anyhow. 'Go shower and head to bed. Your eyeballs are hanging halfway down your face. I'll warn everyone to be quiet around your room.'

'Nice. How come I didn't scare the kids, then? I must look very ugly.' Her smile slipped as a yawn gripped her.

'They're a lot tougher than you'd guess.' Luca felt his usual sadness for these beautiful and gentle people who dealt with so much, then he glanced at Ellie and brightened. 'But they're also very like kids anywhere in the world when you buy treats or play cricket with them.' Things he was always indulging in.

He felt his heart lurch as Ellie stepped through into the ablutions block and shut the door. El. His dearest friend. Damn, but he'd missed her, and he was only just realising how much. No one quite poked the borax at him the way she had whenever he'd got too serious about something she'd deemed to be ridiculous. She was usually spot on too. But now something was definitely not right. He'd never seen her so beaten, as though all the things she held dear and near were gone. Somehow, sometime, over the coming weeks he'd find out, and see if he couldn't help her to get her spark back.

* * *

Ellie woke to knocking on her door. *Where am I?* She looked around at the children's drawings covering the walls and it all came back in a hurry. Vientiane. The amputee centre. She stretched her toes to the end of the bed and raised her arms above her head. She'd slept like the dead and now felt good all over, ready to start her job in this country that was new to her.

Knock, knock.

'Who is it?'

'Chi. Luca said you have to get up. I've got you more water.'

Luca. So that hadn't been a dream. She'd be excited about catching up with him if she didn't know he'd want all the details about her failed marriage. He wasn't going to get them but he'd persist for days; she just knew it. Then again, he had told her why he wasn't married. What a witch that woman had turned out to be. Terminating their baby with no regard for its father. That was beyond her comprehension. But then she'd never faced a similar situation. Freddy had made certain she didn't get pregnant.

'Ellie?'

'Sorry, come in.' Ellie shuffled upright and leaned back against the wall as Chi entered.

'Luca said you're going out at seven o'clock.' The girl spoke precisely and slowly as if searching for the right words.

Damn, she'd forgotten Luca's suggestion of a beer in town. Taking the proffered bottle of water from Chi, she snapped the lid open and said, 'Thank you, Chi.'

The girl beamed as Ellie poured the cool liquid down her parched throat.

'What time is it?' she paused long enough to ask.

'Half past six. Are you still tired?'

'A little bit, but eight hours is more than enough for now. I wouldn't have slept tonight if you hadn't woken me.' As Chi sat down on the chair in the corner Ellie asked, 'Where did you learn to speak such good English?' The girl looked so cute in her oversize shirt and too-small trousers.

'Here. The doctors and nurses teach me.' Pride filled her face, lightened her eyes.

'How long have you been in the centre?' To have learned to speak English to a level she could be understood without too much difficulty she must've been around the medical staff a long time.

'I was this high when I came with my brother.' Chi held her hand less than a metre above the floor. Ellie guessed she was now closer to one hundred and twenty centimetres. 'Long time ago. My brother was this high.' Half a metre off the floor.

'Is your brother still here, too?'

Chi blinked, the pride gone, replaced with stoic sadness. 'He died. The bomb cut off his leg and the blood ran out.'

Ellie shuddered. Reality sucked, and was very confronting. Flying fragments of metal did a lot of damage, and were often lethal. It had been a spur-of-the-moment decision to come here. When she'd heard about Sandra's family crisis she'd thought about the weeks looming with nothing to keep her busy before she took up her next job and put her hand up. Helping people in these circumstances was so different from working in an emergency department back home, where life was easier and a lot of things like medical care taken for granted. Here people, many only young children, were still being injured, maimed or killed by bombs that had been left lying around or shallow buried decades ago.

'Louise and Aaron adopted me. My mother and father are gone, too.'

How much reality should a child have to deal with? Leaping out of bed, she scooped the girl into a hug. 'I'm so happy to know you, Chi.'

'Knew I couldn't trust a female to get my message across without stopping to yak the day away.' Luca stood in the doorway, his trademark grin including both her and Chi in that comment.

With sudden clarity Ellie understood how much she'd missed that grin and the man behind it. Missed their conversations about everything from how to put a dislocated shoulder back into its socket to which brand of beer was the best. They'd argued, and laughed, and fought over whose turn it was to clean the house. They'd cheered each other on in exams while secretly hoping they did better than the other.

She ran to throw her arms around him. 'I'm glad I've found you again.'

'I'm glad, too, because tomorrow's your turn to do the washing.' He laughed against the top of her head.

His hands were spread across her back, his warmth seeping into her bones and thawing some of the chill that had taken up residence on the morning she came home from work to find Freddy and Caitlin in her marital bed, doing what only she should've been doing with her husband. She breathed deep, drawing in the scent that was Luca, her closest friend ever, and relaxed. Friends were safer than husbands and sisters, the damage they wrought less destructive.

'I have missed you so much.' *I just hadn't realised it.* How dumb was that? Who forgot someone important in their lives because they'd fallen out about a man? Not any man, but Freddy. Luca had been right about him, but she wasn't going to acknowledge that. She couldn't bear to see the 'I told you so' sign flick on in his eyes again. Not yet anyway. Even if she could laugh because he'd won that argument there was too much pain behind it for her to be ready to make light of what had happened. That day would probably never come. 'We should never have stopped texting or emailing even when we were in different cities, no matter what we thought about what the other was doing.'

Luca swung her around in a circle, her feet nearly taking out the bed and then the chair with Chi sitting on it. 'I do solemnly swear never to stop annoying the hell out of my best buddy, Ellie, ever again.'

'Look out.' Chi leaped on top of the chair out of the way of Ellie's legs. 'Ellie makes you crazy, Luca.'

Ellie was put back on her feet and then Luca grabbed Chi and swung her in a circle. 'You're right, she does. I'd forgotten how to be crazy until today.'

Chi giggled and squirmed to be put down. 'Ellie, can I be your friend, too? I want to be crazy.'

'Absolutely. We'll be the three crazies.' Ellie reached for the girl and hugged her tight, trying hard not to let the lurking tears spill. What a day. What a damned amazing day. She'd found Luca, gained a new friend and was starting to feel a little bit like her old self. A teeny-weeny bit, but that was a start.

'Okay, crazies, time Ellie got ready to go out. Chi, I'm sorry but you're too young to go to a bar, but I'm sure we'll find somewhere else to take you while Ellie's here.' Luca cleared his throat and when Ellie looked up she'd swear there was moisture at the corners of his eyes, too.

It was all too much to cope with. Seeing Luca get all emotional wasn't helping her stay in control. 'Go on, shoo, both of you. I'm going to take another shower and get spruced up.'

'It's a bar in Vientiane, no need for glad rags.' Luca grinned. Then slapped his forehead. 'Oh, I forgot. Lady El won't be seen anywhere in less than the best outfit.'

She picked up her pillow and threw it at him. 'Get out of here.'

She hadn't arrived in the best-looking outfit, even if she'd started out looking swanky back in Bangkok after a shower at the airport. But hey, in the interest of her self-esteem she wasn't going out in a sack, either. Though maybe here where the temperatures were so hot and the humidity high and everything definitely casual she could let go some of the debilitating need to be perfect. After all, there was no one here that she desperately had to please. Not even her friend. Luca had always accepted her for who she was, even if he did tease the hell out of her at times.

Suddenly she realised she was only dressed in a T-shirt and knickers; her bra lay on top of her discarded trousers. This might be Luca, but she had some pride. Glancing at him, she was dismayed to see his gaze was cruising down her body, hesitating on her breasts. She couldn't read the look in his eyes, but it was different from how he'd ever looked at her before.

Ellie shivered—with heat and apprehension. What was going on? 'Get out of here. I'll see you shortly.' She needed a shower, a very cold one.

* * *

'Like your dress,' Luca told her an hour later as she perched her backside on top of a high stool and leaned her elbow on the bar. 'When did you start wearing red?' His eyes held the same expression they had back in her room.

She chose to ignore it. 'Since I found the most amazing saleswoman in a very exclusive boutique.' It was true. That lady was very skilled at her job and her shop was Ellie's favourite, though lately there hadn't been any call for beautiful dresses.

The one she'd slipped into tonight was a simple sheath that was casual yet elegant. Her new look, she decided there and then. No more going for the tailored, exquisite clothes her husband had demanded she wear even to cook dinner. She'd miss the amazing clothes because she had loved them but hated the criticism rained down on her for not looking perfect enough. But, hey, she wasn't in that place anymore. She was with Luca in Vientiane. Ellie grinned. A real, deep all-or-nothing grin. Life was looking up. Strange glances from Luca or not.

'What's up? You look as if you won the lottery,' Luca pushed a glass of Beer Lao towards her.

The condensation on the glass made her mouth water and that was before she'd tasted the contents. 'As good as, I reckon. I'm starting to unwind and enjoy myself.'

'Things haven't been so great for you recently?' There was a guarded look in his eyes as though he was afraid of overstepping the mark. Something they'd never had to worry about in the past.

A deep gulp of beer and then, 'You were right. Freddy was an a-hole. I left him and now I'm trying to decide what it is I really want from my life.'

'I'm sorry to hear that.'

No gloating, thank goodness, or she'd have tipped her beer over his head. And that would've been such a waste. It was delicious. 'You know what? I'm not sorry.' It had only just occurred to her but, no, she was not sorry that episode of her life was over. Now all she had to do was pack it away completely. If that was possible considering her sister's role in it. Hopefully, being so far removed from the complications of her family, she might find some inner peace. Though she might never learn to trust anyone after what had been done to her.

'Then, find that smile again.' Luca placed his hand on top of hers on the counter. 'You look better when your eyes light up with pleasure.'

Turning her hand over to clasp her fingers around his, she said, 'Seeing you makes me feel good. I couldn't believe it when you said my name.'

'*You* were surprised? I got a helluva shock considering you weren't the doctor we were expecting. How was that for coincidence? Or was it our stars aligning or some such babble?'

'You've been here too long.' As laughter bubbled up Ellie's throat something strange was going on with her hand. The one covered by Luca's. She could feel heat and a zinging sensation that had nothing to do with the weather and all to do with— No way. She jerked her hand free, folded her arms across her chest and rubbed her arms vigorously.

'Ellie? You're going weird on me.' Luca locked his eyes on her.

Looking into those grey eyes, she searched for recognition of what had just happened but found nothing.

Seemed her imagination was running riot. 'I'm fine,' she croaked.

'Phew. For a moment there I thought you were changing on me.' His gaze was intense, as if he was checking her out.

Zing. She felt it again. This time it was as if someone were lightly dancing down her spine. Tearing her eyes away from Luca, she snatched up her glass and drained the beer in one long gulp. The glass banged back on the counter and she stared around the bar, looking at everything and everyone but Luca.

'I'll get you another.' His hand scooped up her glass. The fingers that wrapped around the moist receptacle were long and strong, and tanned. Not that she understood why she was noticing.

Ellie's mouth dried, despite all the fluid she'd just swallowed. *They're only fingers. Luca's, what's more.* She shivered, as though it were cold, except the temperature was beyond high and her skin was on fire. What had just happened? She had to get herself under control. Getting wired over Luca was so not a good idea, let alone sensible. And despite her mistakes she was usually sensible. Or had that attribute flown out of the door and floated away on the Mekong just across the road?

Guess it had been so long since she'd been close to any man that her body had reacted without thought. But this was Luca. *Down, girl, down.* He was the last man on earth she should be having feelings about that had nothing to do with friendship and all to do with sex.

CHAPTER THREE

LUCA AIMED FOR relaxed, trying to ignore that something big was bugging Ellie. The defining strength of their friendship had taken a battering years back and he wasn't prepared to push. Not yet anyway. He'd hate to lose her now he'd just found her again. Not that he'd been looking. He'd kind of shut off most things from his previous life, except the mantra he'd always lived by— Chirsky men were bad husbands and fathers.

'I should head back to the compound,' Ellie muttered.

What happened to spending the evening together? 'Let's have another beer and then we'll eat.' Not waiting for her to answer, he waved at the barman busy with another order and indicated their empty glasses. He didn't want to walk even a few metres down the bar because Ellie looked as if she was about to bolt, and that was the last thing he wanted.

He went with, 'It's unbelievable. I was coming into that room to meet some doctor I'd never heard of and there you were, looking like my Ellie.'

She blanched. Then slowly she slipped off the stool, standing straight—and bewildered. 'I really should go.' There was a wobble in her voice.

Luca placed a hand firmly on her shoulder. 'Sit down.

The heat and travel hits you hard at first, but you need to stay awake till a reasonable hour to get your body clock back on track. The sooner the better.' He doubted those were the reasons for her looking as if she'd been run down by a train, but he played along. 'When I first arrived it took me ages to settle into a routine.'

'How long have you been here?' She still looked ready to flee.

'Nine months, three to go.'

Leaning her elbow on the counter, she propped her chin in her hand. 'Then what?'

'Maybe a spell in Cambodia.' Or Vietnam, or even Australia at a major hospital. He hadn't made any decisions about a whole load of things that involved his future since he'd come over here. He was avoiding them, because it was easier that way.

Her eyes widened and at last she gave him a smile. There were long gaps between those and he was already learning to appreciate them. She asked, 'Since when did you want to give up your goal of being head of the busiest A and E department in New Zealand?'

The problem with changing the subject so Ellie would relax was that he ended up in the hot seat. About to start telling her about the clinic's pet pangolin instead, he paused. They used to tell each other just about everything. Shouldn't he start renewing their friendship by doing what they'd always done? 'Gaylene doing her little number on me was a shock.' *That's an understatement, El, in case you don't realise.* 'I thought I'd made myself invulnerable, invincible, so that no one would catch me out. How wrong could a guy be? Maybe I'd become arrogant. I don't know.' He glanced across at Ellie and smiled despite himself. 'Okay, I was.' Hopefully that had changed. He'd sure as hell been taken down a peg or three, though not for anything to do with his medical work.

'I can understand wanting to protect your feelings but you're sounding as if you don't ever want to let anyone near, into your heart.' She eased her butt back onto the stool.

Luca felt some of the tension in his belly lighten. At least she didn't look quite so ready to run for the door anymore, but did she have to go straight to the centre of his problem? So easily? Maybe he hadn't missed her as much as he'd thought. But of course he had. Strange how he hadn't known that until he'd found her again. Should've done something about looking her up years ago, but he couldn't stand Baldwin. Not at all. 'I've never made any bones about the fact I do not want a family—no wife, no children.' Okay, *want* was the wrong word. He wouldn't risk having a wife and family. That was closer to the truth.

'That was an excuse for bonking every moving female while you were young, but not forever, surely?' She was laughing at him, soft and friendly-like but laughing nonetheless.

'Wrong,' he snapped. Telling her what made him who he'd become was a mistake after all. But then he'd known that, had always kept certain things to himself, even from this woman.

'Hey.' Her hand covered his. 'I didn't mean to upset you. You've got to admit you spent a lot of time chasing females back then.'

'I didn't have to chase anyone.' Yep, maybe he still was a little bit arrogant. A sigh huffed across his lips. 'You want to hear my story or not?'

The surprise in her eyes told him she hadn't expected him to continue his tale. *Well, Ellie, nor did I.* But now he'd started he didn't want to stop. He wanted her to know what drove him and how he'd arrived here. The idea of opening his heart to her appealed, when it had never done so in the past. Never. Which should be a warning.

So he stalled. 'Let's order some food. Want me to choose? Anything you won't like?'

'As I have no idea what the locals eat, you go ahead. I can't think of anything I won't enjoy. Tell you what, though, they brew great beer.'

'Their food's just as good.' He beckoned to the waitress and rattled off a few dishes he thought would be a good introduction to Lao food. Then he drank deeply from his glass and wiped the back of his hand over his mouth. 'My father left before we were born.' Ellie had met Angelique, his twin, when they were sharing that house in Auckland. Ange would often drop in for a night, sleeping on the floor in the corner of the lounge. 'Growing up knowing he'd never wanted to meet us, to be a part of our lives, that he didn't love us…' He paused, looked directly at Ellie. 'It was horrible. I used to look at men who were about the age I thought my father might be and wonder if they were our dad.'

Ellie ran her fingers down his arm. 'That's horrid. Did you never try to track him down through phone directories or electoral rolls when you were older?'

'Mum refused to tell us his name or where he came from, not even what he did for a living. Nothing. It was as though he'd never existed.'

'Her way of coping, maybe?'

'Possibly, but as kids we didn't understand that. Hell,

as an adult I still find it hard to accept.' He wasn't admitting to the equally awful thought that maybe his mother hadn't known who their father was because she'd slept with more than one man at the time they were conceived. As Gaylene had done with him, but they hadn't been a couple until she'd learned she was pregnant.

As far as his mum was concerned, he wouldn't judge her. His mother's life hadn't been easy growing up. Her father had been a bully and a thug to both her and her mother, and was not the kind of man a daughter could rely on for love and safety.

Understanding was blinking out at him from those hazel eyes less than a metre away. 'So when Gaylene declared you were the father of her baby you stepped up because no child of yours would not know their father.'

'Got it in one. Not that Gaylene knew my story, but she sure went for the jugular. In her eyes it didn't hurt that I was destined to become that head of department I'd planned on and would be earning a fat salary when I got there.' He tasted the sourness in his mouth. Thought he was long past letting what she'd done hurt him, huh? Thank goodness he hadn't loved her. That would've really turned him beyond bitter.

'You'd have married someone you didn't love for your child? Wouldn't it have been better for everyone to have remained single but fully involved with that child?' Ellie made everything seem so simple. Was that how she looked at life? A memory rose of her spitting words in his face, defending Baldwin when he'd tried to make her see reality. *He's a real man, of course he's played the field, but now he's settling down—with me*, she'd insisted.

Now she was here, without a wedding ring on her finger, and a change of name. Not so simple, eh?

'Didn't matter in the end,' he sighed. It hadn't been as straightforward as Ellie made it sound. Certainly not when Gaylene had been pressuring him so hard. He hadn't wanted to appear not to be taking his responsibilities seriously but at the same time it hadn't been easy to accept he was going to be a father when he'd spent his adult life doing his damnedest not to become one. 'I would never put any child through what Angelique and I had to deal with. Never.' Which was why he wasn't going to have children. Not only hadn't he known his father, his grandfather had been the worst example of a parent. He'd often wondered if having bad male role models on both sides of his family meant he'd be a terrible father, had inherited some chromosome that made men bad. He wasn't going to find out because if he was like them then it would be too late for any offspring he procreated.

'Oh, Luca, I never knew.' She locked those eyes on his. 'Not that I was meant to. I get that, too. But for the record I think you'd be a wonderful father. Just in case...' Her words trailed off.

Had the bile rising in his throat been that obvious? 'Thanks for the vote of confidence. It's good to know someone believes in me so blindly.'

'Ouch. You're not playing fair. I know you, have seen you working with children when they're in pain and terrified, still remember you cuddling Angelique's wee boy only hours after he was born. You have the right instincts, believe me.' This time she sipped her beer.

He'd like nothing more than to believe her, but that would be a huge leap of faith, right off the edge of the planet, in fact. He settled with, 'Wee Johnny is now at school and whipping up merry hell with his teachers. He wants to be an All Black without having to go through the usual channels.' Johnny was a great kid, so bright and busy and full of beans. He missed him.

'Is he? Got a photo?' Ellie seemed keen to get away from the uncomfortable conversation they'd been having.

He tugged his phone from the back pocket of his pants and tapped the icons. 'There. Isn't he a handsome dude?'

Snatching the phone from his grasp, Ellie stared at the picture. 'Just like his uncle.'

'I'm handsome?'

'I meant cheeky and obviously up to mischief.' She swiped the screen, moving on to more photos of his nephew. And Angelique. 'Oh. Your sister looks so much like your mother now.'

As in sad and bitter? 'Yes, the spitting image.' In every way. 'I tried to make up for Johnny not having a father, but for her I can't be anything but a brother.' Not even a good one now. Anger welled up. 'How could she have done the same thing as Mum? She knew what it was like not having a dad around the place. Hated it, and swore she'd never let her kids go unloved.'

'Hey.' Ellie's hand was back on his arm, warm and soft.

Almost sexy—if she wasn't a friend and that wasn't a friendly gesture. What was going on? Luca blinked. 'What?'

'Angelique's not as strong as you. Never was. Remember when you used to insist she should be studying at university for a career and she wanted to work in a café? She liked what she was doing, and you couldn't change who she was.'

'Yeah, I've finally worked that out.' *Focus, man. On the conversation and nothing else.* He had to be out of sorts because of Ellie's sudden reappearance in his life. He'd missed her. A lot. Yeah, that was all that odd sensation around her touch was about.

She hadn't finished. 'But, Luca, you support her, stand by her and look out for her son. That's huge.' Ellie sounded so sure, it was scary.

'Wrong. I'm over here, not at home, aren't I?' Guilt ramped up, but Angelique had told him to get out of her life and stop interfering with how she raised her son just about the time his carefully planned career was getting on top of him. It had begun to seem a hollow victory when there was no one to share it with. He'd started questioning everything he'd believed in. Except not being a parent. That was non-negotiable. No exceptions.

Hot spices wafted through the air and four small plates of mouth-watering food appeared on the counter in front of them. Perfect timing. This talking with Ellie was getting too deep and uncomfortable.

She was licking her lips and sniffing the air like a dog on the scent. He did what he always did when the going got tough—he grinned. Amazing how that helped all the tension fall away. However temporary, it felt good to be with her knowing she wouldn't try to rip him off or take something from him he didn't want to give. Good friends were rare and priceless. And El was the best. So why did he feel he had to keep reminding himself of that? It was as though something had changed between them that he couldn't fathom. Luca shrugged. He had four weeks to work it out before she headed home again.

The woman distracting him said, 'Tell me more about the clinic.'

A reprieve, then. 'It's heartbreaking seeing what these children deal with, and yet uplifting because of their sunny natures and how they take it all in their little strides.'

'I was really moved today when the kids gathered around me, all chatter and laughter when they'd never met me.' The sticky rice and peanut sauce were delicious. Ellie forked up more and watched Luca do the same. He'd told her more about his past tonight than in all the previous years she'd known him. He'd surprised her, but then today had been full of surprises on all fronts.

Thinking back, she saw where she'd missed little clues about his past. Whenever talk had got around to families he'd been reticent, and she couldn't remember what he'd said about his father except he hadn't been around. Not once had he said that the man had never been there, was basically unknown. Hell, she might've got her marriage all wrong but her family had always been there for her when she was growing up. It was different nowadays, though. Awkward and sometimes downright hostile with Caitlin still coming and going in her parents' lives as though she'd done nothing wrong. But Luca had missed out on a lot, hadn't had that loving childhood she'd had, so why wasn't he wanting to have his own family and make up for that? Had he ever fallen in love? Come close, even? Sad, but she suspected not.

'Are you listening to me?' Luca elbowed her, causing rice to drop off her fork.

'Heard every word.' *I hope, or I'll be asking questions about what he's just told me tomorrow and then he'll give me stick.* 'The clinic is full to bursting at the moment.'

His grey eyes squinted at her. 'I said there are four spare beds.'

'You did not.' She laughed, and even to her that sounded strained. She changed the subject and determined to concentrate on everything he said. 'Who's Baxter?' She'd heard the kids talking about him when she was getting ready to come out with Luca.

'The clinic's pet pangolin.' She must've looked bewildered because he explained further. 'An anteater. They normally live in the trees. Apparently this one turned up one day with one leg half severed off. It was before my time. Aaron operated and now it slopes around minus a leg.'

'So Baxter knew where to go for an amputation.' This time her laughter was genuine.

Luca smiled back. 'The kids adopted him and he's stayed, sometimes foraging for ants farther afield, but he never goes very far. You'll see him soon enough.'

He pushed their empty plates aside. 'Feel up to a stroll beside the Mekong?'

Not really. She'd like nothing more than to fall into bed and get some more sleep. Glancing at her watch, she saw it was only just after eight thirty. And here she'd thought they'd been in the bar for hours. It was too early to go back to her room, especially after having slept most of the day. An evening stroll with Luca would be the next best thing. Maybe even better, and she could walk off the effects of all that beer. What had she been thinking having so much? Hadn't been thinking at all, that was what. Standing up, she slung her bag over her shoulder. 'Sure.'

Outside the air had cooled all of about two degrees. Ellie shook her head. 'To think I was looking forward to the warmth after a particularly cold spring back home.'

Luca caught her hand in his and swung their arms between them. 'I still haven't got used to the heat. Especially at night when I'm desperately tired and sleep's evasive.'

Ellie gently squeezed his hand, enjoying the strength of those firm fingers. This felt good. Being with someone who knew her and wouldn't make up things about her, wouldn't be sniggering behind her back, wouldn't be breaking any vows.

Neither of them talked as they strolled along a path lined with bars and nightclubs. Despite the noise from those buildings the sound of the river seeped into Ellie's mind, a steady pouring of an unbelievable amount of water carrying debris and fish along its path. Where had that branch come from? A few kilometres farther north? Or from another country? China, even? 'Amazing.'

'What is?'

'The river and all the countries it runs through.' Ellie turned towards Luca and missed her footing on the uneven surface.

He caught her waist, held her as she regained her balance. 'Careful. Can't have you breaking your ankle before you've even started working with us.'

'That would make me very unpopular.' Those hands were definitely showing their strength. And their heat. She could feel each finger distinctly from the others. A different kind of warmth than what the climate was producing caressed her feverish skin. Tipping her head back, she met Luca's stunned look. Carefully taking a backwards step, she extricated herself from his hold and dropped her gaze. And instantly felt she'd lost something. Something important. But this was Luca. Not some hot guy she'd want to go to bed with.

Really? Luca wasn't hot? Yes, he was, but she'd never thought of him like that. That would be too— Too strange? Or too hot to handle? She peeked up at him, found him staring out at the river now, an inscrutable look on his face. When had he got so good at those? Not back when she'd last knew him, for sure. Back then he used to make jokes to divert unwanted interest. These days she also had a few of her own special expressions that hadn't been around in those days.

'I think it's time for me to get back to my room,' she muttered and began to turn around.

'No problem.'

Even his voice sounded different: deeper, huskier. Reading way too much into everything? Eek, was she on the rebound from Freddy? The thought slammed into her brain, almost paralysing her. Was that what this was about? Reacting strangely to Luca because she felt safe with him? Could trust him? He'd never hurt her, physically or mentally. No, but she could get hurt by her own stupidity. Because she was being stupid. She mightn't have seen or spoken to Luca for years but she knew him—as a friend, and he was perfect like that. She didn't need or want to have anything else with him. Surely tomorrow she'd wake up refreshed and over whatever was ailing her.

'Ellie, are you all right?' His concern sounded genuine.

Had he not felt anything? Did that mean she could relax? No. Not until she'd stopped these silly sensations tripping her up every time Luca touched her. If she didn't, four weeks working with him were going to be tricky. Luca had always touched his friends whenever he wanted to share something with them or comfort them. 'I think I'm so tired I have no idea which way's up.' Which was completely true. 'I shouldn't have had those beers.'

'They might help you drop off to sleep quickly.' He waved over a hovering taxi. 'Come on, Sleeping Beauty. Time for your bed.'

Huh? Sleeping Beauty? More like droopy sad sack.

Luca handed Ellie out of the taxi and paid the driver. 'I wish they wouldn't turn all the outside lights off,' he growled as they headed up the path to the staff sleeping quarters.

'I'd have trouble finding my room if you weren't with me,' Ellie agreed.

'You'll soon know your way around. It's not a complex setting. The hospital is at the back with long wings off three sides. Ours is on the right and houses staff quarters, wards and our small operating theatre, with the tourist centre at the very end.'

'Tourists?' In a medical centre?

'The museum room. There're photos of bombs in the ground and the craters caused when they explode. Pictures of wounded children and their families hang everywhere. There's a real bomb that's had the detonator removed in the centre of the main viewing room, which is very dramatic and has tourists putting their hands in their pockets for money to fix more kids. Not that we'd stop even if the funds were rock bottom.'

'Is the foundation struggling?' Ellie asked, thinking that she could easily hand back the money she was being paid for her month here. She felt sure she was going to be the winner of her time spent with these wonderful people. Money didn't compare to exchanging hugs with a thirteen-year-old with only one arm who was determined to become a teacher when he grew up, as one lad had told her in her first five minutes here.

'Struggling's probably a bit strong, but there's never a well of cash. The foundation relies heavily on donations. One benefactor in the States has set up an investment fund that pays handsome dividends, and without that I'd say we'd be in big trouble.' Luca spoke with authority, as though he'd dug deep to learn all he could about the organisation helping these kids. No surprises there.

'You are getting quite a kick out of working in such a different environment from what you were used to, aren't you?'

'More than I'd expected,' Luca acknowledged. 'At first I worried I'd been stupid to sign up for twelve months, but it didn't take long to realise that I was enjoying practising medicine outside my usual comfort levels. There's as much drama here as in an A and E department, as you'll soon learn. But more than that, I'm in on the follow-up care, and over here that means getting to know the whole family—if there is a family, that is.' His voice went from excited to sad within a few words.

Ellie wrapped an arm around his waist. 'Reality sucks, doesn't it?'

'It can.' Then he said with what she thought was a smile in his voice, 'Then there are the success stories, like Chi who wants to become a doctor to help her people. She's going to Australia with Louise and Aaron when they decide to return home, which they're saying will be within two years.'

'What happens when they go? Are there replacements queuing to get in?'

He shrugged. 'Who knows?'

Was Luca considering it? 'Would you put your hand up?'

'The idea has crossed my mind.'

'You don't want to return home? You don't miss Auckland?' Now that they'd reconnected she didn't want to lose him again, but that didn't mean she'd be moving over here full time so as to spend more time with him.

Going back to the city where she'd done her internship and had loads of good times with Luca and her housemates had been an obvious choice when the temporary position at Auckland Hospital became available. She'd be housesitting for the specialist she was covering for and couldn't move into the house until he and his family headed away to America for his sabbatical.

A part of her still wanted the house-and-kids package—with a hot man, of course. But that meant learning to trust again, and she wasn't brimming with confidence of that happening. Especially since it wasn't only her husband who'd cheated on her but her sister, as well. Sometimes she thought Caitlin's treachery was worse. They'd been so close. *Not close enough to see she loved your husband.* True. Caitlin and Freddy were apparently talking about getting married when the divorce was settled. They had a wait on their hands because with New Zealand law that couldn't happen for more than another year.

Luca twisted out of her hold, reminding her he was with her. He'd remained silent for so long her mind had taken a trip into things she didn't need to be thinking about right now. Had her question about missing home hit a chord? Should she press the point? Once she would've. But there were years between then and now. She went for the easy option. 'You've gone quiet on me.'

'I don't have a home to miss. Angelique and Johnny have their own lives to lead that apparently don't include me. Auckland is my hometown, always will be, but it'll be there whenever I choose to return.'

'Hell, Luca.' That sounded incredibly sad and bleak. Where was the man who was always happy and making jokes, always acting as though he didn't have a worry in the world? Had he been leading a double life? But then she hadn't known about his father, or lack of one, until tonight, either. She stopped to look up at him, only just seeing his facial expressions in the star-studded darkness. The sadness for him grew into something else, roiling through her so that she wanted to reach out and touch him deeply, to show he wasn't alone, that she cared. 'I will never let you out of my life again.'

His jaw moved as he swallowed. He was staring at her, his eyes unblinking. When he spoke his voice was low and loaded with emotion. 'Thank goodness for that. It's been too long, El.'

Way too long, and the worst thing was that she hadn't even noticed until today. Reaching out to him, she was going to hug him, as she used to whenever they'd celebrated an exam pass or lost a patient or felt a little lonely. But then Luca's arms were tugging her in against his body, his head dipping so that his mouth found hers. With his lips on hers, his tongue slipped inside her mouth.

Ellie breathed deep, drew in Luca, a mix of beer and chilli and hot male. Of safety and—hot male. Surrendering to the need clawing through her, she focused on kissing him back and hoping she was wiping away that sadness that had been rolling off him in waves.

Then as suddenly as it started, the kiss ended. Luca abruptly dropped his arms and stumbled backwards. 'Ellie, I'm so sorry. I don't know what came over me. Look, that door to our right is your room. I'll see you tomorrow.' And he was gone, racing back the way they'd come, out onto the road and still he didn't slow down.

'Thanks very much, Luca. You're sorry? Talk about taking a knife and cutting into me. You're sorry for a mind-blowing kiss that I reckon you were enjoying as much as I was?'

But she was talking to the night. Luca was way beyond hearing her. Staring around the dark grounds, she could only sigh with relief that the lights were out. Doubtful anyone had seen them kissing. But her heart wasn't letting her off that easily. It pounded hard and fast while her hands shook and her skin tightened with need. Luca. What had they done? Whatever it was, she wasn't sorry. But she should be. She'd been kissing the man when only minutes before she'd acknowledged she never wanted to let him out of her life again. *Way to go, Ellie. No one kisses a friend like that, with that intensity and emotion.* It was sexy; very, very sexy. And her body was suffering withdrawal already. Which meant the future of their friendship was now in jeopardy.

CHAPTER FOUR

LUCA STUMBLED ALONG the road, not bothering to look where he was going. What had he been thinking when he'd kissed Ellie? He hadn't been thinking. That was the problem. Not with his brain anyhow. Ellie, of all people. He'd kissed her, his best friend, damn it.

And wanted to do it again.

No, I don't.

Yes, he did. Now. Sooner than later.

Oaths rent the air blue. What had he done to their friendship? As if that was going to move ahead after that particular little fiasco. Damn it. Ellie was—El. His long-lost friend. So lost he'd have been able to get in touch with her simply by going online and looking up her phone number. Or ringing the A and E department at Wellington Hospital. But he hadn't done it. He'd been smarting over her telling him to butt out of her life if he wasn't prepared to accept her decision to marry the man who was now her ex. Being right felt hollow. He regretted walking away. Not even being preoccupied with his own problem in a short skirt was an excuse. He'd let Ellie down.

Ellie didn't ring you, either.

Didn't make it right. But nor was kissing her right.

It had to be way up there with the dumbest things he'd ever done in his whole goddamned life. Worse, they had to work together for four whole weeks. That could prove uncomfortable. Or interesting.

Come up with some good news, will you?

Nope, couldn't think of any at this moment.

His pace slowed and he jammed his fists on his hips, tipped his head back to stare up at the sky.

No answers up there.

He resumed walking at a slower pace, breathing deep, letting the heavy, warm air calm him. There were no answers at all. He'd spent an evening talking with Ellie, sometimes about subjects they'd never touched on before, like about his sorry past. He'd got tied up in the fun of seeing her again and spilled his guts. Then he'd goddamned kissed her.

He needed his head read—only problem there it was such a shambles no one would be able to make anything out of it.

It was some kiss, though.

Shut up.

Go on. Admit it. When did a kiss ever give you an achy feeling in your heart?

There was the answer he was looking for. He hadn't realised just how much he'd missed Ellie, and now his heart was happy. As in how one friend would feel about another after four years' absence and everything that had happened in that time. For Ellie that had been a failed marriage for reasons he had yet to find out, and for him the loss of a child he'd never wanted but hated the opportunity being stolen from him. But Gaylene had only started this sense of not belonging anywhere. Angelique with her outrageous demands that he stay out of her and Johnny's lives had exacerbated his need to question everything he'd thought *his* life was about. Including being the head of a large A and E department.

No wonder his emotions were all over the show. That kiss had come out of nowhere, blindsiding him. Now all he had to do was move on and forget it ever happened.

Yep, that should work. Easy as.

Ellie woke slowly the next morning, her head feeling as though fog had slipped in to fill it while she'd been comatose. Guess the good news was that she'd slept at all. After Luca's knee-knocking, bone-rattling kiss she'd figured she'd never sleep again.

Luca had been late getting in last night. She'd heard him bumping into furniture in the next-door bedroom that she knew was his. Had he gone back to town and found a bar to try to drown out that kiss? Or didn't he care that he'd kissed her and stirred up all sorts of emotions she so wasn't ready to deal with?

Knock, knock.

'Who is it?' *Please don't be Luca.* Not yet while she was still in her satin shorts and cotton top.

'It's Chi. You've got to get up. Breakfast's nearly ready.'

Phew. Sometimes she did get what she asked for. 'Come in, Chi.'

The girl opened the door cautiously and peered around the room before stepping inside and closing the door again. 'Morning, Ellie. You've had a big sleep.'

If only that were true. A certain someone and his kiss had kept her awake staring into the dark for hours until eventually exhaustion had won out and dragged her under for a brief spell. 'I don't know where the kitchen is yet. Do you want to show me around after I get dressed?'

Chi nodded solemnly. 'We have breakfast early before everyone begins working. Then the tourists start visiting at nine.'

'Right. I'm heading for the shower. Two minutes, okay?' She snatched some clothes from her bag that had yet to be unpacked.

Chi was still in Ellie's room when she returned from a fast and cold shower. The bed had been made, every corner tucked in neatly, the pillow perfectly straight and the cover smoothed so as not one wrinkle showed.

'Thank you so much, but you don't have to look after me. I'm sure there are lots of other people here who need you more than me.'

'I like you.'

Tears blocked Ellie's throat. A hug was called for. It was the only way she could show her feelings right now with words backing up behind the lump in her throat, unable to squeeze past. For everything this child must've suffered it all came down to simple observations and reactions. Give and take. Hugs. 'I like you, too,' she finally managed to get out, then focused on getting ready for the day. She slapped on some make-up. Even here she'd try to look her best.

Not for Luca by any chance? *No way.*

'You've got a text.' Chi nodded at her phone on the desk.

Probably Mum or Dad. Despite the rift between her and Caitlin that overlapped into her relationship with her parents they would still want to know how she was settling in. Then another thought snapped into her head. What if it was from Luca?

'Come on, Chi, show me where to go.'

If it was from Luca he could wait until she'd worked out how to handle today after what went down last night.

She couldn't resist. Snatching up the phone as she headed out, she pressed Messages and gasped. It was from her sister, Caitlin. There was nothing she wanted to hear from her. Her finger hovered over the delete button. What if something had happened to Mum or Dad? That would be a good enough reason for Caitlin to text. But wouldn't she ring if that was the case?

She sighed. The message read, Just checking to see you arrived safe and sound.

Why don't you ask Mum? I sent them a message on the way in from the train station.

Ellie shoved the phone into her shorts pocket and followed Chi. What was Caitlin up to now? They didn't do texts or any form of communicating. That had finished the day she'd learned the truth about her sister and her husband. It had been a stunning birthday present; one she'd never forget. But sometimes when she wasn't thinking clearly she did admit to missing Caitlin. They'd been closer than grapes in a bunch, told each other everything. Everything? As in 'I'm sleeping with your husband, Ellie,' everything?

'In here.' Chi took her hand to tug her into a long narrow room that housed the kitchen and a very long trestle table.

'You must be Ellie.' A man in his late forties and of average height crossed the room, his hand extended in greeting. 'I'm Aaron. Sorry for the confusion yesterday about who you were. I've been in touch with headquarters and they admitted the oversight was entirely their fault.'

Ellie shook his hand in return. 'It doesn't matter. I'm here, you've got the bases covered. That's what's important.'

'True. We'll try to break you in quietly today. But there's no telling what will come in the doors at any given moment.' Aaron's smile was completely guileless and relaxed Ellie enough to put her sister aside for a more appropriate time when she was on her own.

Her nose twitched as the smell of something hot and delicious reached her. 'What do we eat for breakfast?'

'*Chew makork*. Eggs, carrots and sticky rice,' Chi told her.

Different. 'Bring it on.'

It was simple and delicious. There were other vegetables with the carrots, and a chilli sauce made her skin heat and her mouth water. For her the food was all part of the adventure.

Unfortunately so was the grim awakening as to why she was here that arrived as everyone was finishing breakfast.

Aaron, who'd headed away to check on a patient he'd operated on yesterday, now stood in the doorway. 'Incoming patients. Two of them. All hands on deck. Ellie, that includes you. We'll show you the ropes as we go along.'

Gulp. She hadn't seen the hospital or the small theatre yet. 'I'm ready.' *Fake it till you make it*. It wasn't as though she didn't know what to do, but she'd have liked a few minutes to learn where everything was kept.

Louise must've seen her hesitation because she said, 'You'll be fine.'

Love it when people who know next to nothing about you except what was in your CV say that. Ellie shook her head and prepared to face whatever had arrived in the little building at the end of the garden. 'Where's Luca this morning?'

His absence had surprised her. Was he avoiding her? That would be plain silly considering they had to spend a lot of time together over the next few weeks. Better to front up to last night and move on.

'He went out early to visit a family in a village who don't have the wherewithal to get in here for check-ups and dressing changes. It happens a lot and we try to accommodate everyone.'

Maybe he hadn't gone to get away from her. Ellie wasn't sure how she felt about Luca this morning. Good, bad or indifferent? Certainly not indifferent. Or bad. Okay, so her feelings were good. As in friends good? Or more? As in used to be friends, now might be something else? Lovers? Well, there wasn't anything else. She wasn't going down the full-blown relationship of being married and contemplating kids track for a long time—if at all. Her skin prickled with the humiliation of her last attempt at that. Then there was the pain she'd known as all her dreams had shrivelled up into a dry heap.

'In here.' Louise turned into a large room busy with people dashing back and forth and someone crying out in agony.

The sight had Ellie drawing on all her strength not to gasp out loud. The young patient being carried across the room hadn't had the benefit of an ambulance crew and a relatively soft ride. The child had been piggybacked in by a small man, the blood from where a foot should've been dripping a trail right across the hospital room. At least someone had managed to tie a makeshift tourniquet around his lower thigh so that the blood flow had been minimised, though not completely stopped.

'Where's the other patient?' she asked, trying not to convey her horror as she and Louise lifted the unconscious boy off the man's back and placed him on a bed. 'Aaron said patients, plural.'

'In front of us. The boy's father. He has an injury to his buttocks.' Louise nodded at a gaping wound that Ellie hadn't noticed as she'd been too busy focusing on the child. 'You can take him over to that bed for an assessment and report back to Aaron. Noi will interpret for you.'

'I haven't met Noi yet,' Ellie said over her shoulder as she approached her patient.

Louise beckoned a young man over and made the introductions. 'Noi learned English at school. He wants to be a doctor and is spending time with us until he can get into medical school here in Vientiane.'

'*Sabaai dii.*' She'd learned the greeting that morning over sticky rice and carrots. 'Lovely to meet you.' Ellie shook Noi's hand.

The way Noi said *sabaai dii* was definitely an improvement on her botched attempt.

She smiled. 'I need practice.'

Noi nodded. 'You'll soon learn. Let's help the father.'

Ellie could not imagine how the man they were easing onto the bed had carried his son on his back with the wound she was now seeing. He'd have been in agony, even without the constant pummelling he'd received from his load, yet he hadn't said a word or groaned out loud. Turning to Noi, she said, 'Can you explain to our patient what I'm going to do? Also ask if he has any other injuries.'

While Noi spoke rapidly in Laotian she cut away what was left of the man's trousers, careful to be as discreet as possible, and hearing the tremor in the father's voice as he replied to Noi.

Noi told her, 'The father heard the explosion and found his son on the side of the road with his foot missing. When he stepped around him to lift him away from the danger another, smaller explosion happened. That's when he was hurt.'

Lucky for him there were no other injuries. This one was bad enough and going to cause him a lot of pain and anguish until it mended.

Crossing to where Louise and Aaron were working on the boy, she reported, 'That wound on the buttocks is the only injury. Muscle damage is severe and will require deep suturing. I need to administer pain relief before cleaning the wound and stitching.'

Aaron replied, 'Louise will get what you require from the drugs cabinet. Later this morning when we're done with these patients I'll show you everything and give you the codes for that and other locked rooms.'

'We'll be in surgery shortly with this lad, trying to save his lower leg,' Louise told her. 'Can you intubate him while I get what you require?'

'Of course.' She swapped places with Louise, and suctioned the lad's airway clear of fluids prior to inserting the tube. Next she attached the mask and began running oxygen, keeping an eagle eye on the boy's breathing. 'Don't the locals know to stay clear of the bombs? Or am I being simplistic?'

Aaron was having difficulty getting a needle into a vein in the thin forearm but eventually managed to get it into a vein on the back of the boy's hand, giving access for saline and drugs. 'At last.' He looked up at Ellie. 'You're seeing things as someone coming from a safe and relatively comfortable society does, as we've all done when we first arrived. These people are extremely poor. Scrap metal fetches on the market what's to them a lot of money. If a child can sell a piece he's helping feed his family. It's a no-brainer for them. It's also why a lot of children are missing limbs. Or worse. Welcome to Laos.'

Ellie surprised herself by finding a smile. 'I'm glad to be here. Truly.' Helping people and animals when they were in need had always been a big deal to her, and was the reason she'd gone into medicine. At first she'd been aiming to become a vet, but as she'd got older she'd swapped frogs and guinea pigs for humans. The idea of going to vet school had been quickly vanquished when her favourite dog had to be put down after being run over by a truck. No way could she ever deliberately put down any living creature, even if it was for the best. She just didn't have what it took.

Louise returned and handed her a kidney dish containing vials and syringes. 'Here you go. Once you've finished there can you move over to the day clinic and help with the day patients? I'm sorry we haven't had time to show you the ropes, but Luca assures us you're very good at your job.'

Luca had? Guess he'd talked with these two about her yesterday while she'd been in dreamland. He was four years out of touch, but she'd take the compliment anyway. Those had been lacking lately, and it felt good to have someone still believing in her without qualification. 'Not a problem.'

'Thanks.' Louise began heading for Theatre, then

paused. 'If Luca's not back when you're ready, ask Noi to introduce you to everyone.'

'Here I go, then,' Ellie whispered as she vigorously scrubbed her hands under a tap. 'The first day of a new venture. The first day after Luca kissed me.' And apparently he was due back any time soon. How would they look each other in the eye? The knowledge of their responses to that kiss had to come between them. So how to move beyond it without making a hash of things? If they didn't, the rest of her days here would be uncomfortable and difficult for both of them.

Ellie, focus on the job and stop worrying about the tomorrows.

If only it were that easy.

It could be. Face it, why did everything have to be complicated? What would be wrong about having a few kisses with Luca? Seeing where they led? Chances were they'd get over each other quickly and return to a relationship they were comfortable with. Not one where they didn't see each other or talk together for years, please. She was done with that. Done with losing the people in her life that were precious to her. Getting one person back was amazing, and she needed to tread carefully or risk losing him again.

So how did one go about retracting a kiss?

A memory of the heat that had zapped between them at his touch told her. It was impossible. As in it was too late. She was fried. The chances of looking at Luca without wondering what it would be like to feel his body against hers, inside her, were remote. This rebound thing had a lot to answer for. Who'd have thought it? The only explanation she could come up with on the spot was that she knew Luca well and would be safe with him while she tried to find her feet in the dating game. But she hadn't been contemplating getting into that murky pool for some time to come.

Luca leaned a shoulder against the door frame of the outpatients' clinic. A yawn rolled up and out, stretching his mouth and making him aware of the grit in his eyes. Damn, he was tired. Sleep had been impossible last night. Every time he'd closed his eyes his mind had filled with images of Ellie.

Ellie blinking at him in astonishment as he'd crossed the room to hug her for the first time in years.

Ellie in that curve-hugging shift dress that emphasised her figure and did nothing to curb the desire tugging at his manhood.

Ellie looking glum when she mentioned her broken marriage. Not that she'd said a lot. But there'd definitely been sadness and despair in those hazel pools that seemed to draw him in deeper every time he locked gazes with her. Like a vortex, swirling faster and faster. He had yet to hit the centre, but it was coming. He could feel it in his muscles—each and every one of them, damn it.

Watching her now as she talked to Noi, obviously getting him to explain to their patient what she had to do to help him, Luca felt that peculiar clenching of his heart again. A sensation he'd only felt once before— yesterday when he'd been with Ellie.

So much for heading out early to avoid her until he'd got his thoughts and emotions into some semblance of order. Only minutes back at the clinic and he was in trouble. Wondering where these feelings would lead him. Hoping nothing was about to come between him and Ellie again. He'd do anything for that not to happen.

So he wouldn't be kissing her again?

Damn right he wouldn't.

Dragging air deep into his lungs, he crossed to help with her patient. 'Hey, need a hand?'

Startled eyes locked on him. 'Luca. When did you get back?'

'Minutes ago.' There were green flecks in her eyes he hadn't noticed before. Could eyes change like that? Or had he just opened his wider? Begun to see things that had always been before him? 'What's the story here?' He tried to shut down the runaway heat speeding through his veins. 'Apart from those buttocks, I mean.'

'Nothing else. This man's been lucky.' Ellie's mouth twisted. 'I mean luckier than his son, and luckier than he might've been. It's unbelievable what's happened to them.'

Touching a finger to the back of her hand, Luca nodded. 'It's okay. I know what you mean. It takes time to get past the horror of bombs blowing up and hurting innocent people. This is for real, and we are so not used to it. You'll never get comfortable with it to the point you stop thinking and wondering why it has to happen at all, but you will come to accept that it does and we're here to help.'

Her teeth nibbled at her bottom lip as she stared down at the wound she was about to repair. 'Thanks. I needed to hear that. Here I was thinking I'd seen it all in the emergency department. Stabbings, shootings, high-speed car crashes. Awful scenarios, but this—' she waved a hand through the air '—children, adults, bombs, severed limbs. It's grotesque.'

'Yes, it is. Now, do you want me to assist while you put this man back together?' One of the nurses could do that but he was hoping with everything he had she'd say yes. He wanted to work with her. Maybe then reality would return, banishing this stupid need thickening his blood every time he so much as looked at Ellie. Time spent doing a medical procedure together would bring back memories of their training days in A and E and hopefully follow on with more reminders of what their relationship was about.

'That would be great,' she answered. 'I've given him painkillers, enough that hopefully he'll be drowsy while I stitch him back together.' Ellie proceeded to outline how she intended going about fixing her patient's wound. 'What happens when we've patched him up? Does he stay here?'

Luca shook his head. 'He will be transferred to Mahosot Hospital. We don't keep adult patients in our ward.'

The man turned his head to stare at Luca. He asked in Laotian, 'My boy. Where is he? Is he safe?'

When Luca interpreted Ellie told him, 'Aaron has him in Theatre. He's lost his foot and ankle. You'll know what to tell him about how Aaron will help his boy.'

Nodding, Luca explained to the father how the doctors would clean the stump and stop the blood flow. He kept it brief and simple. There'd be time later for the family to come to terms with the extent of the surgery going on in Theatre. Then he focused on assisting Ellie.

They worked well together, each anticipating the other's requirements without a word being spoken. And yes, the memories flooded in, unnerving him. A whiff of the past when they worked well together gave a hint of what the future could hold if they went down that track.

Nearly thirty minutes later Ellie tied off the last stitch and reached for a swab to clean the last of the blood on the surrounding skin. 'The risk of infection will be high, especially if this man goes back to his village in the next few days. What's the next step in his treatment?'

'Don't expect him to stay in hospital. There'll be pressing issues back home he'll want to attend to, like earning enough money for food,' Luca told her.

'The people I saw sitting on the front step yesterday when I arrived. They were parents of our patients?' She added, 'I thought *they* were the patients.'

'They'd mostly be mums and dads.'

'What about our man's son? Will he go home, too?' Again horror was reflected in her eyes.

A gnawing need to hold her tight against him and to shield her from all this grew larger and larger, and he had to swallow hard to hold back. 'Hopefully, with Noi's help, we can persuade the family to leave the boy with us until his wound heals. Sometimes a relative will move in to be with their family member, but that depends on if they can afford someone to be away from home for so long.'

'I've lived a very sheltered life.' Ellie lifted sad eyes to him.

'You're not regretting coming here?' He hoped not. Otherwise her month would stretch out interminably for her. But he also didn't want her stressed by what she was dealing with. Not everyone could cope with it, and Ellie seemed to already be under pressure from something else.

'Not at all. It's an eye-opener and I think I needed that. I've been getting too self-absorbed lately.'

Guess a marriage breakup might do that. 'Come

on, we'll grab a coffee while we can. Day clinic starts shortly. I'll be showing you the ropes.'

And working my tail off to forget that damned kiss.

'What do you do for a social life here?' Ellie asked, her eyes not quite meeting his.

'Drink beer with long-lost friends,' he answered flippantly.

'That exciting, eh?'

'Yeah, very exciting.'

'Luca, about last night—'

He shouldn't have said *very exciting*. She was getting the wrong idea. 'Last night was a mistake, okay? I'm putting it down to the shock and surprise of us catching up when we least expected it. Nothing more than that.'

'Fine.' Her gaze dropped, focused somewhere below his chin. 'That's good. I'll do that, too.'

Yeah, except it didn't feel good. Not at all.

CHAPTER FIVE

In Outpatients, Ellie ruffled a toddler's hair while squatting down beside the wee tot to check out a healing wound on the girl's arm. Luca's mouth dried. Ellie was beautiful. More beautiful than ever, even with that wariness that never seemed to completely go away. How could he not have kept in touch? Even knowing that the man she'd chosen to marry was wrong for her, especially knowing that, he should never have let other things get in the way of their friendship.

But he had. Now she was back, in his life, on his turf. And he was having these weird and wonderful reactions to her. Weird and wonderful? Or weird and weirder?

Beside him Noi said, 'The children already love her.'

'She certainly has a way with them,' Luca acknowledged. Not something he'd particularly noticed before. But then why would he? He hadn't been in the habit of taking notes of her attributes.

As Ellie carefully lifted the toddler's shirt she spoke softly and got no resistance to her gentle prods around the child's rib cage.

Luca sighed. 'She'd make a wonderful mother.'

He hadn't realised he'd spoken out loud until Noi asked, 'Ellie doesn't have children already?'

'In the Western world it's not uncommon for women to have children later in life than they do here.' Did Ellie want children of her own? He couldn't remember ever discussing that with her, but then they'd been so busy getting on with becoming doctors they hadn't been looking that far ahead. Until she'd met Baldwin, that was.

Noi shook his head, but refrained from comment. Probably didn't understand the differences between their cultures. 'I'll see you in the ward.'

'Luca, there you are,' a little boy squealed and ran across the room to him.

Ellie jerked around, a startled look on her face. 'Luca.' She gave him a brief nod and returned to her patient.

As he reached for the boy flinging himself at him he winced. Ellie hadn't been falling over herself to be friendly since yesterday when they'd talked about their kiss. While he should be grateful she wasn't pushing for a follow-up kiss, a part of him wished otherwise. He'd like nothing more than to repeat it, to taste her sweetness again, to feel his body fire up in anticipation of something more. No, not that. That desire had kept him awake again last night. Keep this up and he'd be a walking zombie by the time her month was up.

'Luca, say hello,' the boy demanded.

'Hi, Pak. How's that arm?' he asked, watching Ellie and tucking the boy against his chest.

'It's better now. The concrete can come off.'

'No, it can't. You've got another week before I remove it.'

A smile was hovering at the corners of Ellie's mouth, as though afraid to come out fully. 'Concrete, eh?'

'It's what the kids call their casts. Concrete sleeves,'

he explained as Pak wriggled in his arms. 'You want to get down already?' he asked in Laotian.

'Yes.'

'I like that you speak the lingo.' Ellie stood up, admiration lightening those big eyes and lifting her mouth into a full, delicious smile.

Delicious smile? He was deranged. Had to be. Why else was he wanting to kiss that mouth? Again? When he knew absolutely that it would be wrong, would lead to all sorts of complications? 'Not very well.'

The smile faltered, disappeared. 'You've made a start.' She turned away, picked up a stethoscope and knelt down to the toddler, who seemed rooted to the floor as she stared at Ellie. Had she fallen for her, too?

Fallen for her? *No damned way. I have not.* This was getting stranger and stranger. Luca mentally slapped his head. Put Pak down. Strode back the way he'd come, heading for the ward and the children who needed him to check their stumps, needed encouragement to start walking again, or using arms that were shorter than they used to be. Away from Ellie and those eyes that drew him in.

So he was running away? Acting like a coward now? What else was he supposed to do?

Face up to her. Get past that kiss.

Luca didn't miss a step as he spun around and headed back to the outpatients' room, right up to where Ellie was straightening up again. Reaching for her, he drew her close and lowered his head.

Just before his mouth claimed hers he muttered, 'This has got to stop. We need to move past whatever's causing us to act out of character.' Then he kissed her. Long and hard, tasting her, letting her taste him. Feeling the moment when the tension left her body and she melted in against him. Feeling those lush breasts pressed against the hard wall of his chest. Sensing her heightened awareness of him.

His growing need strained against his trousers, about to push against the softness of her belly.

Luca tore his mouth away, dropped his hands to his sides, glared into Ellie's startled eyes, and growled, 'There, we've got that out of the way. Now we can work together without any distractions.'

And he walked away. If he could call his rapid shuffle a walk.

How had he come up with all that stuff? No distractions? He'd just made a monumental error and ramped up the distraction meter to such a level it was off the Richter scale. And he'd thought he couldn't get any more stupid. Went to show how wrong a guy could be when diverted by a beautiful woman. So much for bravery. He had not intended on kissing Ellie when he returned to her.

So why had he gone back?

He seriously had no idea. Other than not wanting to be thought of as a coward. Which only went to show what an idiot he really was. Kissing Ellie again had not dampened down his ardour. Hell no. Now he wanted more. More kisses, more touching, more of everything.

Good one, Chirsky, good one.

Idiot.

Ellie's fingers were soft on her lips, tracing where Luca's mouth had touched hers. *Stunned* didn't begin to describe how she felt. When Luca had charged back into the room with a determined expression darkening his face she'd had no idea what it was about. There'd been a moment when she'd wondered if he was angry at her for some misdemeanour, except she hadn't been here long enough to stuff up anything. But then he'd hauled her into his arms and kissed her—thoroughly. Not angrily.

She'd kissed him back equally enthusiastically. It had been a kiss to defy all kisses. It shouldn't have happened. But it had, and now Ellie had to work out a way forward. In Luca's eyes that kiss should end all speculation and leave them free to get back to being who they were to each other. Friends without benefits.

'Ellie?' Louise stood before her, that worried look of two days ago back in her kind eyes. 'Are you all right?'

I've just been kissed by my best friend. How am I supposed to feel? 'I'm fine.' Uh-oh, had Louise seen her and Luca in that embrace? 'I was checking out Took.' *Before I was interrupted.* 'She's got a chest infection.' *I was checking out Luca, too, but that doesn't count. Not much. I think his chest is okay. Nah, it's hard and muscular and I want to run my tongue the length of it. Much more than okay.*

'That's Took's second infection in three weeks. I don't think there's a lot of clean water at home for keeping the wound site under her arm sterile.' Louise was studying Ellie with a very wise expression on her face. 'When you're done here, would you like me to show you how the outpatients is run instead of you working with Luca in the amputation clinic?'

Ellie knew Louise had been looking forward to a morning off to go into town. Tempting as her offer was, Ellie couldn't accept. She was here to help, not hinder the running of the clinic and the staff's downtime. 'Not at all. I've been looking forward to meeting some of those other patients.'

'As long as you're sure.'

'Louise—' Ellie grimaced '—I'm sorry. Luca and I used to be very close friends and then life got in the way. It's the best thing that could've happened, finding him working here. Truly.' On a long, slow breath she added, 'I've missed him a lot and I think he feels the same. Things have just got out of whack, but we'll settle down. You'll see. I do not want to upset anything going on here. I came to help, not disrupt.'

Finally she got a big smile from Louise. 'Any time you feel like a glass of wine and a girl talk you know where to find me.'

'You're a champ. Now I need to get some antibiotics for Took.'

'I'll walk down to the drug cupboard with you. Aaron wants some mild painkillers for his patient.'

One of the many notches in Ellie's tummy loosened. 'I heard the markets are only open in the mornings. Is that right?'

'That's what the brochures say but I've never found them closed before late afternoon yet. Aaron and I usually go there at least one afternoon a week and carry on to a bar and restaurant. Want to join us this afternoon after everyone's wrapped up here? Luca's coming,' she added quickly.

'I'd love to.' She wasn't going to let that kiss spoil her getting out and seeing the sights and enjoying shopping in the local places. Doing that with people who already knew their way around would be more fun, too. She wasn't into getting lost and trying to find her way around. Didn't have the patience, for a start. 'There's something about markets I adore.'

'You're a softie. I can see you buying from every stall.'

'Could be a long day,' she agreed. 'It will be fun.'

Hopefully Luca would see things in the same light and not get het up about her joining them. Otherwise he could be the one to miss out. She wasn't going to stay back in her room. And the added bonus was more time spent with Luca. She had an itch to quieten.

'Hey, Ellie, come meet Ash,' Luca called out the moment she walked into the clinic. He was all professional and outwardly friendly. Almost as if that kiss hadn't happened. Or was on hold?

He'd got himself all together quick enough. Guess that meant he wasn't as rattled as she'd been. Still was. But then Luca had had plenty of experience at hiding what he didn't want anyone else to know about him. She tried to follow his example and focused on the boy. 'Hi, Ash. Why do we call you that?'

Luca explained, 'Because his name is longer than the alphabet and equally unpronounceable for Westerners. It starts with *A* so he's called Ash.' Luca was squatting beside a boy who couldn't be more than four, and had only one leg.

'Makes a lot of sense—not.'

When Luca looked up at her she found smiling at him wasn't too difficult. There were no recriminations peeking out, no annoyance with her for succumbing to his kiss. So she could even begin to think he might have been right—they'd needed to get that second kiss out of the way to move on. Really? Make that a no, but she'd do her best not to show how much she wanted to follow up on it.

Kneeling beside Ash, she turned to concentrate on the boy's stump. 'This happened recently? Two or three weeks ago?'

Luca nodded. 'Three. We're still getting the hang of using crutches, aren't we, Ash?'

The boy nodded slowly, his huge dark eyes sombre as he studied her, still staying close to Luca. As if he trusted his doctor for everything. That was wonderful.

The boy was so young, younger than most she'd seen around here so far. 'Does Ash stay here all the time or is he a day patient?'

Luca locked his gaze on her and that was when she saw the apprehension in the backs of his eyes. So he wasn't being blasé about her or their kiss, just working on keeping it in perspective. But he answered the question she'd voiced, not the one spinning around her skull about where they went from that moment back in the treatment room. 'Ash is living with us for now. His mum and dad visit whenever they can get in from their village, which is up in the hills north of here.'

In other words not very often. Ellie's heart squeezed for this brave little guy, and she put her own concerns aside. 'How many brothers and sisters have you got, Ash?'

Ash stared at her for a moment, before turning to Luca for an interpretation. 'Four' was the answer.

'I can see why you've learned some of the language,' Ellie told Luca. 'These kids need you to understand them, don't they?' It had to be hideous finding themselves with such awful injuries in a clinic surrounded by people speaking strange words. Yet Luca chattered to Ash as though he was totally au fait with the boy's language. She asked, 'How do you say I like you?'

Luca nodded in understanding and slowly enunciated a phase that was almost incomprehensible.

Ellie grinned at Ash and tried to repeat the phrase. 'Don't think I'm making any sense to him at all.' She laughed.

'Try again after me.'

Same sound, same result, except Ash was starting to smile at her. A slow awakening that lifted his sad face and lightened those eyes to a dark brown, the blackness dissipating.

When Luca told him what she'd been trying to say his little smile grew and he nodded at her before putting his tiny hand on her arm.

That felt like the best thing to happen to her. After Luca's amazing kiss, that was. A quick glance at Luca and she found him watching her so intently her cheeks began heating up.

'Ash likes you, too.' His words were a caress, making her think there was more to what he said. Luca liked her, too?

Right, let's get this show on the road and stop mooning over Luca. 'Can I help him with his crutches?'

'Sure. We've just had a new pair made, which in clinic speak means an old pair cut down to Ash's size. The ones he's been using were way too big for him and he kept tripping, which caused awful pain.' Luca was all doctor mode now.

'So he's not going to be keen to get moving on these newer ones.'

'You got it.' Luca ruffled the boy's hair in that casual yet caring manner he did so well. Had he ever thought about having his own family? A warmth trickled through her at the thought of Luca surrounded by his own children.

'Is there an adult pair somewhere?' she asked and grinned when Luca's eyes widened in understanding.

'Why have I never thought of that? Over in that walk-in cupboard.' He nodded in the direction of two doors butted up together. 'Have you ever had to use crutches yourself?'

'Nope. But that's the point. I can make mistakes, too.'

'This I have to watch.' Luca chuckled as she headed for the cupboard.

Trying the crutches out for size, she quickly had a pair and started back to Ash, swinging between the wooden implements that had seen better days a long time ago. It wasn't as easy as she'd thought it would be, but that was fine. She didn't want to be perfect in front of the boy. She'd rather fall over and laugh. Though she didn't want Ash falling. For him it would be too painful. 'Let's go.' She nodded at him.

Ash stared at her, not making any move to get off the chair. Two big tears slid down his cheeks and he shook his head from side to side.

Ah, hell. Tears would be her undoing any time. She'd rather wrap him up in a blanket and read him a story than make him do this. But, 'Come on. You'll be good.'

Luca held out the small crutches and said something in Laotian. Whatever it was his voice was soothing and encouraging, and slowly Ash stood up on his good leg and took the crutches being held out to him.

Go you, Luca. 'We'll do this together,' Ellie said and, standing on one foot, moved her crutches forward and waited.

Luca interpreted.

Ash bit into his bottom lip and his face crunched up in concentration.

Ellie held her breath.

So did Luca.

Ash lifted the crutches and put them farther in front of him.

'Go you. Now we hop.' Ellie demonstrated, making sure she didn't go too far forward.

Luca interpreted.

Ash hopped. The crutches wobbled dangerously.

Ellie held her breath as Luca held his hands beneath Ash's arms without actually touching him, ready to catch him if the crutches went from under him.

Panic flared in Ash's eyes as he swayed and grappled for balance. When he was standing straight again he looked down at the crutches as though they were to blame for his predicament.

'That's good, Ash.' Ellie kept her tone light and encouraging. 'Now we'll do it again.' And again, and again.

Slowly they progressed across the room, and with every step Ash's confidence grew. The fear softened from his face as determination crept into his eyes, tightened his mouth. He was going to make these crutches work no matter what.

'Don't get too cocky,' Ellie warned. A fall onto the floor would set him back again.

'Take a break,' Luca told her, and then repeated the same thing to Ash in Laotian.

Or she supposed that was what he was saying. 'I'll stop if Ash does.'

Ash said nothing, just turned and began crossing the room back to where they'd started.

Ellie hurried to catch up, nearly tripping over her own feet. Ash looked at her and almost laughed. Almost but not quite. His mouth widened, his eyes lit up and his chest lifted, then everything stopped and he went back to solemn. Guess he didn't do laughing since the devastation that had brought him to the clinic's attention. Life for these kids would become very hard when they grew up and had to struggle to compete for work in an environment not flush with jobs and cash even for the uninjured.

She wasn't going to let that distract them from having fun while he learned to get around. This was only the first step of learning to be mobile again. 'You little ratbag.' She grinned. 'It's a game now, is it?' She held back on racing him. He was not ready for that yet. But it wouldn't be long before he was running around on those sticks as though born with them. Ellie reckoned that soon the staff would be wishing he'd sit down and keep still for a while. 'I am so glad I came here.'

Luca grinned. 'Glad you see it that way. I get such a kick from helping these guys.'

'You're a natural with children.'

He looked shocked. 'I am?'

'Definitely.' And what was more, she really liked that. How come she'd never noticed it before?

'Luca,' Sharon, a nurse, called across the room. 'There's been an accident outside the clinic and the victim's been brought in here. His heart's stopped so there's no time to wait for an ambulance to take him next door.'

Luca said, 'Coming. Get Carol to take over with Ash. Ellie, can you join me?'

'Be right there.' She helped Ash put down his crutches and sit on his seat again. His legs were shaking from the strain of learning to balance and hop, but his eyes were wide with excitement.

'I'm here.' Carol sank down on the chair beside the

boy. 'We'll do some exercises and rubbing on your muscles now, Ash.' Carol was a physiotherapist and had a love-hate relationship with the children for the pain and relief she brought them.

Ellie dashed to the small resus unit, where an elderly man lay on the bed. Luca was already leaning over him performing CPR while a nurse gave oxygen as required.

'There's a defib in Theatre,' Luca told her.

Ellie raced to get it and, returning, opened the kit and began attaching the pads. 'Stand back, everyone.' After checking everyone was out of the way she pressed the start button and held her breath as the mechanical voice recited the procedure that was underway. The patient's body arched off the bed, dropped back. Instantly the cardiac monitor began beeping instead of the flat tone it had been giving.

'Hoorah.' A muted cheer went up.

Luca stepped back and wiped the sweat from his brow with the back of his hand. 'Strike one to us. Might as well sort out those wounds while he's here. I wonder which came first—the accident or the cardiac arrest?' he said as he began examining the man thoroughly.

Ellie shook her head in amazement as she tossed her gloves into a bin half an hour later and watched their patient being wheeled through the building to the hospital annex. 'That's one lucky man. Who gets catapulted through the front windscreen, lands on a pole in a ditch and only gets concussion with lacerations and bruising?'

'You're forgetting the heart attack that probably caused him to drive off the road in the first place.' Luca rubbed his eyes with his fingertips.

'He chose the right spot for his accident,' Ellie said as she watched Luca. There were shadows under his eyes. 'Are you having trouble sleeping?' she asked before she engaged her brain in gear. What if he said he'd lain awake last night thinking about that first kiss? She wouldn't know how to handle that. It was bad enough having to work with him and pretend they hadn't kissed a second time, and that the entire staff probably knew about it because little children knew no boundaries when it came to being discreet.

'It was hotter than usual last night,' Luca muttered without looking at her.

'Really?' A little devil was making her question things best left alone. The same devil that had her wanting more of Luca's kisses. 'I didn't notice.'

'You've only been here a few days. All the night temperatures will be hot to you.' Luca's gloves headed in the same direction as hers. 'Coffee?' he asked, then looked shocked for asking.

The devil replied, 'Sure. Why not? Unless we're needed in the clinic again.' She should be wishing they were. But she wasn't.

'We're due a break.'

Ellie followed Luca to the kitchen. 'What's next on the list of things to do?'

As Luca stirred a load of sugar into his coffee he said, 'This afternoon I'm visiting two villages where we have kids still adjusting to their prostheses. You're coming with me.'

'Great. Seeing where these families live will be interesting.'

'It's a damned eye-opener is what it is. Don't go expecting a pretty picture, Ellie, otherwise you'll get a rude shock.' His voice was laced with anger. At her?

Taken aback, she snapped, 'I said interesting, not exciting or fun.'

'Good. Then, we'll head out after lunch.'

'I'll let Louise know. She's expecting us to join her for the market and a meal afterwards.'

'No need. She knows where we're going, and that we'll catch up with her and Aaron at the market.' His tone hadn't lightened.

'What's your problem? If you'd prefer I didn't come with you then just say so. I won't be offended.' *I might be hurt a wee bit, but I'll get over it.* If he didn't want to be shut in a vehicle with her for the afternoon then he didn't, but he could at least tell her. Didn't need to go all grumpy on her.

'You need to see these people in their own villages. It will help you understand better how much they have to give up when they visit their children, why they often send another child to be with the injured one.'

'Will it help me to accept that these kids have to dig for metal in order to have food at the end of the day?' she growled back. Two could get wound up and snap at each other.

Luca's shoulders lifted as he drew a deep breath. 'Unfortunately yes, but it won't help you condone it. Nothing, no one, would. Those bombs are so destructive. But hunger is worse—or so the villagers think. As they're the ones living with it, who am I to argue?'

Instantly her mood softened. Whatever was going on between her and Luca, her job was about these children and their families, and her time here was about her job. Somehow she'd get through the time spent in close proximity to Luca without going off her head yearning for another kiss. Fingers crossed.

CHAPTER SIX

'WE'RE GOING TO see Lai first.' Luca drove slowly around a group of schoolchildren on bikes. 'She's a fourteen-year-old who had the misfortune to fall into a crater and land on large pieces of shrapnel, piercing her abdomen and perforating her bowel.'

'Unbelievable.' Ellie grimaced. 'Did Lai work or go to school before this happened?'

'She worked the family stall at a nearby market selling vegetables that the village grew. Now someone else does that job and she tries to look after some of the gardens, but she's weak and suffers a lot of pain and inflammation that we haven't been able to control very successfully.' Luca had a box in the back of the vehicle for vegetables he'd buy from Lai to take back to their kitchen. Any little amount helped the village a lot.

'They're a tough people, aren't they?'

He nodded. 'They are. Here we go.' He pulled into a yard where hens were fossicking for any unfortunate worm or beetle. 'That's Lai over in the shade.' The girl looked as though she were dozing but sat upright the moment he stepped out of the four-wheel drive. 'Hi, Lai.'

'Dr Luca. I didn't know you were coming today. Who's that?' She nodded at Ellie.

'This is Dr Thompson. She works at the clinic with me.' He kept the words simple because he didn't understand the language as well as Ellie had given him credit for.

But Lai must've understood. 'Has she come to see me?'

'Yes.'

'She's pretty.'

At least that was what Luca thought Lai said. And if it was he had to agree. Ellie was pretty, downright beautiful really, with her high cheekbones and sparkling hazel eyes that sometimes were more green than brown—like today. Then there was all that dark blonde hair she'd tied in a high ponytail to keep it off her neck. As it swung with her movements it made him itch to let the hair free and run his hands over and through it, to feel if it was as silken as it looked. 'Lai says you're pretty,' he told El. He'd always known that but never got in a stew over her looks. Now they did things to his libido that shouldn't be happening.

'What does she want from me?' Ellie smiled towards the girl. 'Hello, Lai. My name is Ellie.'

Luca translated roughly, and earned Ellie the biggest smile he'd ever seen the girl give anyone. El did that everywhere she went. All the children at the clinic adored her already, their little faces lighting up the moment she stepped into their room. She was so good with them. Like today with Ash and those crutches no one had been able to get him back to using since his last tumble. Now the kid was almost racing on them.

Already Ellie was squatting down, holding Lai's hand and talking softly. It didn't seem to matter that Lai didn't understand her words; she certainly understood that compassion and care radiating from Ellie's face.

'You're like old friends,' he mock growled. 'Yakety-yak.'

Ellie squinted up at him. 'You can join in. It's what friends do.'

Was that a poke at him? Because of that kiss? 'I'll get the medical bag.' Anything to give him a break from those eyes that saw too damned much. He shouldn't have brought her out here today. It had been the perfect opportunity to get away alone for a couple of hours while he relived that kiss and put it to bed in his mind. Put it to bed? He knew exactly what he wanted to put to bed and with whom. Making love to Ellie shouldn't even enter his mind, but it had from around the instant he'd started kissing her the other evening. And it sure as hell didn't seem in any hurry to go away again.

His knuckles were white where he clenched the bag's carry strap. How was he supposed to get through the coming weeks if this was how he felt after only days? Look at her. Chatting with Lai as if she knew the language and making the girl laugh. Now there was a first. Lai didn't laugh, ever.

But hey, he understood perfectly. Ellie made him smile more often than he had lately, so bogged down in what to do next with his career that he'd become unable to find his usual cheery persona. She made him feel other things, too, like excitement for being with her, for being alive. Like this need to hold her and make love with her. His friend, best friend back in the days they lived and worked together. Never had he felt a twinge of desire for her, and yet now his whole body pulsed with a throbbing need that would not go away. Damn it.

He slammed the door shut, the bang echoing through the village. Ellie raised questioning eyes in his direction and stood up. 'You okay?'

'Why wouldn't I be?' Hell, he was turning into an old grump. A smiling old grump. 'I need to take Lai's temperature and check her wounds.'

'Want me to do it?'

No, I want you to take a hike, give me some space and stop looking so damned desirable in that thin-strapped top that barely reaches your waist and those short shorts. 'Come with us into Lai's family home.' He should've insisted she dress in a shirt with sleeves down to her wrists and baggy trousers that didn't out-line her butt so well.

The tiny lopsided dwelling was spotless, an amazing feat considering the dust swirling around outside. Lai's mother was cooking rice and something he couldn't make out by smell or sight. She gave him a shy smile and shifted a stool out from under the table for him.

'Your temperature is normal today,' he told Lai. That was a first. Hopefully that indicated the start of Lai's return to full health.

'The wound looks clear of infection, too,' Ellie said a moment later.

Luca asked to see Lai's pills and gave her some more antibiotics to take if redness returned at the wound site. Then he negotiated to buy some vegetables from her mother and soon he and Ellie were back on the road.

A few minutes along the road and Ellie started laughing.

'What?' he asked. 'Have you got heatstroke?'

She only laughed louder. 'I'm trying to put Luca the

A and E specialist and Luca the Laos clinic doctor together. It's not easy.'

'Thanks a bunch. I don't think I'm a bad doctor. I do an all right job anywhere I'm needed.' Didn't he?

Her hand suddenly covered his on the steering wheel. 'Relax. I wasn't having a poke at you. You're an amazing doctor.'

A different heat from that of the climate seeped into his blood, warmed him deep inside. 'Thanks.' For the compliment? Or the touch? He hoped she forgot her hand was there for a little while.

'I'm still getting used to seeing you working here where the urgency is less—except when new patients turn up bleeding all over the show. I only remember you on full alert, going from patient to patient, giving each of them your undivided attention, and yelling orders to the nurses. Here you're calmer, work at a pace that suits the children and still get to see twice as many patients as everyone else.'

Quite a speech. His chest swelled with pride. 'Coming here has been good for me. But I want to return to emergency medicine some time in the near future.' When had he made that decision? Only a couple of days ago he'd been wondering whether to take up a twelve-month contract in Cambodia. Was Ellie's presence changing everything for him? 'Would you give up what you do back home and spend a year doing something similar?'

She withdrew her hand.

Damn.

Ellie nibbled her bottom lip for a moment. 'I don't think so. But it's early days. Ask me again at the end of my month here.'

One month. It could be a very long time, or it could

speed by. With Ellie he had times when the minutes seemed to whizz past, and then when he was busting to kiss her again and had to work with her instead the minutes felt like hours. Now he had to sit in a car with her so close his skin was constantly aware of her. He should've hosed her off before they left to remove that tantalising scent she wore.

She hadn't finished telling him about what she was doing next. 'I've already got a six-month contract back home starting after Christmas. Any ideas of working offshore will have to wait.'

'Christmas. Being here I'd sort of forgotten about it. You'll be spending the day with your family?'

'I don't think so.' There was a sharp edge in her voice.

'Why not?' She had always tried to get home if she wasn't rostered to work on the twenty-fifth.

'I'll be in Auckland.' A definite 'don't ask' echoed between them.

But this was his friend; he needed to know. 'There are planes.'

'I don't want to be in the same city as Freddy, all right?'

Didn't make sense to him. It wasn't as though Freddy would be sitting down to Christmas dinner with her parents. 'We used to talk about things that were bugging us.'

'We did.' She stared straight ahead.

Okay. He'd fall into line and stop pushing her. He didn't want her wrath, nor did he want to upset her, and it seemed that was where he might be headed, though for the life of him he didn't understand why. 'You're going to love the market. Hope you've brought lots of cash.'

'They don't use EFTPOS?' She looked relieved that he'd changed the subject.

What had that been about? He hoped she'd tell him sometime before she headed back home.

'Buy this one.' Luca passed her a hat from a stall table to try on. 'The kids will fall over laughing if you wear that around the place.'

Ellie took the cotton creation with fabric elephants and bears swinging from the brim. 'The kids or you?' She chuckled. She put down the sane and sensible sunhat she'd just tried and plopped Luca's suggestion on her head.

The woman behind the counter grinned and pointed to a mirror. 'You like? You buy?' The hope in her voice would've had Ellie buying the hat if nothing else would.

'Go on, and this one.' She handed over the sensible one, and picked up two more brightly coloured caps. 'And these.'

'You've only got one head,' Luca quipped.

'They're not exactly expensive,' she retorted, happily handing over some American dollars.

'You're supposed to barter.' Luca shook his head at her. That smile that had started as he followed her around Talaat Sao, the morning market that ran all day, just got bigger and bigger. So he was enjoying her company. On the trip to the villages she'd begun to believe he couldn't wait for her to be gone.

'Next time.' Not. She hated bartering. Wasn't any good at it because she felt it was cheating someone out of their money.

Luca only laughed. 'I'll do it for you.'

Aaron called from farther along. 'Luca, here are some shirts that might be what you're looking for.'

While Luca headed that way Ellie waited for her

change and the hats to be folded neatly and placed in a plastic bag. *'Kowp jai,'* she said, and smiled at the woman's surprise at her butchered thank-you.

The woman nodded and grinned. *'Kowp jai.'*

That sounded nothing like what Ellie had said, but, hey, she'd tried. Turning in the direction Luca had gone, she scanned the heads of the crowd pushing through the narrow walkways between overladen stalls and couldn't see him or Aaron. Luca's height had him shoulders above most people and he was nowhere to be seen. Making her way to where she thought Aaron had called from, she found dozens of shirts hanging for sale but no sight of the two men. Or Louise. Where were they? How would she find them? If she went outside she could end up on the wrong side and not know where to go next.

She stared around, ignoring the bumps from people trying to move through the crowd. *Think, Ellie. Getting freaked out is stupid. It's not a massive market. They won't have gone far.* Looking at the next stall, she saw there were more shirts for sale, as there were at all the stalls along this line. She began walking quickly, suddenly wanting nothing more than to see Luca.

If she didn't find them along here she'd return to the stall where she'd got her hats and wait for them to find her.

'Ellie, come and tell Luca he should buy that shirt,' Louise called from behind her.

Spinning around, she saw the three people she'd been searching for crammed into a back corner of a stall she'd walked straight past. 'You think he'll listen to me?' She gave a lopsided smile and hoped her racing heart settled fast. How silly to get all worked up over not being able to see these guys for all of five minutes.

'Depends what you've got to say.' Luca looked at her across the tiny space. 'Hey.' He shrugged out of the shirt. 'I'll take it.' Then he crossed to her and gripped her hands, bag of hats included. 'Breathe deep. You're okay. You're not in that underground cave now.' His fingers tightened around her hands, his thumbs rubbing her wrists. 'You're fine. Promise.'

See? Her friend understood her, knew why she'd got worked up over nothing. 'I looked around and couldn't find you. I didn't know where to go, where we'd come in.'

'Ellie? You okay?' Louise looked at her with concern.

She let go a sigh. 'Yes, sorry. Years back a group of us went to some caves and when we were all deep inside the guides turned the lights off for a short time so we could see the glow worms. I got a bit lost and panicked. Ever since I get a wee bit stressed in crowds if I'm not sure where I am.'

Luca kissed her fingers before dropping her hands. 'My fault. Knowing how you were that day, I shouldn't have left you at that stall on your own.'

'No, Luca, it's not your fault. I'm a big girl. I should've watched where you went and kept an eye on you until I had my shopping sorted.' She liked that he had recognised her panic instantly and had come to her. That was special, and she felt cared for.

'Should we head out for that drink, then?' Aaron asked.

'No way. I haven't seen half the market yet. And I know Louise is looking for some earrings to send home to her niece.' She wasn't preventing everyone doing what they'd come here for. Anyway, her panic had gone, she was with Luca and all was well in her world.

'Trinkets and jewellery next, then.' Louise nodded her approval.

By the time they all sat down to beer and wine at a local bar Ellie was pleased with her shopping. 'Those earrings are lovely.' She sipped her drink.

'Which ones?' Luca drawled. 'I thought the stall holder was going to faint with excitement the number you two bought.'

'Says the guy who bought five shirts,' Louise said.

'I can't wait to visit the craft galleries,' Ellie enthused. 'Handwoven fabrics and embroidery will get me every time.' And might put a bit of a dent in her bank account, especially if her baggage allowance was exceeded going home. But, hey, what was money for if not sharing around? She knew she was a sucker for the shy smiles on the faces of the women selling their wares.

'He knows you well.' Louise nodded at Luca when he leaned on the bar waiting for the barman's attention so he could order a snack.

'He does.' Better than anyone else, Ellie realised with a start. Not even her ex had known her as well. Whose fault had that been? Hers for not offering up titbits about herself, or Freddy's for not thinking to ask? 'It's kind of good having someone aware of who I am.' It was something she hadn't had for a while.

'And it helps that that someone has a nice butt,' Louise said, grinning in the direction of Luca.

Aaron's eyes rolled.

'What are you trying to do here?' Ellie asked, while trying not to gape at what was truly a very nice butt. She was a butt girl after all.

Louise shrugged through a soft smile. 'Nothing.'

Now *her* eyes were rolling. 'Of course.' Where had

this longing for something more with Luca come from? Kisses were great, but what would making love with him be like? Shock rippled through her, bringing a sweat to her arms, between her breasts, her thighs. Sex with Luca? Yeah, that too-good-looking-to-be-true man. Was it even possible to go from best friends to lovers? Her skin heated further at the thought.

I really do want to find out, want to match my body to his and feel him inside me.

The glass shook in her hand, but she dared not set it down for fear of knocking it over.

Sex with Luca and there'd be problems. Keep him as a friend, and they'd always get along no matter how many arguments they had over the dumbest of things. In her experience friends were more forgiving than husbands. Take Luca as a lover and everything expanded, became filled with tension and the potential for hurt feelings that no one recovered from. She trusted Luca as a friend. It might not be the same if he became her lover. There was more to lose.

A dose of reality was needed about now to stop her head spinning. She checked her phone in a pathetic hope that she was needed back at the clinic. Nothing doing. She reached for her glass and forced her mind to follow the conversation Luca and Aaron were now having about deep-sea fishing in the South Pacific. She hadn't known Luca had tried it. Hadn't known he enjoyed fishing, even.

Next they headed to a restaurant filled with loud tourists, and followed that up with a nightcap at a nightclub so that she could apparently see more of the city.

'Can't have you going home without seeing every side of Vientiane.' Aaron grinned. 'Hope you're into dancing.'

'There's no music.' She stated the obvious, staring at Luca and fighting the sense she was slipping into a deep hole with no way out. She couldn't dance with Luca. That would mean touching him, feeling those muscles moving under her hand.

Luca chimed in. 'There will be. Very loud, too. The band's taking a break.' He leaned close and asked, 'What do you want to drink?'

As she breathed in his scent her mouth dried while her skin heated. 'W-water,' she managed, wanting to grab him to prevent him moving away. She turned her head, her nose brushing across his cheek. 'Luca?' she whispered.

'Ye-es?' He remained perfectly still.

What? Luca what? Her mind was blank, totally absorbed in all things Luca and unable to come up with a single word.

Finally he stepped away. 'Two waters,' he said to the barman before pulling a stool close to hers and parking that very nice butt down.

Her lungs struggled with the whole in-out thing. Air seemed lodged somewhere between her nose and her chest. Was she ill? Could that be what this was all about?

You're kidding. You've got the hots for Luca. That's what it's about, nothing more, nothing less.

Right. Now what? She stared around the club, finally focusing on Louise and Aaron on the dance floor. 'They're a lovely couple.'

Luca's gaze followed hers. 'I wonder sometimes if they don't get enough privacy. Living on the compound all the time means there are always others around.'

'I wouldn't cope with that. I like my own space, and if I was with someone I'd want him to myself some of the day.' Yet she and Freddy hadn't spent hours together at home. One or other of them was usually working long hours or he'd be playing golf or she'd be at the movies. It hadn't bothered her then. Over the past couple of days her marriage had started to look a little different from what she'd believed it to be. Had she been an unknowing part of its breakdown? There were usually two sides to everything.

As that blinding truth struck her, Luca took the glass from her hand. 'Let's dance.' Before she could say no he was leading her onto the floor to join other couples dancing to the fast tempo. Luca held on to her hand and began to move in time to the music.

Ellie found a smile for him. 'You always were a smooth dude on the dance floor.'

His face cracked into a wide smile. 'You bet.' And he grabbed her to spin them around in a wide circle, scattering half the other people nearby. 'Glad you remembered.'

There wasn't a lot she'd forgotten, just things she hadn't known about until this week. What else hadn't he spoken about? She wanted to know it all, felt the need to understand more about him. Why was he here and not in that A and E department? That had nothing to do with Gaylene's betrayal, surely? Why didn't he know what he wanted to do next in his life? That might be because he'd lost his child. Something that big would change her focus, too.

The music changed, much slower this time, and Ellie found herself being tucked against Luca's body, one of his hands around her waist, the other holding hers against his chest, as they stepped in unison to the rhythm. Their hips touched, her breasts moved over his chest as she danced, and she breathed him in. She forgot all the questions she'd wanted to ask. Forgot all the reasons why she shouldn't be dancing like this with Luca. Knew only his heat, his scent, his hard body against hers.

She didn't want to go back to her tiny, stuffy room. Could stay here in Luca's arms all night. Being held so tenderly almost broke her heart. She hadn't known such tenderness before. Yet there was strength in his hands and body, in his face too. His beloved face. How had she forgotten the warmth in his eyes? In his heart, his hands?

She'd never really noticed it. That was how. Luca had been a friend. Now he was more than that. And somehow she had to ignore the desire unfurling deep inside her body, not let it take over and rule her besotted brain. But she'd wait for one more song before she shifted out of his hold. Just one more.

No one told the band that she didn't want to step away from Luca and minutes later they were dancing all over the show at a fast pace.

Ellie's mood lifted as she jived and shook in time to some of her all-time favourite songs, Luca moving right along with her.

'Time we headed home,' Aaron interrupted. 'Unless you want to grab a cab later.'

Luca raised an eyebrow at Ellie.

Yes, she'd love nothing more than to continue dancing the night away, but she really had to remember she and Luca were no more than friends. That to take this any further might help her heart for a while but it would only get broken all over again when Luca had had enough. Or finally made up his mind where he was going next because that wouldn't be in the same direction as she was headed. Unfortunately. Because she was beginning to see a future that involved Luca, despite knowing it was impossible. 'We're coming with you.'

'We are?' Luca stretched that eyebrow higher.

'I am.' She shrugged. 'Sorry, but— Well, I'm sorry.'

He draped an arm over her shoulders. 'Not a problem, El. Glad one of us is thinking straight.'

Couldn't he look a little bit disappointed?

CHAPTER SEVEN

A WEEK AFTER that night dancing at the club Ellie was still vacillating between relief she'd insisted she came back from the nightclub with the others and wishing she'd given into the relentless need to learn more about Luca and that incredible body.

'Ellie, come and play.' A young boy stood in front of her, swinging a cricket bat from side to side.

How incongruous was that? Cricket in Laos seemed unlikely yet someone previously working here had introduced the game to the kids and apparently they couldn't get enough of it. Given the falls and knocks the kids received, the staff had to limit the number of games. She put her laptop aside and stood up, stretching her calves when they protested at the sudden change in position. 'Sure. Who else is playing?'

'Everyone,' she was told. 'They're waiting over the road.'

Over on the vacant land where houses used to stand before they burned to the ground in a dreadful misadventure years ago. 'Right, have you got the ball and the wickets?'

'Yes, Ellie, we have.' This little guy enjoyed practising his English. He wanted to be a truck driver one day and take tourists everywhere. 'Dr Luca got them.'

Of course Luca would be playing. If the kids were involved, then so was Luca. They could have a team each. This was the first time she'd joined in, but she'd seen a game the other day and had admired the kids for their determination and strength. Some swung crutches, another waved an arm that had been cut off at the elbow. All of them carried scars on some part of their body. All of them were laughing and chatting like monkeys in a tree. She loved the lot of them.

Noi called out from the clinic front door, 'You want a wicket keeper?' He'd never admit it but she'd heard he loved cricket as much as the youngsters. He also kept the children in line, gently admonishing them when they got carried away with heaving the ball at the wicket and their pal holding the bat. Even tennis balls could hurt when hitting the wrong spot on a small body.

'You bet,' Luca yelled back.

'I'm first batting,' said the boy who'd asked her to join them.

'I'm throwing the ball,' said another.

'Shouldn't we have teams?' she asked no one in particular.

'I want to be in Dr Luca's,' someone yelled.

'Me, too.'

A girl said shyly, 'I'm playing with Ellie.'

'You know what? I've got a plan. Noi, can you bring some crutches out here? Our size.' She tugged the belt off her shorts and handed it to Luca. 'Strap my leg up so I'm the same as these guys.'

Luca's eyes widened. 'You're kidding, right? That's going to be very uncomfortable.'

'Like it is for the kids all the time,' Ellie parried. 'You can tie one arm to your chest so that you can't use it.'

'You're nuts,' but Luca took her belt and tied up her leg.

She tried not to notice when his fingers touched her skin. Tried really hard. Then he pulled his shirt off and somehow managed to make one arm useless by twisting the shirt around his neck and tying it over his arm. She had to focus on the ground so as to avoid staring at the view created when he'd removed that shirt.

'Completely bonkers,' he told her with the first spontaneous smile she'd received from him all week.

What was bonkers? Oh. Her idea that all the staff out here were now partaking in by incapacitating themselves in some way. Not her longing for Luca. So much for putting the brakes on her highly fired-up hormones the other night. She'd been uptight ever since, and he'd been reacting the same way whenever he was around her. It might've been for the best if they had made love and got it out of the way.

'Bet no one back home has seen a cricket game quite like this.' Ellie laughed half an hour later as she lay sprawled on the ground after tripping over her crutch for the third time. 'Running for the ball and making catches is incredibly difficult but a whole heap of fun.'

'It was a great idea.' Luca nodded as he tried to get his breathing under control after chasing a ball right across the field. 'The kids are loving this more than ever.'

'So are you.' He looked the most relaxed she'd seen him for days.

He nodded. 'You know what I like best about working here?' He didn't wait for her to answer. 'We're not only doctors but physiotherapists, psychologists and friends to these kids. It's the whole package.'

'Changing your thinking about returning to emergency medicine?' It would be a shame. He was so good at it, but then again he was proving to be good at this. He was starting to become involved with people in a way he'd never done before. It suddenly struck Ellie with blinding clarity why Luca had chosen emergency medicine over all other specialties—he could treat people and send them home or to a specialist, but he didn't have to know who they were outside the emergency department. No learning about their family or their job, or whether they liked sports or were couch potatoes. He worked in the immediate picture with no tomorrows.

Ellie sat up and looked at this man she'd thought she knew. Back then she hadn't even started getting behind his facade. He'd fooled her as much as everyone else. Kind of undermined their friendship. When she'd thought they shared most things about themselves Luca had been holding back big time. She should be annoyed, angry even, but no. She was liking him more and more each day. This revelation only made her more determined to get to know Luca better, properly, and not only in the physical way. In fact that could take a hike for a while so that they could spend time together talking and enjoying getting out and about in Vientiane. *As if your hormones are going to settle down while you do that.* No harm in trying.

'You're staring.'

'Yes, I am.' *And liking what I see.*

A loud cry cut off whatever Luca had been about to say. A girl had tripped over her crutch and landed flat on her face. Ellie scrambled upright and raced across on her one leg and the crutch to drop down beside her. 'Lulu, let me see.' She gently removed the girl's hands from her face.

Blood spurted from Lulu's nose, and tears streamed down her cheeks. 'Hurts, Ellie.'

'I know.' Kissing Lulu's cheek, she gently felt the nose, then the rest of her face.

Luca knelt down opposite Ellie. 'What's the damage?'

'Everything seems fine,' Ellie told him, then said to Lulu, 'You've flattened your nose a bit, but it's going to be all right.'

'I don't want to play anymore.'

'Fair enough. Can I look at your back?' Lulu had three wounds zigzagging from her right shoulder to her left hip, caused by an explosion outside her school that had thrown her sky-high then dumped her on top of a wooden fence.

When Lulu nodded, Ellie carefully lifted her shirt. Phew. The stitches had held. Not that Ellie really expected otherwise, but she liked to be sure. 'I'll take you back over the road and get you a drink.'

Luca told her, 'I'll carry on with the cricket a bit longer.'

'See you later.' She began undoing the belt that held her leg bent, grimacing as pins and needles stabbed her muscles when the blood began circulating again.

'Want to go into town for a meal tonight?' He seemed to be holding his breath as he waited for her reply.

'Love to.' They could start on that talking stuff and getting to know each other better. Did that mean she'd tell him what Freddy and Caitlin had done to her? No. She wasn't going there, wasn't ready. She'd become quite adept at ignoring the truth and pretending she didn't have a sister or ex-husband—except in the middle of the night or when she was tired and not controlling her thought processes as well as she might. She wasn't any better than Luca at putting it all out there.

Lulu was crying steadily now.

'Hey, come on, poppet. Let's get you cleaned up.' She took the girl's hand and headed for the building.

Luca watched Ellie and Lulu all the way to the clinic and in through the doors that seemed to gobble them up. Ellie was a marvel, strapping her leg to be like the kids. She'd run—if using one leg and a crutch could be called running—back and forth after the ball whenever it was hit in her direction. No wonder the kids adored her. She was so natural with them. Aaron had hinted at trying to get her to take a twelve-month posting but she hadn't been very receptive.

Slap. The tennis ball bounced off his thigh. Luca looked around to find the culprit and met a pair of laughing eyes. 'Ng, you little tiger.' Reaching for the ball, he threw it at the wickets and missed by a mile, which only made the kids laugh and chase after it.

'You were daydreaming,' Ng said as he ran to the other end of the wicket. 'I got a run,' he shouted at his friends.

If the kids were noticing how distracted he'd become he needed to do something about it. Like what?

Take Ellie to bed.

Or have a long, cold shower every thirty minutes.

Or— He had no idea. Ellie had climbed into his skull and wasn't about to be evicted. And, he huffed, he'd damned well gone and suggested they go into town tonight. Again. They'd been doing quite a bit of eating out but usually one or two of the other staff members went with them. So there was his answer. Ask around to see who else wanted to join them.

'Catch it, Luca,' someone screamed at him.

Hell. He was meant to be playing cricket. He scanned the air between him and the wicket, saw a black shadow dropping towards the ground only a couple of metres away. Lunging at it, his fingers found the ball, curved it into the palm of his hand. When he held it up for everyone to see there were shouts of jubilation and a grizzle from Ng.

'I'm on your team.'

So why am I fielding? Luca wanted to ask. But basically if a person wasn't batting or bowling they were trying to catch the ball. No one really won, but then they didn't lose, either. 'Want to bowl next?' he asked, knowing Ng would never turn down that opportunity.

Glancing at his watch, Luca sighed. Still hours to go before he and Ellie headed into town. Hours when he'd be busy rubbing sore muscles on some of these kids caused by falls and skids in the field. It never failed to amaze him how eager they were to get into the fray, knowing they might hurt themselves. Tough little blighters, each and every one of them.

When he returned home he'd miss them all, even those he hadn't yet met. Returned home? Okay, he meant when he left Laos. Didn't he? Going back to NZ was on the cards but much further down the track. Emergency medicine still held its thrall and when he returned to that he wanted to be at the top of his game, but right now he was getting so much pleasure out of knowing his patients better than a BP reading and a diagnosis. Who'd have believed it? Not him—

Mr Avoid-All-Relationships-That-Involve-Exposing-His-Weaknesses. He liked having the kids hanging around demanding his attention. Who'd have thought it? Not him.

'Your turn.' One of the older girls stood in front of him, holding out the bat. 'But you can't hit the ball too hard.'

He grinned. 'Want to bet?'

Later, when everyone traipsed into the kitchen for food and water Ellie was there with Lulu, who looked decidedly happier now. Again Ellie had worked her magic.

She was so good with children. Where had she learned that? Or was it inherent? She'd be a brilliant mother, seemed to have all the right instincts.

As kids shouted and teased and bumped around him he heard Ellie's laughter. Raising his eyes, he met her amused gaze.

'Look at you.' She grinned. 'Not much more than a kid yourself, the way you've got chocolate icing on your chin.'

Luca ran his tongue around his lips and tried to find the icing dollop she'd mentioned. His tongue wasn't long enough. But when he looked back at Ellie she was obviously fascinated with it. Snapping his mouth shut, he turned away, trying to deny the heat zipping through his veins.

'Who's first for a massage?' he asked above the din.

Everyone got even busier eating and talking. Not one kid looked in his direction.

'Lulu's had hers,' Ellie told the kids. 'Pogo, bring that cake and come with me.'

Pogo, named for the way she usually bounced everywhere, reluctantly picked up another piece of cake and limped out of the door behind Ellie.

'Ng,' Luca said. 'Come on. The sooner we do this, the sooner you can do something more fun.'

'Can we sing?' Ng asked hopefully.

Another thing Ellie had started. Singing while massages were going on.

'Great idea. Come on, everyone. Bring that cake and follow us. We'll do this together.'

Soon the clinic was filled with the less than tuneful sounds of simple English songs Ellie had taught the children being yelled and sung and whispered. Even the other staff members helping were adding their voices. Ellie's voice was there, in tune and strong, the words clear and her face alive with joy. At that moment he'd swear she was the happiest he'd seen her since she'd arrived. Such simple pleasure had a lot going for it, and Ellie was soaking it up. He'd forgotten how much she enjoyed singing, and how she'd been an avid karaoke fan.

'The amputee clinic works a kind of magic on you, doesn't it?' Luca said as they wandered through the city centre later that night.

'It's the children who do that. They're so upbeat at times I want to bottle whatever it is that makes them that way and take it home. They're amazing.' Ellie stooped to stare into a shop window. 'Look at that. The weaving is beautiful. I'm going to have to get a piece before I go home.'

'What would you do with it?'

She lifted her shoulders, dropped them. 'No idea. It doesn't matter. A piece of handwoven fabric will make a wonderful memory of Vientiane.'

He had stored some of those lately. All with Ellie in them, all able to go with him wherever he went. 'Along with the zillion photos you've taken.'

She never seemed to go anywhere without her camera or phone. There were probably as many pictures of the children on her phone as in her camera. 'It's going to take me months to sort through those, and pick the best for an album.'

'Do people still do that?' He was happy leaving the few he occasionally remembered to take on a stick, which meant one day he'd probably lose them. But then photography wasn't one of his passions.

'I guess it's too easy not to get photos printed these days, but I like flicking through the pages of an album. Turning on my laptop and clicking on different folders doesn't give me the same satisfaction.' Ellie continued walking along the street. 'Got loads of you, too. Wait till I show Renee the cricket-doctor shots. She won't believe it's you.'

'Renee? You two are still in touch?' She'd been one of their housemates way back.

'I've been renting a room in her apartment since I found myself single again. She's just as bossy as she used to be.'

'And you still take no notice, I bet.'

'Something like that.' Ellie looked around. 'Where shall we eat tonight?'

'How about the restaurant tucked behind that hedge?' It was more upmarket then anywhere they'd eaten before.

Ellie's eyes widened and she turned them on him. 'Are we treating ourselves?'

'No. I'm treating you.' Out of the blue had come the need to take her somewhere better than a rice and sauce kind of place. Somewhere special with the napkins and wine and waitresses who made a career of their job. He wanted to spoil Ellie. And himself. It'd been a very long time since he'd gone upmarket for just about anything. There hadn't been the inclination because he hadn't had anyone he wanted to share that with. Taking Ellie's elbow, he led her across the road, dodging jumbos and cars, and into the outdoor area of the restaurant.

So much for a quick meal and a couple of beers, then returning to the clinic. So much for not spending too much time with Ellie and getting himself all out of sorts.

When he'd ordered a bottle of wine and they'd perused the menu and given their orders, Luca leaned back in his chair and stretched his legs under the table. 'Are you going to do any tripping around after you finish with the clinic?'

'I'd like to, but I haven't made any plans yet. Have you gone further afield than Vientiane and its surrounds?'

'No. I've been a real stay-at-home kind of guy, always finding things to do with the kids.' Travel hadn't been big on his list of things to do once he'd qualified as a doctor, and now that he was in Indochina nothing had changed. 'I'm probably wasting a golden opportunity.'

'I hear Luang Prabang is wonderful.'

'Some of the nurses who were here in June came back raving about it. You should go. It's only about an hour's flying time from here.'

Their wine arrived and Ellie sipped, her expression thoughtful.

'Something wrong with the wine? I can order another one.' He raised his glass to his lips to taste it.

Ellie's eyes locked on him. 'Come with me.'

'What?' he spluttered into his glass.

'Let's go to Luang Prabang together. It'd be a whole lot more fun going with you. I don't fancy joining tours to see everything and then not having anyone to say do you remember to.' Her eyes were imploring him to agree.

He didn't want to disappoint her. Not at all. Besides it was way past time to get out there and see the country. 'You're on.' He could take a few days. Mid-December wasn't any busier or quieter than the rest of the year and Aaron had been nagging him to take a break.

'That's fabulous.' Her smile was worth everything. Warm and exciting, it wove through him, lifting the tension hovering in his body forever, making him want to laugh out loud.

Instead, he put down his glass and reached for her hands. With her fingers linked between his, he said, 'Thank you for giving me the kick in the backside I've been needing. It's too easy staying here pretending I'm too busy to take time out for myself.'

'I'm glad you're coming with me.' Her smile widened. 'We'll have to go after I've finished my contract.'

'That's not a problem. I'll warn Aaron tomorrow and then we can go online to make some bookings.' Flights, hotel rooms—as in plural. They wouldn't be sharing a room, a bed. The tension returned. He had to be sick in the head. Or looking out for his heart. He didn't do long-term relationships. He had his father's genes but he'd learned something growing up. Best to know his faults and act accordingly, which meant love 'em and leave 'em. He was not loving and leaving Ellie. Leaving might turn out to be impossible for starters. As for loving her? Best not to go there. He didn't want to wake up one morning to find he had a complete family around him, knowing he would one day walk out and break their hearts as he went. Yeah, he'd seen it all, knew the hurt it had caused his mum and sister, and himself, and could say he never wanted to do that to anyone. Especially not to Ellie. But what he hadn't figured into the equation was how much he could love her, and how deep it cut not to act on that.

To think he'd agreed to go away with her. Two nights would be like two months in her company and unable to follow through on the longing he felt for her.

Ellie leaned back to allow the waitress room to put her plate down. 'Yum.' She sniffed the air and grinned. 'I wonder if I can take a local chef home to Auckland with me.'

'Are you looking forward to living in Auckland again?' he asked before forking prawns and rice into his mouth.

Her grin faded. And he felt chilled. He should never have asked. If he'd spoiled the night he only had himself to blame.

'It's going to be different. Last time you were there, as well as the other two in the house. I knew everyone training with us, whereas now I don't really know anyone up there. I'm sure I'll bump into people I used to know eventually. I do like Auckland and the job should be good.' She pushed rice around her plate. 'And it's at the other end of the North Island to where Freddy's living.'

'You'll miss him?' Was she still in love with the man?

'Not at all.' Her eyes met his and she said, 'Promise.' Finally she managed to get some rice into her mouth. When she had swallowed she added, 'I'll be able to relax. I won't be bumping into him at work or downtown. I never seemed to be able to get completely away from him. Not that either of us wanted time together, but at the hospital if we were even on the same floor people would be watching us, waiting to see if we yelled at each other—which we didn't. Not in public anyway, and then it was me doing the yelling. Not Freddy.' The spark of excitement had gone out of her eyes.

'That must've been hell. Having people watching you all the time, I mean.' Ellie tended to be a private person except with close friends and family.

'It was. So yes, Auckland's looking good. And who knows? I might decide to stay there permanently if I get another position when this next one runs out.' Sounded as if she was trying to convince herself.

If Ellie was in Auckland he'd be very tempted to return home. Where was the contract for Cambodia? He needed to sign it now before he gave in to temptation.

Temptation was staring him in the face right that moment. Ellie licking sticky rice from her fingers, then her tongue caught up a grain from the corner of her mouth. And his groin tightened exponentially. Goddamn. They were only halfway through dinner. How could he eat a thing now?

By picking up your fork and putting food in your mouth. Close your mouth—you're looking like a thirteen-year-old in lust with your teacher. Chew the damned prawn, and don't dribble.

He shuffled his butt on the chair, aiming to make everything more comfortable, and only succeeding in making his erection more apparent—thankfully only to himself. He was that teenaged boy all over again. The difference being Ellie was his age and not ten years older and wiser. They were both grown-ups and there was nothing to stop them having sex together. Nothing.

Except friendship and the future.

'More wine?' Ellie asked, holding the empty bottle up.

'Sure.' Might as well overindulge. The evening was already going pear-shaped fast. He nodded at the waitress across the room and leaned back, easing his legs further under the table in an attempt to shift the pressure between his legs. Pear-shaped? He nearly laughed. Not at all.

'Am I missing something here?' Ellie asked. 'You seem to be having a private joke.'

Oh, damn. Forgot she never missed a damned thing. 'You want dessert?'

Those hazel eyes locked on to his, the flecks now green and brown. Her tongue was back to its antics, tracking first along her bottom lip and then over the top one. 'Dessert? As in?'

'As in fresh fruit salad or apple pudding.'

Her tongue disappeared. Her gaze didn't. 'Right. Not as in hopping into bed and finding out exactly where we're headed?'

The shock that ricocheted through his body, crashed into his brain, was reflected back at him from those piercing eyes. He'd swear she hadn't meant to say that. Not at all.

The wine arrived. Perfect timing, or not. Their glasses were suddenly full once more. In need of a huge gulp, Luca reached for his, slopped wine over the edge and onto his hand. He was quick to reach for his napkin to wipe his hand, not needing Ellie to lift his hand anywhere near her mouth and that tongue—if she was that way inclined, and right now he had no idea what she was thinking.

Her cheeks were pink, her gaze had shifted to a spot

in the middle of the table and her glass shook when she raised it to those lips that seemed to have stolen his sanity and left him with the biggest hard-on he could remember.

Luca tugged his wallet from his back pocket and peeled out some notes, tossed them on the table, snatched up the wine bottle and got to his feet. Reaching for Ellie's hand, he said, 'Let's go.'

Her hand was warm in his. 'Where to?'

Good point. The chances of no one noticing them sharing a room back at the clinic were next to none. 'We'll find a hotel room.'

'Sounds sleazy.' She giggled. 'But I think I might like sleazy.'

'Why is every hotel full tonight of all nights?' Luca growled as his frustration increased forty minutes later. It was all very well that there was some big festival on, but they only wanted one bed, one room. Hell, they'd give it back in a few hours.

Ellie leaned her head against his shoulder. 'Guess we'll have to run the gauntlet at home, then.'

'Taxi,' Luca yelled at a vehicle moving off from the other side of the road. 'Wait.'

He was taking Ellie to bed tonight. Nothing would stop this incessant need clawing through his body except making love with El. Nothing. He knew common sense and logic had taken a hike, knew that tomorrow he might regret this, but he had to have Ellie, had to know her better than he ever had before. Ellie was his friend, his sidekick, his—

Say it and you're doomed. Lost forever, to live a life of purgatory, always wondering and missing out, never to be even Ellie's friend. For tonight he had to live in the moment. Not look to the future, not think back on his past. Tonight was about tonight, about him and Ellie and the sexual tension that had been simmering between them from her first day in Laos.

He held open the taxi's door. 'Let's go.'

CHAPTER EIGHT

BESIDE ELLIE IN the taxi Luca leaned forward and swore. 'Looks as if every light in the whole damned place is on.'

Ellie stared out of the side window as they drove up to the clinic. 'What's going on? The children's ward is lit up like Christmas.' She was reaching for her door handle even before the driver stopped. Her heart thudded in her chest, this time with concern for the children, not with lust and need for Luca. How quickly things changed. Though she was still hot for him her need had taken a sideways step, waiting for that moment until they found out what was happening and could hopefully get back to their evening.

They ran inside, heading straight to the ward. 'What's with all this water?' Ellie gasped.

There were people everywhere, mopping, sweeping waves of water through the ward, removing sodden bedding. The children were helping as best they could and getting blissfully soaked as they did.

'Burst water main in the wall,' the physiotherapist told them as she squeezed a mop into a bucket. 'Not sure what happened but there was a big bang and the wall literally blew out, forcing concrete blocks outward. Pogo's bed took the full force and she's in Theatre now with a stoved-in chest from where one block slammed into her corner first.'

Ellie looked around, spied Noi and went to ask, 'Are either Luca or I needed in Theatre?'

Noi shook his head. 'No, Aaron and Louise have got it under control. One of the hospital doctors is there with them. Aaron said if you got back while they were operating you could help in here.'

Luca stood beside her. 'No problem. Any other kids need medical attention?'

'No. They're soaked and their beds are useless but no one else was hurt.'

Relieved at that, Ellie tossed her bag onto a shelf and grabbed a mop. Turning, she bumped into Luca, felt that hard body aligned with hers. Unfortunately this was not how, only minutes ago, she'd envisaged having him against her. 'I'm sorry.'

His finger on her chin lifted her head. 'Me, too. Very sorry.'

'We might get finished cleaning up before daybreak.' How pathetic. She was almost pleading with him to take her to his room. But her disappointment was so enormous, so debilitating she wasn't thinking straight, was putting her own needs before those of the children. She should be ashamed. She was, and she wasn't. But she knew the children would win out. They had to, and she really didn't mind. But why tonight? Why couldn't that blasted pipe have burst tomorrow? Or yesterday? Or not at all?

Luca's finger brushed her bottom lip, sending sparks right down to her centre. 'We'll be lucky to get this dried out and ready for the kids before the end of the week.' His disappointment gleamed out at her from those steely eyes.

'I know.' When she'd finally decided to go for it with him and to hell with the consequences they'd been stopped in their tracks. Was it a portent? And if it was should she heed it? At this moment she could not find it in her to say yes. She wanted Luca. 'If only there'd been one hotel with a bed to spare.'

Luca's chuckle was flat. 'If only.'

'Right. Let's get cracking. We're needed and that's got to be good, even if I wish I was somewhere else.' Ellie slopped through water to the far side of the ward where everyone was tackling the flood. 'It seems the more you're all mopping up, the more that comes out of the wall.'

Noi shook his head. 'The plumber only found the mains tap outside to turn off five minutes ago, and then it was rusted open. The water should stop any second.'

'Where are the children going to sleep until this room is habitable again?' Luca asked.

'The hospital is making room for them,' Noi answered. 'They'll be placed in various rooms with other patients.'

'I hope Pogo's going to be all right.' Ellie shivered despite the warm temperature. 'She's already had enough to deal with for a little girl.'

'A crushed rib cage is no picnic,' Luca agreed as he swept water towards the open doors that led outside. 'She was due to go home on Friday.'

Ellie squeezed her mop through the wringer on the bucket and dropped it back in the water to soak up more. Just went to show that you never knew what was around the corner. One minute Pogo was getting ready to go home, the next she was in Theatre undergoing major surgery.

One minute I was on my way to bed with Luca, the next I'm mopping a floor in the children's ward.

Kind of told her she should grab every opportunity that came along—the ones she wanted anyway. And she definitely wanted Luca. Even as she swept up water she watched him. The muscles in his arms flexed as he lifted a sodden mattress off a bed. Her mouth dried. Ironic given the amount of water around the place. She smiled. Luca did that to her.

'I'll take your bucket to empty.' Noi swung it away and placed an empty one in front of her. 'Sorry your night was interrupted.'

Ellie gaped at him. Did he know? 'It doesn't matter, Noi. Not that this is your fault.'

'I know, but you and Luca seem to be getting on better than your first day.' He flicked looks between her and Luca.

He didn't know where they'd been headed. Relief lifted her spirits. 'That's because we've always been such good friends. I know we lost each other for a while but that friendship was strong, and still is.'

Noi turned his full attention on her. 'Friendship is good. Love is better. You know what I mean.' He wasn't asking, he was telling her.

'Aren't you meant to be emptying that bucket?' *I don't love Luca. Not like that. Not as the man I'd want to marry and have a family with.*

Noi didn't move, his gaze still fixed on her. 'He's different now. Happier and more playful with the kids since you arrived. As if you've made him come alive.'

For a man from a totally different culture from hers

he seemed to understand a lot about this. Too much. 'I didn't know he'd been unhappy.' Luca was always happy, though she'd come to realise these past weeks that had often been a front.

'So were you when you got here. Not now,' Noi said, the seriousness in his voice drumming his words into her.

Of course she'd been unhappy, in fact downright upset, distressed and incapable of moving forward. But to have got past that in such a short time? Not likely. The pain and anger was too much to evaporate so quickly. She bent to push the mop through the water, sent a wave heading across the room. 'Let's get this job finished so we can help the kids settle into their new beds.'

Noi nodded and strolled away, totally unfazed by the storm of emotions he'd started rolling through her.

What a night. She had enjoyed having dinner with Luca in a special restaurant, and appreciated the change from their usual haunts with other staff. Just sitting with him talking about things only they knew about had been relaxing. There'd been no sting in anything he'd said to her, and she hadn't felt the need to defend herself about anything. He accepted her for who she was. It was something she did not want to risk losing again.

Which meant no sex. That would put the risk factor right up there. She had no idea what the morning after would be like. Would she be able to walk away and believe they had had their moment and could return to normal? Or would she wake up and know she'd made a mistake? Realise that it had been too soon after her failed marriage and that she was probably using him to get back on her feet? Rebound sex. Rebound love.

Ellie gasped. Love? No, not that.

'You okay?' the man distracting her from the clean-up asked as he placed a bucket between them.

'Why wouldn't I be?' she growled. Rebound or not, loving Luca was not on. She couldn't love him because— Because she couldn't. It wouldn't feel right to love her best friend. Why not? He was a man, sexy as they came, kind and caring, knew her well, too well at times. There'd be no surprises. That wasn't an issue. She'd had a surprise with Freddy and look where that had got her. Single and here, debating about her feelings for Luca.

'You're pushing water in the wrong direction.' Luca grinned. 'I like it when you're muddled.'

'I don't.' *I can't love him. Not like that. Do I want to set up house with Luca? Be with him day in, day out? Have his babies? Does my heart race whenever I'm near him? My heart races—with desire. Set up house with Luca? I doubt it.* As for babies, she didn't want Luca's or anyone's. She wasn't ready. So, not love, then.

Her head shot up and she stared at him. Really stared, seeing his face, those beautiful grey eyes, that nose that had been broken when he was a kid and bent slightly to the left, that stubborn chin. She hoped not anyway. She'd loved Freddy and this felt different. *Yeah, and look where that got you.*

Noi nudged her. 'Here's your bucket.'

When she dragged her eyes sideways she found Noi nodding slowly. 'Like I said,' he added with a quick glance at Luca.

Ellie turned to run out of the room, and noticed all the people busy trying to clean up the mess and knew she wasn't going anywhere. She had to remain here, doing her share. As much as she wanted to escape and find solitude while she absorbed this new information her mind had thrown up, she couldn't. Leaving when she was needed wasn't in her psyche. So she pushed the mop harder than ever and became totally focused on water and the floor, working twice as hard as anyone else. But every time she looked up she got an eyeful of a wet and gorgeous Luca happily cleaning up the ward, teasing the kids, laughing when they tipped water over him once.

And she'd compared him to Freddy? No way. Her ex would've said to call him when everything was back to order; he wouldn't have picked up a mop. He was a surgeon, not a cleaner.

Gulp. Ellie dropped her gaze to the job in hand. Maybe she'd never really, deeply, loved Freddy at all. So what were these feelings for Luca? Friendship or love?

There was a holiday atmosphere in the clinic the next morning. The kids were hyper after their exciting night, acting as though the whole incident had been put on for their benefit.

Luca scratched his unshaven chin as he tried to eyeball every kid at the long table. 'You still have to have massages and go to school,' he told them over breakfast.

'Good luck with that,' Ellie quipped as she dumped her plate in the sink.

He needed a lot of luck with quite a few things at the moment. Like sorting out what was going on between him and Ellie. Last night they'd come so close to changing their relationship forever. So close. He was still trying to work out how he felt about that.

Sure, he'd wanted to make love with her. No question. He still did. His body had throbbed half the night with the need to touch her, to caress that soft skin, to be inside her. But this morning, in the harsh light of day, his brain had started throwing up some serious thoughts. Like, even with Ellie he had to remember his gene pool and the likelihood he'd be a bad husband and father. Like that Ellie hadn't had time to get over Freddy yet, and that *he'd* probably take the brunt of that when she came to her senses.

'I'm going to see Pogo,' Ellie announced, as though needing to make it clear she was working. Trying to combat leftover emotions from last night?

Had she had a change of heart? Finally decided last night's disaster in the clinic had been a good thing, that it had run interference before she'd had time to think everything through fully? In some ways he could agree. But a huge part of him mourned not having had that opportunity to make love with Ellie. Something in the dark recesses of his mind seemed to be saying she might be the best thing for him, might be the one woman he could risk his heart to. She certainly was nothing like Gaylene, wouldn't deny him his child—even one he thought he didn't want. Whatever it was, he shut it down immediately. Shoved to his feet and stomped across to the sink to rinse his cup and plate.

But his gaze fixed on Ellie as she left the dining hall: her head high, her shoulders tense, her hands clenched at her sides. Exhaustion after the eventful night? Or something deeper? Him? Them and what they hadn't managed to do?

He knew the feeling all too well. Throw in confusion and a need that seemed to be growing every day and he was toast.

'Can we play cricket today?' one of the boys called to him.

'Yes, of course.' That should fill in a few hours.

'Luca.' Ellie stood in front of him an hour later as he was instructing a boy on caring for his wound where he'd lost two fingers.

'Hey, Pogo's not doing so well, I hear.'

Her mouth turned down. 'No, poor wee girl. I've been sitting with her after changing bandages and adjusting her meds. Her parents are with her now.'

'They'll be gutted. Only two days ago they were saying how excited they were Pogo was going home.'

'We need to talk.' Ellie's eyes were wide as she looked at him.

His heart sank. He didn't want this conversation, would prefer to carry on as though last night hadn't nearly happened. 'About last night?'

Her smile was wobbly. 'Sort of. We are going to Luang Prabang, remember?'

How could he forget? Two nights away with Ellie and knowing now that they really shouldn't have sex if they wanted to remain friends. Oh, yeah, he remembered all right. 'Are we still on?' he asked, aware that she must say yes. *Please.*

'I hope so. We need to make bookings—for flights and a hotel.' Her cheeks turned a delicious shade of pink.

He nearly reached out to run a finger down one of those cheeks, only just in time thinking better of it. That would be an intimate gesture and he wasn't sure where he stood today. With her—or with his own thoughts. 'Want me to do them? I've got time now.'

She nodded. 'That'd be great. Do you know anyone here who could recommend accommodation?'

'Aaron and Louise went up there six months ago. I'll check with them. Two rooms, right?'

The pink deepened as she nodded. 'I guess that would be sensible.'

The last thing he felt like being was sensible. He'd done sensible all his life and lately he found it was getting tedious. But this was Ellie he was thinking of breaking the rules with and she could get hurt. That was the last thing he wanted to happen. 'What are you doing after Luang Prabang?' She'd be a free agent then. Her contract at the clinic was due to finish soon and her new one back home didn't start until the New Year. There was plenty of time for her to indulge in travelling around Indochina if she wanted. Or even stop off in Australia, as she'd mentioned one day when they were talking about one of their old housemates who'd moved to Perth.

'I'm going home.'

That was not the answer he was expecting. His surprise must've shown because she explained.

'I keep thinking there are loose ends back there that I need to deal with. I have to pack my gear and move out of Renee's apartment. Spend some time with Mum and Dad before Christmas.' A troubled look came into her eyes at the mention of her parents. Or was that Christmas?

'Seems to me you're making excuses for not staying over here longer. None of those things are going to fill in the nearly four weeks until you start work in Auckland. You don't even have to find a house up there—you've got one fully furnished for the duration.' Did she want to get as far away from him as possible?

'I could go for a coffee break right now.'

Luca took her elbow. To hell with being careful and wary. His friend appeared lost today and he'd step up to the mark for her no matter what it cost him. 'Come on. Coffee out under the tree.' Where hopefully no one would disturb them.

'I'm struggling with not knowing what I want to do,' Ellie told him ten minutes later as she sat down on the grass, not at all concerned about the ants that might bite her.

'The Ellie I remember always knew what she wanted to do about everything.'

'Right up until my marriage fell apart. Then I focused on dealing with that and the shame that followed me around. I was determined to get away from Wellington and the hospital, and here I am.' Her hands were tight around her mug.

'With the first six months of next year sorted. That can't be too bad, can it?' There were things she wasn't telling him, he just knew it, but was reluctant to ask for fear she'd walk back inside.

'Then what do I do? Work in an emergency department? Buy a house, and if so where? Even travel doesn't excite me, and I've always thought I'd do that when I had time. Pathetic.' Her sigh was long and filled with despair.

The urge to wrap her in a hug was huge but Luca sensed she wasn't ready. 'You're not pathetic, so stop feeling sorry for yourself. You've been knocked sideways by your ex, and lost sight of those plans you had with him. Of course you're confused about where you're headed.'

'I'm over here with so many places to visit, and beyond going to Luang Prabang with you I can't find the enthusiasm.' She sipped the coffee, staring at her feet.

'Give yourself time.' She was enthused about going away with him for two nights? His heart melted at the thought. He wasn't on the 'get rid of' list, then. 'They say it takes a couple of years to get over a breakup.'

'I wonder if *they* know what they're talking about.' She wrinkled her nose.

'Want to look at where you could go to after our jaunt north? Hanoi's not far from Luang Prabang.'

'You think I could do that on my own?'

'Asks the woman who did a solo parachute jump because she was dared? I reckon there's nothing in this world you can't do if you want to.'

Finally Ellie lifted her head and gave him the full benefit of a big smile, one that reached her eyes. 'Thank you for that. It was my turn to need a kick in the backside. You book Luang Prabang and I'll make a decision about where I'm going after that.' She placed her hand on his thigh for balance as she stood up. 'Watch this space.'

They were back to being friends, easy with each other. 'Thank goodness,' he muttered even as disappointment rippled through him. He wanted more. He knew that now. Last night hadn't been about just one night at all. But was he prepared to risk it?

No. He could get hurt, but, worse, he'd definitely hurt El somewhere along the way. No doubt about it.

CHAPTER NINE

ELLIE'S CONTRACT WAS UP, and she and Luca were in Luang Prabang. Over the weeks she'd survived the temptation of Luca by keeping frantically busy with the children. Now they were visiting the bear sanctuary on a day trip out from the town, which had been a priority for her. 'I want to set them free,' she muttered to Luca as she clicked her camera nonstop getting photos of the black bears behind the wire fences set in the lush vegetation near the Kuang Sii waterfalls.

'I know what you mean. It seems cruel to keep them enclosed but they'll be killed if they're not protected. Catch twenty-two, I guess.'

'What I don't get is why anyone would want to hunt them in the first place. They're so beautiful.'

'As we've both said often, this is a very different world from the one we're used to.' Luca was holding his camera to his eye. 'Look at me. And smile, woman. I'm not pulling your teeth out.'

'Have you got one of the bears in the photo?' she asked.

'The bear's smiling. Now will you?'

It wasn't hard; despite the ever-present tension in her stomach brought on by all things Luca, she was having

fun. Not even thinking about what she might be missing out on sleeping in separate rooms at the hotel could
wipe her smile away. They'd been on the go since arriving yesterday.

'At last,' Luca growled and clicked a photo. And another, and another until she shifted away. 'I could sell
them on the internet.'

'Good luck.' She laughed. 'The guide's beckoning—
guess it's time to head back.'

'A cold beer would go down a treat.' Luca smacked
his lips. 'This humidity's getting to me.'

'They sell it at the stalls where the van's parked.'
She wouldn't mind one, either. She slipped her arm
through his. 'Let's check them out before we go. Bye-
bye, bears.'

'You're dribbling, and I haven't got anything to wipe
your slobber up with.'

With beers in hand they clambered into the van to
join the three Australian guys sharing the trip. Ellie
stretched her legs towards the door and leaned back in
her seat to enjoy the terrain they'd pass through. 'Next
stop, Elephantville.'

The weather turned wet about the time they climbed
off the elephant they'd ridden through the jungle. Rushing under the shelter, where there were bananas to feed
the animals, Ellie felt the sweat trickle down her back.
'The rain doesn't stop the humidity, does it?'

Luca shoved his camera into a plastic bag and put it
inside his day bag. 'Give it time.'

Suddenly the rain became torrential, pounding the
tin roof of the shelter and making conversation next
to impossible.

Ellie leaned close to Luca to yell, 'Wonder how long this will last.'

'Who knows?' he yelled back, then jerked his head back.

'Luca?' He hadn't shaved that morning and a dark stubble highlighted his strong jawline—and sent waves of something suspiciously like desire rolling through her. What would he do if she ran a finger over his chin?

'Let's go. The driver's waving us over to the van.' He raced away, stomping through puddles, getting soaked from all directions.

Not that there was any choice. Ellie braced herself for the drenching she was about to get and chased after him, wondering at his abrupt mood swing.

'The skies are angry.' The driver laughed as he slammed his door. 'We have muddy ride back.'

Ellie felt a prickle of apprehension. The road hadn't been that great when it was dry. Her hand slid sideways, onto Luca's thigh. His fingers laced around hers and he squeezed gently.

'We'll be fine. This guy will be used to driving in these conditions. They're not uncommon up here in the hills, from what the man at the hotel said this morning.'

'I guess.' The apprehension backed off but she didn't withdraw her hand, enjoying the way Luca's forefinger rubbed across her knuckles. *Please don't pull away. Not yet.* Heat sparked along the veins of her arm. Eek, if having her hand held by Luca did this to her, what would making love be like? She suspected like nothing she'd ever experienced.

On the ride up out of the valley the van slipped and slid on the mud and water pouring down the road. The sound of the wheels spinning filled the van. Ellie wondered if they'd have been better waiting until the deluge slowed, but when she'd voiced that opinion the driver replied, 'Might not stop for days.'

Her grip tightened around Luca's hand. Her jaw ached as her teeth clenched. Leaning against him, she found some comfort even though there was nothing he could do if this trip went badly. Luca's jaw was jutting out, his eyes not wavering from the road ahead. The van was quiet, everyone probably holding their breath as she was.

Then suddenly they popped over the crest of the hill and the van tilted forward as they headed down. The relief was palpable, until everyone realised going down had its own set of problems. The driver braked repeatedly to slow the van but they skidded more often than on the way up.

When the van slid towards the edge of the road Ellie thought she must be breaking the bones in Luca's fingers, her grip was so tight. She tasted blood on her lip where her teeth pushed down. The air stuck in her lungs, her ribs tight under the pressure. 'Oh, no. We're going over the edge. We're going to crash.'

Up front the driver was shouting something incomprehensible as he spun the steering wheel left, then right.

And the van slid closer to the top of the ravine.

A scream filled Ellie's throat, but when she opened her mouth nothing came out.

Luca's hand was strong around hers. His body tense beside her. 'Jeez.' Then he let her go to grab at the latch that was the internal handle on the sliding door. His muscles stood out as he strained to tug the door back on its rollers. His lips pressed together until there was no colour in them. And still he pulled, frantically trying to open the door.

Nothing happened.

The back of the van lurched forward with a thud. The wheels were over the edge.

Ellie's heart stopped.

This was it. The van would drop like a boulder to the bottom of the ravine. *We're going to die.* Ellie jerked in her seat, staring around, frantic for a way out.

Slam. The noise was horrendous. Air whooshed inside.

'Come on,' Luca yelled as he grabbed her arm. 'Jump.'

The door was open. That had been the slamming sound.

'Jump, Ellie. Now.'

She didn't get a chance. Even as she strained against the steepening angle of the van Luca snatched at her, wrapped his arms around her and fell out backwards.

Thump. They landed heavily on the side of the bank. Pain tore through Ellie's side where her hip had connected with something solid and unforgiving. The air whooshed out of her lungs. Her head snapped back, crashed against the ground. Luca's arms were no longer holding her. She cried out, 'Luca?' Then she gasped in air, tried again. 'Luca, where are you?' He had better be all right. She couldn't imagine what she'd do if anything had happened to him.

'El, I'm here. Are you okay?'

She'd never heard such a beautiful sound. 'Yes, I think so. Are you?'

Her relief was snatched away by a loud bang and the noise of metal being torn and bent. The van had come to a halt wrapped around a tree.

'The driver, the Aussies. Luca—' The words dried

up on her tongue. They didn't have a chance of surviving that crash.

A familiar, warm hand gripped her shoulder. 'We'll get help.' That hand was shaky. 'Are you sure you're all right?'

Pain thudded through her hip but when she shifted her leg nothing felt broken. She nodded. 'Thanks to you.' Twisting her head, she kissed the back of Luca's hand. 'What about you?'

'A few bruises but think I got lucky.'

'You're not lying? Not going all macho on me?' When Luca shook his head Ellie began pushing herself up to the road, sliding in the mud as she made hard work of the short distance. Her body was shaking as if she had the DTs. Shock did that, she knew. She concentrated hard, thought about the situation. 'What are the chances of another vehicle coming along in this weather?'

Luca was right behind her. 'That tourist bus was due to leave right after us. Though how a bus will manage on that road when the van was struggling, I don't know.'

Ellie shuddered. A busload of people going over the edge didn't bear thinking about. 'Wait. I hear something.' She strained to listen through the torrential rain.

'Not a bus but a four-wheel drive, I'm thinking.' Luca stepped into the middle of the road, slip-sliding in the mud and waving wildly. 'Hell, not one but three of them. We just got lucky, El.'

Guess luck was relative. Guilt assailed her. They *were* lucky. There were four people still in that mangled van down the bank. The only luck for them was she and Luca were doctors, doctors with nothing but their bare hands and the knowledge in their heads. If they were still in need of medical intervention.

'You're not going down there,' Luca informed her moments later in a do-not-argue-with-me tone. 'It's too dangerous.'

'Right, I'm to stand up here watching you risking your life? I don't think so.' She turned to find people from the vehicles now parked to the side of the road approaching with ropes.

'El,' Luca growled. 'Two of these men are going down with me. If we can get anyone out of the van, the others will pull them up here for you to attend to.' Again his hand was on her shoulder, his fingers gently squeezing. 'There won't be an ambulance turning up. It's up to all of us to get these people stabilised and to a hospital.' His voice was calm, encouraging, not like that of someone who'd barely escaped with his life minutes earlier.

Shame at her outburst had her apologising. The last thing Luca needed right now was a hysterical female on his shaky hands. 'Sorry. You're right. Again. But, Luca, please be careful.' She couldn't lose him now. Even as a friend he was too precious to her. She'd lost enough people this past year for various reasons.

'Promise.'

Standing around waiting, peering over the edge and sucking a deep breath every time one of the men slipped, which was often, nearly drove her nuts. She only let the breath go when she knew for sure that man was all right. When Luca slid down a steep, muddy patch too fast her heart slammed her ribs. 'You promised you'd be careful,' she whispered. 'I should've asked you to promise that you'd be safe and not get hurt.'

'Over here,' a male voice called through the gloom from halfway down the slope.

Luca and another guy veered off to the right, and very

soon were crouched beside a small bush where what Ellie finally recognised as feet were sticking out from.

Soon Ellie's first patient had been hauled up to the road and she had something to keep her mind off Luca. The guy was caked in mud and muck, soaked through from the rain, and still managed to crack a joke. 'Didn't read this bit on the tourist brochure. Must've caught the wrong ride.'

Hot tears filled Ellie's eyes and she had to blink rapidly to dispel them. 'You and the rest of us. You want to tell me where you're hurt so I can check you out?'

'I don't need to be hurting for you to do that, babe. Been eyeing you up all morning.'

'I'm a doctor,' she told him. His face was pale underneath the mud that was slowly washing off in the rain. 'Let's get you into one of the vehicles. Don't see why we need to be getting any more drenched than we already are.'

A man she hadn't noticed standing nearby put a hand under the Aussie guy's elbow. 'Here, lean against me.'

The Aussie was limping and he held the other arm tight against his chest. 'Thanks, mate. Think my arm's broken.'

After slitting the sleeve up with a pocketknife the other man handed her, Ellie noted a large swelling over the tibia that suggested her patient was right. 'I'll create a makeshift sling so that you don't move or jar your arm until you're in hospital.' When and where that was she had no idea. 'What else? You were limping.'

'Everything seems to be working. Think my thigh hit something hard when I was thrown out of the van. Probably only bruised, though it hurts like a bitch.'

Yeah, Ellie could commiserate. Nor was her hip

happy, protesting every time she bumped against the door or moved sharply. 'Let's take a look.'

More vehicles stopped, more people slid down the bank to help extricate the driver and the other two passengers. Luca finally returned to the road and helped Ellie do whatever she could for the injured men. One by one they were taken away in various vehicles, heading for proper medical care. The driver remained unconscious throughout the whole ordeal of being pulled free of his stoved-in van and hauled up the bank. With no oxygen or monitors of any description Ellie and Luca did their best to make him comfortable before seeing him off in a truck that had just turned up.

'I'll give you two a lift into Luang Prabang,' one of the first men to stop told them. 'You look knackered.'

That would be an understatement, Ellie admitted to herself. Sore, soaked through, muddy and still shaking, she desperately wanted a hot shower.

Luca held her hand all the way back to their hotel. Tightly. They were both shivering from cold and fright. Though the temperature was as hot and the air as muggy as ever, Ellie couldn't believe the chills tightening her skin. Her saturated clothes clung to her, pulling at her skin every time she moved.

At the hotel entrance she tugged off her canvas shoes before going inside, but she still left a trail of footprints and water as she crossed to the stairs leading up to where their rooms were situated. Luca still held her hand, his shoes swinging from the fingers of his other one.

They hardly uttered a word all the way, and even when Ellie tried again and again to shove the key into the lock, Luca said nothing. He merely took the key from her shaking hand and tried three times before he succeeded.

He followed her into her room, dropped his shoes on the mat and headed for the bathroom. 'You need out of those clothes and under the shower, like now.'

'So do you.' She was already unbuckling the belt on her trousers, then pushing them down her legs, the wet fabric clinging to her skin.

The sound of running water came from the bathroom. 'Give that a few seconds to warm up.' Luca stood in front of her.

Ellie stopped struggling with her T-shirt and stared up at this wonderful man who'd just been through hell with her. For all the moisture she carried in her clothing and her hair, her mouth was dry. 'That was way too close.'

His eyes widened in agreement as he reached for the hem of her shirt and started to lift it up over her breasts and then her head. 'Yes, it was.'

She shuddered. And slipped her arms up so as he could get her shirt off. Her hands joined behind his neck, pulling his head closer to hers. 'We're alive.'

'Yep.' His lips brushed hers. 'And wet and shivering.' He scooped her up into his arms and headed for the bathroom and all that glorious warm steam that was now beginning to fill the tiny room. One arm was around her back with his hand on her lace-covered breast, the other arm under her knees with his fingers splayed across the top of one knee. Heat filled her, banishing the chills, even where Luca's wet shirt clung to her rib cage. Need poured through her, need to prove she was alive and well, need for Luca.

Setting her down in the shower box, he began unzipping his shorts. 'Move over.'

She didn't need a second invitation. Scuttling sideways, she reached for him, pulled him into the shower even before he'd finished undressing. Gently wiping the mud off his cheeks, his neck, his arms, she felt him unclasp her bra at her back.

Luca pushed her thong down, his hands taking it past her thighs, over her knees and down to her ankles, where he lifted one foot then the other to free the thin scrap of lace. Upright again, those strong hands she adored touching her gripped her buttocks. 'We're alive, El. And I'm going to prove how much.' Then he lifted her so she could wrap her legs around his waist.

Her mouth sought his, her tongue instantly inside the hot cavern of his mouth. Hot. Heat. Real. This was real, making the blood pound through her veins, in her ears, deafening yet wonderful as the regular thumping beat the rhythm of life. *We're alive.*

Pushing her breasts hard against his chest, she rubbed back and forth, absorbing the exquisite sensations blasting her as she felt Luca's skin sliding against hers. Feeling each individual finger where he touched her backside, knowing the sensation of his palms on her soft skin. Feeling, feeling, feeling. Nothing, no one, had ever felt so wonderful, so full of promise.

Now she wanted all of him; needed to feel his length slide inside her, fill her. Then, and only then, would she truly believe they had survived. His erection was pulsing between her legs, against her opening. Ellie began to slide down over him, drawing his manhood into her, gasping with wonder at the strength and length of him. 'Luca,' she cried. She was more than ready. As the tension coiling in her stomach, at the apex of her legs, everywhere, began tightening farther, Luca tensed, then thrust upward, hard, driving into her, again and again, proving he was here, alive and well, and with her.

As the tension gripping her exploded into an orgasm Ellie screamed, 'Luca. Luca.'

'El, oh, yes. That's it. That's good.' He rode her hard and deep, and when he came his eyes snapped open to lock with hers. Eyes full of understanding and longing and bewilderment—and gratitude. For being here, and not down that ravine? For sharing this with her?

'El' was all he said as he held her tight against his body, his hands lightly rubbing her buttocks, shivering through the end of his release. 'El.' The tiniest word meaning so, so much.

They dried each other off, taking their time to discover the other's body. 'You are beautiful,' Luca whispered as he carefully ran the corner of his towel beneath her breast. The small, heavy globe filled his hand to perfection. Her nipple peaked even as he stared at it and he lowered his mouth to savour her. One swipe with his tongue and that peak tightened further. So did his penis. *Down, boy.* This time they were going for long and slow and getting to know each other better.

Something like hope filtered through the postcoital haze blurring his mind. Never had he known such excitement with a woman, so much release and relief and care, so—different and special. Almost loving. Had he been driven by the need to acknowledge he'd survived a horrific crash? Or something more? Something to do with Ellie herself? Had she always been his future? Had he been blind to what was right under his nose?

His gut clenched into a tight knot. Ellie was soon leaving Laos, bound for Perth and then home. Which was a good thing; it had to be. They didn't, and couldn't, have a future other than their rekindled friendship. That was the only way he could ever continue with her in his life. The other—becoming lovers beyond today—was unthinkable, would break every rule he'd made for himself. Would open him up to his vulnerabilities. He wasn't prepared to do that. Not even for Ellie, not even to have her by his side forever. Because she was a 'forever' kind of girl. He suspected that was why she hurt so much about Freddy leaving her. The commitment she'd made to him and their marriage had been broken.

Forget her failed marriage. Right now his body was humming with after-sex lethargy and the need to repeat the whole thing. As soon as possible. His body was going in the opposite direction to his mind, and he couldn't stop it. His body, that was. Why did he say making love when with Ellie? Every other time in his life he'd had sex. When he'd driven into her, pumped his soul into her, he'd known he was safe in every way. Hell, he'd felt complete for the first time in his adult life, maybe since the day he was born. As if he'd found home, which was plain untrue. Home was where the heart was, or something like that, according to a saying out there. But his heart wasn't up for grabs. Not even Ellie was going to snag it. Though these past few weeks it'd been getting harder and harder to deny he wanted and needed her in his life on a regular basis. As in a partner. A life partner. His heart.

'Luca.' Her soft voice skidded across his skin. 'You still with me?' She dropped his towel and ran her palms over his chest, her thumbs lightly flicking his nipples and sending sparks flying out to every corner of his body. Those warm, tender palms cruised lower, over his abs, and lower.

The breath caught in his lungs.

Her hand wrapped around him. Slid down, up, down.

His brain went on strike. The time for thinking was over. His body took up the challenge. He had to have El. Again. Now. The need to taste her, to feel her hot moistness surround his desire was rampaging along his veins, through his muscles, weakening his ability to stay upright—even when his hands were fondling those beautiful breasts.

'El, I need you.' Snatching her up into his arms, he carried her the short distance to the small double bed filling the tiny room and laid her down. Had he really said that?

It's true. I did and I do.

Hopefully Ellie hadn't heard, or if she had then she'd pass it off as something he'd said in the heat of the moment. Which it was. If his brain had been in good working order he'd never have uttered those words.

Truth will out.

Yeah, so they said. He lowered himself beside Ellie and reached for her. His fingers caressed a trail from her lips to her throat to her breasts to her belly button and beyond. El.

CHAPTER TEN

'I'M STARVING.' ELLIE STRETCHED the full length of the ridiculously small bed to ease all the kinks out of her muscles. Pain erupted in her hip. 'Ow!' she cried out. 'Why didn't I feel that when we were making out?'

'Because I'm a bigger distraction?' Luca raised up onto an elbow and lifted the sheet to study her hip. 'That's a piece of work. More colours than the rainbow.' His lips were softer than a moth as they brushed over the tender surface of her beleaguered hip.

She did an exaggerated eye roll. 'Oh, please. Your ego needs controlling.'

He grinned. 'I know.' Then he turned all serious. 'Sorry I threw you onto a rock on the way out of that van.'

There was a lot behind those flippant words. He had saved them from a worse fate. Instead of freaking out in that tumbling metal box that was their transport he'd done something about the situation, done his absolute best to save them. He was her hero. She thought of the driver. 'I wonder how Palchon is. If he's regained consciousness.' *If he's alive.*

'We could go find out on our way to Luang Prabang's airport this morning.'

'I'd like that.' Ellie sat up, groaned as pain again reminded her of her hip. 'My upcoming flight to Perth is looking less exciting. Can you get me some painkillers in Vientiane, and something to help me sleep?' Not that she'd been thrilled about leaving Laos anyway. *Be honest.* It was Luca she didn't want to leave. But that shutdown look that had just appeared on his face told her more than anything that he did not want to carry this on any further. What they'd had together in this small hotel room was all they were going to have.

Her heart shattered. She loved Luca. She'd loved him as a friend, and now as a lover. But most of all she loved him as a man, for all the pieces that made him who he was. For his tenderness, for the way he had always listened to her grizzles and cheered her up when the world came tumbling down on top of her, the mess of dirty clothes he never put in the wash for days on end, his skill as a doctor. She loved him completely.

Ironic really, when she'd come to Laos to sort herself out and instead got herself caught up in love with Luca, when he'd made it plain he did not reciprocate her feelings. She'd be going home flattened and filled with despair. Home would now be in Auckland, a city filled with memories of Luca.

Unless this was love on the rebound, and then she could hope that eventually, hopefully in the not too distant future, she'd get over Luca. It was debatable whether they could ever go back to be best friends again. So whichever way this turned out, she'd lost someone else important to her. The sooner the year finished, the better. She was going to dance and drink and sing the new year in like never before, welcome it with open arms, then get on with her new job and creating the career that'd take her through the next twenty years without falter.

'I'll head back to my room to shower and pack my toothbrush.' Luca stood up from the bed in full naked glory.

'Sure.' He was beautiful. Had he always looked like this beneath his snappy shirt and fitting trousers? She'd seen him in running shorts and T-shirts, in track pants, in jeans, everything a normal well-dressed man would wear, and she'd had no idea what he was covering up. Blind? Or had she been that unaware of her feelings for him? Went to show this love thing was new, not something that had been lurking in the back of her head.

'If we're going to have breakfast and visit the hospital we need to get a shake along, Ellie.' He wrapped a towel around his waist.

'Sure,' she repeated, still drinking in the sight of toned muscles and long, strong limbs. How could she have missed those? 'See you in thirty,' she muttered through a salivating mouth.

'Make that twenty. We don't want to miss the flight back to Vientiane. Who knows when we'd get another one? We were lucky getting this one.'

And tomorrow she was heading to Australia. Tossing back the sheet, she leaped up, ignoring the protest from her hip. Funny how that hadn't been a problem while making love with Luca. 'Twenty it is.' An exciting thought snagged her, Miss the flight and have more time in bed with Luca. But looking at his face showed that wasn't going to happen.

Slamming the bathroom door shut, she jerked the taps on and stepped under the cold water. Gasping, she crossed her arms over her breasts and gritted her teeth until the water warmed up. She tried to put aside thoughts of Luca and her new-found love and concentrate on the mundane, like getting clean, dressed, her make-up on and the few items she'd brought here back in her bag. Forget everything else for now. There were many hours in the air when she'd have nothing else to do but think. Or sleep if Luca got those sleeping pills for her.

According to the American doctor at the local hospital their van driver had regained consciousness but he wouldn't be going anywhere in a hurry. Both femurs were broken from where he'd impacted with the dashboard, and ribs had been fractured, presumably by the steering wheel as he was thrown forward.

'What happens?' Luca asked. 'Does he stay in hospital until he's back on his feet? Or will he be sent home within a day or two?'

'I'll keep him here as long as possible, but—' the man shrugged '—it won't be nearly long enough.'

'I'd like to help out financially,' Luca said quietly. 'How do I go about that?'

As Ellie listened to Luca and the other doctor discussing how to give the man's family money to see them through the next few weeks she looked around at the basic hospital emergency room. Nothing like what she'd trained in: not a lot of equipment or any up-to-date beds. There was little privacy for the patients, and families sat on the floor by their loved ones. Yet everyone seemed grateful for any attention they received. Also not like home where some patients and their families felt no compunction over telling medical staff what they expected of them.

'Right, let's go. That plane won't wait.'

That plane was delayed for nearly an hour. Sitting on a cold, hard seat, Ellie watched Luca pace up and down the departure lounge. It was as if he was busting to get back to the clinic. He sure as hell didn't have anything to say to her. He'd gone from caring, loving and sexy to cool, focused and resolute. She'd been cut off.

Beside her a baby kicked her tiny legs and made gurgling noises. Ellie turned her attention to the cutest little girl she'd ever seen and made cooing sounds. Swathed in pink clothes and blanket, the baby had to be sweltering but Mum seemed unperturbed.

'She's gorgeous,' Ellie said.

While it was obvious the mother didn't understand the words she'd picked up on Ellie's tone and smiled broadly. Nodding her head, she spoke rapidly in a language Ellie hadn't heard before. Not Laotian, for sure.

'Can I?' Ellie held her hands out, fully expecting to be rebuffed.

But the woman happily handed her precious child over, adjusting the blanket around the baby's face when Ellie settled her in her arms.

More kicks and gurgles came her way from the warm little bundle. 'What's her name?' she asked without thinking.

The mum stared at her, a question in her big brown eyes.

Ellie tapped her own chest. 'Ellie.' Then she lightly touched the baby's arm. 'Name?'

The woman said, 'Ellee?' Or something that vaguely sounded like her name. Then she tapped her chest and said, 'Sui.' Nodding at the baby, she added, 'Bubba.'

Bubba as in baby, or was that her name? Something in

a foreign language that Ellie couldn't decipher? 'Bubba.' She copied the mother and grinned down at the baby.

What would it feel like to be holding her own baby like this? Her heart slowed, squeezed gently. It would be wonderful, precious. And not something that was about to happen in the foreseeable future. She didn't seem to do so well choosing the men she fell in love with. One hadn't wanted a family with her despite reassuring her in the beginning he did, and Luca didn't want a relationship with her at all, when he'd be brilliant as a dad. He didn't want a family of his own at all. Maybe she should abandon any hope for a husband and her own children. That could save a lot of heartbreak in the future. Except her heart had begun to ache for those things. With Luca.

The PA system announced their flight was ready for boarding. Ellie looked around for Luca. She stilled as she found those intense grey eyes fixed on her, flicking between her and the baby. What? Had she done something wrong? Was it not the done thing to hold another woman's baby for a few minutes? To enjoy feeling the tiny girl squirming and kicking? Whatever Luca thought, it had been a magical moment she was glad she'd taken.

Another look at Luca and she saw it—the longing fighting to get out. Luca wanted children. She'd swear it. But as she locked her gaze on his he shut her out. The blinkers were back in place and he was giving nothing away. Instead, he tipped his head in the direction of the door leading out onto the tarmac and mouthed, 'Ready?'

Handing Bubba back to her mother, Ellie said, 'Thank you for letting me hold her.' Then she put her hands, palms together, in front of her chest, nodded and said, 'Goodbye.'

The woman rewarded her with a huge smile.

A smile that Ellie wore in her heart on the hour's flight back to Vientiane. Luca might be withdrawing but she wouldn't let that dampen the feelings holding that baby had evoked. No way.

If only Luca would admit to feeling the same. About babies. About her and him.

Luca knew he was behaving badly but he didn't know how else to keep Ellie at arm's length. He was afraid that if he let her close he'd haul her into his arms and never let her leave his side.

That night in Luang Prabang should never have happened, yet he couldn't find it in himself to wish it hadn't. Making love to Ellie had been off the wall. Like nothing he'd ever experienced before. That sense of finding himself had increased when they'd gone to bed for their second intimate connection.

With Ellie he thought he probably could face his demons and even keep them at bay. But reality sucked. Beneath the surface lurked those genes he'd inherited from his father and his mother's father. More than ever he did not want to hurt anyone when that person could be Ellie. She'd had her share of pain. She didn't need him giving her a relapse. Which was why when they'd finally got back to Vientiane yesterday he'd made himself busy at the hospital until long after Ellie had headed to her room for the night.

'You can smile.' Ellie leaned against his arm. 'Everyone else is.'

Aaron and Louise were having fun, drinking copious quantities of wine and cracking mediocre jokes. They were at a restaurant and bar, enjoying the evening despite the fact they were losing Ellie in a few hours. 'Seeing

Ellie off in style' was how Louise had put it on the way into town nearly two hours earlier.

It was the nature of the clinic, people coming and going with monotonous regularity. Not many stayed for a year like him, while Louise and Aaron set the record for how long they'd been here.

'I guess our misadventure has caught up with me,' Luca murmured as his nostrils filled with that particular scent he now recognised as Ellie's. Floral without being too sweet, reminding him of the spring air back home. Reminding him of what he could not have.

'Great,' Ellie snapped, tipping her head away from him.

Hiding? Then he thought about what he'd said and shook his head. 'That wasn't a criticism of you or us or how the night unfolded. I am tired, but, more than that, I'm trying to deal with having found my best friend only to be losing her again.'

'Come on, you two. Let's all dance together one last time.' Aaron stood up and reached for Ellie's hand, but Louise took one look at Ellie and then him and dragged Aaron away, leaving them to this conversation that sucked and had no possible outcome that would please either of them.

'You haven't lost me,' Ellie argued, now back to facing him. 'We've changed the nature of our relationship but we're not breaking up.' Was that hope in her eyes?

'I've lost my friend,' he reiterated. He was being cruel to be kind. He couldn't give her anything but friendship and she appeared to want more. Lots more.

The colour drained from her cheeks as she gasped. Hurt glittered out at him from those eyes that followed him into sleep every night. 'No. You can't do that to me.'

I can't save your heart? Give me a break here. I'm thinking of you, looking out for you. 'Ellie, go home and start that new job, find an apartment or a house to make yours, give yourself time to get over your marriage and then start dating again. One mistake doesn't mean you can't find happiness again.' *Only, it won't be with me.*

Ellie lifted her glass, drained it of water and banged it back on the table. 'I don't want to lose anyone else. I just got you back.'

'We made a mistake.' At least he'd had the good sense not to realise that until after he'd learned what it was like to make love with Ellie. He'd never forget, even if he was now spoiled forever.

'I'll tell you what a mistake is.' She held one finger up in front of him. 'Marrying a man I believed loved me enough to want to be there when I got old and grey and used a walking stick.' A second finger went up. 'Trusting Caitlin not to sleep with my husband.'

Shock stunned him. 'Your sister slept with Freddy?' He'd always believed the worst of Baldwin, but this? Luca couldn't get his head around the idea of the guy going with his wife's sister. That went way beyond bad. No wonder there was always wariness and despair lurking in Ellie's eyes. She and her sister had been close.

Ellie hadn't finished. A third finger rose, and her whole hand shook. 'Freddy loves Caitlin. Caitlin loves Freddy. They want to get married as soon as the divorce goes through.'

Luca wrapped both his hands around the one wavering in front of his face. 'El, don't torture yourself. They're the bad guys here, not you.' How did she get up every morning? When did she plaster her smiles on? Seconds before bumping into the kids waiting for her to appear outside her room at the clinic? Who did she trust these days?

Him. It struck him with blinding certainty. Ellie trusted him. *Wrong, girl, absolutely wrong.* Which was why he was fighting the churning need to take her in his arms and kiss her better, never to let her go again. To forget everything he'd been trying to tell himself moments earlier.

'I need a friend, Luca. You.' She swallowed. 'But there's more to what I'm feeling. I've always loved you as a friend.'

Don't say it. Don't. Please. It was going to hurt them both, and then he'd hurt her some more. But he couldn't look away, couldn't find the right words—if they existed—to stop her from laying out everything between them.

'My feelings for you aren't like they used to be, and yesterday kind of underlined that. Making love with you was beautiful.' She paused, staring into his eyes. Searching for what? Waiting for what? Finally, on a long, sad sigh, she continued, 'You know what I'm afraid of, Luca? That for me this is rebound love, and that I'll wake up one day and wish my friend back and my lover gone. The pain would be enormous, but I'm prepared to risk it. Because I believe you—we—are worth it. Because I'm not so sure that this isn't the real deal and what I felt for Freddy was the lesser.' Her head dropped. 'Which doesn't put me in a good light at all.'

'We all make mistakes.' Though not always as big as what this sounded like—on both sides of the marriage. 'You've got to learn to let go, El, drop all that hurt caused by Freddy and Caitlin, and then you'll see our relationship for what it is. Friendship. Nothing more. Or less.'

'You make it sound so easy.' Acid burned in her words; pain flattened her mouth.

Luca stood up, pulling Ellie up with him. He needed fresh air, to walk, to stare at the stars. To explain to El that she was so wrong about them, had got everything completely back to front. Because of what Freddy and Caitlin had done she was searching for someone to make her feel better. Sounding more and more as if her rebound theory was correct. 'Come for a walk.'

'There's not a lot of time before I have to head to the airport.' Suddenly she sounded reluctant, as if she knew she'd gone too far.

'This won't take long.' At least it wouldn't if he could get the words out. He was afraid. Because the moment he said what had to be said he'd lose Ellie again, this time probably permanently. When he reached for her hand she stepped sideways and folded her arms as though she was cold and not avoiding him. But he knew different.

If he waited a while longer there'd be no time, and he owed her an explanation. Dread lined his stomach, making it heavy and tight. 'In Luang Prabang, that was glad-to-be-alive sex. We'd both had a huge shock, were grateful to get off that hillside in one piece, and naturally we celebrated in the most obvious way. It was great sex, the best I've ever had, but, Ellie, you must see that there's no future in it. We're friends, I care a lot for you, but nothing's changed. I still won't get married or have kids.' If he said it all fast enough it started to sound right. 'Those are the things you ultimately want in your life. Not yet. I get that it's far too soon. But I'm *never* going there.'

He was breathing fast, as if he'd run a marathon or something. His heart beat hard and erratically. As for what was going on in his head, the kaleidoscope of emotions and need mocking his words—he wasn't going there, couldn't go there. He'd hate to find he'd got this all wrong.

Ellie rounded on him, stabbed a finger at his chest. 'Aren't you going too far with your assertions that I want to marry you?'

He held his hands up. 'Just laying it all out right from the get-go. I come from a line of lousy commitment-phobes. I'm trying to save you here.'

'Pathetic.' Her hands banged onto her hips, and she winced. Must've hurt the bruised one. 'You're blaming the men in your life for your avoidance issues when deep down you want to love and be loved. You want a family of your own, but you're too damned afraid to reach out and try for that.'

'You don't know what you're talking about.'

'Really? Then, why have you only ever dated the kind of women that won't want the whole nine yards?' Ellie turned away, turned back, her face softening as she gazed at him. 'You've proved yourself time and time again, Luca. You did everything you could for your nephew. You haven't given up on him despite his mother kicking you out of his life. I've seen you with young patients, never letting them down, always ready to stay hours longer than required to make sure they're coping.'

'That's not the same.' Why couldn't she understand he wasn't doing this for the hell of it? That, yeah, he'd like to make happy families—with her, what was more—if only there was a spitting chance in hell of it working. 'Even Angelique proved we've got bad genes by doing to Johnny what Mum did to us—refusing to acknowledge his father.'

Ellie shook her head at him and began to walk back towards the restaurant. Her time was almost up and she had to get to the airport. Luca's heart was breaking. This time was different from when they last went their separate ways. Then she'd been going to Freddy, and he'd had Gaylene on his back. He'd always believed that one day they'd get back in touch. Tonight he knew this was the end for them. 'Ellie,' he called softly. 'I'm sorry.'

She had to have supersensitive hearing because she came back to him and placed her hands gently on his cheeks. 'So am I, Luca. So am I. Do me one favour? Let go of some of that control you hold over your emotions. Start taking some risks with your heart. Stop blaming everyone else.' Reaching up on her toes, she kissed him, not with the passion of yesterday, not lightly as she used to as a friend, but as a woman who loved him and knew she'd lost him before they'd even started.

CHAPTER ELEVEN

ELLIE STARED AROUND the apartment she'd been sharing with Renee since the day she'd moved out of her marital home. 'I'm going to miss this, you, even Wellington,' she told Renee. 'But not the hospital.' Though now, after Luca, it almost seemed easier to stay here in the same city as her ex and Caitlin. At least here she had Renee and a handful of casual friends she enjoyed evenings with at five-star restaurants or going to shows.

She had this awful feeling that wherever she went her heart was going to take time to put all the pieces back together. All she could hope for was that some day way ahead she'd stop feeling this debilitating pain. Hell, she'd thought Freddy and Caitlin had hurt her. She'd had no idea.

Renee gave her a tired smile. Three gruelling nights with an extremely ill two-year-old requiring two emergency operations had done that to her. 'You can change your mind any time you like. Save me the hassle of finding another roomie.'

It was tempting. Running away didn't come naturally. 'I've signed a contract.'

'Six months isn't exactly long-term.' Renee never minded firing the shots directly at her target, which was why Ellie liked her so much. No bull dust. 'I'll keep your room for you that long.'

'Stop it. I might do a Luca next and go overseas, though not to Asia.' Australia or the UK appealed more at the moment.

'I still can't get my head around Luca ditching his super career and going over there for a year. Back when we were all sharing that house he drove the rest of us bonkers with his plans for running the biggest and greatest A and E department in the country.'

'That Luca's gone. Or missing in dispatches at the moment.' Whether he'd ever return to those goals she had no idea. 'He's not easy in his new skin, but I now wonder how comfortable he was in his old one.'

'Backstory. I wonder what his is. He never talked about his family, did he? Even when we'd been on the turps and talking a load of nonsense about ourselves.' Renee looked pensive. 'Does that mean there are some nasty skeletons in his cupboard?'

'Luca definitely thinks so. Certainly lets them rule how he lives his life.' Anger rose suddenly, unexpectedly, nearly choking Ellie. He let his unknown father dominate him. He'd pushed her away because of a man he hadn't met. *Thanks a bundle, Luca.* He didn't deserve her. Yeah, way to go. Her anger deflated as quickly as it had come, replaced by sadness—and despair. 'He does have issues, but until he decides to talk them through they're not going anywhere.'

'And you? You've come home broken-hearted.' Renee handed her a mug of milky coffee even though she hadn't asked for one. 'Are you going to be okay?'

'I'm an old hand at this. At least in Auckland I won't have to put up with knowing nods and snide remarks about my model sister and how awful it must be trying to keep up with her fashion sense and stunning figure.' Ouch. *More than bitter, Ellie.*

Renee growled, 'Stop it. It's over now.' She was repeating Luca's words. 'Even if you stayed on in Wellington I think you'd find no one cares anymore. In fact I've lost count of the number of people asking me how you're getting on and when you're coming back.'

'So they can talk about me again.'

'Ellie, give it a rest. I thought you were moving on from all this, then you return from Laos all in a pickle again. If Luca's upset you, that's one thing, but to carry on about Freddy and Caitlin still is another. It's been nearly a year. Don't you think it's time to accept they are serious about their relationship? Even if they did go about it all wrong and hurt you so badly.'

'There would never have been a right way to go about it,' she snapped, and banged her mug down. Time to throw her bags in her car and get out of here. It was a long drive to Auckland, and she intended on dropping in on her parents first.

'So you'd rather have continued being married to a man who was no longer in love with you just so you could feel righteous. What about your feelings for Luca? Are you going to walk away from them? Not fight for him, show him how much you love him?'

Ellie's mouth fell open. What? 'Have you gone crazy?'

'Probably.' Renee's stance softened and she pushed the mug of untouched coffee back towards Ellie. 'But you know me, never one to keep my mouth zipped.'

'I thought I liked that about you.'

'Changed your mind?' Renee smiled. 'When was the last time you saw Caitlin? Talked to her?'

Months ago when she'd been in a shop trying on leather jackets Caitlin had strolled in with a friend to look through the racks of clothes on sale. Ellie had tugged out of the jacket she'd been admiring in the full-length mirror, left it on the counter and stormed outside, ignoring Caitlin's pleas to stop and talk. 'The last time I said a word to her was January. When I demanded she get out of my bed, out of my house and away from my husband.' That had been the day she'd learned that the house no longer appealed to her and her husband wasn't really hers in anything but name. She'd ditched the name by the end of the day.

'Go see her.'

Ellie gasped. 'Next you'll be telling me to forgive her.'

Renee shrugged. 'If that's what it takes.'

'To do what?' This conversation was getting out of hand, but she couldn't help herself wanting to know where her friend was headed with it.

'What happened with Luca?' Renee asked.

'He sent me packing, said we had no future together.'

'And you came away. Didn't fight for him. Oh, Ellie, you need to sort your stuff out. Starting with Caitlin and Freddy.'

Ellie couldn't get Renee's words out of her head as she drove north. It hadn't helped that Mum and Dad had asked her to give her sister a call sometime. Everyone made her feel as if she were the guilty party. That she'd gone off and had an affair behind her husband's back with someone close to him instead of how it had really gone down.

You need to sort your stuff out. Renee might be back there in Wellington but her damned criticisms were in the car, going to Auckland with her.

Luca had told her to drop the ball of pain directing her life. *It's not pain.* She slapped the steering wheel with her palm. *It's anger.*

Actually it was red-hot, belly-tightening rage. The people she loved most in the world hurt her. Freddy. Caitlin. And now Luca. They did it so effortlessly. They picked her up, then tossed her aside as they chose.

Only one reason for that. She let them.

She needed windscreen wipers for her eyes. The road ahead was a blur. Lifting her foot from the accelerator, she aimed for the side of the road and parked on a narrow grass verge.

Every time she had pangs of longing to see her sister, to talk with her, she turned them into a ball of hate and hurt, put the blame squarely on Caitlin. Shoved the past aside: the nights when they'd sat in bed together talking about the guys they'd dated, the drones they'd dumped, the bullies at school or the teachers they'd hated. The clothes they'd shared—mostly Caitlin's because she had such great style, with the added bonus of being in on bargains at the right places because of her modelling career.

The tears became a torrent. 'Do you miss me, Caitlin? Like I miss you? What did I do wrong that you had to fall in love with my husband?'

Tap, tap. Ellie looked up to find a traffic cop standing beside her door. Flicking the ignition one notch, she pressed the button to open her window. 'Yes, Officer?'

'Is there a problem, ma'am?'

Quite a few actually. 'No. Am I parked illegally?'

'No, but it's not the safest place to pull over if you

didn't have to.' The woman was staring at her, no doubt taking in her tear-stained scarlet cheeks. Her mascara was probably everywhere but on her lashes by now.

Ellie stared around, saw she had stopped only metres from a sharp corner. 'I was in a hurry to stop, I wasn't thinking clearly.' Would the cop stop her from driving on, or hurry her away from here?

'Can I see your licence?' When Ellie widened her eyes the cop explained, 'Routine. I have to ask every time I stop a driver.'

Ellie handed the licence over. While she waited for the cop to go check her details on the car's computer she blew her nose, finger combed her messy hair and tried to wipe away the black smudges of mascara staining her upper cheeks.

'Thank you, Doctor.' The licence appeared through the window.

'That was quick,' Ellie commented.

'I've just had a call. There's been an accident two kilometres further up this road. Truck versus car. An ambulance has been called but it will take a long while to arrive. Could you help in the meantime? I'll take you with me.' Her thumb jerked in the direction of the blue-and-yellow-striped car with the lights still flashing.

'Of course.' Ellie was already closing the window and grabbing her handbag to hide in the boot. Vehicular accidents were the thing at the moment—for her at least.

The speedy trip had Ellie's heart racing and her mouth smiling. 'I should've been a traffic cop.'

Rose—she'd given her name as they set out on this crazy ride—laughed. 'I'm not supposed to admit this, but I love the high-speed moments.' Then her smile switched off. 'Until I get to the accident and have to see all that gore. I couldn't do your job for all the money in the world.'

'So we're both doing what we enjoy, though I still hate the sight of mangled bodies. Usually I get them when they've been straightened out on a stretcher, not shoved awkwardly into a car well or around a steering wheel.'

Rose weaved around the stationary traffic already forming a long queue. 'Look at that. This isn't going to be pretty.'

Ellie had already taken in the car squashed under the front of a stock truck. 'How can anyone survive that?' she asked as she pushed out of the car. 'The car roof is flattened down on top of the occupants.'

Making her way directly to the accident site, she looked around to see if anyone had been pulled from the wreckage, saw only a brawny man standing with another traffic cop answering questions and rubbing his arms continuously.

'Hey, you can't go there,' someone called out.

'I'm a doctor.'

'She's with me,' Rose added from directly behind her.

'You don't have to come any closer,' Ellie told her. 'You go do the traffic thing and I'll see what I can do for the driver of this car.'

Two men stood up from the driver's side, allowing her access. 'We've found two men in the front. No one in the back,' one of them told her.

The driver's head was tipped back at an odd angle and his eyes were wide-open. Not good. Ellie felt sure he was deceased but she went through the motions in case. The carotid vein had no pulse. Nor was there any at his wrist. Leaning close, she listened for any sound of breathing.

Nothing. Gently closing his eyelids, she looked across to the other seat at a young man also not moving.

Then his lip quivered. Just the smallest of movements, but movement nonetheless. Thankful she'd seen it, Ellie reached over to find his carotid and sighed with relief when she felt the thready beat of his pulse. How long that would last considering how much blood there was seeping from under his shoulder was a moot point. 'This man's alive,' she called as she gently probed his chest to ascertain if his ribs were broken. A punctured lung would not help his chances of survival. Nothing to indicate a rib forced into the lung cavity, but she'd go warily as only an X-ray would confirm that. 'Can we get his door open?'

'We've tried but it's stuck,' she was told.

'Then, we need to move this man out so I can get to his passenger.' Standing up, she eyeballed the two men who'd been here when she'd arrived. 'He's gone, I'm afraid, so this won't be pleasant for either of you, but the other man needs help. Fast.'

'There's a tarpaulin on the truck we can wrap him in,' a policeman said. 'Let's get this guy out of here so you can work some magic.'

Magic. She hoped her imaginary urn was full of that, because it really looked as if the passenger was going to need it all and then some. She said, 'Rose mentioned an ambulance was on its way but this man needs to get to hospital fast.'

'I told them back at base to get the rescue helicopter out here, but it still takes time for the crew to scramble and get airborne.'

'Yes, but at least they'll get him to where he needs to be faster than if he goes by road.'

'Exactly.'

Ellie steadied herself. This was so different from the accident in Laos where everyone had relied on the help of passers-by. There this man wouldn't have had a chance; here he might. 'I don't want to shift him out of that space without a neck brace and a backboard. We really need the car opened up.'

'That's our cue.' A large man dressed in a fireman's uniform stood beside the car, holding a set of Jaws of Life in one hand. 'We've got a first-aid bag with your brace. And a board.'

'Our man's chances have just gone up a notch.' Ellie wished the words back the moment they left her mouth. Talk about tempting fate. She crawled inside the mangled wreck and tried not to listen to the screeching metal as it was slowly and carefully removed by the firemen, and instead concentrated on finding the source of all that blood.

One of the firemen leaned in from the new gap in the car's exterior. 'Tell me what you require from the kit and I'll hand it through.'

Once again she was doing the emergency medicine she'd trained for in very different circumstances from what she was used to. Her admiration for ambulance crews and firemen rose higher than ever.

After an interminable time when Ellie despaired of that flying machine ever arriving it was suddenly all over. She stood with hands on her waist watching the helicopter lift off the road with her patient. 'That's that, then.'

Beside her, Rose shook her head. 'Now the fun really starts. We've got to get this lot moving again.' She nodded towards the traffic, many with their motors already running. 'I wonder how far out the coroner's vehicle is. The sooner we get that other man taken away, the sooner we can investigate the scene and open the road completely.'

Sadness rolled through Ellie. A man had died here today because, according to the truck driver, he'd come round the corner halfway across the median line. Because of that there were going to be people whose lives would never be the same again. People that the police had yet to go and break the sad news to. 'It's so heartbreaking.' The speed at which lives could be taken, or others altered, was shocking. Everyone should hug their loved ones every day.

'I'll get someone to take you back to your car,' Rose said.

Ellie looked around, saw the impatient drivers desperate to get going, the firemen pulling what remained of the car free of the truck, the police working hard to sort everything out, and felt humble. 'You know what? I'll walk. It was only a couple of kilometres.'

'What if that had been Luca?' Ellie asked herself as she strode along the grass verge. They'd argued and were in disagreement over where their relationship should go from here on in, but he was fit and healthy back in Laos. She could talk to him just by picking up her phone. She could even hop on a flight and be able to see him, touch him, in less than twenty-four hours. She could tell him she loved him. But the family and friends of that young man had lost those opportunities forever.

Why she was thinking like this now, today, she had no idea. It wasn't as though death was new to her. She'd seen it in the department far too often. Probably the fact that she was already feeling despondent over Luca had made this worse. He'd been the first face to pop into her mind when she'd seen that crash site.

Her phone vibrated in her back pocket. It was her mother texting.

Are you safe? Caitlin's worried, says there's been a fatal accident near Levin.

Ellie pressed the phone icon. 'Hey, Mum, I'm fine. Got caught up in the traffic jam but should be on my way any moment.' Not a lie, just stretching the truth. She didn't want to say she'd been attending to the victims, didn't want to hear her mother's questions.

Her car was around the next corner.

'Mum, I've got to get going. I'll call you when I get to Auckland if it's not too late.' Which it probably would be now. She might have to look at other options. 'Love you.'

Flicking her automatic key lock, she slipped into her car. The last thing she felt like was driving for the next eight hours. A shower would be good. She could stop halfway at Taupo, hole up in a motel for the night.

She tapped her phone. Caitlin had told Mum. Caitlin. Should she let it all go? Forgive Caitlin? No way. How could she do that? The betrayal had been huge.

But so was the void in her heart. Damn it, but she missed her sister. Caitlin had told Mum she was worried about her today.

Another worrying thought struck Ellie. Was her anger and grief over her failed marriage going to hold her back from achieving more with her career, with finding love again?

You love Luca.

Yeah, she did, but could she trust herself with that

love? There was that rebound theory spinning around her skull. What if she took a chance and ended up flat on her backside again in a few months' time?

That particular risk was always there. Look at her and Freddy. She'd believed that was forever. Big mistake. Or bad judgement? Or— Drawing air into her lungs, Ellie slowly let the disturbing idea enter her mind. Had she not loved Freddy as much as she'd believed? Look how soon she'd fallen for Luca. Less than a year since her world had imploded and she was in love with him. She'd been quick to believe Freddy hadn't loved her as fervently as he'd claimed in the beginning. But what if she hadn't loved Freddy as much as she was capable of? As much as she now loved Luca?

Have I always been a little bit in love with him? So what if I have? Neither of us recognised it, so nothing was lost.

Except she'd made the mistake of marrying Freddy.

Her husband—the man her sister had fallen in love with and wanted to wed as soon as it was legally possible, and whom until now Ellie had been determined to hate for that.

Ellie turned the key so that she could lower the window and let in fresh air. She wasn't ready to start driving.

Luca had hurt her with his quick denial of their relationship. He wasn't prepared to give a little on his stance, wasn't ready to take a chance with her.

Yeah, well, she hadn't been rushing in to hug her sister and say she understood. Because she didn't understand how someone that close could fall for her husband. But— Always a damned but. Caitlin did love Freddy. She got that. Had heard her parents talk about it, had learned that Caitlin and Freddy had moved in together months ago and were as happy as sparrows in a puddle.

A shiver rocked Ellie. The skin on her forearms lifted in bumps. Was she stuck in a holding pattern? Unable to forgive and move forward, unwilling to let it all go and take control of her life again? As if she was afraid of something. Hard to believe that.

But she wasn't ready for Luca, for sure. She needed to sort herself out and get back on track before she could expect him to become a part of her life. He'd been right to tell her to go home, away from him. She was not ready. She had a lot to do first—starting now.

Ellie pulled on the handbrake and let the engine idle. Staring up at the small house on the side of the hill in central Wellington, she felt her heart almost throttling her. Her hands gripped the steering wheel so tight her knuckles were white.

Could she do this?

She had to.

It was time, way past time, really.

This was the first step of her recovery.

Still she sat staring beyond her car at the quiet suburban street. Nothing like she'd ever have believed Caitlin would choose to live in. Her sister had been about fancy apartments and patios, not overgrown lawns and tumbledown houses that had been built in the 1930s.

Move your butt.

Ellie sighed. Yep, she was procrastinating because that was way easier than facing up to Caitlin. But until she did she wasn't going anywhere with her life.

Shoving her door wide, Ellie clambered out quickly, not allowing herself a change of mind. The concrete steps leading up to the front door were uneven and crumbling at the edges. The grass hadn't seen a lawnmower in months. So unlike either of the two people living in this house. Trouble in paradise? She hoped not. Sincerely hoped not.

Have I done this all wrong? Should she have had it out with them way back at the beginning?

Too late. All she could do was work on moving ahead. Who knew what was out there for her? But until she settled the past she had this strong feeling that she wouldn't be finding out.

The door swung open as she raised her knuckles to knock. 'Ellie? Really?'

Ellie's heart rolled as she stared at her sister. Caitlin looked the same, yet different. More grown up. Major life crises did that to a person. 'Can I come in?' She knew there was reluctance in her voice, felt that the moment she stepped over the threshold she'd have conceded something—but that was why she was here. To start forgiving, start getting her family back, start accepting that she and Freddy had made a mistake, that they hadn't been right for each other.

Caitlin stepped back, pulling the door wide. Tears streamed down her face while hope and caution warred in her eyes. 'You were on your way to Auckland,' she finally said in a strangled voice so unlike her usually vibrant, cheeky tone.

'I'm making a detour.' Ellie ran her tongue over her suddenly dry lips, tried to still her rolling stomach that felt as if it was about to toss her breakfast. What was she doing here? This was way too hard. She hadn't forgiven anyone. *But you want to. You want your sister back.*

Caitlin turned away abruptly, almost ran down the hall towards the kitchen. 'I'll put the coffee on.'

Ellie's feet were rooted to the floor. Should she stay? Should she go? An image of the young man she'd declared deceased snapped on in her mind. Were there people out there he hadn't apologised to for something? Had he told his girlfriend or wife or kids this morning that he loved them?

She moved forward, one shaky step at a time, to the door of the kitchen. 'I've missed you.'

That wasn't what she'd meant to say at all. She'd been going to demand an explanation for why she hadn't been told about the affair. But now that she'd uttered the words her whole body started to let go the tightness that had been there since January.

The bag in Caitlin's fingers hit the floor, spraying coffee beans in every direction. Then Caitlin was leaping at her, wrapping her arms around her, crying, 'Ellie, I'm so sorry. I didn't mean to hurt you. I love you. I've missed you every day since.' Her tears soaked into Ellie's blouse as she clung to her.

Ellie couldn't stop her own tears from streaming down her face. But nor could she find any words: her throat was blocked and her brain on strike. She so wanted to forgive Caitlin, but to verbalise that didn't come easily. Didn't come at all. Finally she lifted her head and dropped her arms to her sides. 'I'll see you on Christmas Day.'

Then she left. And started her journey all over again, this time with her heart feeling a little lighter.

Slipping a CD into the car stereo, she even hummed as she drove out of the city and along the highway past the ocean—for the second time that day. Definitely stopping the night in Taupo now. Listening to The Exponents brought other memories crowding in—all of Luca. Luca dancing. Luca laughing. Being patient with the kids at the clinic. Kissing her, making love to her. Luca. She sighed with longing clogging her senses.

What would he say if he knew she'd been to see her sister? Now she'd been to see Caitlin, would he think better of her for it? Would he work at letting go some of his hang-ups now that she'd started on hers?

Nah, of course he wouldn't. He was determined never to change, never to take a risk.

'Well, Luca, that's all fine and dandy, but I've started to turn my life around, and you can do the same, even if it doesn't bring you back to me.' She sang the words almost in tune to the song blaring from the stereo. A sad song, she realised, just as a fresh bout of tears began splashing down her face.

She'd reached Levin again, and looked around for a place to park. Strong coffee was needed. And food to stop the shakes and settle these stupid crying bursts. What was wrong with her anyway? She'd started patching things up with Caitlin, which had to be good. She might want Luca but that wasn't going to happen any time soon, if at all, and no amount of bawling her eyes out would alter that. Blowing her nose hard, she scrunched up the tissue and stepped out of the car to head for the nearest café. 'Auckland, here I come. Life, here I come.'

CHAPTER TWELVE

LUCA TOOK OVER from Aaron, suturing the wound on the right leg of their latest bomb victim while the other man drew deep breaths of air. 'It never gets any easier, does it?'

'No,' growled Aaron. 'What I wouldn't like to do to those bastards that left the bombs lying around in the first place.'

'Come on, Aaron. We've had this discussion a dozen times. You know there's nothing to do about it except what you already do.' Louise's eyes were on their patient but her words were with her husband. 'You're getting yourself all wound up again.'

Luca concentrated on his work. He'd spent many hours lying awake at night thinking about what the Laotian people had to live with but understood there was nothing he could do to remove all those bombs. The suture needle clattered into the kidney dish and he straightened his back, feeling the aches from the continuous bending over. Doctoring was what he did, had spent years learning how to do, but he hoped he'd never see another damaged limb, never perform another amputation.

'Let's wrap this up,' Aaron said.

'Could go for a plate of sticky rice and peanut sauce right about now,' Luca replied as his stomach rumbled. Dinner had been hours ago, a meal they'd barely had a mouthful of before rushing into Theatre with this teen-aged boy.

Louise shook her head at him. 'Nothing puts you off your food, does it?'

'Not much.' Except Ellie. Since she'd left after giving him a speech on how she thought he should be living his life, he hadn't been as interested in food as usual. Nor in beer, sightseeing or playing cricket with the kids. It felt as if she'd taken the sun with her. Everything—or maybe only he—was gloomy. Downright depressing some days. He'd gone and fallen in love with her. Like really, deeply in love. The sort of love he'd always known he was capable of and determined not to have.

Let go some of that control, she'd railed at him. If only Ellie knew how much self-discipline he'd lost over the weeks since he'd first seen her with Louise on the day she arrived. Try as hard as he could, he wasn't getting it back. He wasn't able to push aside his love for her, no matter how it burned him to try. He did not want to love Ellie. It broke the rod he'd used for living his whole life. Snapped it clean in two. He still didn't want to love and yet now he did.

So all he had to do was ignore it, and hope that eventually he'd be able to manage getting through an hour at a time without thinking about Ellie, without wondering where she was and what she was doing. Wondering if she missed him half as much as he did her. Hoping for her sake she didn't, and pleading with the stars for his sake she did.

What a mess he'd become.

'Let's go into town for a beer and that rice you're hankering after,' Aaron said as they pulled off their scrubs. 'Louise will stay with the boy, and Jason's here if there's any change in his condition.'

Jason. The next doctor in a long line of short-term doctors. The guy was cool, eager to help and join in all the fun with the kids, was a better bowler of the cricket ball than Ellie had been—but he wasn't El. 'Good idea.' Anything to take his mind off her for a few minutes.

But so much for that theory. Aaron plonked two bottles on the counter in a bar they used occasionally on Sethathirath Road. 'Heard from Ellie lately?'

'No. You or Louise?'

'Got an email yesterday. She was heading to Auckland today. Guess she'll be there by now. How far is it from Wellington?'

'It'll take all day. Though with Ellie at the wheel you can cut an hour off the time.' Unless she'd quietened down recently. He wouldn't know. Didn't know a lot of things about the woman he loved, when he thought about it. Which was all the damned time.

'Bit of a speedster, is she?'

'She had this fire-engine-red Mustang that she got a kick out of taking for a spin. That thing went like a scalded cat, only with a lot more revs. It was her pride and joy, and her only real indulgence. Cost her a bundle in speeding tickets, though.' *Wonder what happened to it.*

Aaron was lifting one eyebrow in his direction.

'What?' he demanded.

'You're smiling for the first time since Ellie left.'

'Of course it's not the first time.' He raised his beer to his lips. He always smiled and laughed, didn't he?

Right now he felt relaxed and happy because of those memories. Yeah, but when was the last time he'd felt remotely like this?

Aaron shook his head at him. 'I must've been looking the other way.' Then he changed the subject. 'You made up your mind where you're going after Laos?'

While it was a different topic, it still brought Luca back to Ellie. Hopping a ride down to New Zealand was at the top of his list. Seeing Ellie would be the best thing to happen to him since she'd left. Then what? He'd have to leave again. They couldn't return to a platonic friendship after that mind-blowing night in Luang Prabang. Even he knew that. So staying on in Auckland, which was the only city he wanted to work in at home, was not an option. It might be a large city but Ellie would be there and he'd never be able to forget that, always be looking for her.

He told Aaron, 'I'm liking the look of Cambodia.' Sort of. Though returning to his career as an emergency specialist seemed to be teasing him more and more every day. 'Maybe Australia.' Closer to home and more in line with his career ideas.

'If you're thinking of Cambodia why not stay here for the next twelve months? Not a lot of difference, when it comes to working with the locals, if you think about it.' Aaron had tried to convince him of this on several occasions, and was now flagrantly ignoring the Australian component of his reply.

Luca's phone vibrated in his pocket. Pulling it out, he saw he had two texts. 'Noi says our boy's doing fine.'

Aaron grunted. 'I got that, too.'

Luca's mouth dried. Ellie had texted him hours ago.

He hadn't checked his phone after they'd finished in Theatre. Hadn't thought there'd be any messages.

Visited Caitlin today. Late leaving Wellington for Auckland, stopping over in Taupo. How's everyone at the clinic? Ellie. XXX

'Wow. Ellie visited her sister.' That took guts.

'What's so odd about that?' Aaron asked.

Damn, he hadn't meant to speak out loud. 'They've been estranged all year. Like, seriously.' But Ellie had gone to see her. Had taken the gauntlet he'd thrown down to get on with sorting out her life. Good on her.

What about the challenge she set you?

What about it?

Going to run with it? Or away from it?

'That's sad, but Ellie's obviously had a change of heart.' Aaron was watching him closely. Looking for what?

'They used to be very close.' It wouldn't be easy talking to anyone who'd had an affair with her husband, but Caitlin? She hadn't said how it had gone. They might've had an even bigger bust-up, but he didn't think she'd be telling him if that was the case. 'I don't know if the girls will ever get back what they had.'

'Christmas is only one week away. That's always a good time for families to be together.'

Ellie would hate spending the day on her own. Christmas had always been a big deal for her. 'What do we do here for Christmas? Get a tree and lots of presents for the kids?' They would this year, if he had anything to do with it.

'All of that and loads of food, though it's hard to find anything like what we're used to back home. You going to be here?'

'Why wouldn't I be?' The guy knew he had less than two months to run on his contract.

Aaron stared at something across the other side of the bar. 'Thought you might want to go spend it with Ellie.'

Luca spluttered the mouthful of beer he'd just taken. 'You what?'

An eloquent shrug came his way. 'Most men I know would do almost anything to be with the woman they love for Christmas.'

Luca wanted to deny it, wanted to shout at the top of his lungs that Aaron didn't have a clue what he was talking. But he couldn't. *Because it was true.* Which didn't lessen the urge to hurl his bottle across the room and shout at somebody. Gritting his teeth, he held on to his sanity—just. Counted to ten, again and again. When he finally believed he could speak without spitting he said, 'That obvious, huh?'

'Neon.'

'Great.' So everyone knew what had taken him four weeks to work out. Or was that ten years? Had he always loved Ellie? That little gem didn't feel wrong. Or a shock. Maybe he had. Talk about a slow learner.

'What are you going to do about it?'

Any time you want to shut up, Aaron, I'm not going to stop you. 'Nothing.'

'Fair enough.'

Huh? What sort of answer was that? 'How long did you know Louise before you realised you loved her?'

'Minutes. It was as though she hit me over the head

or something. Instant, man.' A smile lit up Aaron's eyes. 'Never regretted it for a second. Not even when she burns my bacon.'

'True love,' Luca drawled. 'No challenges, then. No problems to get over before you got together permanently?'

'Ha. A ton of them. But we weren't going to be deterred by anything. Life's too short, as that accident you were in shows. What would you have felt if Ellie hadn't made it out of that van? Think you might've spent the rest of your life regretting not telling her how you feel?'

'I think you make a better doctor than a psychologist.'

Aaron picked up their empty bottles. 'Another?'

'Sure. Why not?' Luca picked up his phone and tapped the screen, reread El's text. Short and to the point. Why had she contacted him when they'd more or less agreed to go their separate ways when she'd left Vientiane? She'd have struggled to visit Caitlin, and it wasn't something she'd have done just to prove a point so she must just be keeping in touch, treating him like the close friend he'd insisted he was.

He'd been adamant they weren't getting together and she'd got the message, loud and clear. She'd even said how she wondered if this had been a rebound thing. Sex with a man she knew well and could trust to look out for her. Yet at the same time she knew he had his limitations and would never ask her to set up house with him.

Control, she called that. Told him to let it go. Hell, if he did who knew when he'd stop unravelling? Everything he'd struggled to gain would go down the drain. Right now he was out of plans for the next year or two; let go of that control Ellie despised so much and he would be lost forever.

Ellie didn't sound lost after seeing Caitlin.

He wasn't really thinking when he began tapping in a message.

How did it go with Caitlin? Did you talk?

The moment he sent the text he wanted it back. Getting involved wasn't his greatest idea. Before he knew it he'd be wanting to be there to help Ellie through the minefield that getting back onside with Caitlin entailed. How would El handle seeing her sister with her ex? Then he saw the time. She wasn't going to read it for hours yet. It was early morning back in NZ. He had a few hours to regret his move.

We hugged. I made a date for Christmas and left.

Got that wrong. Was she lying awake worrying about her sister?

Christmas is good. Family time. Why are you awake?

Might as well ask since he'd started this.

She came straight back: Missing you.

Right then Aaron slid a beer in front of him. Perfect timing. 'Thanks.' He closed the phone and slid it into his pocket. He had no reply to that text. Not one that he was prepared to make. That would mean laying his heart on the line.

Christmas was a week away, right? Luca stretched his legs to increase his pace as he strode along the path winding beside the Mekong. Seven days, to be exact. Then it would be over and life could go back to normal.

Except Christmas wasn't going to be normal for Ellie, which meant the days afterwards wouldn't be, either. Spending time with her family would be hard, and if Baldwin was there, which he had to presume he would be, then, hell, Ellie was in for a terrible day.

She needed support. But who from? He was here, and fighting the urge to give in to go home for a few days. He coughed. Time to start being really honest with himself. It was the need to see Ellie that he was fighting. Acknowledging he loved her hadn't taken the edge off that need. It had made him supercautious when answering any more of her many texts. El hadn't taken a back step when he'd told her to go home and get on with her life without him. Oh, no.

Pulling his phone from his pocket, he went through the past three texts. His pace slowed as he reread the challenge she kept waving in his face.

How are the kids? Say hi to them from me. Missing them and you.

Of course every time he mentioned Ellie to the kids he'd be bombarded with questions about where was she, when was she coming back and could they all text her, too—on his phone? Kids. He'd seen the hunger in her eyes at Luang Prabang Airport as she'd held that baby; the hunger that had wormed into him and made him think about having children with Ellie. Him? Having kids? El had said he was good with children, but how far could he take that?

Won't know if I don't try. Suddenly that idea didn't

seem so impossible. With Ellie by his side he could con-
quer seemingly insurmountable problems. She was his
rock, believed in him—knew him too well, which was
grounds for a solid relationship. Wasn't it?

The next text.

How's your nephew? Missing you.

She knew damned well he didn't have any contact
with his sister's kid. Did she think he'd suddenly start
emailing the lad because she thought he should? Of
course she did. She was challenging him to sort his life
out. As she'd started to do with hers.

Then the text that had thrown him when he'd first
read it.

Saw the house I'm moving into for six months. It's stunning and has me thinking about buying my own here
in Auckland. Missing you.

Two decisions in one sentence. Buying a house spoke
of putting down roots, and obviously she was happy to
be back in Auckland. Far enough away from her family
to avoid awkward get-togethers but close enough to see
them occasionally if she felt so inclined.

Luca read that one again. Missing you. She used that
at the end of every message. It hit him hard in the heart
every single time. Stuffing his phone back in his pocket,
he stared at the brown river pouring past in its timeless
way. 'Hell, El, I'm missing you fit to bust. You'll never
guess how much.'

Unless he told her. Could he do that? Find the courage to commit to her?

I want to. More than anything I want to be with Ellie Thompson for all the years to come.

Which meant some sharp gear changes in the head. Did he have the guts to do that? Ellie had shown courage by visiting Caitlin. Somehow he had to find the same within himself.

His gaze cruised the rushing water again. Water that came from the north, through countries, towns, communities, the flow barely changing from one year to the next. The river moved on, from yesterday to tomorrow, returning to calm after floods and storms and wars, making allowances for small changes in direction. Like life.

Except his was lacking something, someone. Ellie. It spooked him to think he might've always loved her but had been too tied up in his determination to avoid commitment that he'd pushed his feelings so deep it was a wonder they'd come to light. He could try just jumping in—sort of a leap of confidence in himself and Ellie. And if it backfired? That was where the courage would come in. He'd have to start over, but was that such a bad thing when the alternative might be to never experience a wonderful relationship with the woman already sitting in his heart? He'd told Ellie to let go of what Caitlin and Freddy had done, to make some decisions for herself about herself.

Why couldn't he do the same with Gaylene? She was a shield. He stopped walking to stare up at the sky. Hell. Had he been hiding behind her? Using what she'd done to him as an excuse to stay away from getting hurt again? Because she had hurt him—badly. He mightn't have been head over heels in love with her but he'd been willing to try. He'd wanted some say in their child's life. Had been devastated when she'd terminated it with no regard to his feelings. Of course he'd been hurt and angry. But that was no reason to push Ellie away. None at all.

Another left-field thought dropped into his head. Why not follow El's example and get in touch with his sister? A friendly email with no demands, just 'hi, how are you, this is what I'm doing' stuff. If he didn't try he'd never get back the family he missed.

Ellie rolled out of bed and dropped her head in her hands. Christmas morning usually made her smile with excitement. But not this one. Her stomach was roiling, making her nauseous.

Today she had to face up to Caitlin and Freddy over Christmas lunch with Mum and Dad. Play happy families. Ugh. Why had she said she'd do this?

Because if she wanted to have a life with Luca she needed to move on. Luca. All very well for him to say she should sort herself out. What had he done about doing the same with his own life? Huh?

Fumbling on the bedside table, she found her phone and checked for messages. Nothing. Not a word from Luca for days. Guess that would teach her to keep telling him she missed him. But she'd only been truthful, even when knowing he wouldn't be comfortable with it. So much for thinking he might give in and accept she wasn't going to change her mind about loving him.

'Morning.' Renee strolled into the room looking rumpled and relaxed in her cotton PJs. 'Merry Christmas.'

Ellie jumped up and hugged her friend. 'Merry Christmas to you. Thanks for lending me the bed.' She'd flown in late last night and come straight here, having turned down her mother's plea to stay with them. There was only so much time she'd be able to face spending with her sister and ex. She might be making headway but she wasn't ready for full-on happy families yet.

'It's still got your name on it.' Renee laughed. 'I've got the coffee brewing or there's bubbles waiting to be opened.'

'Think I'll start the day with coffee. Need to keep my head straight until after Christmas lunch is over.'

'You know you can come back here to join my lot if it all gets too much for you today.' Renee hugged her back.

'You're a great friend.' Her other great friend seemed to have forgotten all about her, not even sending a Christmas message in reply to the one she'd sent after falling into bed last night. Ellie tugged her bag close and pulled out the sundress she'd planned on wearing today. 'I'll grab a shower first.'

Renee was already half out the door. 'Don't take too long. I want to give you my present.'

But when Ellie made it to the kitchen Renee was in no hurry to hand her anything except a steaming mug of coffee after quickly putting her phone aside.

Instead, Renee made a great fuss of opening the exquisitely wrapped box that contained the opal earrings and bracelet Ellie had bought for her.

'They're gorgeous.' Renee grinned, slipping the bracelet over her hand. 'Beautiful.' She slowly removed one earring from the silk cushion it rested on and slipped it through her earlobe. As she plucked the second one up the doorbell buzzed. 'Someone's early for breakfast. Get that for me, will you? I'm heading for the bathroom.' Renee disappeared so fast Ellie didn't have a chance to say a word.

The buzzer sounded again.

'I'm coming,' she muttered and swung the door wide. 'Merry— Luca.' She looked behind him but no one else was there. None of Renee's family. Only Luca. Her heart rate stuttered, then sped up. Luca was *here*? In Wellington?

'Merry Luca. That's novel.' He grinned at her.

'Are you? Merry, I mean?' *Are you Luca? Or just a figment of my imagination?*

'Merry ho-ho, yes. Merry boozy, no.' Uncertainty replaced that grin. 'Are you going to invite me in, El?'

She stepped back so quickly she banged up against the wall. 'Renee thought one of her—' No, she hadn't. She'd been dilly-dallying over coffee and her present, then suddenly, when the buzzer went, she'd headed for the shower. 'Renee knew you were coming, didn't she?'

Luca nodded. 'Yes. I rang her to find out where you were staying. I wanted to surprise you, El.'

'You've certainly done that.' She led him into the kitchen, all the time trying to get her heart rate and breathing under control, but it seemed impossible. Luca was here, not in Laos. With her and not the children. 'Why?'

'Why am I here?' His eyebrows rose and he reached for her hands as she nodded once. 'I'm going with you to your family Christmas lunch.'

Her head shot up. 'You're what?'

'I'm going to be there for you, with you, supporting you. I know it's not going to be easy being with Caitlin and Baldwin.'

She should've been relaxing, getting excited. She wasn't. 'You're being a good friend.'

Luca stepped closer, finally taking her hands in his. 'No, El, I'm your partner.'

'What do you mean?' Was she being thick? The sense of missing something important nagged her. 'My partner? As in lover, kids, house partner?' *Or 'sex when he was in town' partner?*

His smile was gentle and—dare she admit it?—full of love. He said, 'I'm done with being just your best friend. I want the whole shebang. With you.' His hands were warm, strong yet soft. Enticing her closer.

Even as she held back, a glimmer of hope eased through her. Had Luca come because he loved her? It sounded like it. 'You stopped answering my texts and emails.'

'I'm not good with words, especially not in messages. But I missed you so much it started driving me nuts. I had to come see you. Nothing could've kept me away any longer.'

'Have you decided what you're doing after Laos?' What did it matter? Why was she being so cautious?

'Moving to Auckland to be near you, or with you if you'll have me.'

She gasped. 'Luca? What are you really saying?' Pulling her hands free, she folded her arms across her chest. She did not want the distraction of him holding her while she absorbed whatever he was about to tell her.

'El—' he locked his eyes on hers '—I'm saying I love you. I've missed you since you told me to get a life. You are my life. I want to share everything with you. Starting with your Christmas Day.'

Now her heart was really pumping. 'Everything?' He couldn't mean that. He'd gone to great lengths to make her understand he didn't want the same things she did.

His hands were on her wrists, unfolding her arms. Then he was holding her hands again, his thumbs caressing her. 'You, the babies, the house and cats and dogs or pet rabbits. The whole works.'

If Luca could say all that, then it was time she opened her heart and laid everything out there for him, too. 'I want all those things, too, with you. I love you so much it hurts when you're not with me. These past two weeks have been horrible.'

His arms went around her and he gently drew her close. 'Tell me about it.'

'I have missed you.'

He chuckled. 'Yeah, I got those messages loud and clear.'

'You didn't reply to them.'

'I was too afraid to. Once I told you I was missing you I'd be committed to you, and I had to be sure. I've done a lot of soul searching, but in the end I can't deny how much I love you and want you. Loving you is easier than not. I promise not to let you down.'

'Luca, I never thought you would. All that was in your head, not mine.' She gave him a little shake.

'Good answer.' He gave a lopsided smile. 'Seriously, thank you for believing in me and giving me the boot up the backside I needed to see what has been in front of me for a very long time. I've done something else, too. I emailed Ange and she replied saying to drop by while I'm here. As in visit her in Auckland, which is where you're going after today, right?'

Ellie nodded. 'Yes.'

'Then, so am I. I've finally worked out I've loved you for years. Then I had to tell you face to face. So here I am.'

Ellie reached her arms around his neck and raised up to place her mouth on his. 'Shut up for a moment.' Then she kissed him.

His arms wrapped around her, his chest hard against her breasts, his mouth open to hers. Ellie slid her tongue between his lips, tasted her man and melted further against him. Luca was here. He'd always been in her heart, but he was here in her arms, kissing her as ardently as she did him. All her Christmases had come today. All of them.

'Merry Christmas, Ellie.' Renee's voice broke through her euphoria.

Peeling her mouth off Luca's, she turned in his arms to stare at her friend. 'Best present ever.'

'That's what I thought.' Renee had the cheek to wink. 'I'm popping the champagne. What I just saw requires celebrating.'

'I agree.' Ellie grinned, finally letting all the fear and hurt and need fly. Luca loved her. What more could a girl want?

As the three of them raised their glasses Renee said, 'To Ellie and Luca.' She drained her flute and put it down. 'I'd better go and get those croissants and bagels I ordered for breakfast. My family will start arriving shortly. See you.' She waved a hand over her shoulder as she headed for her front door. There she turned around and, looking very pleased with herself, she gave Ellie a big wink. 'One hour to yourselves. Merry Christmas, my friends.'

* * * * *

A FATHER
THIS CHRISTMAS?

BY
LOUISA HEATON

MILLS &
BOON

Published in Great Britain 2015
by Mills & Boon, an imprint of Harlequin (UK) Limited,
Eton House, 18-24 Paradise Road, Richmond, Surrey, TW9 1SR

© 2015 Louisa Heaton

ISBN: 978-0-263-24745-9

Harlequin (UK) Limited's policy is to use papers that are natural,
renewable and recyclable products and made from wood grown in
sustainable forests. The logging and manufacturing processes conform
to the legal environmental regulations of the country of origin.

Printed and bound in Spain
by CPI, Barcelona

Dear Reader,

I *love* Christmas. I love the countdown to the big day, the wishing and hoping for snow, the excitement of my children as they try to guess what they're getting… shaking and weighing up presents under the tree. I love the food, the putting up of the decorations, and laughing at my husband as he tries—and struggles—to put up the Christmas lights each year.

As a child, I thought Christmas was special—but it meant even more when I watched my own children experience the season. For Eva and Jacob, Christmas means different things. For Eva it's a time that makes her feel even more separate from the family she was once with, and for Jacob it's a tragic reminder of a cruel event.

In this story we accompany them on their journey to find their own magic at Christmas—their own happy ending that they never believed could be possible. I hope you enjoy it.

Love and best wishes,

Louisa x

To Mum and Dad,
who bought me a beautiful manual typewriter
one Christmas and released the story-writing bunny.

Lots of love, your loving daughter. xx

Books by Louisa Heaton

Mills & Boon Medical Romance

The Baby that Changed Her Life
His Perfect Bride?

Visit the Author Profile page
at millsandboon.co.uk for more titles.

CHAPTER ONE

'QUICK, EVA, TAKE my pulse!'

Eva turned to her friend. What was wrong?

'What? Are you ill?'

She placed her fingers on Sarah's pulse point on her wrist and looked with concern at her friend as she counted beats. But Sarah wasn't looking at *her*—she was focussed on something or *someone* behind Eva, across the minors department, towards the entrance. She was seemingly fascinated, with a sparkle in her eyes and a slow smile creeping across her face as she looked someone up and down.

'Sex on a stick at one o'clock.'

'What?'

Why was she being ridiculous? Eva swivelled in her seat to see who was making Sarah act like that and her eyes fell upon the one man she'd thought she'd never, ever see again.

Jacob.

Dressed all in black, in what had to be tailored clothes, considering how well they fit, with his tousled dark hair and a five-o'clock shadow, a red-tubed stethoscope draped casually around his neck, he looked stunning.

Well dressed, powerful.

Virile.

More so than four years ago, if that were possible. Time had been overly generous to Jacob, bestowing upon him masculine maturity in a well-defined body that simply oozed sex appeal.

She'd begun to believe that she'd imagined this perfect man. That her one hot night with him that Christmas Eve four years ago had been a figment of her imagination. Despite the obvious, startling reminder that it *hadn't* been imaginary.

Their son.

Eva wanted the earth to swallow her up. Because then she wouldn't have to face him. Wouldn't have to explain to him that he was a father.

She could hardly believe that she had slept with a man she had only known for such a short time. Just because of something she'd felt when she'd looked at him. Taking him at face value—because, really, what else had she had to go on? He'd been in her arms, and they'd danced together in a slow, sultry melting of bodies… The way his hips had swayed, his groin had pressed against hers, the *feel* of him…

But now she was different. Stronger. She was no longer the young woman who had given her heart to a man who had only been a fantasy for just one night—a man she'd dreamed of after the fact.

Now she was more mature. A strong woman. A confident doctor. And there was no way she was going to let Jacob know how she was really feeling.

Terrified.

Still attracted…

I'm not! Just because it feels as if my heart is trying to leap from my chest…

She let go of Sarah's wrist and deliberately turned her back on him.

There was so much he needed to know! So much she needed to tell him. She'd searched for him. Tried to let him know about Seb. But it had been impossible! Would he understand?

Her mouth felt dry, as if it was full of sawdust, and she knew if she were to talk to him her tongue would just stumble over the words. She groaned as her stomach flipped and swirled like snowflakes in a snow globe.

'It's probably that new doctor Clarkson mentioned earlier.' She tried to sound as casual as she could. When Dr Clarkson, clinical lead of their A&E department, had mentioned they were getting a new doctor she'd initially been thrilled. Who *didn't* need an extra pair of hands in A&E after all? Even if it *was* just temporary cover for Christmas.

But he hadn't told her who was coming. Who the new doctor actually was.

Jacob Dolan.

The doctor who'd slept with her and then run off to Africa. The doctor who'd got her pregnant and then disappeared without leaving a trace!

Why did he have to look so good?

Sarah leaned forward to whisper to her, 'Oh, my goodness, I'd really love to find *him* in my Christmas stocking...' She licked her lips. 'How on earth are we going to get any work done with him hanging around? I'm going to be spending all my time wiping drool off my chin and hoping the cleaners have enough wet-floor signs to dot around me.'

Eva grimaced a smile, but went back to her paperwork. All she had to do was write these notes. Write these notes and then maybe get the earth to open up and swallow her or something. Once he realised she was here—once he realised that she was the woman who had slept with him four years ago...

She could grab her coat and go. She could say she was sick or something.

No...that wouldn't work. You only get a day off if you're dying—nothing less...

Their son.

She could tell Dr Clarkson it was something to do with Seb.

This was her dream come true and her worst nightmare all rolled into one! Whilst once she had dreamed about what life might have been like for the pair of them if Jacob hadn't disappeared, she was now faced with the fact that he was back. Here. In her department. And he would eventually need to be told about Seb.

She'd tried to tell him before.

I tried. I tried to track him down. But there was no trace! This isn't my fault! He can't hold me responsible for this!

She didn't have to think about him being here. About him actually being in her A&E department. Standing mere metres away, looking even more alluring than he had before, if that were possible.

She'd hoped her imagination had got it wrong. That her memories of him were impaired. That perhaps he'd *not* been that stunning. That perhaps he'd have more in common with Quasimodo, or a troll, or something hopeful like that.

'*Look* at him, Eva.' Sarah glanced at her friend and frowned. 'Eva? Why won't you look at him? Oh, he's coming over...' Sarah scraped back her chair and stood up.

Eva sucked in a deep, steadying breath and felt her heart pound against her rib cage. This couldn't be true! This couldn't be happening! Not now. She wasn't prepared for it. She'd dreamed about finding him and telling him about Seb for years, but now that the opportunity was upon her she was terrified.

'Eva?'

That voice.

Chills trembled down her spine and she felt every single goosebump that prickled her skin.

She could see Sarah glance at her in surprise that somehow Eva *knew* this man. No doubt there would be an interrogation later, and she'd want all the details, but Eva was mindful that not only was this her workplace but she was a professional—and what business was it of anybody but her?

She dredged up what she hoped was a pleasant smile from somewhere—hoping it didn't look like a ghastly rictus—and turned around, praying to any god that existed that she didn't flush like a menopausal woman or look as if she was going to pass out.

Those blue eyes...

'Jacob! Nice to see you again. It's been a long time.'

Was her voice as strangled as it sounded to her? She hoped not. She was determined to be as professional as she could be. Professional and *distanced*. She was at least grateful for the fact that her voice was actually working. She'd felt so trapped and cornered suddenly she was amazed her voice hadn't disappeared altogether, in a case of phobic aphasia.

She held out her hand for him to shake, as one colleague would to another. He raised a quizzical eyebrow and shook it, smiling that kilowatt smile.

Oh, help...

Eva kept the smile plastered on her face, not knowing what else to do. She had momentous, life-changing news for this man. But how could she tell him? Everyone knew she was a mother—it was bound to be mentioned to him at some point. All she needed was for someone to mention how old Seb was and Jacob would do a little maths, and then—

'How have you been?' he asked, smiling, looking her up and down. 'You look great.'

She lifted her chin and smiled. 'I've been fine. You?'

What had she expected? For him to say that his life had been awful without her? That after their one night he'd dreamed about her the way she had about him? *Hah!* Jacob Dolan had most likely coped absolutely fine without her!

'I've been good. I can't believe you actually work here.'

'Well, I do.' She struggled to think of something else to say. Something pleasant. Something...*neutral.* 'This is Sarah Chambers—another A&E colleague.'

She introduced her friend and Sarah practically melted over him, shaking his hand as if she'd never let go, as if his hand was somehow magically feeding her oxygen or something.

Eva rolled her eyes at her friend's blatant fawning, and when she could finally stand the overt flirting no longer she deliberately walked between them, so that their handshaking had to be broken off to allow her through.

'Let me introduce you to everyone.'

Jacob dropped into step beside her. 'Thanks. So... you're going to be my new boss?'

She shook her head. *No. Definitely not.* 'Dr Clarkson is clinical lead.'

'How long have you been here?'

'Since before I met you.' She grimaced at how easily she'd referred to when they'd met. Now he would be remembering it, too.

She almost stopped walking. Couldn't believe she'd referred to it. Her stomach became a solid lump of cold ice. Her feet felt as if they were inside concrete boots and walking was like trying to wade through molasses.

How do I tell him?

'How was Africa?'

There. That was better. Turn the focus back onto him. It gave her time to breathe. Time to think. Time to formulate the answers she knew she'd have to provide.

'Hot. And dry. But amazing. Life-changing.'

There was something odd in his voice then, and she voluntarily turned to look at him, trying not to be pulled by the lure of those sexy blue eyes that had got her into so much trouble in the first place.

'It's been life-changing here, too. But it sounds like you might have a few stories to tell?'

She could tell *him* a few! About what had happened after he'd left. About the decisions she'd had to make. How she'd done everything alone—as always. But she couldn't right now. How could she? He'd only just got here. He'd only just arrived. Let the poor guy take his coat off before—

'I certainly do. We ought to catch up some time.'

He paused briefly, then reached out to catch her arm. Electricity crackled along her skin like a lightning strike.

'I'm glad you're here.'

His touch burned her skin and she stared at him in

shock before pulling her arm free. Unable to stand his close contact, and the effect it was having on her breathing and pulse rate, she stepped farther away, putting a trolley between them and distracting herself by fiddling with the pressed bed sheets, pillowcases and yellow blankets piled upon it.

She picked up one or two and took great interest in folding and refolding them, giving herself time to recover from his touch. To cool down. For her heart rate to slow.

Time to think of something to say.

How *did* you tell a man that he was a father? Completely out of the blue?

By the way, you ought to know...you're a father.

No! She couldn't say it like that. It wasn't something you could come straight out with. There had to be some sort of preamble. An introduction.

Jacob? You remember that night we spent together? Look, I know we used protection, but somehow it didn't work and...

Hmm... That didn't seem all that marvellous, either.

Jacob...there's no easy way to say this, so I'm just going to come straight out with it...you're a father.

'Let me show you around the department' was what she came up with.

That was easier. By being professional, by not actually looking at him, she could almost forget...almost pretend he was someone else. A junior, maybe. A complete stranger.

She led him around the Minors area and then into Majors, Resus, Triage, the waiting room, stockrooms, sluice and cubicles, talking nonstop about all kinds of things—hospital policy, staff rotas, tricks to know when dealing with the computer—anything and everything but the one thing she wished she *could* talk to him about but was afraid to tell him.

She was talking so he didn't have the chance to ask questions. And all the while aware of his proximity, his dark brooding outline, his expensive clothing, the feel of him near her once again.

She knew she was babbling. He was playing havoc with her senses. It was as if her body had been awoken by his presence. The way a flower reacted to the sun.

Her mind devilishly replayed a memory of his kiss. How his lips had felt upon hers. How they'd drifted ever so lightly across her skin, sending shivers of delicious delight through her body, arousing her nerve endings to touch in a way they had never been before, making her ache for more.

Eva could remember it all too well.

Every sizzling second of it.

Jacob had made her feel so *alive*! She'd had a long day at work that day, and when she'd made it to that party she'd felt exhausted—bereft of feeling. Yet in his arms she'd become energised, had tingled and yearned for his every touch, savouring every caress, consuming every desire and gasping her way through her ecstasy.

Feeling alive once again.

That one night had changed her entire life.

She shivered at the thought, those goosebumps rising again and her nipples hardening against her bra in expectancy. He was the only man who had ever made her feel that way. The only man she'd ever slept with since that night. The memory of him, the experience of him, had stopped her being intimate with any other. No one could measure up to his memory.

Not that there'd been anyone to challenge it, really.

Eva mumbled her way through the details of the filing system and how to operate the computer patient files, work through any glitches on the system, then asked him if he'd like to take on his first patient.

He cocked his head as he looked at her, trying to get her to make eye contact. 'You okay? I mean, I hope our having to work together isn't going to be uncomfortable?'

No, I'm not okay. You're back! You're back, and I had no warning. No time to prepare. And I have something momentous to tell you. And it will change your life. And I'm so aware of that and—

'I'm fine. It's...just been a difficult morning.'

He nodded in understanding. 'Anything I can help with?'

'No.'

He raised his eyebrow in such a perfect arch it was all she could do not to race into his arms there and then.

'Are you sure?'

How are you with kids? Do you even like children? Because I have some news for you...

Eva sighed and shook her head.

No, she wasn't sure.

She wasn't sure at all.

How to tell him that he was father to a beautiful, bright, funny, gorgeous three-year-old boy, who obsessed over lions and tigers and looked *exactly like him*?

She swallowed a lump in her throat as fear overturned her stomach. Nausea unsettled her. A close sweat beaded her brow as guilt and shame overflowed from the box where she normally kept all those feelings tightly locked away.

What was she to do?

* * *

Eva slammed a patient file down hard on the doctors' desk, the slap of cardboard on table echoing around the department, then sank heavily into a chair. Her fingertips punched into the keyboard as she began to write up some notes. She had no time. They were already running behind. Patients were filling up the waiting area and two were about to breach the four-hour limit.

Patients who had turned up because there were no district nurses to unblock catheters. Patients who were filling the corridors because there were no beds to put them in. Patients who were turning up just because they didn't want to be alone at home and they needed someone to talk to just a couple of weeks before Christmas.

The need to immerse herself in work and forget about the new doctor was overwhelming.

If she absorbed herself in work it wouldn't give her any time to think about *him*.

The guy who'd turned her neat little world around in just one night.

Even now she told herself she still didn't know what had happened that night. How had he managed to put her under his spell? She knew it had been a difficult and long day at work. She'd almost not gone to that stupid party. But it had been Christmas Eve, and she'd put herself down to work on Christmas Day, and the need to celebrate the season, despite not having any family of her own, had made her go. Just to have a drink or two with friends. Chill out for a moment.

And she'd done that. Had actually been enjoying herself for a brief time when she'd noticed him across the room.

Those eyes. Those piercing blue eyes. But she had noticed something in his gaze. A loss—a grief so deep it had called to her.

She'd recognised emotional pain. And, having been in a similar place herself, she'd hoped she could soothe him. No one had ever helped *her*. But maybe she could help him? Just for a moment, if nothing else.

Then, when he'd noticed her, something had happened. Something weird and dreamlike. As if the rest of the world had melted away and it had been just the two of them, standing in front of each other. Close. Almost touching. He'd said his name and then she'd been in his arms. Dancing with him. Swaying with him. Their bodies mirroring the other, blending together, matching the other.

Melting into one.

There'd been something magical that night.

And it seemed he was still magical now!

How involved would he want to be with his child? He might not even care! He might not want anything to do with them! Perhaps he'd be the type of guy who only paid child support. She wouldn't hate him for that. She'd be disappointed, but in fact she quite liked the idea that she wouldn't have to share Seb. She enjoyed it being just the two of them. It had always just been the two of them. She'd never had to share him.

Jacob could be in a relationship already with someone else. A man who looked the way he did? Of course he would be! A man like him wouldn't be single. If she'd ever entertained any grand idea that they would somehow end up together...

Her hand holding the pen trembled. She put it down for a moment and just sat for a second or two to pause and gather herself, to take in a deep breath and steady her jangled nerves. She could feel her heart slowing, could breathe more easily. Could act the professional doctor she believed herself to be.

Picking up her patient notes, she strode off to Minors.

Leo Rosetti had been brought in by his wife, Sonja. His knee hurt, and despite his taking painkillers at home nothing would touch it.

Eva entered the cubicle smiling, and closed the curtain behind her. 'Good morning, Mr Rosetti. I'm Eva, one of the doctors here in A&E. Can you tell me what's happened this morning to bring you in?'

There. That was better, she thought. Focus on the patients. Not on the fact that a certain someone had re-entered her life and turned it upside down and inside out.

'Well, Doctor, I've got this terrible pain here.' He leaned forward on the bed and rubbed at his left knee through his trousers. 'It's awful, I tell you. Really hurts.'

'And how long has it been like this?'

'Since the beginning of December now, and I really don't feel well in myself, either. It's not good for a person to live with pain day after day.'

No. It wasn't. Especially the emotional kind.

'He's diabetic, Doctor,' the wife interjected. 'And he's got osteoarthritis in both his knees. Had it for years. But he says this is different.'

Eva asked if he could roll up his trouser leg and she examined the grossly swollen knee. 'Are you on any meds, Mr Rosetti?'

'Leo, Doctor, please. I'm on metformin for the diabetes.'

She gave him a general check and then carried out a primary survey, asking questions about his general state of health, taking his BP and arranging for a full blood count and an X-ray, even though Leo said he hadn't knocked or damaged the knee as far as he knew.

'Will he be all right, Doctor? We're going away this weekend.'

'Oh, yes? Anywhere nice?'

'Africa—well, Kenya specifically. We're going on safari. Thought we'd do something different for Christmas, now that the kids have flown the nest.'

Africa. What *was* it with Africa?

She coloured as she thought of Jacob and what it had been like to see him again. That intense look in his eyes. Still with the power to make her go all weak at the knees as it once had.

Feeling guilty at having let her mind wander whilst she was with a patient, she smiled quickly. 'I'll be back in a moment to do the bloods.'

She pulled the curtain across and exhaled quietly and slowly, closing her eyes as she tried to gather her thoughts, her hand still clutching the curtain.

Seriously—what was going on here? Why was she allowing herself to get so worked up?

So Jacob was here? Big deal! He was just a guy. Just a…

I need to pull myself together!

This was not like her! She was normally an organised person. Efficient. She didn't get distracted at work! There was too much at stake to let personal feelings get in the way whilst she was there.

A distracted doctor was a dangerous doctor.

She hurried back to her seat to write up her notes, managing a weak smile as Sarah settled next to her.

'You okay?'

'Sure!' She tried to answer cheerily. 'Just…you know…busy.'

'Really? You seem a bit flushed about that new guy. Anything I can do?'

'Short of growing another pair of arms? Seriously, I could really do without having to babysit a new doctor—'

'So how do you know him?'

Her cheeks burned hot. 'I don't—not really. We only met once before.'

'Come on! He knew your name! You *know* him. How come?'

Eva stared hard at her friend, afraid to give the answer. Afraid to voice the thing that mattered the most to her in the whole world.

Because he's Seb's father.

She muttered something unintelligible and hurried away.

Her patient, Leo, had his bloods done and sent off, and also an X-ray that showed osteoarthritic changes and some mild widening in the joint space of his knee. The blood cultures wouldn't be available for three days, but his Hb levels were normal.

As the knee itself was hot and swollen, she felt it was wise to do a fine needle aspiration to draw off some of the fluid for testing. As she did so she noted that the fluid was quite cloudy, and she marked the tests to check for white blood cell count with differential, gram stain and culture.

She suspected a septic arthritis, and knew the joint would probably have to be drained until dry, as often as was necessary.

'It shouldn't affect your holiday as it's important you keep moving, Leo.'

Mr Rosetti and his wife smiled at each other, and she was about to leave them alone and send the aspirated fluid to Pathology, when Jacob pulled open the curtain and asked if he could have a quick word.

Excusing herself from her patient, she stepped outside of the cubicle with him, feeling her heart race once again. What did he want? Had he found out about Seb?

Her brain quickly tried to formulate an answer about that. 'Look, I meant to—'

'There's been a road accident. We've been phoned to let us know that a number of child casualties are coming our way.'

Children? Eva's heart sank. She could only hope that the children about to come into the department would have simple minor injuries.

They began a hurried walk to Resus. Eva's mind was focused firmly on the news. 'Any idea of the number of casualties?'

'Not at this stage. But it was a school minibus carrying a number of children across town. The police suspect they hit some black ice.'

Her heart thumped hard. She knew Seb's school had been attending a Christmas church service today.

'What age range?'

'We don't have any more details yet.'

It *couldn't* be Seb's school, Eva thought. Someone would have phoned her already.

'Has anyone let Paeds know?'

He nodded. 'I did. They're sending a team down as soon as they've got people to spare.'

'There's no one free *now*?'

What was she doing? She shouldn't raise her voice at him. It wasn't his fault, was it?

They burst through into Resus.

'What's the ETA?'

A nurse put down the phone. 'Seven minutes.'

'Let's get organised. Check equipment trolleys, monitors, sterile packs, gauze—everything and anything. We've an unknown number of paediatric casualties coming in and I want this to run smoothly. Let's prepare for crush injuries, possible fractures, whiplash and maybe burns. Have we ordered blood?'

Sarah and another doctor, Brandon, arrived in Resus. 'We're on it.'

She nodded at both of them. 'I'll lead team one—Sarah, you can be team two... Brandon three.'

'Where do you want me?' asked Jacob.

Ideally as far away from me as possible.

'Work with Brandon.'

'Okay.'

He wrapped a plastic apron around himself and grabbed for gloves before glancing at the clock, walking away to join Brandon.

She watched him go, knowing that at some point she was going to have to tell him the truth.

Just not now.

Six minutes to go.

Eva pulled on her own apron and donned gloves, her heart pounding, her pulse thrumming like a well-oiled racing car.

Five minutes.
All eyes were on the clock.
Watching it tick down.

CHAPTER TWO

Ambulance sirens grew louder and closer as the staff waited, tense and raring to go. These were the moments that Eva both loved and hated.

Loved because of the way Resus went quiet as they all waited, pensive, with adrenaline urging their muscles to get moving.

Hated because she never quite knew what horrors she might yet encounter.

Still the paediatric team had not arrived.

Outside, there was the sound of rumbling engines and then the distant beeping sound of a reversing vehicle. Hospital doors slid open as the first patient came in.

Eva spotted a small dark-haired child, wearing a neck brace and on a backboard, and heard the paramedic firing off details about the patient.

'This is Ariana, aged three. Ariana was restrained by a seat belt but endured a side impact of about thirty miles an hour. Head to toe: small abrasion on the forehead, complaining of neck pain, score of eight, bruising across the chest and middle, due to the seat belt, lower back and pelvis pain, which is secured with a splint, GCS of fifteen throughout, BP and pulse normal.'

Ariana? Didn't her son Seb know a girl in his nursery school called Ariana?

Eva tried not to panic. She had to focus on the little girl in her care. Surely the school would have rung her if anything had happened to Seb? Although her phone was turned off, of course, and in her locker. She'd run and check as soon as she got the chance. Ariana was her priority right now.

'Ariana? My name's Eva. I'm one of the doctors here and I'm going to look after you.'

The way you dealt with any patient was important, but when it came to dealing with children—children who didn't yet have their parents there to advocate for them—Eva felt it was doubly important. You *had* to let them know it was okay to be scared, but that they would be looked after very well and that the staff would do their utmost to get the child's parents there as quickly as possible.

Ariana looked terrified. She had a bad graze on her forehead, probably from smashed glass, and her eyes were wide and tearful. Her bottom lip was trembling and it was obvious she was trying not to cry.

Eva's heart went out to her. How terrifying it must be to be that small, alone and hurt, in a strange place that smelled funny and sounded funny, surrounded by strangers who all wanted to poke you and prod at you and stick you with needles, saying they'd make you feel better.

'We need to check you're okay, Ariana. What a pretty name! Now, I'm just going to use this—' she held up her stethoscope '—to listen to your chest. Is that all right?' Eva always made sure her paediatric patients understood what she was doing.

Ariana tried to nod, but her head's movement was restricted by the neck immobiliser. 'Ow! It hurts!'

'Which bit hurts, honey?'

'My neck.'

'Okay, I'll check that out for you in just a moment.'

Ariana's chest sounded clear, which was a good sign. However, neck pain was not. It could simply be whiplash, but with neck pain you never took a chance.

'We'll need to take a couple of special pictures. But don't you worry—they won't hurt. It's just a big camera.'

She looked up at the team she was working with, awaiting their feedback. One was checking the patient's airway, another was checking her breathing, another Ariana's circulation. One would get IV access for the admission of drugs or painkillers or blood, if it was needed. Each doctor or nurse was calling out a result or observation. They all worked as a highly efficient team so that patients were quickly and perfectly assessed as soon as they arrived in Resus.

Ariana was looking good at the moment. With the exception of the neck pain and the pelvic brace she was doing well, and she was responsive, which was very important. Her blood pressure was stable, so hopefully that meant no internal bleeding at all for them to worry about.

Behind her, Eva heard the Resus doors bang open once again as another patient arrived from the accident. She risked a quick glance to see who had come in. She knew Sarah or Brandon would take care of the new patient and she could focus all her attention on Ariana.

'Have the parents been called?'

One of the nurses replied, 'We believe the school are trying to contact parents now.'

'Good. Did you hear that, Ariana? We're going to find your mummy and daddy.'

She couldn't imagine what it must be like to get that call, being a mother herself. Luckily, so far, Seb hadn't been involved in anything serious like that. The only time she'd ever been woken by a phone call was when he'd gone for a sleepover at a friend's house and the mother had rung at about eleven o'clock at night to say that Seb couldn't get to sleep without his cuddly lion.

Nothing like this, thank goodness.

But having Ariana in front of her was making her doubtful. This sweet little girl looked familiar, and she felt *so sure* that Seb had a girl in his nursery class called Ariana…

If it *was* the same preschool as Seb… If he'd been hurt…

Her stomach did a crazy tumble.

She glanced across at the other teams. Sarah was busy assessing a patient and Brandon and Jacob were looking after their own little charge.

She turned back to Ariana, who was now holding her hand, and showed her the Wong-Baker FACES pain-rating scale—a series of cartoon faces that helped really young children scale their pain.

'Which one of these are you, Ariana? Zero? Which means no hurting? Or ten? Which means hurting the worst?'

She watched as Ariana looked at all the little cartoon faces and pointed at four—'Hurts A Little More'.

Good—the painkillers were taking effect. Hopefully that four would drop. Earlier, the paramedic had said her pain score was eight, so it was better, even if it wasn't perfect.

Eva continued to hold Ariana's hand. It was a soothing thing to do whilst they waited for their turn at CT and X-ray. If it had been Seb trapped in a hospital bed she would hope that the doctor caring for him would do the same thing, too, until she arrived.

Ariana's CT scan was clear. The computer tomography scan showed internal slices through the body, so that breaks or bleeds could be seen much more clearly. Her pelvis was fine, as was her neck. Eva decided that she'd wait until they got back to Resus before she took off the immobiliser from Ariana's neck and the brace from her pelvis.

As they wheeled her out of CT one of the nurses let Eva know that Ariana's parents were on their way.

When they arrived back in the department Eva made the decision to take Ariana to the cubicles. Minors was busy, as some of the lesser injured children from the minibus had filled it up, and they still had a waiting room full of patients who hadn't been involved but had come in with various ailments or injuries.

'We'll wait in here for Mummy and Daddy. This is much less scary than where we were before, isn't it?' She smiled at her patient.

Ariana was looking much happier now that the immobiliser and brace were off. She'd been a very lucky girl.

'Ariana...I know you were going on a trip with your nursery. Which nursery do you go to?'

Please don't say Pear Tree Pre-School!

'The one next to the big school.'

Pear Tree Pre-School was next to an infant school...

'What's your teacher's name?'

Seb's teacher was Miss Dale. She was a very pretty

young woman, with the sweetest nature, and Eva secretly wondered how she managed to keep her perfect composure all day long when surrounded by thirty-odd preschoolers.

'Miss Dale.'

Oh, my God! Seb!

'Ariana, I just need to check on something. Stay here, honey.'

She yanked open the curtain and fled from the cubicle, flagging down a passing nurse to sit with Ariana before heading straight to the minors board, looking for her son's name.

Her eyes skim-read all the names until she saw it: Corday, Sebastian.

Please let him be all right!

She was about to rush off and find him when she did a double take, noticing the name of the doctor tending to him.

Jacob Dolan.

A sick chill had pervaded her body and her limbs felt numb and lifeless.

Jacob was with his son and he didn't even know it!

Seb was talking to his father and he had no clue!

She forced her limbs to move. Forced her heavy body to start making its way to the cubicle where her life would change drastically.

Cubicle number four.

What were they talking about? Seb couldn't be that injured if he was in Minors, but how bad was he? Was he sitting up in bed, chatting with his father? Was her secret out already?

No, not possible. Surely...?

Eva walked towards the cubicle with its closed curtain, a feeling of dread sitting low and heavy in her stomach. She could hear laughter inside, and Seb's gentle chuckling.

She was just about to pull the curtain back when she felt a hand on her arm.

Sarah and Brandon wanted to give feedback. One child had a small fracture of the wrist and severe bruising where the seat belt had crossed the body. Another had dislocated her shoulder, but it had been reduced and put into a sling. The teacher driving and all the other adults had got away with nothing more than whiplash and bruising.

'Nothing more severe? Thank goodness for that. They've been lucky, all of them.'

As Sarah and Brandon went back to their respective charges Eva couldn't help but relax her shoulders, but she took a deep breath before she whipped back the curtain.

Seb was sitting up in bed, a broad smile on a face that was peppered with cuts. Jacob was seated on a stool next to him, about to glue a cut on his scalp.

'Mummy!' Seb saw her and lifted his arms for a cuddle.

Eva hurried over to him, waiting for the axe to fall, waiting for Jacob to do the maths and accuse her of being some heartless witch...

'Seb! Are you okay?'

Jacob held off with the glue, giving them a moment. 'Hello, Seb's mum.'

She chose not to look at Jacob, knowing that if she did her eyes would give her away. Instead, she rapidly checked her son over, her hands grasping at his limbs, feeling for hidden injury. Apart from the cut on his scalp, he didn't seem too bad.

She picked up his chart from the end of the bed and read through it. 'Nothing serious, thank goodness.'

Jacob was watching her. 'Just some minor cuts and scratches, thankfully. His head was banged against the side window, which has given him the small laceration that I was going to glue. He should be fine.'

'Does he need a head CT?'

'Dr Ranjit has checked him and said it wasn't necessary.'

Dr Ranjit was a paediatric neurologist, so she had to assume he was right. 'I see…'

'Seb and I were just talking about lions. Apparently they're his favourite animal.'

'He loves lions.'

Jacob tilted his head at her curt tone, looking at her curiously. Then he asked Seb to put his head back against the pillow so that he could administer the glue. 'Be brave, now—this might tingle a bit.'

Eva gripped her son's hand tightly, smiling brightly into his face to encourage him to be brave.

He looked *so* like Jacob! Couldn't Jacob see it? They both had the same almost black hair, slightly wavy. The same bright blue eyes…the same nose and mouth. It seemed that when genetics were being decided upon Mother Nature had decided to give Seb only his mother's skin tone—very pale and creamy, with hints of pink in his cheeks. Apart from that, he was the spitting image of his father.

And this was not how she'd wanted Jacob to find out. She'd wanted to be able to tell him somewhere peaceful and neutral—perhaps the hospital grounds in a secluded corner? To buy him a coffee and ask him if he had time for a chat, and then slowly drip feed the information about what had happened after he left.

Not like this. Not in front of her son!

Seb winced as the glue went onto the edges of his wound and Jacob pinched them together to help them adhere.

'You're doing great, honey.' Eva rubbed his hands in hers and wished she could take away the pain. The discomfort. Do what she could to make her son feel better.

'I didn't know you were a mother.'

She looked at Jacob quickly, and then away, guilt flooding her cheeks with heat. 'No, well…things change.'

'How old are you, Seb?' he asked, frowning.

'Three.' Seb smiled. 'It doesn't hurt now.'

Jacob nodded and let go, and the wound's edges stayed together. He pulled off his gloves and smiled. 'There you go. It doesn't need a plaster or anything. Just don't get it wet. Well done, Seb! You're very brave.'

Seb beamed with pleasure.

'Can I take him home now?' Eva started to gather her son's things. His backpack had been put on the end of his bed, and his jacket.

'He needs to stay here for an hour or two for observation. He *has* had a bump to the head.'

He was staring at her, his eyes full of questions.

He knows!

She had to get out of there! She did not want to have this conversation in front of Seb! She would *not* have this conversation in front of him. No. Not at all.

But he had to stay. For observation. Couldn't she observe him at home? She was an A&E doctor after all…

'May I have a word with you, Dr Corday?'

Oh, this is it. Here it comes…

'Sure. But…um…later, maybe? I need to arrange cover if I'm going home.'

'Could we talk *now*?'

She looked at Seb. Then back at Jacob.

'Let me get him sorted first.'

She rummaged in his backpack and found his reading book. She passed it to him.

'Have a read of your book, Seb. I'm just going to step outside the curtains and have a talk with Dr Dolan.'

Eva followed Jacob from the cubicle and went with him over to the quiet corner by the Christmas tree.

It looked beautiful this year. The team had really done themselves proud. For years they'd had a tired old fake tree that had been packed away each year in an old cardboard box, battered and unloved. But this year they had a real tree, beautifully decorated in gold and silver, with lots of pretend presents underneath.

Eva and Seb had been really looking forward to Christmas. This year it seemed Seb really understood what was going on, and what was happening, and the story of Santa Claus had got him so excited! They'd already put their own tree up at home.

But Eva wasn't excited right now. She felt dread. And guilt. All those emotions she'd kept hidden away for years, since that first night with Jacob, neatly locked down, were now threatening to overwhelm her with their enormity.

She stood in front of Jacob like a naughty child before the headmaster. But then she thought about how he was guilty, too. About his part in all of this.

She squared her shoulders back and looked him in the eye. 'Yes?'

'You seem a little…distracted.'

She said nothing. Just stared at him. Waiting for the axe to fall.

'Seb's a great kid.'

'He is. The best.'

'You weren't a mother when we met.'

Her cheeks flamed. 'No.'

'But you are now. And he's three?'

'Yes.'

Jacob seemed to be mulling over his next words. Thinking about what he might say next. Whether she would rebut his words or accept them.

'He looks like me.'

Eva stared deeply into his bright blue eyes...eyes so much like Seb's. She couldn't—wouldn't—deny him the truth. He deserved that.

'Yes.'

Jacob's voice lowered. 'Is he mine, Eva?'

Of course he's yours! Surely it's clear to everyone?

She wanted to yell. She wanted to confirm it to him angrily. Rage at him for all he'd put her through after he left. But she didn't. She knew that could come later. Right now he just needed the plain facts.

'Yes. Seb's your son.'

He stood staring at her, his face incredulous.

The Christmas tree twinkled between them.

She couldn't help but notice how his broad shoulders narrowed down into a neat, flat waist. How his expensively tailored trousers moulded his shape, his long, muscular legs. He looked mouth-wateringly good. The years he'd spent in Africa had obviously been good to him. He was vital and in peak condition.

Years before, when they'd met at that party, there'd been only hints of the man he was to become. But even then he'd been delicious... Now the heavier muscle and perfectly toned body looked amazing on him...

She swallowed hard.

All she'd known about him that night was his name and that he was going to work for some charity. That he was a doctor, like her, and was going to Africa. But just because that was what he'd said, she hadn't been sure it was true. People lied. Especially at parties. To make themselves sound better or more interesting than they actually were.

Jacob. In *her* A&E. Standing there. As large as life. As gorgeous and as sexy as he'd ever been. A hundred times more so.

He was just staring back at her, his mouth slightly open, as if he'd had something he was about to say only it had never come out.

She couldn't just stand there! Waiting for the axe to fall. To see his reaction. Waiting for him to reject them.

So Eva turned and headed in the opposite direction—back through the curtains of the cubicle that held her son.

Their son.

If she just accepted right now that Jacob wasn't going to be sticking around—he was just a locum after all, here for the busy Christmas period—then it wouldn't hurt as badly. She couldn't expect him to stay. She and Seb deserved to be loved 100 percent. Eva refused to accept anything less.

'Seb will be okay to go home soon. I'll have to take the rest of the day off. There's no one else to take him, and I can't get my neighbour Letty in—not after this.'

'The new doc can pick up the slack,' Sarah said.

'Jacob.' Her mouth and lips and tongue flowed over his name like a caress.

Eva turned to go and get Seb, then realised her coat and bag were in her locker on the other side of the department. She hurried to get them, flushing as she went past the double doors to Resus.

She had to be quick. Her fingers fumbled over the combination lock and her hands were shaking by the time she managed to open it.

She'd worried so much about how Jacob would react upon finding out he had a son that she hadn't given a thought as to how *Seb* might react if he found out! He didn't even know he *had* a father. Seb hadn't yet asked, and she'd been too afraid to broach the subject with her very young son, deciding to wait until he was older to tell him what little she knew about Jacob.

Eva hurried from the staff locker room and headed for the cubicles.

She wanted to go home *now*!

CHAPTER THREE

HE HAD A SON? A *son*!

That little boy. Seb. He'd just been *talking* to him, taking care of him, and he'd not once suspected that he was his son.

But why would he? Just because the boy had had the same hair as him and the same eye colour…that didn't mean he should have suspected at all…

Why the hell hadn't Eva told him about Seb? Why had she kept him a secret?

He couldn't bear that. Secrets were dangerous.

He had to talk to her. Find out more. Find out what had happened after he left.

Walking away from the Christmas tree, he headed back to the cubicles—only to find Eva there, putting on her coat and scarf.

'Where are you going?'

'Home. I can observe Seb there. I *am* qualified.'

'He needs to stay here.'

She looked at him. 'This is nothing to do with you. You don't have to pretend to care.'

'Seb is *everything* to do with me—and not just as his doctor. And I do care.'

Eva stared at him, and as he waited for her to say something Seb peeked at him over his book and smiled.

Jacob couldn't help but smile back. Seb was a cute little guy.

Then he looked back at Eva. 'You both need to stay. We need to talk.'

She shook her head. 'I'm not ready for this right now.'

'Tough. It's happening.'

He dared her to defy him. If she chose to walk away right now, then he had no idea what he would say. He'd probably have to chase her until she gave up and headed back to A&E. But thankfully he didn't have to do any of that.

Eva let out a big huff, and then removed her scarf and unbuttoned her coat. 'Fine.'

Jacob let out a breath and his shoulders sagged down. He hadn't realised how tense he'd been. He couldn't help but look at Seb now.

He looked tall for a three-year-old. Like himself, he supposed. He could remember his mum saying that he'd always been tall for his age. Then again, Eva wasn't short, either. But now, the more he looked at his son the more he could see himself in the little boy. Seb's eyes were the same shape and colour as his, he had the same wavy hair, the same shaped mouth...

It was like looking at a mini-me.

And he was *three* years old...

Three years that he had missed out on. Three years of important milestones—his first word, his first steps, his first tooth, his first Christmas!

I've missed everything. Birthdays and Christmases...

How had he not known about his own son? More important, why had Eva kept it from him? For three years!

The last woman who had kept a secret from him had almost destroyed him.

Jacob called for one of the healthcare assistants to sit with Seb. 'Don't let him out of your sight,' he said, then guided Eva into the staff room and slammed the door closed behind them.

Three years! I've had a son for three years and she never told me!

Fury and rage that he'd never thought it possible for one human being to contain filled his body, making it quake, and he had to grit his teeth to try to bring it under some form of control.

'What the *hell* have you done?'

She looked up at him, her eyes wide and defiant as a solitary tear dribbled down her face. Even crying she was beautiful, and he hated her for that. Why couldn't she look wretched? Why couldn't she look awful, as if she were suffering for the pain she'd caused him?

He recalled Michelle standing in front of him, crying, begging for his forgiveness...

'I've done nothing wrong.'

He looked at her, incredulous. 'Nothing *wrong*?'

'I'm raising a boy on my own and I'm doing a damned fine job, thank you very much!'

'Oh, I'm sure that you are—but what about me? Did you not think our son deserved a father?'

'Of course I did!'

A horrible thought occurred to him. 'Are you with someone else? Is another man raising my child?'

She shook her head. 'No.'

'Then, why didn't you find me and tell me?'

'I tried! Believe me, I tried! But I only had your name,

and I knew you were going to work for a charity in Africa. I had no way to track you down.'

'Did you even try?'

She wiped the tear from her cheek. 'Do you know how many charities do work in Africa? Do you know how much research that would have taken?'

'You could have asked my friends from the party! They would have known!'

'I did! They told me you were working with Change for Children, but when I contacted them, they told me you'd already left!'

He stared at her. It was true. He had worked for them, but only for a little while. And then he'd met that doctor working for a different charity and he'd gone with him, hoping to assist with an eye clinic...

Had he told anyone? Had he told anyone the specifics of where he was going next? He couldn't remember. Surely he must have said something? But even if he had, would she have been able to track him down? He'd still been running then. He would not have left a way for himself to be traced by his family...

Was all this *his* fault? If he'd only thought to leave a forwarding address... Only he hadn't, had he? Because he'd been trying to avoid his family tracking him down and sending him letters, bothering him with all their worry and their 'Are you all right?' and 'Are you coming home?'

He'd always assumed that when the time came he would be there for his children. As his father had been for him. He'd imagined what it might be like to hold his baby in his arms... And Eva had had his child, not found him to tell him about it, and his own son had been without him for three years. If he'd known he wouldn't have stayed in Africa for so long...or even gone there in the first place!

Words couldn't adequately describe how angry he felt right now.

And for it to be *Eva* who had done this to him. The woman who had sashayed into his life one night, blown his mind and made him feel more alive than he'd felt in a year! The woman who'd filled his dreams for many a night subsequently. The woman who'd made him regret leaving England. The woman he'd thought about coming back home for.

He'd never have expected that *she* would do this to him!

'So...what does Seb know about me?'

She folded her arms. 'Nothing yet. He's too young to have asked about his dad. I had planned, when the time came, to tell him that you were in Africa, with no means of communication.'

'Africa...'

He'd loved it there. It had been such an education for him—would have been for any doctor—to go from a high-tech medicalised hospital to work in a ramshackle, dusty building that barely had instruments, lights or monitoring equipment. Many a time he'd been so frustrated at the lack of equipment, at the numbers of people they'd lost because they didn't have adequate resources, that he'd decided to come home again and again, after every loss, but he never had.

If only I had...

Then he might have learned about Seb sooner. Learned about Eva. Could he forgive her? This was Eva—the woman he'd...

Jacob cleared his throat. 'I've lost so much time with him already. He needs to know who I am.'

She stood up instantly, her body blocking the door. 'You're not going in there to tell him right now.'

He raised an eyebrow. 'He needs to know.'

Eva nodded. 'Then, I'll tell him. At home. In his own space. Then maybe… I don't know…perhaps you could come round later? Get to know him? Next week, perhaps…'

'Give me your address. I'll be round tonight.'

'Tonight? I don't—'

'Tonight. I've already lost three years.'

She looked down at the ground. 'I need more time.'

Jacob stepped forward so that he faced her, his nose mere inches away from hers. 'You've already had three years. Tell him today. Or we both tell him tonight, when I come round. Your call.'

Eva backed away from the intense, angry stare of Jacob's eyes. She'd had no idea of how angry he'd be. Or, really, what type of man he was. She'd allowed herself to be seduced by a stranger that night. She only knew one side of him.

'I'll tell him. I was the one who kept it from him after all.'

The way she looked at him then, with those beautiful crystal blue eyes of hers—the palest of blue, like snow ice on the polar caps—he had a flashback to how those eyes had looked into his that night they'd spent together, and a smack of desire hit him hard and low in the groin.

How could he still desire her when she'd just driven him mad with anger?

'You know what hurts the most, Eva?'

She shook her head, her full, soft lips slightly apart,

so he had to fight the urge to kiss her. It was as if there was a battle going on in his body. Half of him wanted to be furious with her; the other half wanted to take her to bed and make her gasp with delight.

'Not only did you keep Seb from *me*, you also kept Seb from my parents. Grandparents who would love him. Aunts and uncles who would adore him. Cousins who could be his friends. My family would *adore* Seb.'

'They still can…'

'But only because I came here.' He reached up and removed a wave of red hair from her cheek, then realised what he was doing and dropped it like a hot coal. 'How much longer would you have kept the secret if I'd gone elsewhere?'

She seemed nervous of his touch, her breath hitching in her lungs and then escaping when he let go of her hair. She was breathing heavily, and he felt empowered to know he had that control over her. That she still responded to his touch.

He'd never forgotten that one night…

'Jacob, I—'

'What's your address?'

Reluctantly, she told him.

He stepped past her and yanked open the locker room door.

'I'll be round at six.'

And then he left, leaving her alone.

Eva stood gasping like a landed fish after he'd left the locker room. As the door slowly closed behind him she sank down onto the bench and let out a long, slow, breath.

Jacob knew. And it had been every bit as horrible as she'd feared.

She felt she should have told him when she'd had that moment in Resus. Perhaps it might have gone better? If she'd been honest with him when she'd had the chance? But, no, she hadn't said anything. Instead, she'd sneaked away like a frightened mouse. And now look what had happened.

She'd *wanted* to tell him. She'd wanted to tell him ever since she'd discovered she was pregnant! But…

She hadn't been able to find him. She'd blamed him for being untraceable.

She'd wanted Seb to have it all! A mother *and* a father. As she'd *never* had. She'd promised herself that whenever she had kids her children would have the firm foundation of a loving family. Of growing up surrounded by love and security.

When she'd realised she couldn't trace Jacob she'd quickly accustomed herself to the idea of raising Seb alone. Of relying only on herself—the way she'd always done! Seb would be able to rely on her. She'd be the best mother she could be. Her child would have the certainty that she was there to stay and she would love him more than life itself. Do the job of both parents.

Her feelings for Jacob she could control. What had they been but fantasy? He was a man she'd been able to put on a pedestal because she hadn't known him long enough to discover otherwise. Who knew what he was really like?

She could *do* this.

It would be easier now. They would be able to work together and she wouldn't have to worry anymore about him finding out about Seb. The worst was over.

Wasn't it?

She caught her own worried gaze in the mirror.

Maybe it wasn't. Maybe Jacob would let Seb get to know him and then he'd disappear again? He had a temporary post here—perhaps he'd be a temporary father?

Eva got up and went over to the sinks to splash cold water on her face. She stared again at her reflection in the mirror, dabbing her skin dry with the paper towel.

'Jeez…you really didn't handle *that* very well at all,' she told herself, trying out a tentative smile.

That was better. She needed to look human again before she went to collect Seb. She didn't want him to notice she'd been crying. After today he needed to see his normal mum—the one in control. The one who soothed his brow when he was sick…the one who read to him at nights until he fell asleep. He'd need everything to be normal after the frightening start to his day in the minibus.

But I'm going to have to tell him about Jacob…

Exactly how *did* you tell a three-year-old about his father? Would he even be able to understand what she was telling him? Or would he accept it easily? In her experience her little boy was very adaptable. Maybe he'd take it in his stride?

She threw the paper towel into the bin and continued to look at herself in the mirror. She blinked quickly. The redness in her eyes was almost gone now. By the time she got out there to Seb she should look fine.

Eva opened the door.

Seb was still in his cubicle, but Jacob was with him, holding on to Seb's little fingers as he spoke to him. Seb looked intrigued. So happy. She wondered what they were talking about. She watched them together. The way Jacob spoke, the way he laughed—he was so like Seb. And Seb looked *so* like his father, with his wavy dark hair and intense blue eyes. They were the spitting image of each other. He was so obviously Jacob's little boy.

And I didn't persevere in trying to find him. I should have! We could have had everything we ever wanted...

Yeah, right. As if *that* would ever have happened...

Seb spotted her and waved. 'Can we go home now?'

Jacob didn't smile at her.

'Soon. We need to stay for a while so the doctors can keep an eye on you.'

'Because I banged my head?'

'That's right.' She glanced at Jacob.

He looked to his son. 'You know what, Seb? I'm going to come round to your house tonight. Is that okay?'

Seb nodded emphatically. 'Yes! You can tell me more about lions.'

He smiled. 'I will. I'll tell you anything you want to know.'

Eva stared at him hard, but he looked away from her and down to his son, ruffling his hair.

He'd kept them there as long as he could, but eventually Jacob had watched as his son and Eva left the department.

Hell of a first day!

He'd expected fireworks. He'd expected ups and downs. But not this. Never this!

Three years. He'd been a father for three years. Years that he'd spent in Africa, tending to the poorest and sickest of people, with almost no modern medical facilities. Watching people die needless deaths, getting depressed, drinking too much...

Thank goodness he'd stopped with the alcohol. That had been a stupid path to go down. But what with

Michelle and The Wedding That Never Was, he'd felt entitled to a drink. And the drink had helped numb his thoughts. About Michelle. About Eva.

She'd been the last thing he'd expected at that party.

He'd gone there expecting to say goodbye to a couple of friends—people who had been there for him after Michelle, who had let him crash on their floors despite the stuff going on in their own lives—and there she'd been. Standing on the far side of the room, in a dress that hugged in all the right places. That flaming red hair had made her stand out in a room of mousy browns and she'd had the bluest eyes he'd ever seen, her lips curved in a half-smile.

Something about her had intrigued him.

Who *was* she? What was she doing there?

The very fact that he'd actually been thinking those questions had woken something in him. Something that he thought had died along with Michelle. And when he'd held her in his arms to dance, her soft curves moulded into his body, as if she'd been carved specifically for him, he'd turned to mush.

He'd wanted to kiss her. Had wanted to taste her. Possess her. All other thoughts—all the pain, all the grief, all the torment that he'd spent months trying to get rid of—had suddenly dissipated.

All there had been was Eva.

And she'd kept quiet. Not told him he was a father. Not tracked him down. If she had he could've been... He could've had...

He shook his head to clear his thoughts.

She was doing it again. Muddling his mind. What *was* it with women who did this?

He had to think clearly again. There was a reason he didn't like to revisit his past.

Jacob strode back into the department and picked up a patient file. No matter what, life was now going to be different. He'd get to know Seb. Slowly. Not rush it. He'd get to know his son. Let Seb get to know him. *Do I want to see my family again?*

The last time had been on his wedding day. The day that Michelle had died. Almost five years ago.

Since then, he'd been running. Running from his family…running from those who said they loved him because he couldn't cope with them. Couldn't think about dealing with their pity and their sympathy and their sad looks, their supportive pats on his back. He'd not wanted to face any of that. Nor would they have wanted to give it if they knew the whole truth of what had happened that day…

But he could be different now. Couldn't he? It wasn't just him anymore—he wasn't alone now. He had a son, and his son would need him. He refused to let Seb be without his father for a moment longer.

And it was nearly Christmas. Traditionally a time for family. Perhaps now was the time for him to start building some bridges? Maybe let his parents know about Seb? Maybe Eva would let him take Seb for a visit? They'd love that. Love Seb. And Seb would love Jacob's old childhood home. The smallholding. The animals there. The old orchard where Jacob had spent so many hours himself.

I can't go. There are too many memories there of Michelle…

It was too much to think of going there.

Michelle had grown up right next door. His English

rose, with her gorgeous straw-coloured hair that had floated and billowed in the breeze. He could picture her everywhere there. In the orchard. The barn. The house. He could hear her laughter even now, as she danced away from him, always out of reach.

His parents' grief and Michelle's mother's grief would be too much to deal with! How they all managed to still live there, he had no idea!

I bet they still have that picture of us both on the kitchen mantelpiece...

Their engagement picture. He'd felt so happy when she'd said yes.

If only he'd known of the pain she would eventually cause.

CHAPTER FOUR

TELLING SEB ABOUT Jacob was a lot easier than Eva had been expecting.

He sat there on the couch, looking up into her face with those eyes that were so like Jacob's, and she told him the momentous news.

'Seb, I want to talk to you about your daddy.'

'My daddy?'

She'd never really heard him say the word, and to hear it now felt strange. Odd. But she guessed she ought to get used to it. Jacob was back, and from what she'd seen so far he was going to stick around long enough to meet his son. Whether he *stayed* around... Well, that could be another thing entirely. When had anyone ever stuck around for her?

'Yes. You know the man today at the hospital, who helped glue your head?'

'Yes.'

'Well, that was him. That was your daddy.'

Seb seemed to think about it for a moment, his head tilted to one side and his eyes screwed up with concentration. Eva knew she had to say something else to make things clear for him.

'Daddy has been working away since you were born,

Seb. In Africa. Remember he told you all about the lions? Well, he was doing very important work, being a doctor like Mummy, so he didn't get a chance to meet you. But now he's back, and he's excited to get to know you, so tonight he's coming to see you.'

'Okay,' he said, and simply went back to watching his television programme.

Eva sat next to him quietly. Waiting to see if he'd say anything else. Ask anything else. But Seb seemed engrossed.

Assuming he was fine, she got up and went into the kitchen. She was thrilled he'd taken it so well, but children were very accepting, in her experience. Until now she had been all that Seb needed.

Eva knew what it was like not to have parents. Growing up in the foster system had been a lonely experience. Some places she'd stayed longer than others, but as she'd been pushed from pillar to post she'd always felt alone and separate. Dependent only on herself for her own happiness.

She'd got used to not relying on other people. Used to people walking away. And she'd known that those who did stay, stayed only until she was sent elsewhere. She'd been a foster child. The families she'd gone to had known she wouldn't be staying forever, so there had always been that detachment. They'd never got close. Never cared for her too much, or loved her too much.

She never got attached to anyone. There was no point. The only person she'd allowed herself to love was Seb, and he meant the world to her. If Jacob was here for now, then great. But she knew she had to hold a piece of herself back from him. A piece of *Seb* back from him.

Just in case.

Because what had life proved to her so far? People pretended they were going to be there forever. Some would even promise it. They'd promised Eva that she would never have to get used to another home ever again. And what had happened? Real sons and daughters had been born and suddenly she'd been cast out. They'd sit her down, then have *that* talk with her about how things weren't working out.

There was no point in getting attached to people.

They just let you down.

And she'd promised herself—and Seb—that if she ever did meet someone she thought could be the great love of her life, then that person would have to love her and Seb 100 percent. She refused to be anyone's second best. Refused to be the 'reserve' love interest.

Eva spent the afternoon getting the place ready for Jacob's arrival. Due to her working full-time, and being a single mother, the house wasn't as presentable as she would have liked. There were stray plastic bricks and action figures everywhere. There was even a platoon of storm troopers guarding the bottom of the stairs.

She cleared away what she could and vacuumed through, polished and cleaned. The Christmas tree was looking a little sad in the corner, so she rearranged some of the ornaments and switched on the lights to give it some life. She laid the dining table with her best china, in case he stayed long enough to sit and eat with them. She cleared the hallway of coats and shoes.

It had become a veritable graveyard of outdoor stuff, even though there was just the two of them, but there was a mix of wellingtons, work shoes, Seb's shoes, trainers and slippers there, all waiting to be tripped over.

She was quite pleased with how neat it all looked when it was cleared away. She'd never been much of a housekeeper, having never had a real home except for this one, and she did her best.

Now, the big question was whether to get dressed up for Jacob's arrival?

If she tried too hard he'd know it. If she dressed casually would that take away from the enormity of the occasion? But didn't Seb need as much as possible to stay the same?

She certainly didn't want Jacob thinking she was dressing up especially for *him*, so she decided on casual. After a quick shower, she dressed in blue jeans and a fitted white T-shirt. Over that she wore a short taupe cardigan. And even though she'd decided not to make herself up especially for Jacob she painted her toenails, because she liked to go barefoot in the house. After a quick blow-dry of her hair, a swipe of mascara, lip gloss and a squirt of perfume, she felt ready.

Two minutes before six the doorbell rang.

Eva swallowed hard and felt her already jangling nerves turn into a cacophony of chaos.

He was here.

Seb's father.

'It's him! It's him!'

Seb rushed past her to get to the door first and she followed sedately after him, to give herself a few last seconds of trying to calm her nerves. She almost felt as if she was walking up to the gallows. She had no idea of how Jacob would be with *her*, but she hoped he would be pleasant in front of Seb.

The mirror in the hall told her she looked just fine. If a little apprehensive...

Seb pulled open the door and beamed at his father. 'Hi.'

'Hello, Seb.' He stood in the doorway, wearing jeans and a T-shirt with a black leather jacket over the top.

She was glad he'd chosen casual, like her, but *his* casual managed to look oh-so-sexy.

In his hands he held a gift-wrapped present, which he handed to Seb. 'This is for you.'

'What is it?'

Seb gave it a shake and Eva recognised the sound of many somethings with many pieces waiting to be built—or eventually, knowing them, sucked up into her vacuum cleaner.

'You'll need to open it to find out. Hello, Eva.' He was now looking at her, his gaze intense and unreadable.

She had to be welcoming and friendly, especially in front of Seb, so she smiled. 'Jacob. Come in. It's cold out! No need to stand in the doorway.'

She held the door open for him, inhaling the scent of him as he passed, the smell sending her back to that night she'd spent naked in his arms, writhing and tingling and gasping her pleasure...

She blinked rapidly. 'Go straight through. Seb, why don't you show your daddy into the lounge?'

She closed the front door and watched Jacob and his son disappear into the room ahead of her.

Get a grip!

She let out a harsh, short breath, then squared her shoulders and headed into the room with them.

Seb was ripping off the wrapping paper on the parcel to discover a large jigsaw puzzle of his favourite cartoon characters. He dropped to the floor in delight so he could study it better.

'You bought him exactly the right thing. He loves jigsaws,' she said, glad she hadn't already bought it and put it under the tree.

Jacob knelt on the floor and watched his son. 'My sister has a son. I tried to remember the sort of thing he was into at this age.'

At the mention of his sister, of Jacob's nephew, Eva felt chastened. She stood in the doorway, not sure what to say next.

Seb looked up from his present and beamed a smile, then ran over to Jacob and threw his arms around his father's neck. 'Thanks, Daddy!'

Jacob looked surprised at how easily Seb was being with him, then relaxed and hugged his son back. 'No problem.'

Seb let go, and then took a step back and looked at his father. 'I'm Seb.'

Jacob smiled. 'I'm your dad. Pleased to meet you.'

They shook hands, and then Seb giggled and went back to his puzzle.

Jacob looked up at Eva and smiled hesitantly. 'He took it well, then?'

'Yes. Easier than I expected.' She sat down on the couch near him. 'It's been a big day for him, what with the accident this morning and then you. I'm sure all his questions will come later, when it begins to sink in.'

'I'm sure they will, too. He's still okay? After this morning's accident?'

She nodded. He seemed fine.

'Hey, Seb… Want me to help you do it?'

'Yes, please!'

As they huddled together on the carpet, with Jacob pretending to struggle to find pieces, she watched him—this man who had fathered her child. She'd always wondered what he would be like with his son, and here he was, playing it out live in front of her. Jacob seemed at ease with Seb, which was good, and Seb, in turn, seemed comfortable with Jacob.

Eva headed into the kitchen to make them all a drink.

She made up a tray of tea for the two of them, including a real teapot, and a juice for Seb, before heading back out into the lounge. She put the tray down on the coffee table and asked him whether he'd like sugar and milk.

'Milk without, thanks.'

She poured the drinks and sat back.

It was strange. It was almost as if they weren't strangers at all. Seb was laughing and chatting with Jacob, trying to show him how the pieces fitted together and which pieces matched which, and Jacob was laughing and smiling, and it was like watching friends who had known each other for years.

She almost felt like an outsider. The way she had felt as a foster child. Being apart from the family unit, as if she was a visitor.

Her stomach coiled in on itself at the too-familiar hurt and, feeling uneasy, she decided to interrupt. 'Is there anything you want to ask?'

Jacob looked up at her, as if he'd forgotten she was even in the room. She saw him look her up and down and then away. 'I…er…have a lot of questions, actually.'

'Okay. Fire away.'

'You were on your own? For the pregnancy? How did it go?'

She nodded and took a sip of her tea. 'Yes. Totally

on my own. When I found out I was pregnant I was shocked. The doctor said I was about two months gone, and pretty much after that the morning sickness started.'

'Was it bad?'

'Pretty bad. I was okay in the mornings, but late afternoons and evenings were the worst—which weren't great whilst I was working shifts at the hospital and getting tired.'

'But you coped?'

'I always do.'

He looked at her then, his eyes holding hers just for a moment longer than was comfortable. 'Any cravings? My mum craved apple pie and custard with me.'

She shook her head. 'No. Not really. But I couldn't stand the smell or sight of blood...which isn't ideal for an A&E doctor.'

He smiled as he clipped his jigsaw pieces together. 'What did you do?'

'I made sure there were plenty of those cardboard sick bowls in the room with me and got on with it. I wasn't going to have the hospital make special provisions for me.'

'Why?'

'Because I wasn't special.'

She wasn't going to tell him the real reason. That when she was growing up no one had ever made special provisions for her. That she was the one who made provisions for others. Fitting in around everyone else. She'd never received special efforts from anyone. Why would she have expected her colleagues at work to do that?

'And the birth? How did that go?'

Seb looked up. 'Mummy borned me in the water.'

Eva smiled. 'That's right, Seb. It was a water birth. After an extremely long and tiring labour.'

'How long?'

'Forty-two hours.'

'Ouch.'

'Ouch, indeed.' She smiled at him.

He was smiling, too.

When they realised they were smiling at each other they stopped, Jacob looking back down at the jigsaw pieces and Eva down at her cup.

What was she *doing*? She wasn't meant to be getting friendly with him. She was just meant to be polite. For Seb's sake. Nothing else was going to come of this.

'And…er…he was healthy?'

'Very healthy. Nine pounds in weight. Were you a heavy baby?'

'No. A seven-pounder. You?'

'I don't know what I was.' She could see he looked confused. Most people knew how heavy they were when they were born. Their parents usually told them. But she didn't have that information. Had never thought to ask for it, either. 'I didn't have parents,' she explained. 'I grew up in foster care.'

'Mummy had lots of homes!' Seb said, passing Jacob a piece he needed to complete the corner of the picture.

'I'm sorry to hear that.'

He sounded it, too. Genuinely. Which made her look at him carefully. He really had a kind face. It was easy to see in the wide openness of his eyes, the laughter lines around them and the generous smile of his mouth. His features were soft and rounded. There were no sharp lines, no bony angles, no harshness to his features.

She'd always believed you could see the kindness of

a person in their face. If someone was a nice character, kind and gentle, then you could see it. But if someone was cruel or nasty or vicious, then you could see that, too. The meanness would be plain to see.

Jacob had a good face. A beautiful face.

And she felt a small amount of hope. That he would be a good dad to her son and remain that way. Seb deserved it. Not that she'd ever let him want for anything. He wasn't spoiled. But he *was* loved. And he knew that he was loved, and she'd tried to love him enough for two. Her guilt at not being able to give him the father he needed had hurt for a long time. But he did have *her*. He had his mother. Which was more than she had ever had.

Jacob hadn't known about his son for three years, though! He'd missed so much! How could she ever make up for that?

'I'll just check on dinner. Would you like to stay?'

Jacob looked up at her…*so* delectable. Heat flooded her cheeks at the thought.

'That would be nice. Thanks.'

'It's just pasta. Crab linguini. Is that all right with you?'

Jacob smiled. 'That would be great. Anything you're having will be fine.'

At that moment he looked so charming and approachable she had to remind herself that even though she'd once slept with this man, made a child with him, they were still strangers.

It was hard for her to get up and move away from them, from their sudden cosy family unit, to go and cook the pasta. But she figured she needed to leave them—to give them some time together without her there. A bit of father and son bonding.

Just cook the pasta. That's all you have to do.

She was successful at that, then hurried to the fridge to prep the crab. She mixed the crab meat with fresh herbs, salt and pepper and a small amount of chilli. It was good to be doing something with her hands, because before she'd been beginning to feel like a spare part. Now she felt useful. As if she was contributing.

She figured she'd better get used to it, because there were bound to be more meetings like this as Jacob and Seb got used to one another. They had so much to learn about each other. Three years of catching up to do.

How many times were you meant to apologise to a man when you'd kept him from knowing his child?

She felt incredible guilt. She'd apologised, but now she was trying to put everything right. But there was no need for her to feel beholden to him. They were both at fault for Seb not having had his father around.

The fork she was using slipped from her fingers and clattered to the tiled floor. Sighing, she bent to pick it up—but Jacob got to it first.

She'd had no idea he'd followed her to the kitchen and she was surprised and shocked to find him there.

So close…

They stood up together and he held the fork out for her to take.

'Thank you.' Her fingers brushed his and she tried not to show how much his contact affected her.

Such an innocent, brief connection.

But such an effect.

Her heart pounded—so much so that it sounded as if it was in her ears and not her chest. Her mouth went dry, as if she'd spent months in the desert, and she fought to stop her hands from trembling as she put the fork into the sink and got another one.

Could he see her hands shaking?

Now was probably not the best time to pick up a heavy pan of pasta, but it was done and she needed to drain it. The pan wobbled slightly, but she hoped he couldn't see.

'Why don't you get Seb to wash his hands? This'll be done in a minute or two.'

She heard him go and let out a pent-up breath. At the same time the steam from the water billowed up around her face as she strained the pasta.

How had it come to this? Yesterday she'd not had a care in the world. She and Seb had been good. School was good. Work was good. Home life was good. They'd been looking forward to Christmas, just a couple of weeks away—Seb praying for snow, as always.

It had all been *good*.

And yet today… Today her son had been in an accident and had been brought to her A&E. Jacob had turned up out of the blue. Her body had fired off little shots of adrenaline every time he came near and now he'd discovered he was father to her son!

How could just one day change so much?

Eva mixed in the cooked crab, then took the bowl of linguini and the side salad into the dining room and called them through.

Jacob came in with Seb on his back and set him down by his chair.

'This looks great.'

She nodded her thanks and bade them sit. Seb helped himself first, and Eva served up salad to everyone's plates as Jacob served the pasta.

They all began to eat, at first in silence, enjoying the food, and then Seb asked his first question of the night.

'Were there big lions?'

Jacob finished his mouthful of food before answering, 'In Africa? Yes, there were!'

'Whereabouts in Africa were you?' Eva asked.

Jacob smiled at her. 'Lots of places, but mostly I was in the Manyara region of Northern Tanzania. Do you know where Tanzania is?' He looked to his son.

Seb shook his head.

'It's between two countries called Somalia and Mozambique. I'll show you on a map later, if you'd like?'

'And you were doctoring people?' Seb pushed a huge forkful of linguini into his mouth, sucking up a stray strand of pasta.

Jacob laughed. 'I was. It was a lot of hard work!'

Eva watched the pair of them talking across the table. Seb looked so much like his father. It was hard to think that they had only met today. They even held their forks the same way.

Seb nodded. 'Why didn't you phone me?'

Jacob looked awkward. What would he say? Eva wondered.

'There were *some* phones there, Seb, but they were old, and lots of them were broken, so a lot of the time they were useless. And I couldn't use my mobile because... Well, there just aren't any antennae over there. I'm sorry. I would have phoned you if I could.'

Jacob glanced over at Eva and she looked down and away, thankful that he hadn't blamed her outright, in front of their son, for his not even knowing about his existence.

Jacob *would* have called his son if he'd known about

him! That was what he'd been trying to say with that look. With just a single glance from those blue eyes of his.

The pasta suddenly seemed inedible to her, sticking in her throat, and she had to take a large drink of juice to wash it down. Then, feeling very uncomfortable and needing some fresh air, she quickly stood up. 'Excuse me a moment,' she said, and disappeared back into the kitchen.

Leaning back against the kitchen units, she held her hand to her mouth. Would Jacob ever let her forget what she'd done? Would he always try to punish her for not trying harder? She wasn't sure she'd be able to put up with those reproachful eyes of his for evermore...

She opened her fridge to check on dessert. The chocolate mousse was set, so that was fine. All she had to do was go back into the dining room and continue to pretend to Seb that everything was fine...

Back at the table, Jacob was showing Seb something on his phone. 'Do you see? That's my parents' place. Your grandparents. They own over ten acres there, and have it full of all the animals you'd find on a farm. Chickens, goats, alpacas...' He sounded wistful.

'What are *they*?' Seb was flicking through the pictures on Jacob's phone.

'They're like llamas.'

'Don't they spit?' Eva cringed.

Jacob laughed. 'Sometimes. But alpacas are gentler, I think. Or so my parents used to tell me.'

'Can we go?' Seb looked to Jacob, then to Eva.

Eva saw the look of joy and hope on his face. How could she say no?

It would give Seb a chance to get to know his grandparents. Now that he *had* some. All he'd ever had family-wise was her. Now he had grandparents and uncles, aunts and cousins. Seb's world was about to get a whole lot bigger. And though she'd wanted that for him, now that it was a reality she worried about it.

She'd have to get to know them. She'd have to sit in front of them and be judged. Like before. When she was a child. And she wanted no one judging Seb like that. Seb was her son. The one thing in this world that she had to protect. Jacob's family were strangers and she knew nothing about them.

'I suppose… But maybe in a few weeks? If Daddy is happy to take you?'

Jacob looked down at the floor. 'Er…sure.'

Eva could see that something wasn't right. Jacob didn't seem too keen on the idea. Why did Jacob seem apprehensive?

Seb's his son, too. Remember that.

She'd never shared her son. *Ever.* And now Jacob would introduce him to his new family. And she had no idea how far away their place was, or what type of people they were, and there was black ice on the roads. Today had proved how dangerous it was to travel.

What would they make of him? His grandparents?

What was she thinking? They'd *love* him. Of course they would! A new grandson to spoil. They'd love and adore Seb, surely. Welcome him into the Dolan fold without a backward glance.

Hopefully…

She had no idea what it was like to have grandparents. She could only imagine what they would think of *her.*

They'll judge me. Keeping their grandson from them for all these years…

Seb looked disappointed at her response. She could see he was keen to go. Jacob was staring at her.

'They *will* look after him.'

'I'm sure they will. It's just—'

'They're his grandparents.'

'I know they are. So…why don't *you* seem to want to go?'

Jacob looked down at his plate and she could see he was clenching and unclenching his jaw.

'It's a long story.'

'Well, maybe I need to hear that story before I let you take my son somewhere that might not be safe.'

'It's safe!' He almost laughed out loud. 'What…? You think there are monsters there or something?'

Eva glared at him. Talking about monsters in front of Seb! He had no idea how his son might feel, hearing his daddy talk about monsters! Seb could be terrified— Jacob wouldn't know!

'People aren't always the nicest.'

'My family are *very* nice.'

'So why don't you want to go?'

He looked cornered, looking to Seb first, then back to Eva. Eventually, he let out a breath. 'Because they don't know I'm back in the UK yet.'

'Why not?'

'I have…reasons.'

'I'd like to know what they are.'

Seb sucked up another long piece of pasta and grinned at his dad.

'We haven't spoken for a while. There wasn't a falling out—there weren't any arguments—it was just that I needed to get away for a while, and I didn't contact them or speak to them in the time I was away. The lon-

ger it got, the more difficult it became and now it's…
almost impossible.'

Eva considered his words. 'You haven't spoken to
them for *four* years? If there were no fallings-out, then
ring them. I'm sure they'll be thrilled to hear from you.'

'I'm sure, too.'

'Yet you still haven't done it?'

'No.'

Jacob pushed some pasta round his plate. She watched
him as she absentmindedly used her fork to twist and
turn her own pasta. Seb was still eating hungrily. Her
son's eyes were gleaming and bright, full of childish
enthusiasm.

Jacob watched his son—gazing upon his mirror
image, taking in all the details of Seb's face. The chicken
pox scar above Seb's left eyebrow. The small mole below
his ear. The light smattering of freckles across Seb's nose
that were more Eva than him.

Eva thought back to when she was pregnant. Desperately trying to track him down and let him know about
his child! Unable to find him. She'd been so upset at not
being able to give her son his father! But he'd moved on,
as people always did in her life, and the disappointment
at that fact had hit her so hard. She didn't know why
she'd expected it to be any different with him.

And it was then and only then that she had truly understood just how alone in the world she was…

She'd so wanted him to know! So wanted to have
someone else there. To hold her hand. To reassure her
that she could do this. To let her know that someone else
cared about this baby with her—wanted to nurture it
and love it and take care of it. To tell her that no longer
would she have to walk through this world alone and on

the edges of everyone else. That she would be a part of something. A team. United against the world.

But no. He'd gone. And so she'd faced it alone.

Until now.

Those two were already bonding. Quicker than she'd ever imagined. She knew Seb had been excited to learn his father was back, but she'd expected him to question it further. To hold something of himself back, taking his time to decide whether or not he could trust his father. But, no, Seb hadn't been like that at all! He was happy his father was here and he was carrying on as if they'd been together for always!

Or maybe those were her own thoughts?

While she'd carried Seb in her belly she'd tried over and over again to find Jacob. But eventually she'd had to admit defeat. As far as Eva had known, Jacob might never come back. As far as she had known his note might have been a lie—he might not have even been going to Africa, but slept with her and then disappeared because that was the type of man he was.

Though there had been that look in his eyes that had told her he was different. She'd wanted to find him—she really had—but after she'd hit that dead end...life had got in the way. Looking after herself and then Seb had taken over, and then too much time had passed, and...

She began to understand a little as to why Jacob had not contacted his family. The more time that passed, the more difficult it got. Perhaps they were more alike than she'd realised?

Eva excused herself and scraped back her chair, taking away the pasta still on her plate and then coming back for theirs. Jacob and Seb had both cleared their plates—a first for Seb, who usually left something. She raised an eyebrow at his empty plate and was rewarded with a grin.

'Ready for dessert?'

They both nodded and looked up at her at the same time, and the looks were so devastatingly identical she felt her insides contract.

In the kitchen, she scraped the plates and put them in the dishwasher, then she got the mousse from the fridge. She served it into three bowls and carried it back out to the table, serving Seb first, then Jacob. She sat opposite and mutely spooned up the chocolate.

Normally it would have been delightful...enjoyable. But right now, she couldn't taste anything and she might as well have been spooning sawdust into her mouth. It felt cloying and heavy and she didn't enjoy it at all.

Perhaps this was what second-guessing yourself felt like? Whatever it was she was doing, it wasn't pleasant.

Somehow she finished the mousse. So did Seb and Jacob. She took their dishes into the kitchen, only to hear Jacob follow her in and set down the condiments he'd brought through from the table.

'Thank you for dinner. I didn't know you were such a good cook.'

'Well, there's probably a lot we don't know about each other. But when you're alone you either learn how to cook well or how to cook quick, and I never was one for microwave meals.' She turned to face him and once again tried to ignore the effect of his looks. He was effortlessly attractive and she found that annoying. Or was it the fact that she was still attracted to him that irritated her?

The father of her child stood mere inches away, after all this time. A man she hadn't seen for years now back, tanned, matured and still making her nerve endings sing like a performing choral act.

The last time I saw you we were naked.

And that was the problem. She could still picture that night. Still remember the effect of his touch…still recall how he'd made her feel, how he'd made her yearn for more. How they'd made a child that night and how it had been magical.

The way he looked at her now wasn't innocent, either. Could he remember, too? Did he remember how she'd ground herself against him? The way she'd gasped in delight at his touch?

'I'm sorry, Jacob.'

He raised an eyebrow. 'For what, exactly?'

'For not finding you. For letting you work with me this morning and still not telling you until I was backed into a corner.' She bit her lip. 'I should have persevered. I should have kept trying to find you.'

He said nothing. Just stared at her. His eyes bored into her soul so intensely she got lost.

'Okay. Thank you. Seb wants me to stay for a bit longer. So I can be here when he goes to bed and read him a story. Is that all right with you?'

She nodded. 'Of course.'

Seb's bedroom was a little boy's dream, as far as Jacob was concerned. The walls were blue and covered in lion posters. There was a small low bed, and Jacob could see tubs and tubs of toys. There was a giant beanbag in one corner, and a small desk and chair piled high with books. A garage set lay under the window and from the ceiling hung many different plane models and home-made paper chains.

Seb's room was perfect for a boy, and he could imagine what it must be like to enjoy this room as a child.

'Wow! Great room, Seb.'

'Mum painted it. I did this bit.' Seb pointed.

Jacob made a point to study the windowsill. 'You've done a great job. You sure you haven't done this sort of work before?'

'I paint pictures in nursery.'

Jacob nodded. Seb was already in his onesie and had climbed into bed. 'So what book are we reading?'

'That one.' Seb pointed at a book.

Jacob settled down next to his son and felt envious of all that he'd missed. Cinema trips, meals out, watching Seb grow... Being there for illnesses and birthdays. And for all those other times when nothing actually happened but you were just in each other's company, watching television or sitting on the sofa.

Christmases...

All those magical times he'd not been there. It made his heart feel leaden even to think about it. But was it best that it had happened this way? Would he have been ready for this kind of responsibility three years ago?

Jacob picked up the book, found the bookmark and opened up the pages. 'I've not read this one.'

'We've read it lots of times.' Seb fiddled with his quilt. 'Will you go back to Africa?'

Jacob looked hard at his son and saw fear in Seb's eyes. 'I said I would, but... You've grown so big and I've missed so much... I don't want to miss a single second more.'

Seb smiled and snuggled down into his bed. 'Will you read to me *every* night now?'

'I'll try. I'd better ask your mum first—if I can come round every night.'

His son propped himself up on his elbows and frowned. 'But don't you *live* here?'

How could he explain? How could he explain to Seb that his father and his mother had never even been in a proper relationship? That it had been one night when he'd let himself get carried away by a redhead with a body that wouldn't quit and the kind of lips that ought to have come with a health warning.

It was all too complicated. And he didn't want to blame Eva in front of Seb, either.

'I wasn't sure if your mum would have room, so all my things are at my flat.'

'But now you can bring your clothes here.'

Jacob ruffled his son's hair, marvelling at the softness of it under his fingers. 'Maybe. Settle down, then—let's read you the next chapter of this story.'

But his private thoughts lingered on how to sort out this situation between himself and Eva.

Clearly Eva hadn't told Seb the truth about their relationship. How could she? Seb was so young still. He could understand that. *He* wouldn't want to tell a child about that, either.

He'd been so apprehensive about coming here tonight. Learning about Seb had been such a shock to his system. One minute he'd been a single guy, with his only commitment being a temporary contract with the hospital, and the next, he'd found out that he was a father! And not to a baby about to be born, but to a three-year-old child!

He'd been furious after Eva had left the hospital. Livid. But then, after a bit of fresh air up on the hospital roof, other thoughts had entered his head. What if he wasn't a good dad? What if he had no idea of how to do it? It had been so long since he'd last allowed himself to care for someone. To love someone. He'd spent so long with his heart locked away in a box...

But a child needed love. *Deserved* to have it!

He wished he'd found out about Seb sooner, but there was no way he could have done—no way he could have predicted the consequences of that night. He'd used protection with Eva. He'd only known her first name, and he hadn't taken her number or found out where she worked. It had been first names only and one hot, unforgettable night. He hadn't asked her any questions, because he hadn't needed to know.

She'd been his gorgeous redhead, his mesmerising siren, and he hadn't wanted to talk, or to think, or to second-guess. He'd wanted simply to go with the flow and enjoy the ride his body was taking him on. To allow her to soothe his soul. And though it had only been one night, it had made him feel alive once more. He'd hardly been able to believe it had made such an impact on him.

She'd filled his dreams for weeks afterwards. Every now and again he would think he'd caught the scent of her perfume, even though he'd known she was on a different continent!

He'd have had no way of tracking *her* down, the same way she hadn't been able to find him. Although he supposed he could have asked his friends. The ones at the party. Though actually they had been more friends of friends. But he could have asked them who the mesmerising redhead was, who Eva was...

Which, technically, he *had* done when he'd got back to the UK.

He shifted slightly and turned a page of the book, not really in the story, but lost in his own thoughts.

Upon his return to England he'd called a friend from the party that night. He'd asked him vaguely, as if it weren't important, if he could remember that night. If he could remember someone called Eva.

Mark had joked and joshed with him about it, and said that he couldn't, but then later that day Jacob had received an email from him, with Eva's full name.

It had been as simple as that to find out where she was currently practising. Thank goodness she wasn't called Smith or Jones. Thank goodness she wasn't married! Because she might have been—there was no reason why she wouldn't have met someone else in the time they'd been apart. She probably wouldn't even remember him.

But he'd wanted the chance to see her again. Because for some reason—even after all those years—he'd never been able to get the image of her out of his head. She'd done something to him that night—something other-worldly that had brought him back to who he really was—and he'd wanted to feel that way again. Being in Africa had taught him that something was missing in his life—and he'd thought maybe, if he was brave enough to seek out Eva, he'd find it once more.

But he'd come back and discovered that he had a son...

Wow.

He wanted to know his son—although just looking at him it already felt as if he'd known Seb his whole life. It was like looking at a mini-me, only with paler skin and freckles.

The burden of responsibility hit him hard. A *son*! A

three-year-old boy who would want to look up to his father and emulate him. Could he be that role model?

There was no question about it.

It was a tough situation, and he'd had enough of those to last him a lifetime: Michelle... The Wedding That Never Was...

Over time it had been easier to lock away his heart for good, to disappear when things got tough—to take a breather and throw himself into work until he could get his head around how he was feeling.

But finally he'd felt ready to come back. Strong enough to find Eva and to continue to be the best doctor he could be. Only now he could add another role to the one of doctor.

Father.

And he wanted to be the best father he could be...

For Seb...and for himself.

Eva had cleared away the dishes downstairs, cleaned the kitchen and sat down on the sofa, fidgeting with her mug of tea as she waited for Jacob to reappear.

This was the first night in a long time that she had not read her son his bedtime story.

Because his *father* was doing it! Jacob. The one man all other men had had to live up to. Not that there'd been many other men. Not seriously anyway. She'd had the odd dinner date, or been invited out to coffee, but she'd always stopped it at that. Though it had been nice to know that men still found her attractive, she'd made it clear to each and every one of them that it would not get serious. Because after a couple of dates they'd always wanted to get more involved in her life than she was prepared for—they'd wanted to meet Seb.

And none of them had been Jacob.

She'd fantasised about what might have been for so long—had stupidly almost fallen in love with her one-night stand and allowed herself to put him on a pedestal.

The night they'd spent together had been the best night she'd ever had. Of course she was bound to be sentimental about him. He'd made her *feel* for the first time in ages! Besides, they'd made a child together. Without Jacob there'd be no Seb. And her son was her world. By having her own child she'd discovered how it felt truly to love for the first time ever. To feel connected to another human being.

Of course Jacob had known nothing of the feelings he'd engendered in her. He'd slipped away into the night, never to be seen again.

Until today.

She'd always been sceptical about people who believed in love at first sight! What a cliché! Things like that didn't happen in real life, did they?

Only it had. She'd gone to her friend's party out of a sense of obligation, really. But once there she'd decided to live a little, to have a few drinks and, for once, to lose herself in the moment.

And suddenly, across the room, her gaze had collided with his. He'd stood there, half a foot taller than everyone else, and those piercing cobalt eyes had pinned her to the spot with their intensity.

The music had been blasting out, people had been talking loudly and laughing all around her, but, caught in his gaze, all she'd been aware of was her mystery man.

Her body had tingled with awareness, each nerve ending lighting up like a beacon. And when she'd realised he was coming across the room to her, without breaking eye contact, her limbs had turned to jelly, her mouth had gone dry and she'd had to physically remind herself to keep breathing.

Up close, he'd been devastatingly handsome. Tall, broad, athletic. A shock of dark hair. He'd lifted up a tress of her own hair, letting it run through his fingers, his gaze focusing on her open lips before he'd said, 'I'm Jacob. Dance with me?'

It was as if time had stopped. As if everyone else had no longer been there and it was just the two of them in that airless room. The heat, the lights, the music and them.

A slow tune had come on and he'd led her into the small dance space, his fingertips deftly pulling her after him, and then he'd spun her around and pulled her into his arms, so that she was pressed up close against his body, her hands against his chest, feeling his heart beat…

It had been magical! His touch… The connection she'd felt with him… As if that moment had always been meant to be. If she'd said that to anyone else they might have laughed at her, but she'd felt it to be true.

He'd held her in his arms and she'd rested her head against his chest and listened to his steady heartbeat, moving with him, against him, moulded into him, fitting into him perfectly.

And then the music had stopped.

She hadn't heard the next tune. She'd just been aware of his eyes, of the heat in his gaze as he'd lowered his lips to hers…

Even now, thinking about it all these years later, she could feel a shiver down her spine as she recalled how he'd slowly lowered his mouth to hers and finally—*finally!*—claimed her lips for his own.

That soft, gentle kiss had turned into a hungry demand for more, and with her silent consent he had led her out into the candlelit garden and found a summer house.

After closing the doors they'd ripped at each other's clothing, tossing it to the floor, and tumbled onto the futon inside, a mass of laughter and limbs. And then he'd taken her, his mouth insatiable as he'd tasted every inch of her, making her writhe and contort and gasp his name. She'd unashamedly clasped his hair as he'd tasted her intimately, and when he'd kissed her again she'd tasted herself on his lips. The taste, the scent of their sex had driven her on, and she'd clambered on top of him, riding him so forcefully and so deeply she'd noticed bruises on her knees days later that had made her smile with the memory of their night.

Afterwards they had lain side by side on the futon, laughing and giggling into the early hours. Eva had fallen asleep briefly, and when she'd woken Jacob had been gone. His clothes had been missing. Her own naked body had been covered by a crocheted throw.

She'd found a folded note on the pillow next to her.

Had to leave. Africa calls!
You were amazing!
Love, Jacob x

She'd dressed quickly, ashamed at what she'd done, but glad that the party was still in full swing so she could sneak out without anyone noticing.

Eva had been forlorn. How typical of her to fall for someone who had disappeared to another continent…to Africa. Unless his note had been a joke…?

But, no, he'd left without a trace.

She'd tried to forget him. To forget that night. But then she had discovered that she was pregnant.

She hadn't believed the little blue cross at first—they'd used protection; there was no way she could be pregnant, and from one night, too.

Abortion had never been an option. She hadn't been able do it—she'd wanted her baby. No one else was going to make the decision for her. She would make it work—she would *have* to make it work. She would try to find Jacob. Try to track him down. How hard would it be?

Eva had craved to hear Jacob's voice, to feel his touch upon her one more time. She'd cried when he'd not been there to see the first scan, or to help her with nursery decoration ideas, or to help her through her contractions during labour, or to be there to hold his son after he was born. But as time had passed it had become easier. She'd become more able to bear the pain and the longing.

Until now.

And she could still feel that pull. That pull of attraction that hit her low and deep in her gut each time she looked at him. That *need* she had for him—still with her after all this time. How *could* he still have that effect on her? How did one man hold such sway over her emotions? It was like living in an emotional pinball machine, being ricocheted from one feeling to the next—fear, excitement, doubt…arousal.

But what was going on with his family? Why had he been out of contact with them for so long?

When he'd first found out about Seb he'd said to her that one of the worst things she'd done was to keep Seb from the family who would love him. Adore him. Jacob had given her that whole speech about uncles and grandparents and cousins. And yet he showed obvious reluctance to connect with that family.

Why?

She didn't need anyone else's drama. She didn't need anyone else's family issues impeding on the life she lived with Seb. They had a good life—a happy, stable life. She didn't need to take Seb down that road. The road of being judged and found wanting. Of being rejected. She wouldn't allow it.

What were they talking about up there?

She longed to be able to hear. But then she heard Jacob's footsteps on the stairs, and soon he was standing in the doorway, looking as irresistible as when she first saw him.

'How did it go?'

'He's asleep.'

'Good.' She smiled.

Jacob perched on the edge of her sofa. 'He wants to know why I'm not living here.'

Her breath caught in her throat. 'And what did you say?'

'Just that all my things were at my flat.'

'I see…' That was a difficult one.

'He wants me to read to him every night. Would that be okay? To come round in the evenings?'

That could be awkward. 'Erm…'

'I've missed enough nights, don't you think?'

'You'd practically be living here.'

'Just when my shifts allow? If it's really late maybe I could sleep on the couch?'

She'd never get a wink of sleep, knowing he was so close!

'I don't know…'

'I think we should do it. For Seb. I'd do anything for him. Now that I know I have a son I'm not going to let him down. If he wants me here every night, then I'd like to be. I'll keep out of your way.'

She stared back at his beautiful blue eyes. *How?* How would he stay out of her way? The place wasn't that big.

'Okay.'

Had she really just said that?

'Thank you. I'll go home tonight, but I'll bring a few things over tomorrow for when I have to stay.' He attempted a smile. 'I promise my toothbrush won't take up too much room.'

'Right...'

This was all moving so fast! The man she'd wanted for the past four years was practically moving in!

Jacob closed Eva's door behind him and let out a big sigh into the cold night air. The evening had gone better than he'd thought it might. He hadn't been sure how Eva would be with him. Whether she'd be treading on eggshells around him or whether she'd have loads of questions that he just wasn't ready to answer yet.

About that night. The one they'd spent together. About him leaving and never saying goodbye.

She had every right to challenge him about it. He would in her position. There was plenty she could choose to ask about, but she'd not said a thing. She'd given him the time and space he'd needed to be with Seb, and for that he was grateful.

Seb was a great kid, from what he could see. Eva had done a fabulous job in raising him thus far. But now Seb would have his father in his life and things would be different.

Jacob smiled as he walked to his car. Seb was a good-looking boy, with his wavy dark hair and blue eyes, and that alabaster skin. Girls wouldn't stand a chance when he was older! Eva had skin like that... The palest of skin tones, clear, unblemished, to the point where it almost didn't look real. The type of skin you wanted to reach out and touch, just to make sure.

He'd known he was going to find Eva in that A&E department. And, yes, he'd wanted to know more about her. There was something about her that called to him, as if she was some sort of siren singing an enchanted song that only he could hear. He'd never stopped thinking of her in Africa and that had scared him. How could a one-night stand feel like so much more?

What if they became close? What if they had a relationship? Could he keep himself emotionally separate?

Not from Seb. Seb was his son, and already he could see how easy it was going to be to love that boy, and he'd protect him to the ends of the earth if he had to. But Eva? What would happen there?

She'd already got under his skin. She'd ignited something in him that he hadn't felt for a long time. And the last time he'd felt that way... Had *thought* he felt that way...

No...I don't want to think of that anymore.

Could he even trust his own judgement? How could he know that he was making the right decisions? When he'd trusted himself before he'd been blind to what had truly been going on...

He closed his eyes and pictured the way Eva had moved that night. The way she'd felt on top of him, writhing and sweating as he'd felt himself deep inside her, as she ground him into her with a steady, yet deep rhythm. How it had made him feel to hear her gasping, to feel her hot breath blowing into the side of his neck, her fingernails scratching into his back as she'd clutched him to her as if she'd never wanted to let go...

That night had been amazing. But then he'd watched her fall asleep, her back to him, and he'd felt immense guilt, knowing he was going to have to slip away to catch his flight.

He should never have slept with her before he left for Africa. He should never have slept with *anyone*. He'd known he was leaving in a few hours and he'd not been in the right headspace—so what the hell had happened?

He hadn't even considered how she might feel afterwards. That she might feel used or abandoned when she woke up alone.

No. That wasn't true. He *had* thought about it. Worried about it. Had felt guilty about it. He'd treated her badly. Should have told her the truth from the start. He'd never forgive himself for that, even if she did.

But now he needed to be the best father that Seb could ever have. To be there always for his son. Never to let him down. Never to make a promise that he couldn't keep. To make Seb feel cherished and adored by *both* his parents.

He could do that.

Easily.

But he'd treated Eva badly once before—how would he know not to do it again? Perhaps if he stayed away from Eva and focused just on Seb, then that would be safer for them all?

He'd once felt this way about Michelle. A deep-down attraction that had pulled at his very being. And look how wrong *that* had turned out to be.

She'd seemed a safe option. The girl next door…his childhood sweetheart. Michelle had seemed so right. And yet it had all gone wrong! She'd professed to love him, professed to be true to him, and she'd ended up sleeping with somebody else. His friend! The one person he should have been able to trust most.

It had been a huge shock. Yes, Michelle had seemed more and more distracted, but he'd put it down to the wedding and how all the preparations had needed so much organising. Brides were *meant* to worry about their weddings—he'd thought her preoccupation was normal. But it had been something else…the sordid details of which she'd finally disclosed to him on their wedding day.

He hadn't seen Michelle's affair coming… Could he trust his instincts now?

CHAPTER FIVE

EVA HAD BARELY been at work for five minutes before Sarah found her and turned her round in her chair.

'So how's Seb?'

Eva thought about how best to answer her. He'd had a few aches and pains this morning, a bit of a headache, but generally seemed fine. In fact he'd seemed more than fine, and she put that down to the fact that he'd spent a few hours getting to know his father.

But did she want to tell Sarah that Jacob had been round at her house last night?

'He's good, thanks.'

'No after-effects from the accident?'

'Nothing much.' She smiled and tried to get on with her work, but Sarah wasn't going to let it go. Apparently her questions about Seb were only a preamble for her questions about Jacob.

'And Dr Dolan?'

Her fingers froze above the keyboard. 'What about him?'

'Well, you never did get the chance to tell me how you know him.'

Eva looked about them, to make sure no one else was

listening, but the only witnesses were the Christmas decorations, already wilting.

'He's…um…Seb's father.' She looked up guiltily at her friend, hoping and praying that she wouldn't over-react whilst they were at work.

'Seb's dad? Really? Wow, you kept that one quiet.'

Eva nodded, her cheeks aflame. 'And there's more to it than that. I, er, only told him about Seb yesterday.'

'*What?*' Sarah looked totally amazed, her eyes wide, her mouth gaping, until she closed it promptly. 'What did he say when you told him?'

'He was…shocked.'

'I bet. What did he say?'

'He said I had to tell Seb. That he was going to come round.'

'And?'

'And what?'

'How did it go?' Sarah asked, as if she were an im-becile.

'Fine.'

'*Fine?* What? That's *it*? No furtive, lingering looks between the pair of you? No unfinished business?'

'We finished our business nearly four years ago. All that matters now is Seb.'

'But aren't you going to find out if he's single?'

Eva frowned. 'Why?' There was no point, really. It would be too much to expect that life would actually start working out well for her. That they could be a happy family unit with Jacob. *Hah!* As if *that* was ever going to happen.

Sarah shook her head in disbelief. 'Because *you're* single, Eva! And don't forget…he's hot.'

'He's unreliable. Disappears when you want him and

leaves no trace. It was like trying to track down a spy. And he's only here temporarily. Once his contract is over he'll move on and we'll never see him again.'

She felt awful for saying it, but it was what she truly expected. No one ever stuck around for her. No one ever wanted to keep her in their life. Why would Jacob be any different? No matter how much she wanted him to be.

Sarah picked up a treatment card for the next patient. 'If he really was a spy that would make him hotter.'

'You're incorrigible!' Eva laughed. 'Why don't *you* get a boyfriend so you can stop trying to fix me up?'

'I'm married to my job.' She skipped off without a backward glance and left Eva pondering over Jacob.

What did she really know about him? Okay, so he was a doctor—which gave him brownie points from the get-go, didn't it? His interest in medicine meant that he spent his day helping people, and he'd even flown off to a developing continent and offered to help people there, in what must have been difficult conditions. He'd discovered that he was a father and, after his initial shock, had showed up, played with his son, eaten with them and read Seb a story. He'd even promised to come round every night, when he could, so there were signs of commitment there...

But he *had* seduced her and then left without a trace. He'd given her the barest information about himself, so that she'd been unable to track him down. Although she'd *known* it was going to be a one-night stand. She'd *known* it was going to be a one-time thing. But it hadn't mattered. She'd wanted it as much as him—had succumbed to their primal connection and lost herself in the moment.

She'd wondered then, as she had many times since,

what had been driving him that night. And what had he been running away from…? She'd seen that he was in pain emotionally. In some torment. And rather than scaring her off it had drawn her to him. Two damaged souls merging together, soothing each other, before they parted ways, never to see each other again.

Although now she knew that he had turned his back on his family—but why?

He had family who cared about him—he'd mentioned that earlier, and that there hadn't been any huge falling-out. But he'd stayed away from them when quite clearly they would have supported him through whatever it was. And if there *was* something he was still running from, was he the sort of person she wanted around her son? Did he flee when the going got tough? Should she be letting Seb get to know him? Because if Jacob was going to bolt then she needed to know.

She brought up the staffing schedule for the day and saw that Jacob was supposed to be at work in Minors again today.

I need to get on with my work. I can talk to him later.

She picked up her next patient file and headed off to call the patient through, but as she walked through Minors a cubicle curtain swished open and there he was.

'Hello.'

'Hi. You okay?' he asked.

His patient smiled and hobbled past them on crutches, one ankle bandaged neatly.

She waited until the man was out of earshot. Then blew out a breath to calm herself, tucking her hair behind one ear and using the moment to try to focus.

'I'm fine. I'm glad I ran into you, though. I wanted to have a quick word about our…situation.'

'Oh…?'

She looked up into his eyes and once again found herself cursing his parents for giving him the most startling blue eyes she'd ever seen on a man. He had sickeningly long lashes, too, all dark and perfectly outlining his almond-shaped eyes. Any woman would kill to have lashes like his.

'Have you got a minute?'

'Sure. Fire away.'

'I need to know your intentions.'

He looked puzzled. 'My what?'

'Your intentions. With Seb. With the future.'

'I'm sorry, I don't under—'

'You're on a temporary contract here. For the Christmas period. I…er…I need to know if you're going to be temporary elsewhere, too.' She babbled her words, rushing to say them, to get them out of her mouth so that they wouldn't be clogging up her brain any more.

Jacob looked at her, his brow furrowed with lines.

'Are you a stable influence for me to have around Seb? Because if you're not, if you're going to disappear again, then I don't want you around him. Getting to know him. Being in his life for five minutes and then disappearing. Leaving me to handle the fall-out again—only this time with a small child in tow, who will ask questions and be hurt that his father couldn't stick around.'

He looked annoyed that she would even suggest it. 'I'm going to be there for my son.'

'Always?'

'Always.'

'Good.'

She'd believe it when she saw it. She wanted to trust

him. Desperately so. But life had taught her that it didn't always work that way.

He laid a hand on her arm and looked her deeply in the eyes. 'When I came back I didn't expect to discover that I had a child. But I do, and I'm thrilled, and I'm going to be the best father he could ever have.'

She tried not to think about his hand on her arm. Warm and reassuring.

'Right. Glad to hear it.'

'Don't ever doubt me when it comes to Seb.'

She looked up into his dark blue eyes and nodded.

Somehow, magically, there was a brief lull in patients. The waiting room had almost emptied and Jacob took a brief moment to sit outside, cradling a hot cup of coffee and wrapped up tight in his jacket and scarf.

He could feel the weight of his phone in his pocket. Could feel it burning into him as he debated making that call back home. Imagining the scenarios, the conversations, the questions he would no doubt receive.

Could he face them and tell the truth finally? He'd decided in Africa that he could. But now that the time was upon him—the time to pick up that phone and make the contact that he knew his parents and family would crave—he felt anxious.

He knew they'd ask. He knew they'd want answers. So would he in their position.

I should never have let so much time pass without contacting them.

He was angry with himself for that. Angry with himself for a lot of things. He'd been responsible for what had eventually happened. He'd worked too hard, he'd taken for granted Michelle's feelings for him, and once he'd got that engagement ring on her finger he'd stopped trying. Stopped showing her how much she meant to him. No wonder she'd ended up with another man. His best friend!

That betrayal had hurt. The woman he'd professed to love and his best friend... It had been obvious afterwards. The amount of time they'd spent together... And to think he'd been so pleased that Michelle and Marcus got on so well together! Working together to plan the wedding!

I pushed them together. It was my fault.

Accepting his part in it had been a major trigger point for his coming home. He'd spent a couple of years blaming *them. Their* betrayal, *their* deceit, *their* cheating. It had been uncomfortable to turn that questioning on himself. But when he had... He'd taken some time to admit it, but he had found *himself* wanting. Had accepted what he'd done on their wedding day, yelling at her like that, causing her to rush off in tears, crying at the wheel...

He pulled the phone from his pocket and brought up his list of contacts. He scrolled down to M and found the listing he wanted.

Mum and Dad

Jacob let out a sigh and looked about him. An ambulance had just pulled up and was offloading a new patient, strapped to a backboard. Briefly he thought about going in to help out, but dismissed the idea.

He needed to do this. Make contact. He'd spent too long shutting the door on painful things in his past and he'd vowed to himself that when he came back from Africa he would face everything. He'd call his parents.

He'd tell them the truth of what had happened that day. He'd tell them what he had done wrong. He would tell them everything…

He could imagine hearing their voices. How delighted they'd sound. He knew they wouldn't be cross. They weren't that type of people. His parents were easy-going and caring. They'd have *worried*, sure. They'd have fretted. Big time. But they wouldn't greet him with anger.

So just do it already!

He pressed his thumb to the screen and then put the phone up to his ear. He felt odd. Not nervous. Apprehensive…? But he sucked in a breath and knew he could handle this. He was ready now. He never had been before. But now he needed his family as he never had before. Now that he was a father himself. Now was the time to reconnect. Because of Seb.

'Hello?'

'Dad?'

A pause. *'Jacob?'*

He smiled. 'Yeah, Dad. It's me.'

A little boy had been brought into A&E by his terrified father. Separated from the mother of his child, he'd been looking after his son and had woken him from a sleep to find a lump on his forehead that had appeared suddenly.

Eva had called the mother in from work and the two parents had been at loggerheads from the get-go.

'You must have *some* idea, Lee! Did he fall? Have an accident? Go out on the ice?'

Lee looked utterly perplexed. 'No! *Nothing!*'

'Were you drinking again?'

Eva stepped in between them as their voices began to carry across the department. 'That's enough!' She eyed both of them, the look on her face the only warning they'd get, watching them both, making sure she had their attention. 'You can argue later, but right now we have to look after Ben. Okay?'

The father nodded quickly, the mother reluctantly, mumbling under her breath, 'I should never have trusted you in the first place.'

Eva could understand her distress. It was a mother's worst nightmare to find out that something was wrong with her child whilst she was at work. The most obvious explanation for Ben's large bump would be an accident, but Ben's father had denied that—and if things were as bad between them as it seemed from the way they were acting, she could see why the mud-slinging had begun and why the father was in the line of fire.

'Let's concentrate on Ben, shall we?'

His father gripped the handrails of the bed. 'I was with him all the time, Doctor—he didn't fall or bang his head anywhere.'

'Was there any time when you weren't watching him? Any chance he could have had an accident without your noticing?'

'No. Apart from when Ben fell asleep for a bit, and I caught forty winks myself. It's been manic recently, getting my new place ready for Christmas. But I woke up before he did and when I checked on him I noticed this lump that had appeared whilst he was still asleep.'

Strange, Eva thought. So if there was no chance of trauma, what else could it be? A sebaceous cyst? Pott's puffy tumour? A cyst was unlikely, as it would have been present for some time before becoming infected.

'Has he had a cold recently?'

The mother answered, 'For over a week. He's had a badly blocked nose.'

Eva bent down to look at her patient. 'Is your head sore, Ben?'

Ben nodded sadly.

She knew she needed a CT scan to confirm her diagnosis, but before she could say anything the parents began again.

'This would never have happened if he'd been with *me*,' the mother sniped.

'Well, you were at work, weren't you? He had to be with me.'

'I should have asked my mother.'

'I can look after my own son!'

'*Can* you? Because we seem to be in hospital—and I don't really think that means you looked after him very well, does it?'

Eva raised her hands. 'Please keep your voices down.' She stepped from the cubicle and sighed. These two parents were obviously struggling to share custody of their child.

Would she and Jacob become like that over time? Would she be ringing him, wherever he was, and yelling at him down the phone for not being there? She hoped not. All she'd ever wanted was for Seb to be happy, and having warring parents wasn't the way. She'd seen too much of that growing up in foster homes. If Seb ended up in hospital ill, she hoped they would pull together for their son and not bash heads like these two parents were doing.

Jacob seemed a reasonable man. So far. He'd promised he would stick around for Seb. But people made promises they couldn't keep all the time. If things got tough and Jacob left…

I hope he doesn't. I hope he can prove me wrong.

He was a very handsome man; she'd be stupid to think he would remain single. What would happen if he fell in love with someone? If his life was filled with someone else? Would Jacob still want to be around her and Seb? She was his past. They'd only shared a bed once. Made a child together. The likelihood of him having feelings for her was small.

She'd always, *always* been the one in control of Seb's life. Both mother and father to him. Now that responsibility was going to be shared and it scared her. What if Jacob did something wrong? Jacob wanted a say in his son's life. What would *that* be like?

She wasn't sure she could see it going well.

We need to get together and talk about this. It's all changing so fast.

But she wanted desperately for it to go smoothly. For Seb. He was a good kid. Responsible and very mature for his age.

I definitely don't want us to be like Ben's parents.

She set her shoulders and went off to order a CT scan for Ben.

Jacob was there, waiting for a patient of his own. He took her to one side. 'We need to talk.'

'Yes, but not now. I've got a patient.'

'So have I! But I don't want to talk about this at your home, Eva. Not with Seb in earshot.'

'So you do care about what he hears?'

'Of course I care. I'm here for Seb forever. He's part of me. He's part of my life. I've just called my parents.

Told them I'm back. Told them about Seb.' He let out a huge sigh. 'Big phone call for them.'

'You did?' Surprise filled her face. She wondered how they'd reacted.

'They were…very happy.'

'They were?' Eva felt a warm feeling in her gut. A small spark of happiness. She could accept that people had rejected *her* in her lifetime, but for Seb she wanted nothing but acceptance and welcoming arms.

'Yes.' Jacob nodded.

Eva looked at him, shocked at this turnaround. She hadn't suspected this. 'Big day for the Dolan family.'

He nodded and smiled. 'Yes, but telling my mum she's a grandmother again tended to make everything all right. When I rang off she was getting excited about shopping for more Christmas presents.'

'But they were thrilled?'

'Very. Although it did make me think that I need to get Seb something for Christmas, so I wondered if you'd do me a favour?'

'Depends what it is.' She smiled to show she was joking. But she did want to hear what it was before she agreed to anything.

'I don't know what he'd like, so I wondered if you'd come Christmas shopping with me? There's only a couple of weeks left till the big day.'

'When?'

'Later today?' Now it was his turn to smile. 'When our shifts are over? Well?'

She couldn't think of any reason why not. She had a good couple of hours before she had to pick Seb up from her neighbour's and she needed to go shopping herself, really. Christmas was looming fast and she didn't know when she might next get some free time. She didn't want to leave it to the last minute. Plus, it would give her an opportunity to talk to him. Learn more about him.

'Okay. I'll meet you after my shift ends.'

He drove them both into town. It wasn't too far from the hospital, but it would have been impossible if they'd tried to walk it. Once he'd found them a parking space, after circling a car park for ten minutes, they got out and headed into the shopping centre.

The first thing they heard, apart from the noise of chattering shoppers, was Christmas music. A beautiful rendition of 'Silent Night' was being sung live by a group of choristers at the base of the elevators.

The interior of the shopping centre was bedecked in beautiful glittering decorations in silver and white and an enormous tree stood at one end, festooned in white fairy lights with an enormous silver star at its apex.

'Wow! That looks amazing!' Eva gasped in wonder, instantly sucked into the atmosphere of the season and forgetting all about the pressures of work—the clock-watching, the reports to write out by hand as well as on the computer, the endless stream of patients, the sickness, the damage that people could do to one another. 'You almost forget there's life outside of the hospital.'

'There's a grotto.' Jacob pointed at a small wintry woodland display, festooned with mechanical bears and a snowy wood cabin. 'We should bring Seb.'

We.

She liked that. It sounded strange after being the only one to think about Seb. That he already seemed to see them as a family unit felt surreal. But good. Seb had loved having his daddy there last night, and Eva had to admit that she had been looking forward to him coming again.

It was nearly Christmas. And here she was, shopping with the father of her child, and it all seemed so simple and so easy—if she would just let it be that way.

'Where do you want to look first?' she asked.

Jacob pulled off his hat and gloves and shoved them into his pocket, running his fingers through his gorgeous hair to straighten it out. 'I don't know. There's just so much!'

'That jigsaw was a hit. And he likes playing football. Maybe a small trampoline?'

'I don't want to get him another jigsaw. I'd like to get him something fun.'

'Shall we just browse?'

He looked about him, overwhelmed by all the places they might have to go. 'Why not?'

They set off into a huge store that specialised in children's toys. It was so noisy in there! Filled with parents doing the same thing, along with children testing out the toys on display, watching robotic dogs and hamsters whizzing about on the floor. They sidestepped those and headed down one of the aisles, where there seemed to be an abundance of educational toys.

'What sort of things did *you* like as a child?' Eva asked.

'I played outside a lot. In the orchard. I made up a lot of my own games. Bits of wood for a sword, made my own bow and arrow—it was useless, but it was fun! You?'

Eva shrugged noncommittally. 'I never really had much. I was hardly ever in a real home for Christmas, and the children's home I kept going back to just got us practical things like clothes or shoes. I got a copy of *Black Beauty* once and I read it over and over until it fell apart.'

'I'm sorry to hear that.'

He looked it, too, but she didn't want his pity. She shrugged it off. 'It's okay. Anyway, this Christmas Seb really has a sense of what's going on and he's excited. I want to make it special for him.'

'Me, too.'

There seemed to be plenty of things to choose from. Games that would teach children about shopping, about telling the time, about learning the days of the week or the months of the year, or what the weather was like. Jacob didn't want to get his son anything like that. He wanted to get Seb something that was really fun.

'Three's a difficult age. What sort of things can he do?'

'He's very active. He likes physical things—going to the park, climbing on the frames, riding on the swings and things. I bet you made yourself a rope swing in that orchard of yours?'

Jacob laughed and nodded. It was good to see him smile so broadly. His face lit up with genuine joy and it felt good to know she'd made him feel that way.

'I did.'

'Was it any good? I've never tried one.'

'Never? We'll have to remedy that one day.'

One day. That implied he was sticking around, didn't it? She hoped so. Because she liked this. Being with him. Shopping together for Seb. Doing stuff to make their son happy. It was like being united. Wanted…appreciated.

Valued.

It made her feel good. This had to be what everyone else felt.

They headed into another aisle that was filled with cuddly toys of all kinds. A large fuzzy lion was an obvious choice.

'We *have* to get him this.'

Eva nodded. Seb would like that. 'Good choice.'

Jacob tucked it under his arm and they carried on looking, ignoring the aisles full of dolls and anything pink. 'Unless he *wants* any of this?' Jacob asked.

'Er…no. Seb wouldn't be interested.'

'Just checking. Equal opportunities and all that…' He smiled.

She laughed and realised she was enjoying herself. Jacob was turning out to be the nice guy she'd hoped for. She was actually living one of the scenarios she'd once dreamed about. Being in that happy family unit… being that perfect family.

Almost.

She didn't want to spoil it. It felt good. Strangely comfortable. Pleasant.

They stood in the queue and Jacob paid for the lion. They headed back into the shopping centre and he bought them both a hot chocolate. They sat on a bench that suddenly became vacant, quickly slipping onto the seats before anyone else could, and watched the shoppers rushing by.

'This is nice,' Eva said.

'The hot chocolate? Or resting?'

'Resting!' She laughed and took a sip of her drink. 'No—this. All of it. Christmas shopping for our son together.'

Jacob looked at her and smiled.

He really was a handsome man and, looking at him now, she could really see how he and his son shared the same smile.

'I'm glad. You know, you've mentioned your childhood… What was it like?'

She glanced at him. 'You really want to know?'

She didn't mind telling him. It hadn't been a perfect childhood, but she'd made peace with that a long time ago. The past wasn't important now. What mattered was the future. And she didn't think he'd judge her if she told him. Being a doctor, he'd probably be quite understanding.

'I do.'

'The reality of it wasn't that great. I went to ten different foster families. Some of them were okay. One was really nice and I really didn't want to leave them. A young couple—the Martins, they were called…Sue and Peter. I really thought I'd get to stay with them. Be their daughter. But then Sue got pregnant with twins through IVF, and when she was about six months pregnant I suddenly found myself back at the children's home again.'

'That must have been difficult.'

'It was. I didn't understand what I'd done wrong.'

It was an understatement. She'd been incredibly hurt. And it had been a turning point for her. The point at which she'd decided never to rely on other people to make her happy. That she'd just look out for herself. No more performing seal acts to make potential foster carers think she looked cute and adorable. No more behaving well because the staff at the children's home had told her to. She'd behaved well before and look where that had got her!

'How old were you?'

'About nine. It was a tough time. I thought I'd done something wrong and cried for what seemed like forever. Then I got used to not being wanted.'

'It had to have been a tough decision for Sue and Peter.'

She looked at him, searching his face for hidden meaning, but she didn't see anything. There was no guile there. He genuinely thought it must have been a tough decision for the couple. But she'd never thought of it that way. She'd only seen it from her own—hurt—point of view.

She thought of what they must have gone through now…making the decision to send her back. 'I guess it was.'

'Did you ever learn what happened with your own parents? Your biological parents, I mean?'

She sipped her chocolate. 'Wow. You *really* want to hear a sad story at Christmas time, don't you?'

'No. But I want to hear *your* story.'

He looked steadily at her and she eventually met his gaze.

'I was told that my mother was a young girl. A teenage runaway. She got pregnant, no one knew who the father was and she didn't want to raise a child on the streets. So she gave me up.'

'I'm sorry.' He looked at her with sadness in his eyes.

'It's not your fault.'

'No, but it must have been hard.'

'Not at first. I just sort of accepted the story. I've thought more about it since having Seb. I couldn't imagine giving him up. My mother, whoever she was, must have gone through hell to make that decision.'

'I think you've probably got her spirit and bravery.'

Eva smiled, then they both got up, throwing their polystyrene cups into the bin.

They wandered through a few more stores and she noticed that he kept looking at her when he thought she wasn't watching. She wondered if he pitied her. She didn't want that. She didn't need it. Pity did nothing for anyone. It certainly never made things better.

When they finally got to the last store and saw a beautiful blue-and-silver bike that was the perfect size for Seb, Jacob's face broke out into a broad smile.

'A bike for Christmas! His *first* bike. That'll be perfect.'

Eva beamed, too. 'I agree. But he'll need a helmet, too—and stabilisers.'

'You're happy for me to get it?'

She nodded and looked at him. 'I'm happy.'

Back at Eva's home, they unloaded their shopping and Jacob helped her hide the bike away in her bedroom closet, draping it with clothes for extra camouflage.

It felt odd having him in her bedroom, near her bed. In her most intimate space… With the gifts put away, they stood a few feet apart, just looking at each other.

'Well…I guess I ought to go. Shall I come back later? To read to Seb?'

'Yes. That would be great. He'll enjoy that.'

'So will I.'

She stared at him some more, her fingers fidgeting, unsure of what to do. She started when he took a step towards her. Then another. Tentatively, he reached up and stroked the side of her face.

'I've enjoyed this afternoon. Spending time with you. Being with you. Thank you for telling me your story.'

The feel of his fingers stroking her face sent tingles down her body. Her breath caught in her throat and she became hyperaware. Aware of his solid gaze, of where his hands were, how close he stood, exactly what he was doing.

'I enjoyed it, too.'

'I'd like to…kiss you.'

She breathed in, her chest feeling so full of air, so full of hope for what he might do next, what it might suggest, she almost wasn't breathing at all.

'You would?'

He came nearer still. They were centimetres apart and she could breathe in his scent. Her body was doing something strange inside, with the excitement of his proximity. It was as if there were tumblers and acrobats in her stomach, and tiny, tiny dancers in each and every blood cell, pirouetting and twirling their way through her system. And their spinning was getting faster and faster the closer Jacob came.

Her lips parted.

She wanted him to kiss her. She wanted him to so much!

'There's something about you, Eva…'

She was hypnotised. His face was so close. His eyes were upon hers, burning her heart with their intensity; his mouth was so near, so tantalisingly near!

Was she doing the right thing? It didn't *feel* wrong… but surely this couldn't end well? Whenever she thought everything was going right for her, the world would pull the rug from under her feet.

She wanted his kiss, though. It was the way she'd felt once before. But this time there wouldn't be anyone jetting off to another continent straight afterwards.

This time it wouldn't be a one-night stand. This would be something else. A couple reconnecting. A woman and a man who had already made a child together, who had been parted by geography and mileage, who could now be together. Who could be stepping towards the future together.

'But…' He reached up and threaded his fingers into her hair, his hands gently holding her face.

'But?'

'I don't want to ruin this friendship we're creating. I don't want to ruin it for Seb.'

'You won't.'

She looked deep into his blue eyes and saw his soul. He was a tortured man still. She could see that. Sense that. He carried pain within him, something he still hadn't shared with her, but she knew deep in her heart that if she just gave him some time, gave him some room to feel comfortable with her, then he would share it. And once he shared she could help him. She knew she could.

It was probably the lust talking, telling her it wasn't a problem, but she couldn't help it. Being this close to Jacob was electric.

How bad could it be? It wasn't as if he'd murdered anyone. He wasn't a bad guy. Something had hurt him. Something or someone had taken hold of his heart and crushed it.

Eva wondered if she could help him mend it. But what would happen if she did? If she let him in, if she started to care, then she would be taking a chance on him that she'd never, ever taken with anyone else. She would be opening herself up to being hurt again. There *was* that risk, wasn't there? Every other relationship in her past had failed. What would make this one so special?

But what if *this* was a relationship with the potential for something amazing?

That tantalising thought hypnotised her. Blindsided her doubt for a moment.

Jacob pulled her towards him.

Her body pressed up against his and then her eyes closed as her lips met his. Elation flooded her system with ripples and waves of intoxication as the reality of kissing Jacob again sank in.

Their shared kiss, though tender, opened up something inside her that she hadn't been expecting.

A fervour. A *need* that she'd never experienced with any man before.

She burned for him. Breathed him in. Melted into him as she felt his hands caress her and hold her against him. The solidness, the hardness of his male body against her soft femininity was a beautiful yin and yang.

The last time she'd kissed this man she'd lain naked in his arms and allowed herself to fly through the skies with him, soaring amongst the clouds and the heavens as he'd taken her to fever pitch and back again. Being in his arms again felt so *right*, and strangely so *familiar*—as if it had been seconds since they had last held her and not years. His lips were warm and soft against hers; his body was against hers... It made her come alive...

He pulled back to look at her with glazed eyes.

She had no doubt that she looked the same.

Eva touched her lips. 'Will you be with us at Christmas?'

'I'll need to see my family, too, but, yes... I'll be with you for Christmas.'

His family. The people she hadn't met yet. These strangers she would now have to share Seb with. Leave herself open to inspection from. It didn't seem too scary right now, with Jacob, but she was worried about what would happen later.

What would he be like with them? What did she know about him? Really?

Eva craved for all this to work out, but experience told her not to get her hopes up. She wanted not to be afraid. But she'd been hurt so many times before…

I want to be part of a family so much!

But did she dare hope she could actually have it?

Jacob had come back for the evening. They were sitting together in the lounge, whilst Seb played on the floor between them.

'I spoke to my parents again. Said we'd probably take Seb one day before Christmas.'

She frowned. 'Oh?'

Before Christmas? She only had one weekend free between now and Christmas, and spending it with a family she didn't know didn't sound very appealing. Besides, these people probably wouldn't even like her.

'Don't you want to take him on your own? I'm sure they don't want me hanging around—'

Jacob shook his head. 'It'll be fine!'

'No. It's probably best it's just you and Seb at first.'

'They'll want to meet you. I'd really like it, too, if you came. They're very friendly! If anyone is going to get questioned it'll be me. I'm the one who stayed away.'

She smiled at him. 'I know. It's just…difficult for me. Isn't it hard for you, too? You stayed away for a long time. Aren't you worried about going back?'

Jacob nodded. 'I am. There are lots of memories

there.' He thought for a moment, his eyes dark, and then he said, 'Someone I loved...she died.'

'I'm so sorry.'

'It's fine. I've accepted it now. That's the whole thing about going back. I need to face my demons over being there again.'

'And you don't want to go alone?'

'I could go alone...but I'd like you to be there. It's not just Seb who's a part of my family now. You are, too.'

She could feel her cheeks flame with heat. 'Really?'

'Really.' He laid his hand on hers.

'Thank you. Do you...want to tell me about her?'

He looked away. 'She was a childhood friend. Someone who came to mean a great deal to me.'

She nodded. It was understandable that he should have someone like this in his past. And now she could understand some of his reluctance to go back home. It had to be a past love. A love affair that somehow went wrong, perhaps.

A tinge of jealousy announced itself, but she pushed it away. She had no right to feel jealous about this.

But was he over this woman? She wasn't sure. Obviously the pain of loss was still there. She'd seen it in him before. The night they'd met.

They watched Seb play on the floor, silent for a moment, Eva sipping at her tea and Jacob looking back at her darkly, stuck in his memories of the past.

He was hurt. That much was clear. But surely he must have moved on? She didn't want to be his soft place to fall just because he was hurt—she wanted to be his because he wanted to be with *her*. Heart, soul—everything.

Anything less was too risky.

If she suspected he wasn't over this woman then she'd walk away from a relationship with him.

Why did he have to tell me about her? It was all going so well...

Eva needed certainty in her life. Needed security. If Jacob and events in his past somehow threatened that, then she'd separate herself from him immediately. Better to keep him at a distance until she knew for sure. Better to tread carefully.

It wasn't just about *her* anymore.

CHAPTER SIX

A WEEK LATER Jacob took them some Christmas lights. Small white fairy lights to hang outside, around the guttering and over the small fence in the front garden. Eva had told him she hadn't decorated the outside of her house as she hadn't felt safe going up a ladder on her own with just a three-year-old to steady it.

That morning frost had covered everything, making surfaces slippery, and as he worked he could see his breath billowing out around him and his fingertips turning redder and redder as they lost more and more feeling. The little plastic grips that would secure the lights along the guttering were fragile, and he lost more than he used as he tried to force them onto the edge.

But he didn't mind. He felt *useful*. The past few nights when he'd turned up to Eva's home he'd noticed that she was about the only person in the street with no Christmassy outdoor lights so he'd offered to do it, knowing Seb would like it, too.

Eva stood at the bottom of the ladder, holding it, looking up at him and laughing every time he cursed as another clip skittered away from his fingers and fell to the ground.

'Will I need to get you another packet?' she asked, laughing.

He grimaced as he forced another clip into position. 'Maybe. At this rate I might start suturing them on.'

The last clip went into place and he descended the ladder to collect the lights so that he could trail them across the front of the house.

'Can you believe people go through this madness every year?'

'Christmas is a time to make everyone happy, isn't it?'

He nodded. 'Kids, maybe.'

Eva frowned. Surely *he'd* had good Christmases? 'Is Christmas not a happy time for you?'

She seemed genuinely interested in his experiences. But he felt bad about talking about them. His child-hood Christmas memories were great, and he knew hers weren't. She was the one who'd been in foster care—not him. It was that one Christmas Eve he'd experienced five years ago that really bothered him.

'It wasn't for you.'

'My Christmases were…different. I ended up in so many places I lost track of all the varying traditions people had.'

'But were you happy?'

She shrugged. 'I never belonged. I always felt I was intruding on someone else's memories.'

Someone else's memories… No. He didn't want to mess with those.

'Christmas was just fine for me until a few years ago.'

He picked up the knot of fairy lights and began to untangle them, handing Eva one end so he didn't lose it.

'We made Seb on a Christmas Eve. That's a good memory, isn't it?'

His numb fingers stopped moving as he looked at her. She was bundled up tight in her winter coat, her red hair just peeking out from underneath her woolly hat, and her nose was bright pink over her thick, fluffy scarf. She looked like a model posing for a winter-clothing campaign, and he almost wanted to take a picture of her to capture the image.

'Yes. But Christmas Eve isn't all jolly excitement and meeting hot chicks at parties.'

She stared at him, amused. *'Hot chicks?'*

Jacob managed a smile. 'You *were*! I'd not expected to see anyone like you at that party. I hadn't gone looking for a one-night stand, you know.'

She looked about them to make sure there were no nosy neighbours listening in. 'I'm glad to hear it.'

'I was looking to…escape. Forget for a while.' Jacob pulled at more of the wire. 'What were *you* doing there? That night?'

'Well, I hadn't wanted to go, either, but decided to make the best of it once I got there. From what I remember, your eyes looked…sad.'

Jacob headed back up the ladder, so that she wouldn't see the look on his face. He didn't want to talk about Michelle right now. He didn't want to tell Eva about what had happened. Not yet. Not what he'd done. Because if he did then she might be horrified with him. She wouldn't see Jacob the doctor, father of her baby.

If he told her the truth she'd be appalled.

Because he'd killed a woman.

A woman he'd supposedly loved.

No one got to do that and then be entitled to happiness. This life—this chance with Eva and Seb—he *wanted* it, but he wasn't sure he'd be allowed to keep it if he told her the truth. What if he took *her* for granted, too? Or, worse still, Seb? What if they argued and she ran off? Or drove off and…?

The thought of Michelle's blood in the snow smacked him straight between the eyes.

'That someone special I told you about…she died on Christmas Eve. Each time it rolls around I tend to think about it. That night we met, the party was a great excuse for me to say goodbye to a few friends and hopefully forget for a while.'

'Did it work?'

He looked down at her from his perch atop the ladder. 'It did. I met *you*.'

Eva looked up at him and felt her heart flutter in her chest. He'd met her on the anniversary of this woman's death, and though he'd been hurt, though he'd been pained by the day, she had helped manage to soothe him—if only for a short while.

She'd always known she'd seen something in his gaze that night—before she'd spoken to him, before they'd got close. He'd been grieving! It seemed so obvious now. And they'd made something beautiful out of something painful.

They'd made Seb. And here they were, years later, together. Who knew how it would end?

She hoped it wouldn't.

The days running up to Christmas began to pass much too quickly.

Jacob spent as much time as he could at Eva's—playing with Seb, having dinner with them and then reading Seb his bedtime story. He also took him out for walks on his own.

Eva began to learn more about the father of her child—he liked reading and photography, and had taken loads of photographs in Africa, some of which she thought he should enter into competitions, they were that good. And she learned about the work he'd done in Africa—first in an eye clinic, saving the sight of thousands by performing simple cataract operations, and then he'd helped build a new school.

He was certainly handy around the house. The dripping tap in her kitchen had been fixed, and he'd shaved a few inches off a door that had never shut properly and he'd even offered to help repaint a room.

But she was wary of taking advantage of him. Of letting things move too fast. He was there for Seb, after all, not her—though they were getting along well as a unit, and she couldn't help but notice how attractive he still was to her.

Since that kiss after their shopping expedition she'd felt torn about experiencing it again. She wanted to. Very much! But she was afraid of what would happen if she did. Too many times she'd thought she could have something and keep it forever, and it would always be torn from her grasp.

It was difficult to concentrate sometimes, with him in the house. He'd be reading to her son, lying on Seb's bed with his arm wrapped around him, and she would watch them from the doorway and marvel at how homely it looked and how it made her feel all warm inside and safe. But then he'd come downstairs and put his coat on to leave, and there'd be that awkward moment at the door, when he'd kiss her goodbye on the cheek and then look longingly at her, as if he wanted to do more.

She'd been keeping him at arm's length. Trying not to let herself get carried away by his being there and the thrill of the season. Letting him know, subtly, that she wasn't rushing into anything. Believing that if she kept him at a distance she'd be able to stop the pain before it came if anything went wrong—that somehow it wouldn't hurt as much.

But it didn't stop her yearning for another proper kiss. She could feel the tingle in her lips at the idea each time he came round, wondering if maybe today he might kiss her again, but Jacob seemed determined to respect her boundaries.

And still Eva was determined to crack his exterior. To delve deep inside this man who had fathered her child and find out more about his past. She wanted to understand him. Know the pain that he carried. Because if she did then she would know if she and Seb were safe from being left behind. She wanted to know about Jacob, and the fact that she didn't know him as well as she could frustrated her.

Perhaps if she did go and meet his family then it might provide her with the opportunity she needed.

Jacob was sitting next to her on the couch. Wine had been poured and the fairy lights twinkled outside the window and, in the corner of the room, twisted around the Christmas tree.

The television had been turned off. It was just the two of them. Seb was fast asleep upstairs.

'I'm glad you came back from Africa when you did, Jacob.'

'So am I.'

'I was terrified, you know—at first, when I saw you standing in Minors that day. All I could think of was how was I going to tell you about Seb.'

He smiled at her. 'You managed it.'

Eva laughed and sipped her wine. 'Just about. What was it that made you come back? From Africa? Did something happen? To make you come?'

She watched as his blue eyes darkened.

'Something. *Someone*, actually. You have to understand I met a lot of patients over there. Heard a lot of sad stories. The people there were brave. Proud. Each one touched my heart, day after day, but there was this one story that I just couldn't get out of my head.'

'What was it?'

Jacob poured more wine into their glasses and put the bottle back on the table.

'This man brought his wife into the hospital. His name was Reuben and he was in his seventies. You could see the *life* in his face. The wisdom and the pain etched into every line. But he held himself tall and proud. His wife was dying of malaria and we watched her fade every day for about a week.'

Eva listened intently.

'Reuben told me that he'd met his wife, Zuri, when they were teenagers. They'd fallen in love, but Reuben's family had arranged a marriage for him to another woman and they forbade him from seeing Zuri. It broke his heart, but he had to do what his father ordered. He married this other woman and they had children and he said it was a good life, if not a loving one. His wife died when Reuben turned seventy, and he thought that was it for him. That he would die lonely because his children had all grown up and flown the nest. Until he met Zuri again in the market.'

Jacob smiled.

Eva smiled, too.

'Zuri had lost her husband long before. She had been unable to bear children and he had walked out on her. She'd been alone for years. But Zuri and Reuben got together and married within weeks of meeting each other again. They'd been married only three months when he carried her into my hospital, exhausted and spent. When Zuri died, just a week later, Reuben stood with me at her funeral, and he turned to me and thanked me. He said that life was short and that if I had any loved ones at home then I should return and be with them. Because you never knew when life could take them away from you.'

'Poor Reuben.'

'He told me those three months with Zuri had been the happiest of his entire life. His story stuck with me... eating away at me. I kept thinking about Reuben for months afterwards. The twists and turns of his life. How he'd ended up with the one woman he should have been with from the beginning. How he'd known it was special with her. How the short time he'd had with Zuri was the happiest he'd ever had. I kept thinking of you. Of the night we met. How it had felt...special. How you'd made me feel. I wanted to come back and find you. Tell you. See if there was something we could make of that connection we'd felt.'

Eva nodded. 'Because life is short?'

'Exactly.'

He reached up to stroke her face and she leaned into his hand. His gaze was intense as he focused on his fingers, tracing her jawline and then moving down her neck, over the pulse point there that was throbbing madly and down to the neckline of her top. As her pulse accelerated his hand dropped away and he looked up at her, suddenly uncomfortable.

'What is it?'

'Nothing.'

'There's something, Jacob. Please…please tell me. It could help.'

He still looked at her, uncertainty in his eyes.

She could tell that he wanted to say something but was afraid to. *Why?* Surely he trusted her? Had he done something terrible? Because if he had then she needed to know. Not just for her, but for Seb, too. She had to know who she was getting involved with. It was the only way to protect her own heart.

'I *want* to tell you…'

She reached over and took his hand in hers, cradling his fingers with her own, wrapping her hand over his. 'You can.'

'I've never spoken of this to anyone.'

'Then, it's time. If you keep pain inside it eats you alive, Jacob. You can't live with pain all the time. You know what they say about a problem shared?'

He squeezed her fingers. 'It's a problem halved?'

'That's right.'

He let out a big sigh and then nodded. 'A year to the day before I met you was supposed to be my wedding day.'

Eva tried not to show surprise. 'Okay…'

He let out another breath. It was clearly getting easier to say the more he spoke. 'I was getting married to Michelle. She was a childhood friend. She lived next door

to my parents' smallholding and we grew up together...
and then we became something more.'

Eva tried to imagine him with someone else. Loving
another woman intensely enough to want to marry her.
The idea of it made her feel uncomfortable.

'You loved her?'

He nodded. 'Yes. I thought so anyway.'

Eva frowned and took a sip of her drink.

'I proposed and we set a date. December the twenty-
fourth. It seemed romantic. We'd hoped for snow and
we got it, too. For the first time in years it came down
quite thick. It had been raining the previous day, so no
one thought it would settle, but it did. It made everything look beautiful.'

She could picture it in her head. 'I can imagine.'

'I was at the church, waiting. You know how brides
are meant to be late? Well, I waited outside for her to
arrive, thinking I'd head into the church when I saw
the bridal car. She was a bit late, but I thought that was
because she was getting ready on her own. She didn't
have a father or any brothers to give her away. She was
going to walk up the aisle alone.'

Eva sipped her wine. It all sounded lovely so far. But
she knew something was coming. Something bad. She
could tell from the way he was telling the story. The
fact that he'd never spoken of this. She could hear it in
his voice. See the pain in his eyes. The same look he'd
had four years ago, when she'd met him at that party.

He looked away. 'She never made it.'

'How do you mean?'

'She was hit by a heavy-goods vehicle. Side impact
on black ice. She wasn't wearing a seat belt and she was

thrown from the spinning vehicle. She died on the tarmac, bleeding into the snow.'

Eva covered her face with her hands. How awful! 'Oh, Jacob, I'm *so* sorry!' No wonder he hadn't wanted to speak of this! His bride…? Dying on their wedding day…?

He wouldn't meet her gaze. He just stared at the carpet.

Now she understood. Now she understood the look that had been in his eyes at the party. The most horrific thing had happened to him. Of *course* she could understand it now. Understand why he had kept this in for so long.

But she was glad that he'd felt able to tell her. To confide in her. It meant something. That they were getting closer. That he trusted her with this information.

It all made such sense. His childhood friend, this Michelle, a woman he'd grown up with. A longtime friendship becoming something more, something more intense. Love. Commitment. And he'd lost her on what should have been the happiest day of his life!

She wondered briefly what Michelle had been like. The woman who had been Jacob's friend…who had become his love. What hopes and dreams had she had about their married life together? She would have got ready that morning, ready for church, for her wedding— and how happy she must have been.

Now Eva understood why he didn't look forward to Christmas. Why it held bad memories for him.

'Perhaps now…with us…Christmas can become a good time for you again?'

He looked at her. 'I hope so.'

'Thank you for telling me, Jacob. I know it must have

hurt.' She squeezed his fingers. 'I really feel we can move forward now. I'd like to go with you to your parents' place.'

Though she still felt nervous about it—and would continue to until they'd been. Until she'd seen how his family were with her. But if Jacob could make this huge step forward by confiding in her, then she could do this for him. It would help him. Her, too. And it would give her the opportunity to learn more about this man she wanted to trust implicitly.

Jacob focused on her as she spoke, nodding. 'I'd like that. So would they.'

He continued to stare at her and she stared back. They were so close to each other on the couch. Their legs had been touching the entire time Jacob had been speaking and while they'd sipped at their drinks.

She hoped that now he had started to open up about himself he would continue to do so. Perhaps back at his childhood home, confronting old memories, he would do so. She could learn more about him. About Michelle.

What if he still loves her?

The horrible thought impeded on her warm feeling inside and she tried to crush it down. Ignore the fact that she'd thought it. But the more she tried to ignore it, the stronger it seemed to get.

Jacob had had the love of his life ripped from him! It wasn't a love that had slowly died. It hadn't ebbed away with the years. She hadn't cheated on him.

She'd *died*!

He *had* to still love her!

And if he loved a dead woman how could they ever truly be together? She wasn't going to try to compete with a ghost.

She couldn't afford to get involved with him. She couldn't risk her relationship with him. It would end badly.

Perhaps it would be best if she kept her distance from him until he'd sorted out the feelings he still had.

She looked down at his lips, at his smooth mouth amongst the small forest of stubble that grew around his jaw. A small scar marked a brief valley on his chin. How had he got that? Shaving? A boyhood accident?

What if he *wasn't* still in love with Michelle?

Would she be risking ruining their relationship by creating distance between them when she didn't need to? Would she be fulfilling her own prophecy by keeping him at arm's length?

Life is too hard!

Her gaze went back to his lips. Then to his eyes. He was looking at her so intently. All she had to do was lean closer, close the gap, close her eyes and then he would be hers...

Eva stood up abruptly, placing her wine glass on the table. 'It's nearly time for you to go.'

'Of course.'

This was best. To have the distance they both needed. *It's the right thing to do.*

So why did it hurt? Why did she want him to stay? Because if he stayed who knew where it might lead?

It was best this way. He was clearly still grieving— he was the last person she should be letting herself get involved with right now. She knew that.

He nodded and grabbed his jacket, pecked her on the cheek and headed into the hallway. She heard the front door open and close.

She pressed her hand to her cheek. The warmth from his lips was fading away.

It felt awful to create space between them, but it was the best thing to do.

The house was normally quiet when she woke up in the morning, and she could sit and read a newspaper quietly with a cup of coffee before Seb came bouncing down the stairs, full of life and noise.

But this Saturday morning Jacob had arrived early, and the smell of frying bacon filled the house, causing her to salivate. Even though she didn't normally eat fried breakfasts—she was a cereal and half a grapefruit kind of girl—she wolfed down bacon, two sausages, scrambled eggs and toast.

Jacob was a good cook, and Seb was enjoying having his father around for breakfast.

They could talk to each other for hours, and Eva had often found herself having to grab a book and go off and read somewhere while Seb got to know his father. It was only fair after all. They had three years to catch up on, and Eva no longer felt as if she was being left out.

Jacob had learned that Seb enjoyed nursery, loved sport and animals and wanted to be a doctor one day, like his parents. Seb was also hoping for snow on Christmas Day. Lots and lots of snow. And Seb had learned that his dad had gone on safari and met a real-life leopard, seen a lion pride and even been charged at by an elephant.

It was only as they talked, as they chatted, that Eva realised they were so alike in their mannerisms. Why had she not realised that Seb rubbed at his chin when he was thinking, the same way Jacob did? Why had she not noticed that that they both stuck out their tongues slightly when they were concentrating?

Silly things. Inconsequential things. But everything she noticed was amusing and quaint. Familiar. Things *she* didn't do but Seb did. Why had she never wondered if they were traits from his father?

Jacob was clearing away their greasy, tomato ketchup–smeared plates when he asked Seb a question. 'Seb, do you remember I told that you my parents have a small farm with lots of animals?'

'Yeah,' Seb answered.

'Well, your mum and I have been thinking, and we thought you might like to visit there today. Stay the night. Get to know your grandparents and see the animals.'

Eva nodded as Seb looked to her, as if for permission. She was pleased that she'd agreed to take this step. But it was a huge about-turn for her. The idea of meeting Jacob's family had at first been scary. She'd never wanted to stand in front of strangers and be judged again. But since Jacob's revelations about Michelle, and with the way their relationship was developing, she'd begun to accept that this was the right thing to do. Especially for Seb. These people she didn't yet know were his family, and whether she and Jacob became something or not his family would always be there for her son.

This was an opportunity that she had never had. It was an enormous step forward for them both.

'Can we?'

'Course we can.'

Seb beamed a smile at them both. 'Cool!'

'We'll need our wellies!'

Eva was still anxious at the thought of meeting

Jacob's parents. Even though he'd told her they were nice and friendly. They would assess her.

But she had to remind herself that she was an adult now—not a child. If Jacob's parents and family didn't like her, it didn't matter too much. What mattered most of all was that they knew Seb and adored him. If they didn't like *him*... Not possible! Of *course* they would love Seb. They *had* to.

So she was off to the Dolan smallholding. Where everyone who had no right to judge her lived. Perhaps Jacob was pleased she was going because then his parents wouldn't be able to have a go at *him*?

This weekend was going to be truly uncomfortable for her. Jacob had apparently already told them that they'd need separate beds...

Going to meet a new family again... How many times had she done *that*? Stood outside on the pavement, by a social worker's car, whilst a new family came out to greet her. Assess her. Judge her worth.

They'd all be looking at her. Deciding if they liked her or not. Deciding if she was worth keeping.

It shouldn't matter what they think. I am part of their family now. Because of Seb.

But it did matter.

It mattered a lot. She *wanted* them to like her. She *wanted* to be accepted. She really wanted to be welcomed into the Dolan family.

It was a two-hour car journey that became nearly four. Everyone was driving slowly and more carefully due to the ice still on the roads.

Eva sat in the front seat as Jacob drove them in his sleek black car, with her stomach knotting with nerves at every mile. Jolly Christmas music played over the car stereo—music that she would normally sing along to. But not today. She was a bag of nerves—as jittery and shaky as a naked person in the Arctic.

The last time she'd felt this nervous she had been taking the pregnancy test. Her stomach was clenched tight, her mouth was so dry she could barely speak and she had to keep stretching out her fingers to prevent cramp as she was clasping them so tightly.

And to think I thought I was being relaxed about this!

Outside, the world was doing just fine. Only a week to Christmas and it was a beautiful, crisp winter's day, with blue skies and bright sunshine. They passed fields of grazing horses and cattle or sheep as Jacob drove them down winding lanes through the countryside. There were some flowers growing at the roadside that she'd never seen before. Winter honeysuckle? She wasn't sure. She'd never been green-fingered.

It all looked so beautiful and serene, but as they passed a sign for Netherfield Village—the place where his parents' smallholding was meant to be—she could almost feel her blood pressure rising all by itself. The village was picture-postcard perfect. Literally, she could have taken a photo of its village square and used it as a Christmas card. It was sickeningly beautiful. The type of place you wanted to move to the second you saw it.

Jacob seemed nervous, too, as he drove. He was going home to his family, but he seemed edgy. She supposed that was to be expected. He'd been away from home for years. And he knew that by going back he'd be facing old, painful memories. She was proud of him for doing it, and pleased that he was able to do it with her at his side.

Her stomach rolled as she thought about how she'd kept his parents' grandson from them. Not deliberately— but would they readily accept the fact that she'd not been able to find Jacob? If they were going to have a go at her she hoped they'd do so out of Seb's eyeline and earshot.

She hadn't kept their grandson from them on purpose. They'd lost three years of their grandchild's life. Three years that they'd never get back. Three years of memories and photos and home videos that didn't exist because she'd not persevered in finding their son.

Had she given up too easily?

No. I tried my best.

The thought of meeting them filled her with nerves, and though the fried breakfast had seemed a wonderful idea a few hours ago she could feel it sitting heavily in her stomach now, the grease swirling around inside her like an oily whirlpool, making her feel extremely queasy.

'Nearly there now, Seb!' Jacob called over his shoulder to his son.

'Great!'

Seb leaned forward in his booster seat and looked between the two front seats through the windscreen as Jacob steered his car through the quaint village, past a pub called The Three Horseshoes, a post office, a grocery store, some quaint thatched cottages and then down another lane.

'There's the alpacas!'

'Wow!' Seb exclaimed from the backseat.

Jacob laughed. 'We keep them in the fields where we have the chickens and the geese and ducks. They keep away the foxes and my mum uses their fur to make quilts and baby blankets.'

'They keep away foxes? What? Like guard dogs?' Eva enquired.

'Exactly.'

Seb wound down his window for a better look, letting in a blast of cold air. 'They're funny!'

Eva smiled at his amusement. They were close now, and she could feel Jacob's apprehension building.

Just past the alpaca field he turned into a smaller lane, with lots of lumps and bumps. The car jolted them around as its suspension system struggled with the holey road, but then they were pulling up in front of a redbrick farmhouse with window boxes and a border collie dog lying outside, panting heavily, its breath fogging in the chill air.

'That's Lucy,' Jacob said. 'Come on, Seb! I'll introduce you!'

Father and son got out of the car and had gone over to the happy dog, making a big fuss of it, before Eva could even remove her seat belt. The dog wagged its tail madly at Jacob and lasciviously licked at Seb's happy face.

Eva took that moment to look around her.

To the side of the house there was a rotary washing line, empty and frosted, there were plant pots and tubs filled to overflowing with winter bulbs and early crocus and there were blue gingham curtains at the windows, tied back with sashing.

Eva almost expected to see a hot apple pie cooling on a windowsill!

There was a ginger cat curled up on an outdoor chair in the winter sun, and it opened a lazy eye as she closed the car door and blinked in the bright sunshine.

With the rolling fields set as a backdrop to the old redbrick house, the place was beautiful!

Seb and Jacob were still ruffling the dog's fur, Seb beaming, when the front door opened and Jacob's parents emerged from inside the house.

Eva felt her hesitant smile freeze on her face at their appearance. This was it. The moment she'd been worrying about. She looked to Jacob to see how he'd react, and saw him stand back and stare at his parents, a half smile on his face.

They stared at each other for a moment. Eva could see that Jacob's mum was dying for her son to speak, but Jacob seemed incapable of saying anything.

Needing to break the tension, Eva stepped forward, away from the car. 'Mrs Dolan?'

His mother turned.

Her son looked so like her. Jacob's mother was tall and slim and had the same dark colouring, though her hair had a grey streak in the centre, but his father was already grey haired and slightly plumper.

And they were both smiling.

'Eva!' Mrs Dolan stepped towards her and embraced her firmly, pulling her into a bear hug she couldn't escape from. 'You must be tired from your journey. We were expecting you hours ago! Come on in! We've got freshly baked biscuits and mince pies inside, and a fresh pot of tea.'

She released her and beamed a smile at her.

Eva was delighted. 'Er...lovely... Thank you.'

This was more like it! Eva felt instantly accepted! Where had *this* sensation been as a child? Where had the warm bear hugs been then? Where had the home-baked biscuits and the welcome and the *acceptance* been?

'Jacob!'

Jacob's mother pulled him to her, squeezing him tight,

as if she never wanted to let him go, and then she kissed him on both cheeks and looked at him for a long time, her hands cradling his face.

'You've come *home*! You've changed…'

Then she turned to Seb and pulled him into a hug.

'And you must be Seb! We've been *so* looking forward to meeting you!'

Jacob looked relieved and managed to smile fully at last.

Jacob's father walked over and gave him a hug and a quick back slap. Then they stepped apart.

'Hi, Dad.'

'Son… Good-looking boy you've got there!'

Once Seb had stopped ruffling the dog's fur and rubbing its belly, they stepped into the farmhouse. The front door took them straight into the kitchen, which was made up of old wooden units, with dried flowers and copper-bottomed pots hanging from a rack above. There were two metallic strips on the walls, holding a line of knives and shiny utensils, and in the centre of the kitchen a huge oak table that had been laid for guests.

Candy-cane bunting decorated the walls and a huge spray of holly erupted from the vast copper pot set in the fireplace. Christmas cards lined every available surface. Clearly the Dolans were very popular people!

A vase in the centre of the table held a beautiful bouquet of pine stems, interspersed with cinnamon sticks and dried orange slices. Unusual, but very aromatic, and around it were the promised plates of pies and biscuits. A hot teapot with a knitted Christmas-bauble cosy sat at one end, where Jacob's mother now stood.

'Do sit down, everyone—and help yourself.'

Seb tucked in with gusto—which was surprising,

considering the size of his breakfast—whereas Jacob took nothing, only accepting a mug of tea. Eva noticed that Jacob's gaze kept flicking to a photograph on the mantelpiece that looked like a picture of him with a blonde woman.

Michelle?

In the picture Jacob sat with his arm around the woman's shoulders as they both posed on what looked like an old country stile. She had long honey-coloured hair, almost down to her waist, and they had their heads together, grinning for the camera.

She had clearly been cherished. And was obviously much remembered, with her picture having pride of place in one of the main rooms of this home.

Eva accepted tea and politely took a biscuit, wondering if the Dolans would ever put *her* picture up? She hoped so. It had started well, so far…

'It's so wonderful to meet you at last, Seb,' Mrs Dolan said. 'Your daddy has told us so much about you. Are you looking forward to Christmas?'

Seb nodded, his mouth full of mince pie.

She smiled broadly. 'We hear you like animals?'

Seb nodded again, stuffing in another mouthful.

'We'll take you out later and show you them all, and then you must visit the orchard. It's where your father used to play.'

Seb looked at his dad and grinned.

Jacob smiled back. 'It's also where I first broke my arm, trying to jump the small stream that's there, so try not to be *too* like me. We don't need to take you to A&E again.'

Mrs Dolan took a biscuit for herself. 'Of course! You

had an accident, didn't you? Bumped your head? Were you scared, Seb?'

'A bit…'

Mrs Dolan looked up at her son, then at Eva. 'You're both at the same casualty department, aren't you?'

Eva nodded and smiled. This was so *odd*! They were talking to her as if everything was normal. As if she was *wanted* there. It felt great!

'We've been here in this house forever, it seems. Ever since Jacob was a little boy himself. A bit younger than you, Seb. You must get him to show you the tree where he carved his name.'

'If I can still remember which tree it is.'

'Of *course* you remember. You might not have been here for a while, but you know this place like the back of your hand.'

'You mentioned an orchard, Mrs Dolan? What do you grow there?' Eva ventured her first question, feeling her cheeks flame with heat as everyone turned to face her at the table.

'Bits of everything, really. Apples, pears, greengages, plums—you name it, we've got pies made of it in the freezer! In the spring it looks amazing, when it's all in blossom. And you must call me Molly, dear. Mrs Dolan makes me sound like my mother-in-law!'

Molly Dolan smiled and her whole face creased with delight and happiness.

These people were being *nice* to her! It seemed so strange! It wasn't what she'd been expecting from them at all! A childish delight was filling her on the inside as she soaked up their warmth.

'I'll show you around,' Jacob suggested. 'Fancy a walk? Stretch the legs?'

'Oh, finish your tea first!' Molly urged. 'Always in a rush to get away, Jacob. You've only just got in and sat down.'

'We've been sat down for nearly four hours, Mum. In the car.'

'But Eva needs time to absorb everything. This is all new for her.' She turned to Eva. 'He's always the same when he gets here. It's as if he can't wait to shrug off the city—he has to go out and roam around the place and get the country back into his blood. How he got any work done in Africa, I'll never know.'

She'd mentioned Africa. Jacob's bolthole. But she hadn't mentioned it with any discomfort. She'd not said it as a preamble for launching into a round of questions for her son. She looked as if she was comfortable sitting and waiting until Jacob was ready to talk about it.

Eva sipped her tea. It was perfect. Not too strong. And as she looked across the table at Jacob she began to understand him a bit more. He had a lovely family. Warm, welcoming parents. And he was clearly loved.

Maybe she would be, too?

Eva and Jacob were strolling through the orchard. Seb was with his grandfather, learning the whistles that were used to control the sheepdog, and they could hear them faintly in the distance.

The sun was shining down brightly, but there was no warmth in the cold air and Eva was glad she'd chosen a long coat, hat and scarf. She could feel the sun on her face only barely, and her toes were going numb with cold. It was a strange feeling. But it didn't bother her too much.

She loved the winter. The shortening of the days, getting cosy in front of a fire at night, drinking hot cocoa and being warm and dry inside whilst outside the weather was doing its worst. Wondering when it might snow...

This was the first opportunity she'd had in ages to enjoy the season. She'd been working so much just lately, and had been covering extra shifts until Jacob's arrival. It always got busier towards Christmas in A&E. People and alcohol didn't always mix well, and there was a reason it was called the 'silly season'. There weren't often moments when she could feel carefree and relaxed, and this was a bonus.

All those hours spent worrying in the car... Wasted! She could have sung along to those Christmas songs after all. Mr and Mrs Dolan were lovely. And now she was here, at Jacob's home, with him walking alongside her.

It was hard not to keep stealing glances at him, wondering how he was doing being back here, surrounded by memories. She was enjoying the warmth of his family and feeling she belonged.

'It's very beautiful here, Jacob.'

He nodded and smiled at her. They were walking at a slow pace, with no apparent direction. Just ambling together through the trees.

'You have a wonderful family.' It was true. 'The type I used to dream of having.'

'Thank you.'

She looked directly at him and stopped walking. 'Can I ask something?'

He nodded, squinting at her in the winter sunlight. 'Sure.'

'Why did you have no contact with them? They clearly love you. Care for you. I can understand how you didn't want to be facing old memories by *being* here, but why didn't you keep in contact with them?'

He stopped walking and faced her. They were in a bit of a glade, surrounded by bare, knobbly trees. A robin chirped near them, singing its melody to mark its territory for any other robin that might be listening. It was a happy sound.

He sighed, looking about him. 'It's difficult to say. I know they love me—and please don't think that I take that for granted. I don't. It's just…I knew what it would be like after my wedding day. After Michelle died. They'd look at me with pity, and they'd want to support me and look after me, and I just felt that I didn't deserve it.'

'I don't understand. *Why* didn't you deserve it?'

'It was my fault she died.'

'But you weren't driving that truck that hit her. You couldn't have known that would happen.'

'I know, but…' He trailed off and stuck his hands into his pockets, obviously wrestling with telling her more.

Why wouldn't he say it? Did he not trust her enough yet? Or—her heart sank—perhaps he didn't want to say it because he knew the admission would hurt her.

He still loves Michelle.

'I can't tell you.' He shook his head.

Her worst fears were realised. He still had feelings for his dead fiancée! That *had* to be it. It couldn't be anything else. It was the only thing she could think of that would stop him from confiding in her.

The knowledge of what he was hiding pained her like a punch in the gut. Trying to be brave, trying not to show how much the realisation hurt, she decided to be magnanimous. She would still be his friend, and she was here to help him get through his memories.

'You've made a big step forward by coming here today. You should be proud.' Her voice almost broke as she thought about how she would have to step back from him.

'The place reminds me so much of Michelle…'

As he looked about him Eva tried hard not to show how much his words hurt.

'We played here.' He gestured at the ground. 'Right in this spot. That tree over there… We climbed it. Many times. Tried to build a tree house in it. That small stream… That was where we built the rope swing. And inside the house in every room there's a reminder of her.'

Of course there is! I should never have come today. I could never compete with her memory.

'I saw the picture on the mantel. Is that her?'

He nodded.

'She was very beautiful.'

'She was.'

'What happened to you after she died?'

He let out a big sigh. 'I shut down. I couldn't face anyone. I couldn't bear their sympathy and their pity. I headed up north. Went to Scotland. Somehow managed to find a B & B that had a room and spent the New Year there. Then I just wandered around, basically, though I came back for the funeral.'

She swallowed a painful lump in her throat, realising the depth of his feelings for Michelle. She couldn't compete with this kind of love.

'That must have been difficult.'

'It was. I didn't want to see anyone. Didn't want their words of comfort. Michelle was dead because of *me*.

Her mother was alone, crying, her heart in pieces, because of *me*.'

'I've told you—it wasn't your fault Michelle's car got hit.'

'Wasn't it?'

His eyes had darkened and the mood had shifted. She could tell he still had a lot of pent-up feelings about what had happened.

'No. It wasn't. Jacob…' She stood in front of him and took his gloved hands in hers. The sun was shining into her eyes and she was having to squint to see, but she could see his tortured face in front of her. 'What happened to Michelle *wasn't* your fault. You've got to let go of that thought. Stop running from it.'

'That's the problem with running. You take your problems with you. They're still in your head.'

'I know. When Seb was born I felt so much guilt. Guilt that he didn't have a father, as I hadn't had a father. Guilt that he didn't have a family around him, the way children should. And even though I did what I could to be a dad as well as a mum, I carried that guilt around with me like a millstone. It's still there. I still feel it even though you're here now. I still worry. What if you leave? What if you're not ready? I've let you in, I've let Seb get to know you and love you, and yet you could still leave. I know what it feels like to lug heavy thoughts around.'

He squeezed her fingers and lifted them to his lips, kissing her hands. 'I won't leave.'

Mesmerised by the action, wanting more than she knew he could give, she looked up into his eyes. 'You won't?'

He shook his head. 'No. I couldn't. Not now.'

'You'll stay for Seb?'

I know he's not staying for me.

He released her hands and stroked her face. 'I'll stay for you both.'

He lowered his head to hers to kiss her, checking her reaction for any sign that she might refuse him—checking that she welcomed his kiss.

Oh, she welcomed it! Wanted it. Wanted *him*! Despite her fears, despite her worries, she embraced the warmth of his soft lips as if it was the last kiss she would ever have from him.

It was bittersweet. Knowing now how he felt about Michelle, she accepted that she would have to take a step back from him. Just let he and Seb be close. There was no room in his heart for *her*, too. Not now. He was a man wrapped up in the past, tethered by his pain to a ghost.

His lips claimed hers, and as his tongue hesitantly entered her mouth and licked her own she almost groaned with wishful yearning and grief for her loss of him.

The orchard was forgotten. Netherfield Village. The house. Jacob's family was forgotten. Here beneath the weak winter sun, in Jacob's arms, was exactly where she should be. But her heart was pained. She knew she couldn't have him. This might be their final kiss. The end of their romance.

'Eva…I'm so glad I met you.'

Eva took a step back—away from his arms, away from what she wanted. Breaking contact, she managed a weak smile. 'I know. Me, too. But…I'm not sure I'm ready for this. And to tell you the truth I'm not sure that *you're* ready for this, either.'

He frowned as the sun shone down on his dark hair, and she couldn't help but notice how delicious he looked in his jeans and boots and a heavy black jacket. Still tanned and healthy from his African adventure.

She sidestepped a snail that had not yet made it into hibernation, unwilling to ruin another life as she moved farther away from Jacob.

'We both made our choices in the past, but it was easier to do so then. It was just us. Me alone. You alone. But now we have Seb, and we have to make the right decisions. The right *choices*. So we'll get it right for *him*.'

He nodded, studying her face, clearly hurt by her words. She watched him look at her, no doubt noticing the smattering of freckles that she could never quite hide with make-up, the way her mouth was curved into a false smile. He'd focused on her lips...

'We should get through Christmas and then...start making some decisions,' she said.

Jacob nodded. 'Okay. I'll ask Dr Clarkson if there's a chance to extend my contract.'

'Right. Okay.'

'And what should we tell Seb? Do we tell him we're together or...? Kids are perceptive. Do we say anything at all?'

She didn't want to tell Seb anything! Why would she risk devastating her son? She would die before she let that happen!

'I think we should keep quiet for a while. We can discuss what's happening later.'

'Later?'

'When you've worked through everything. When you're finally...free.'

He looked at her and slowly nodded. And she knew that he could see she was putting the brakes on their relationship.

* * *

Seb was out exploring the farm with Jacob and his dad, and Eva was in the farmhouse kitchen with his mother, helping her to clear up. There was an easy atmosphere between them and they worked well together—Molly wiping down the kitchen surfaces as Eva dried the dishes and put them away.

They'd had a lovely home-made soup for lunch—carrot with coriander that had been grown by the Dolans—accompanied by Molly's rustic bread rolls, filled with sun-dried tomato and onion seeds, which had taken the simple meal to another level. Now she was sated.

If I were a cat, I'd be curled up in front of the Aga.

Eva put the last of the dishes away, folded the tea towel and stood by the kitchen window. Looking out, she could see Seb and Jacob, chasing each other in the grounds, and she smiled.

Molly came to stand next to her. 'I never thought I'd see the day.'

'Me, neither.'

'Jacob…here…back on the farm. With his family. Where he's meant to be. It's going to make this Christmas really special, having him back.'

Eva glanced at the older woman and saw a sadness in her eyes she'd never noticed before. Was it sadness at not having known about Seb? Was this going to be it? The moment Jacob's parents told her how they really felt about missing out on their grandchild? Was this the point when the nice family turned on her?

'I'm so sorry, Molly.'

'What for, dear?'

'For not persevering in trying to find Jacob—or any

of you—to tell you about Seb. If you're mad at me, I'll totally understand—'

Molly turned to look at her in shock. 'We're not *mad* at you! Oh, my dear, we couldn't be happier! All right, we missed out on Seb's early years and we'll never get those back, but you've given us the greatest gift in Seb, and because of him we've got our Jacob back.' She patted Eva's arm. 'Sit with me. I want to tell you something.'

They sat down together at the broad oak table.

'We never thought we'd see Jacob again after what happened—' She stopped short, clearly unsure as to whether to say anything more, glancing over to the picture on the mantel.

'I know about Michelle.'

Molly nodded gratefully. 'I didn't want to say anything unless he'd told you. Michelle was a wonderful girl. She was lovely and she and Jacob made a happy couple. She grew up next door and was always in and out of our house. She never had any siblings, and we used to think she enjoyed all the family chaos she found here. It wasn't till later we realised it was all because of her feelings for Jacob. She seemed so carefree and full of life, and we were all surprised when she became a trainee barrister—it all seemed so very serious for such a sweet girl. When they got engaged our Jacob was head over heels in love. It looked like his life was becoming sorted. A doctor…engaged to be married… The future looked great for them both. When they set a date for the wedding we were all so happy for them. Our son was going to be settled and we wouldn't have to worry about him anymore.'

It was painful to listen to, but Eva could picture it all too well. 'But then she died…'

'Then she died,' Molly repeated, nodding her head softly. 'We were all devastated—most especially her mother. I did what I could to help her through it, but Jacob just disappeared. We were *so* worried. Frantic! We didn't know where he'd gone.'

'Grief does strange things to people.'

Her eyes went dark. 'It does. I've seen it. I never thought we'd get back the Jacob that we know and love so much, but here he is, with a son of his own, and he's smiling again. We have *you* to thank for that, Eva. We can never thank you enough.'

Molly took Eva's hands in her own and held them tightly, squeezing hard.

Eva smiled back, and then gave Molly a hug. Was this what it was like to be hugged by a mum? It felt so good, and Molly was so soft and warm and welcoming. A part of her didn't want to let Molly go!

Tears painfully pricked her eyes at this feeling of being so near, yet so far. Of almost having become a part of the only family that had ever welcomed her.

The next day they all sat down to a hearty breakfast together, though Eva didn't eat much after a sleepless night. Molly stood over the cooker, making a full English breakfast, wearing a flowery apron and beaming at them all like the cat that had got the cream.

Eva could see why she was so happy. She not only had her son back within the fold of her family, but a new grandson, too.

Jacob suggested they might go for a walk into the village and have a look around before lunch.

Molly thought that was a great idea. 'We'll come, too!

We could have lunch at The Three Horseshoes before you have to go home.'

They all set off, wrapped up in their winter coats, with Seb splashing through ice-covered puddles and making a nice muddy mess of his trousers.

As they got closer to the village of Netherfield, Seb began to complain that his legs were getting tired.

'Come here, champ.' Jacob lifted him up into the air and over his shoulders for a shoulder ride.

'Watch your jacket!' Eva warned, noting the muddy rivulets running down Seb's boots.

'That doesn't matter. The jacket will wash.' He held on to Seb's hands and they walked ahead of the others, Seb giggling happily, perched up high.

Molly fell into step beside Eva and threaded her arm through hers. 'Don't they make a wonderful sight, the two of them?'

She smiled. 'They do.'

'You must be so happy they're getting on well?' Molly asked.

Eva nodded, forcing a smile. 'Oh, I am! Christmas is going to be so special this year for Seb.'

'And for Jacob, too, I suspect. He deserves a happy Christmas again. Things are looking up at last for the Dolans!'

Eva said nothing. Were things looking up for *her*, too?

Jacob stood with his father at the bar of The Three Horseshoes. They'd given their group's food order and were waiting for their drinks to be served so they could take the tray to their table.

His dad patted him on the back. 'It's good to have you back, son. We've missed you.'

Jacob smiled. 'I'm sorry I went AWOL for so long, Dad. It wasn't fair on you and Mum.'

'We understood. We know you felt guilty about Michelle, but so did everyone else. You felt guilty... We felt guilty...'

'Why did *you* feel guilty?'

'Because we couldn't protect you from the pain you were in.'

Jacob could feel his eyes welling up. The burn of tears was being held back from bursting forth by sheer will. He was suddenly overwhelmed. Glad to have come home. Glad to be back with family and glad that they understood him.

Eva had been right from the beginning. About him coming back. She'd known more about family than he had.

He turned and looked at her across the pub. She sat with his mother, was smiling at something Seb was saying. But he could see that she was holding back. She had been ever since that moment in the orchard. They'd kissed and then...something had happened. She'd created distance between them and now she seemed to be... apart from them all.

It was probably for the best, even if he didn't like it. He couldn't be with Eva the way he wanted to be unless he told her the whole truth of what had happened. That was the only way he could fully give her his heart. By being honest. But if he *did* tell her... His heart sank at the thought. She would turn away from him. She would be appalled at what he'd done. She would want nothing to do with him and he couldn't risk that.

But she's already turning away from me and I don't want to lose her!

Their gazes met across the bar. Eva looked at him for a moment and then glanced away.

And he knew, in that moment, that he was already losing her.

CHAPTER SEVEN

LEAVING NETHERFIELD HAD almost made her cry. For the first time in her life she had felt welcomed by another family. Jacob's parents had managed to put right, in a single weekend, the years of hurt and pain she had felt every time she'd been sent back to the children's home. She could remember every occasion of being placed in the back of the car, solemnly refusing to turn back and wave at the family she was leaving.

But that Sunday as they'd left Jacob's parents she *had* turned round. She'd waved, she'd fought back tears, and she'd felt as if she was waving goodbye to them forever.

Being in Jacob's company was becoming more difficult. She *wanted* to be with him! Had developed feelings for him. Wanted to connect with him, physically and emotionally. But she knew she had to hold herself back until his feelings for his dead fiancée had been resolved.

If that were possible.

She'd died in such tragic circumstances… Jacob would probably always feel *something* for her.

Her yearning for him was intense. It was as if her body *craved* him when he was near. She would breathe more heavily, she would tighten her hands into fists to stop herself from reaching out to touch him, she would lick her lips in memory of his sweet kisses…

It was torture…

She felt scared. She'd never wanted a man so much! Never wanted to be with his family so much! To turn up again at Netherfield and know she'd be welcomed. That people would smile and be overjoyed at her arrival.

Eva had never had that before. And she wanted it back. Not just for her, but for Seb, too. For all this time they'd been alone, never knowing what they were missing out on, but now they could be a part of that. A part of his family.

But how much of a part? Even Molly had asked what was going on between her and Jacob.

She knew what she would *like* to be going on. But he wasn't ready. Jacob had shared things with her. Personal things. Thoughts. Emotions. The events of his past, as she had with him. But there was still the ghost of Michelle.

Did Michelle rule Jacob's heart? Would he ever let her go? Was he holding himself back from her because deep down he still loved Michelle?

Was she trying to compete with a ghost?

Because that wasn't a battle that anyone could win.

Jacob was generally happy with the way the visit to his parents' place had gone. He'd really not known how his parents would react. He'd expected his mum to go over the top, to cry a bit, maybe gush about having him back and ask him to promise never to go away again.

But she hadn't. She'd been just fine. Dad, too. They'd been thrilled to have him back, but they'd made the weekend more about Seb—about welcoming him and his mother into the family and making them feel comfortable.

He'd observed, as if from a distance. Letting it all be about them unless his mother had particularly asked his opinion on something or deliberately involved him. It had been so good to be back. He hadn't been overwhelmed by memories, as he'd expected himself to be. It had been bearable.

Because of Eva and Seb.

If it hadn't have been for them he knew he would never have managed the weekend without feeling haunted. But their being there had somehow stopped all of that.

Because of them the visit had been about the future. About how much Seb and Eva could be involved. About how much they were now a *family*.

Of course his mum had fed them all as if they'd never seen food before, and had insisted on packing them off for the journey home with freezer bags full of sausage rolls and pastries and pies.

They'd stood in the doorway and waved him off with tears in their eyes. Eva had looked tearful, too, but she hadn't wanted to talk about it.

He'd promised his parents he would call within a couple of days.

And he had.

They adored Seb, as he had known they would, but they also adored Eva, and that meant a lot to him.

Eva meant a lot to him. Finding her again had turned his life around. He'd known that first night at the party that she was something special, but to have thought that she would bring him this much happiness... He'd not expected that to happen.

He'd hoped that when he found her again she would be his friend, but other things were happening. As he got to know Seb more, and the more time he spent in their home, the more he was getting to know Eva, and he knew she was more special than he'd ever believed. Could feel it in his heart.

He so wanted to be able to tell her the truth. The *real* truth about what had happened on his wedding day and not the sanitised version that everyone else *thought* was the truth.

But how would she react? That was his biggest concern right now. If he told her before Christmas… But he so wanted to spend this precious time with them— he couldn't tell her!

She would view him with horror. Look at him differently. Judge him. And he couldn't bear the idea of not being with Seb over Christmas. It was just a week away—he could keep it inside until after the Yuletide season, couldn't he?

I should have been honest with her from the start. But how exactly do you say that to someone? That you are responsible for someone's death? It's not the kind of thing you drop into conversation with someone new.

And now that he hadn't told her the truth for so long… it would be harder to say anything at all.

He wanted to be with Eva. He wanted to be with her in a *relationship*.

But he knew that if he unburdened himself of his guilt, she might walk away…

Eva had had enough pain in her past. Did he want to cause her more?

Their days at work began to pass quickly. With Christmas-party season in full swing the doctors were rushed off their feet, dealing with what felt like a swarm of drunk and disorderlies they had to keep an eye on, as well as dealing with all the usual illnesses and injuries.

There was a slew of norovirus lockdowns on various wards, so they had to limit who they admitted into hospital and where they sent them, causing the corridors to be filled with patients on trollies, moaning and groaning to their paramedics that they hadn't been seen yet.

It was a heady mix of patients filled with Christmas cheer and patients who were grumpy and angry. Everyone's temper was getting shorter and shorter.

In the evenings Jacob would come round to Eva's to read to Seb, and Eva would cook them all a meal that they would eat together. It all appeared quite domesticated and happy, but there was a palpable tension that they could both feel, and both of them refused to mention it in their fear of ruining Christmas.

At work, it was getting harder and harder for Eva to be normal around him. Their relationship—whatever it was—was confusing. Jacob was being polite, keeping his distance, and she was feeling hurt by it. She sneaked looks at him when she thought he wasn't watching, and yearned for his touch.

But she knew they had to be absolute professionals, who showed no familiarity, no favouritism, who showed no attraction to each other, and this just further reinforced to Eva the wisdom of his pushing her away.

She knew it was for the best.

But that didn't make it any easier when all she truly wanted was to be in his arms.

One night they were both tidying up in the kitchen after their meal.

Eva was loading the dishwasher and Jacob was passing her the dishes after scraping them clean over the bin. Their fingers kept touching as they passed and accepted plates and other items, and tiny frissons would ripple up her arms each time. She tried to ignore them. Tried to tell herself that she *could not* have this man. Not right now. Not whilst his feelings were so confused.

Politely, she thanked him for each item, and then, when it seemed she was saying 'thank you' too much, she just looked at him and smiled a thank-you. But then he'd smile back, and then those smiles and glances became longer and longer, until they were just standing over the open dishwasher, both holding the same plate and just looking at each other.

The way Jacob was looking at her—as if he was hungry for her, as if he wouldn't be able to breathe unless he kissed her—made her feel all giddy inside. How long had it been since that kiss in the orchard? Not long at all. And yet it felt as if decades had passed.

Her lips parted and she looked at him, desperate to tell him how she felt about him.

Suddenly Jacob stepped around the open dishwasher and kicked the door closed with his foot. He grabbed her and pulled her into his arms.

Eva was backed against one of the kitchen units, could feel the edge of the work surface digging into her bottom as Jacob's body pressed up against hers. She could feel *him*. Every wonderful inch of him. He cupped her face in his hands and tilted her lips up to his. Kissing her, devouring her face with the force of his passion.

Oh, yes!

Kissing him felt so good! As if they were meant to be! His soft lips, his stubble gave her a sweet, yet burning sensation that flowed from her lips down through her body and ignited a fire deep within her that made her crave more of him. More than just a kiss. More than just lips touching.

She wanted everything about him. His hands, his mouth, his *body*. She wanted all of him. To be with him the way they had been when they'd conceived Seb. Naked and entwined. Unable to get enough of each other.

As their kiss deepened her hands found their way under his shirt, feeling the burning heat in his skin, the powerful muscles contained within him moving smoothly as he kissed her.

I want you!

She wanted to say it. She wanted to take that step and just *tell* him. That she was here. In his present. A real woman who loved him. Yes, *loved* him—if only he would give her the chance.

Remember he's in love with someone else.

Eva pushed him away and was left gasping from the force of his passion.

He looked confused. Hurt. But then his glazed eyes finally got some sense back in them and he stepped away, out of the kitchen.

She heard the front door open and close with such finality that she couldn't stop the tears. She cried. Cried for the fact that she would never have him the way she wanted to. That until he got over Michelle he would never be hers.

I should have kept him at arm's length. It's too painful.

'He's in cardiac arrest!'

Jacob's patient lay prone on the bed, his eyes closed, his mouth agape. Greg Harper had been brought in by his wife, Ginny. He'd been feeling unwell all day, and after an hour of trying to work the ground in his frost-hardened allotment had come in complaining of being short of breath. Ginny had said that he'd looked extremely pale and had felt clammy. She'd called for an ambulance as her senses had told her it was something serious.

It had been a good decision. Because now Greg was in a hospital setting as his cardiac arrest occurred, and therefore theoretically stood a much higher chance of survival.

Jacob lowered the head of the bed and called for the crash team. This was his first case of leading a resuscitation since he'd joined the department a few weeks ago.

Eva came running over, along with two other doctors and nurses.

'Compressions!' Jacob requested, his voice stern and clear.

Eva stepped forward to do them, clasping one hand above the other and placing them centrally to Greg's chest. She began to compress his chest, maintaining a steady rhythm, as Jacob called out further orders to the rest of the team.

'I want pads on, and venous access. Sarah—you take the airway and get an oropharyngeal airway in.'

Jacob took a step back and oversaw it all. He stood in front of Ginny, who had hidden behind him, not daring to look.

The defibrillator pads were soon attached to Greg's chest and Eva stopped compressions momentarily for the machine to assess Greg's heart rhythm—if any.

'He's in VF. Shocking.'

The doctor in charge of the machine checked to make

sure no one was touching the patient and then pressed the button with the little lightning rod on it. Greg's body juddered slightly.

'He's still in VF.' Sarah looked up at him.

Jacob stood firm. 'Continue CPR. Adrenaline.'

The drug was administered into a vein and Eva continued pumping the chest. Her red hair swung back and forth with the force of her compressions and her breathing was becoming heavier. Compressions could be exhausting—especially if resuscitation took a long time—so they liked to rotate staff every two minutes.

'Please don't let him die! Please save him!' pleaded his wife, Ginny.

'Pulse check, please.'

A nurse checked the radial pulse. 'Weak.'

'Continue.'

Jacob's voice rang loud and clear in the department. Cardiac arrests were dramatic, especially to an onlooker, like a family member or friend, but to a doctor they were some of the easiest cases to deal with in A&E, because there was a recognised pattern of treatment. You knew exactly what you had to do and when you had to do it.

Not every case in the department was so clear-cut. People came in with mystery ailments all the time, or didn't tell the doctors all their symptoms, or lied. Cardiac arrests were obvious and they knew how to deal with them.

'Assess rhythm.'

A further shock was given, then oxygen pumped in via a bag valve and mask.

Jacob glanced at the clock. 'Amiodarone. Three hundred milligrams.'

Greg groaned and his wife gasped, peering round

Jacob to see if her husband was showing any signs of waking up.

'Pulse check?'

The nurse felt the patient's wrist. 'I have a strong pulse.'

Sarah, managing the airway and monitoring the machines, confirmed that the patient was making respiratory effort and that blood pressure was slowly rising.

'Well done, team. Once Mr Harper is stable I want him transferred to ITU. Until then I want him on fifteen-minute obs.' Jacob turned to Ginny. 'We've got him back, but we need to make sure we keep him with us. He's in for a difficult twenty-four hours.'

Ginny nodded. 'Yes. Can I speak to him?'

He nodded. 'Of course.'

'Thank you, Doctor! If I'd lost him...'

'You didn't.'

She looked shocked at his abrupt tone, then said firmly, 'He's my *life*.'

The look in her eyes softened his mood and Jacob understood. He laid a hand on her arm apologetically. 'I know. Talk to him. Sit with him. When he gets a bed in ITU I'll come and let you know.'

Ginny smiled her thanks.

He turned at the doorway and looked at her, sitting beside her husband's bed. They were lucky. They'd had each other for years, it seemed. The love. The comfort. Why could *he* not have that? Didn't he deserve it?

What he felt for Eva... He'd allowed his physical desires to overwhelm him the other night. He hadn't been able to help it. She was just so beautiful, and the way they were both holding back had been killing him.

I need to tell her the truth.

No one knew the real truth. Except him and Michelle.

Could he wait until after Christmas? He wanted to. Knew it was probably the best thing. But it was so hard! He loved her and he couldn't have her. Not until she knew the truth—only then could they be together.

If she isn't scared away.

And Eva didn't come alone. She came as a package. With Seb.

He couldn't hurt that boy.

That boy was his life now. If she took him away from him… No. No, she wouldn't do that to him.

Then, what have I got to lose?

Those first nights under the vast African sky he'd thought about Michelle and the way he'd treated her. What he'd done to drive her into the arms of another. He hadn't been able to bear to admit the truth. And his thoughts had always come back to Eva. The woman who had briefly brought him back to life. Thoughts of her had pervaded his mind, but he'd tried to dismiss them as the thoughts of a mixed up, grieving man.

Those nights alone in Africa had made Jacob re-evaluate his life. Think about what he wanted. Not only what he could do for others, but what he needed to do for himself. And all he'd been able to think about was his own family, back on the farm, and the woman with red hair…

Eva.

She'd done a great job with Seb. And all alone, too. She was a strong woman. He had to believe that her internal strength would help get them all through this.

He needed her.

Knew it as he knew the sun would rise in the east.

He burned for her. Couldn't think straight around her anymore.

I should just be honest with her. Get it over with. Then we can move forward. Together.

Jacob spotted Eva across the department. As always, she looked gorgeous. Her curtain of red hair fell in a perfect wave and her crystal-blue eyes looked up at him in question as he walked across to her. She'd made a small nod to the season and was wearing tiny dangling Christmas trees in her ears. They might have looked ridiculous on anyone else, but not her.

He stood in front of her. 'Hi.'

'Hello.'

His fingers itched to touch her. To hold her. Since that kiss in the kitchen it had been killing him to keep himself from touching her. From being with her. How he'd managed to walk away from the house the other night he'd never know.

Her reaction to that last kiss the other night hadn't lied. She'd wanted it, and had responded to it in a way that he'd liked. As his lips had trailed over the delicate skin at her neck he'd inhaled her scent and had almost drifted away on a cloud of ecstasy. She'd smelled so good and she'd felt so right and he'd wanted her again.

He could see no reason to keep punishing himself by staying away. Didn't they both deserve more?

'Eva? May I have a word with you?' His voice was thick and gravelly, as if he was finding it difficult to talk.

'What's up?'

'In private.' He made eye contact and enforced it, staring hard at her, making sure she understood him.

But she seemed nervous. 'Talk to me here.'

She stood up and put her hands into the pockets of the long cardigan she wore.

'Well?'

She was looking up at him, and he so wanted to cup her face and bring those sensuous lips to his own, but he controlled himself and took a step back. 'I need to speak with you.'

'You are.'

'Privately. I thought tonight, when I come round, I could cook *you* dinner for a change.'

'Oh. Okay. That would be nice.'

'I need to tell you *everything*.'

She swallowed. 'Everything?'

He nodded. 'You need to hear it all.'

Eva watched him walk away from her.

He was going to tell her tonight. Tell her that he could not give her his heart. Not until he was over his grieving. He would tell her that he would still like to be there for Seb, but that whatever had been happening between the two of them had to be over.

She bit her lip as she felt tears threaten, but then pushed away her grief.

She wouldn't cry over him anymore.

She would get through tonight and she would be strong. For Seb.

This didn't have to ruin his Christmas. It was only a couple of days away.

Eva set her mind on being strong. On keeping a safe distance. On remaining upbeat.

At least she tried.

Eva came home from her long day at work to gentle piano music on the stereo system, fairy lights and candles lit throughout and the most delicious smells emanating from her kitchen.

She hung up her bag and her jacket and kicked off her shoes, padded barefoot into the lounge. There was no one there so she headed into the kitchen, where Jacob stood stirring something on the hob.

'Where's Seb?'

'With Letty. And she said he could sleep over, too.'

Eva raised an eyebrow. Really? He'd sent Seb on a sleepover? Just how upset did Jacob expect her to be?

He passed her a glass of white wine. Whatever he was cooking smelled mouth-wateringly good. Like Jacob himself.

Stop it!

But it was true. Jacob had a wonderful scent, and when she was up close to him and he held her in his arms...

Eva shook her head to clear it. She needed to think straight. But the idea that there was wine, good food and Jacob... It was all muddying the waters!

Only a few weeks ago life had seemed simple. It had been her and Seb against the world. Then Jacob had come back. And since he'd found out he was a father he'd practically moved in and turned her world upside down! She wasn't even sure she was the same person anymore. She knew she'd changed.

Jacob looked particularly delightful this evening. He wore dark trousers and a crisp white shirt, and his tousled dark hair just crept over the edge of the collar. He had broad, powerful shoulders and a neat waist, and she could only try to remember the powerful, muscular legs beneath the cloth...

He was a sight for sore, tired eyes.

And she wanted him.

The knowledge that he also wanted her, that he'd got himself hot because of her, had barely contained himself because of her, was an aphrodisiac she tried to ignore!

'What's cooking?'

Jacob turned, and the beam of his smile lighting up his face brightened her heart. He was trying to put things right. He was trying to give her a good night before he ruined it with whatever news he thought he still had to share.

'An African specialty. Yam and crayfish risotto, inspired by my time in Gabon, followed by a *malva* pudding.'

'What's a *malva* pudding?'

He smiled. 'It's very rich, very buttery, and filled to the brim with syrup. You'll love it.'

She nodded. Sounded good. 'Wow. You really did learn a lot in Africa. When did you go to Gabon?'

'In between my times at the clinic.'

'And what did you discover?'

Her mouth dried as Jacob took a few steps towards her. He was literally millimetres away from her, towering above her and staring down into her eyes as if he'd just discovered the most beautiful jewel in existence and was hypnotised by it.

'I discovered that I'd left behind the one person who could've changed my life.'

Her. He meant *her*.

And, boy, was that electrifying stuff! She felt so alive with him standing right there, looking down at her, devouring her with his gaze. She felt as if she was waiting for him to inch those last few millimetres closer, so that her body could lock into his, like a key in a padlock.

Were they made for each other? She felt that it might be that way. Physically anyway. But what about the other stuff? The boring stuff that grown-ups had to think about. Like trust and reliability and dependability. And love.

Did Jacob love her? She knew he loved Seb. He was definitely there for his son, and it seemed he spent every spare moment he had at her house. But what of his feelings for *her*? There was a definite attraction between them, but was he still in love with his dead fiancée?

'Jacob, I don't know what I am to you.'

He tilted his head, as if questioning her. 'You're very important to me.'

'Important? Is that all?'

Jacob looked shocked and upset. 'You're Seb's mum. You're the woman I can't stop thinking about. You chase every other thought out of my head and, believe me, that's difficult to do.'

She put her wine glass down and turned to face him. '*Every* other thought?'

He smiled. 'Most of them.'

'It's the ones you don't tell me about that worry me.'

'I *will* tell you. But I'd like us to enjoy our evening first. Let's allow ourselves that. Forget the difficulties for a moment. Just enjoy being with each other for now.'

She could do that. She didn't like postponing the pain that she knew was coming, but she wanted to enjoy him whilst she could. If pain was coming, then so be it, but there was no reason why she couldn't just let go and enjoy being with the man she loved for a few moments more.

She smiled. 'So what do we do now?'

Jacob smiled back at her. 'Eat dinner. Start afresh. Can you do that with me?'

Maybe. It was scary still.

But perhaps I'm tired of being alone?

She stood up and grabbed her wine glass. 'Let's eat dinner.'

Jacob nodded, smiling.

The crayfish and yam risotto was divine! The yam was sweet and soft and the crayfish was succulent and melted in her mouth.

Eva glanced at Jacob. 'This is lovely, by the way. You might not have noticed from the way I've gobbled it all up like a hippo.'

Jacob picked his fork up and grinned. 'I had noticed, and I didn't for one minute compare you to a hippo. And thank you. It's a compliment.'

She took another mouthful, and when she'd swallowed it she looked at him across the table. 'Tell me more about Africa. Your work there.'

He met her gaze and nodded slightly, his face thoughtful. 'Well, you know about Reuben. But there were so many people out there who all changed my life in a small way.'

'I'd like to hear about it.'

'Cataract surgery was the first thing I did. There just seemed to be a never-ending line of people with the need for eye surgery. Not just old people, but kids, too. Seeing a child regain his eyesight was amazing, each and every time.'

'I can imagine.'

'There was this one kid who saw his mum for the first time when he was eight years old. The look of happiness on his face afterwards…' Jacob had a faraway look in his eyes and simply smiled.

Eva could only imagine how he must have felt. 'You said you helped build a school?'

'That was much later—but, yes. Again, there were just so many kids who'd never even seen inside a classroom and we could quickly build one in about a week. To see them all go in and meet their teacher, start writing on blackboards… It made me appreciate all that I'd had in my life. All that I'd taken for granted.'

'Sometimes we need reminding.'

'With each patient I met, each story I heard, it just made me realise that I was getting ready to come home. To find *my* happiness again. To believe that I could have it.'

Eva nodded.

'The African people are so noble. And proud. But in a good way. They're honest and heartfelt…and even though most of them hardly have any material things they're intensely happy if they have family.'

'Did you feel alone out there?'

'To begin with. But I ignored it. I've always been headstrong, but being in Africa taught me that sometimes you need to pause and reflect. Think things through.'

'Before you came back?'

He nodded, intense blue eyes staring back at her from across the table.

'And what do you want from life now?' Her breath hitched in her throat as she half hoped he'd say her, but she was half afraid he'd say something else.

'You. And Seb. I came back intent on finding you and I did. I'm going to be really honest now and say it—

and hope I don't sound like some kind of mad stalker. It was no accident that I walked into your A&E. I knew you were there.'

She gasped. Shocked. He'd *known*? Then that meant he'd known exactly where he would find her when he came back! He'd pretended it was a surprise to walk in and find her!

'But you had no idea about what happened after you left. About Seb.'

'No. And once I was over the shock it was a wonderful surprise. Regret, yes, for the lost years…' Eva's eyes were downcast, so he reached out and grasped her hand with his own. 'But joy at having more family. An amazing son with the woman that I…'

She looked up. 'Yes?'

What would he say? That he loved her? She almost couldn't breathe, waiting for him to say it.

He stared at her intently. 'That I have feelings for.'

Eva exhaled. Slowly.

'Feelings? What kind of feelings?' She licked her lips, watching as his eyes tracked the movement, then moved back up to look into her eyes.

'Strong feelings. I want us to try to be together. Properly.' He stood up from his side of the table and came round to hers.

She watched him move, aware that her heart was pounding and her breathing was getting heavier, her mouth drying in anticipation. 'Jacob—'

He took her hand in his and bade her rise from her seat. 'Would you come with me?'

'Where?' she croaked, her voice almost not working at all.

'Upstairs.'

Upstairs. To bed. Sex. That was what he meant.

She wanted to. Physically, her body wanted that very much, as did her heart, but her head was telling her to think twice. Tomorrow was Christmas Eve. The anniversary of his wife-to-be's death. The anniversary of the night they'd slept together for the first time. Did she want to sleep with him knowing that he didn't feel for her the way she felt about him?

She shook her head. 'I can't be anyone's second best, Jacob.'

He stroked her face. 'You could never be second best for me.'

Jacob gazed down at her, his eyes glazed with a sexual hunger that she wanted to satisfy. Feelings be damned! Why *shouldn't* she have him? The last time she'd slept with him had been all those years ago, and though the memories of that night were awe-inspiring, she wanted to be with him one last time—no matter what happened afterwards.

Jacob scooped her up into his arms and carried her easily up the stairs and into her bedroom, closing the door softly behind them.

Eva, laughing, allowed Jacob to set her down on the edge of the bed. She looked at him, watching as he stood before her, undoing the buttons of his shirt from top to bottom.

It was mesmerising.

He pulled his shirt from his trousers, and as soon as she saw the smattering of dark hair that dipped beneath his belt buckle she quickly stood up, unable to stay away from him a moment longer, and helped him off with his clothes.

To have him before her, totally naked, as she slowly

slipped off her own clothes, was magical. The memory she had of him, of a younger, less muscular Jacob, was stunning enough, but to see him now—more heavily set, broader, stronger—was a powerful aphrodisiac.

And he wanted *her*.

Eva slowly reached out to touch him. Her doubts silenced.

Eva blinked and opened her eyes. Frosty sunlight was streaming in through the open curtains at her bedroom window and her body felt deliciously exhausted.

Christmas Eve!

What time was it?

She felt as if something had woken her, but she couldn't think what. Had there been a sound? Her alarm clock?

Blinking, she turned and glanced at it. Ten minutes past seven. Still early. Yawning, she turned back to look at Jacob, asleep in the bed beside her. His dark hair was all tousled and wavy. From sleep? Or from her fingers? It could easily be both. There'd been moments last night when she'd held his head in her hands as his tongue had worked its magic and she'd grabbed hold of him, her fingers splaying in his hair as he'd brought her to ecstasy.

What a night!

His face looked so relaxed this morning, and he had a five-o'clock shadow darkening his jaw. She'd felt that stubble last night and it had been delicious, tickling her skin and her tender places. Her inner thighs felt roughened and sore. But in a good way.

He was lying on his stomach, his head resting on his hands, and he looked so peaceful, his suntanned skin set healthily against the white of her sheets. His muscled arms and powerful shoulders a delightful addition to her bedroom. And farther beneath the sheets… *Oh, my!*

Last night had been even better than the night she'd spent with him four years ago. She wanted to reach out and touch him just once more, to prove that this was real. As she did so, and her fingers touched his jawline, his eyes opened and he smiled slowly.

'Morning.'

'Good morning.'

He was blinking at the half-light coming through the bedroom curtains. 'The night got away from us.'

'It did.' Swinging her legs out of bed, she grabbed her robe.

'Where are you going?'

'To make some tea. Want one?'

He pulled himself into an upright position, the sheets just barely covering his modesty. 'Sounds great.'

Smiling, she headed downstairs and into her kitchen. The remains of their meal last night were still there, and she smiled at the memory of the food and what had come after…

Then her thoughts darkened. They hadn't talked. They hadn't discussed what they'd meant to. Should she raise it now? Was this a good time to remind him of her doubts?

Look at what had happened last night! It had been amazing! Skin tingling, electrifying. The passion that had been between them…

That's how it could be between us if we let it. If we refuse to face what we don't want to face.

She wasn't sure if they could do that. Surely the lies they were telling themselves would soon creep to the surface and ruin what they had?

No. They *had* to talk. It was the only way.

She couldn't quite believe it. Everything was going right in her world. She'd gained the family she'd always dreamed of. They could be a unit. They were both striving for the same goals. They were both there for Seb.

They were there for each other.

Mostly.

She laid her hand on her heart as she looked out of the kitchen window, waiting for the kettle to boil. She could feel it beating. *Dum-dum. Dum-dum.* It didn't have to beat alone anymore. She'd lain her head on Jacob's chest last night as they'd fallen asleep together and it had beat with the same rhythm. *Dum-dum. Dum-dum.*

She was no longer alone!

Eva wasn't sure what she'd done to deserve so much happiness. Perhaps after all her years of suffering as a child, of being alone, being the outsider, this was her reward now? This sense of belonging that she felt being with both Seb *and* Jacob?

Whatever it was, it was amazing.

She made the tea, and some toast, and prepared a tray to take upstairs. For the first time in her life she would have breakfast in bed, and then *she* would be the one to cause her life to come crashing down around her ears.

She'd let him have a shower. Then she'd had one and now they were both dressed.

As he pushed his belt into its buckle, he looked at her. 'What's wrong?'

She looked up at him from her seat on the bed, nerves racing through her body, causing her heart to pound like a jackhammer as the possibility of abandonment crept ever nearer.

'We never did talk last night.'

His eyes darkened. 'No, we didn't.'

'I think we ought to.'

Jacob stared at her. 'But last night... We...we were so good together! I'm not sure I want to taint that with what I have to say.'

Eva wrapped her cardigan tightly around herself. Neither was she. But she couldn't move forward in a relationship with him if she was lying to herself and allowing him to lie to her.

'Nor do I. But I think we both need to be truthful. For Seb as much as for ourselves.'

He sighed and settled down on the bed across from her. 'You're right.'

She sucked in a breath. Okay. She was ready.

'Tell me.'

He nodded, thinking, his eyes downcast. Then he looked up at her.

'On my wedding day something happened that...that no one knows about.'

Okay. That wasn't the direction she'd thought this would start, but she'd go with it.

'What?'

'Michelle made it to the church. She didn't die on her way to the service like I told everyone. She made it there.'

Eva was confused. 'She *made* it?'

'Remember I told you that I was outside, waiting for the first glimpse of the wedding car? I'd been too fidgety inside, so I was walking around to rid myself of the nerves. Then suddenly she pulled up in her car.'

'You *saw* her?'

He nodded. 'She wanted to speak to me before the

service. She told me that she'd cheated on me. With my best friend Marcus. She said that I hadn't loved her the way I ought to and so she'd looked elsewhere.'

Eva hadn't expected this! 'She *cheated* on you?'

'She said she still loved me, that she wanted to go on with the wedding but wanted to enter our marriage honestly.'

He paused for a moment, then stood and began to pace the room.

'I was furious! Furious that she'd cheated on me, but furious with myself, too—because I'd *known* something wasn't right and I'd ignored it. I knew there was no way I could marry her still. We argued. I said some things... *horrible* things. I don't know what came over me, but I ripped into her verbally. I couldn't bear to look at her. The more I looked at her, the more I hated her. I ordered her to go away. Told her I never wanted to see her again for as long as I lived. She was crying, mascara all over the place, begging for my forgiveness, but I told her to—'

'What?'

'Something *horrible*. She ran from me. Ran back to her car and screeched off. I knew she was driving recklessly, but I was so angry I didn't care!'

Eva covered her mouth with her hand. They'd argued and then she'd died? No wonder he felt awful!

'Jacob...'

'I stood outside the church for ages. Trying to think of how I was going to go inside and face everyone. Tell them the wedding was off.'

'So what happened then?'

'The police arrived.'

She knew what was coming.

'They said that Michelle had died. That she'd been in a car crash, had been thrown from the vehicle. Everyone assumed that she'd died on her way to the church. They were all crying and weeping and dabbing at their eyes with tissues and I just couldn't bear it! It was all so false! None of them knew the truth and all of them wanted to pity me. Wanted to see me collapse in a heap of tears.'

'You must have been in shock.'

'I didn't know *what* to feel. I'd been furious with her and sent her away and she'd got killed. *My* fault. If I hadn't sent her away… If I'd given us a chance…'

Eva couldn't believe it! She could see now how difficult that must have been. For him to have known the truth—that Michelle had cheated—and yet for absolutely everyone else to think they'd been so in love. As she had. But if this was what he'd been hiding, then perhaps he *wasn't* still in love with Michelle!

'*This* is what you've been keeping from me?'

He stood in front of her. 'I'll understand if you don't want anything to do with me,' he said.

She stared at his face. At the pain in his eyes. Seeing the way he was so bowed down by the guilt he'd been carrying all these years.

She was about to say something when there was a furious banging on her front door.

'Eva! *Eva?* It's Letty! Hurry—it's Seb!'

Letty…? Seb…?

She flew down the stairs, Jacob following close behind, watching helplessly as she fumbled over her keys to unlock the front door. Then she flung the door wide.

Letty stood there, with Seb draped in her arms, pale and unconscious.

'Oh, my God!'

'I can't wake him!'

Eva stared at her almost lifeless son and felt her legs give way.

'Seb?' She shook his shoulders gently, then with more force. When he didn't respond she pinched his earlobe. Nothing. She placed her ear over his mouth.

He was still breathing!

The doctor inside her started to analyse, and her gut filled with a nasty sensation as she just knew that something bad had happened.

'Call an ambulance.' She turned to Jacob, but he was already on his mobile.

This was wrong. So very badly wrong.

She kept trying to rouse her son as Jacob spoke on the phone to ambulance control.

'He won't wake up. Not responding to voice commands. Not responding to pain. He's unconscious.'

Eva looked up at him. 'Wouldn't it be quicker to drive him in ourselves?'

'In rush hour? No. Let's wait for the ambulance.'

It was agonising just to sit and wait. To know what they knew and think of all the horrible things it might be. Meningitis? Encephalitis? An infection? Something caused by the earlier accident?

It took an age, it seemed, before the ambulance arrived outside her house.

The paramedics, at least, were familiar to her. Friendly faces. People she trusted. Letty quickly relayed how she'd found him that morning and told them that he'd seemed okay the night before, except for saying he had a headache.

'What?' Eva frowned. 'He had a headache? Why didn't you tell me?'

Letty looked upset. 'I'm so sorry. I didn't think it was that bad.'

The headache could be vital. Different diagnoses flashed through her mind...all the things it could be. But her brain kept telling her just one thing.

Meningitis.

She knew it in her heart, but didn't want to admit it. Not Seb. Not her boy. *No.* It was Christmas. This couldn't be happening at *Christmas.* It was wrong. He shouldn't be like this. He should be getting excited about presents under the tree and Christmas carolling, or looking out for snow...

The paramedics quickly gave him oxygen and bundled him into the ambulance in double-quick time. They allowed Eva in, but held their hands up at Jacob.

'Sorry—only room for one. Can you get to the hospital under your own steam?' And they set off with lights and siren going.

Eva sat in the back with her son, reeling as they went around corners and bollards and through traffic lights, knowing that Jacob would be trying to travel separately behind them in his own car. But he wouldn't be allowed to speed, or to go on the wrong side of the road, and would be delayed in getting to the hospital by traffic lights that they could just speed through.

Briefly she thought about what he'd just told her. About his wedding day. About what had really happened with Michelle. But she pushed it away. That didn't matter now! She needed to focus on Seb.

They got to the hospital fast, and yet it also seemed to take an age. Seb still wasn't responding, but the ECG leads told them he had a good heart rate. That was good. *Something* had to be good in all this.

She was feeling incredibly sick. And guilty. Her son had been dreadfully ill next door, deteriorating, and she'd not known because she'd been sleeping with Jacob!

Eva exhaled heavily and stared at her son. Willing him to read her mind.

Stay strong. I need you, Seb. I need you.

Jacob gripped the steering wheel tightly as the ambulance sped away from him, its lights turning the street blue, then black, in an ever-flickering wail of pain that seared straight to his gut.

What was wrong with Seb? He was no paediatrician—the headache could be anything. But it was the only clue to this whole mess.

Everyone had headaches at some point in their lives—it didn't necessarily mean anything. What did it mean for Seb? He was pale, unconscious. There were a variety of things it could be. An infection…something wrong with his brain. A blood disorder. It could be anything. Something to do with the bang on the head he'd received during that accident on the day he'd found out about his son.

He was a doctor, and all those possibilities were popping into his brain and then out again as he dismissed the thought that it could be any of those things.

He couldn't lose Seb. Not now. He'd only just got to know him. He'd only just begun to appreciate what it was like to have such a wonderful son. To lose him now would be life's cruel trick…

Christmas Eve! It's Christmas Eve again! I'm not going to lose him!

He'd only just found his son… What man wouldn't be thrilled to find out that he had a handsome, strapping young boy? And he was so clever, too—and popular at nursery. Everyone wanted to be Seb's friend. Everyone wanted to sit next to him. He was a good kid. Diligent. They didn't want to know him because he was the class clown. He was a good friend. A nice boy.

The best.

Only now he was lying in the back of an ambulance, speeding to A&E. How had that happened? How had two doctors—two *accident and emergency* doctors—not noticed that their child was ill? Sickening for something?

Had there been earlier signs? Had they missed them? Jacob cursed.

His stomach roiled with nausea and he rubbed at his forehead as a sharp pain shot across his brow.

The ambulance was way ahead of him now. There was no chance he could keep up. Not safely anyway. He wasn't trained to drive like that, and if he wanted to get to the hospital in one piece himself he knew he had to be patient. Had to be careful.

The traffic lights ahead of him turned red and he cursed them out loud in Afrikaans.

The lights took an age. Or so it seemed. It was probably only twenty seconds or so that he waited, but for Jacob, watching the ambulance disappear in front of him, it was tantamount to torture. His heart was in that ambulance. If he knew anything right now it was that.

His whole life was in that ambulance. Seb. Eva. His future.

What would happen if he lost either one of them? He shook his head, refusing to go down that avenue. It would drive him mad with insanity. He couldn't tolerate the thought—it was just too painful. He felt his heart almost shudder at the thought and bile ran up into his throat.

No. Not that. No. I forbid it.

He couldn't lose them. Not now. He'd only just found them. He'd only just expanded his world to allow them in. And now that he had, his life shone bright. Like a brand-new star in the night sky. He couldn't imagine the future without either one of them.

He'd come back to find Eva. To set things right again. Surely it wasn't all about to go wrong a second time?

The lights turned green and he gunned the engine, shooting forward. He had to remind himself to be careful. He overtook a slow driver and glared at the young man behind the wheel of the car as he passed. Did he not *know* he had to be somewhere? That his son could be *dying*? *Get out of the way!*

Just a mile or two from the hospital now. Not long and he could be back by Seb's side. Standing with Eva to be there for their son. Together. As they always should have been from the start.

He would not be leaving her to fight this fight on her own.

He briefly thought about calling his parents. Then everyone who loved and cared for Seb could be there at his bedside to support him.

We'll get you through this, Seb. We need you to get through it. I need you to.

There was the exit he needed for the hospital.

Jacob looked out through the windscreen at the bleak landscape. It was all greys and dark browns. The ground was hard and frosted, the trees lifeless and still. He could just see cars and exhaust fumes and frustrated drivers, impatient people hurrying everywhere, trying to get home to their families. To their warm hearths and jolly Christmas jumpers and repeats on the television.

He was frozen in time.

He paused for a moment, pulling over onto the hard shoulder briefly, whilst he fought against nausea and the fear.

He hesitated, took a breath, then pulled back out into the traffic.

CHAPTER EIGHT

THIS WAS SO ALIEN. So strange. To be the one standing back and watching other doctors fuss around her son.

Her son.

This was no random stranger, brought in from the streets. This was no drink-addled unknown blaring out 'Silent Night', or a faltering pensioner with a dodgy ticker. This was *her child*. Her *son*. Her reason for living.

And they were sticking him with needles. Each piercing of his skin pierced her heart, causing her to flinch. She watched him bleed as they searched for venous access and felt her heart breaking into a thousand tiny pieces.

An intravenous drip—a bag of clear fluid—hung by his bedside... Always so innocuous before, but now seeming so threatening. He clearly needed fluids.

How long since he'd last drunk anything? She didn't *know*. She hadn't been with him. She'd been with Jacob!

Machines beeped. Doctors fussed. Vacutainers popped. Voices called out.

'Stat.'

'Do it now!'

She glanced at the readouts on the machines. His pulse was high, his pressure low.

They kept pushing her back. Politely. She was getting in their way, she knew it, but she *had* to see him. *Had* to keep contact with him. Hold his hand. See his face.

As he lay there she thought back through his whole life. Her pregnancy… Waddling her way through work at the hospital. Those blissful few weeks of maternity leave when she'd been able to put her feet up and rest…

Only she hadn't rested, had she? She'd shopped for baby clothes, for nappies, for equipment—a pushchair, a cot. She'd got the nursery ready, decorating a room for the first time and tipping paint all over her shoes. Then there had been all that palaver with getting the mural on the wall. By the time she'd finished it she'd hated all the characters, only loving them again when she'd taken a step back to marvel at the finished room.

She'd wanted the world perfect for her son. Fatherless, she'd wanted him to have everything else.

The day he was born… Hours and hours of labour, during which she'd been determined to give birth naturally, in her longed-for water birth. The pain had been intense. She'd almost caved and asked for pain relief. She'd always thought she was a tough cookie. But then Seb had been laid in her arms… His chubby arms and legs, his scrunched up fingers and toes and his button nose. His shock of dark hair… He'd looked so much like Jacob she'd almost dropped him.

Almost.

But she'd never let him go. How could she? He'd been perfect. Gazing up at her with eyes so blue she'd thought that the whole world's supply of the colour had gone into his eyes and she would never see a blue thing ever again. Kingfishers would be dull. Bluebells would be just…bells. So blue his eyes had been…

Then there'd been the first time he'd said *mama*. He'd been on the verge of saying it for a long time. Sounding out the *m* for ages, saliva dribbling down his chin as he chomped his lips together over and over, and then... 'Mama.' Heavenly. Perfect. She'd scooped him up and smiled at him so broadly, and he'd smiled back, giggling, and she'd known then, as she knew now, that the perfect little boy she held in her arms would hold all the power over her heart for the rest of her life.

His first attempt at walking—toddling on his chubby legs. Each new day in his short life had given him more and more independence, taking him further and further away from her as he learned what he could do for himself. And still her love for him had grown and grown...

Only he looked lifeless now.

Sleeping, but worse. Pale and unresponsive. Not how he'd ever been and not how a three-year-old should be.

He should be awake, getting excited about Christmas Day tomorrow, sitting in front of the television set or playing outside. Doing a final bit of Christmas shopping with her, perhaps. Helping her make biscuits. Licking out the bowl when she made the icing...

Not here.

Not in a hospital bed with needles and cannulas and IV drips and heart monitors and ventilators and all manner of other things going on.

I can't do this. I can't see him like this.

'He needs a CT.'

She glanced at the doctor and felt alone. *So alone!* Where was Jacob? She *needed* him. Needed him more than she'd ever needed anyone. She shouldn't have to face this alone. Whatever was happening to her son. Whatever the CT might reveal. This wasn't the sort of thing she should do by herself. Hadn't she put herself through hell so she could rely on him? Hadn't she let him in so she could share this responsibility with someone else?

She'd always thought herself strong. Independent. Looking out for herself and Seb in the best way she knew how. And she'd done well at that. But this…? This was something else. This was a torment and a cruelty that she couldn't face alone.

I need you, Jacob!

Eva couldn't tear her eyes away. She needed to see what they were doing to her son. What they *weren't* doing.

They were good doctors. The best. She *knew* these people. It wasn't as if she'd put him into the hands of strangers.

She knew what they suspected.

Words wouldn't soothe. Reassurances didn't matter. Not until your child was whole and well again did anything matter.

Eva felt awful for the way she'd always been so detached with everyone else's kids. But she'd had to be. If she'd got attached, or personally involved, allowed her feelings to interfere, then she'd have been a worn-out wreck.

Only now she was on the other side. Not the doctor. The relative. *She* was the grief-stricken mother. *She* was the one with tears staining her cheeks, her eyes red, searching for hope. *She* was the one grasping at straws and hoping beyond anything that today's doctors and today's medicine could save her child.

Eva felt so alone. So isolated.

But deep down she knew she wasn't. There was Jacob. Somewhere…

Where *was* he? Why wasn't he here yet? Was he still driving to the hospital? Madly searching for a parking bay? Who cared about getting a parking ticket? He should be here by now. Perhaps even now he was running to the A&E department?

Her shoulders went back and her chin came up as grim determination strengthened her.

He's coming. I know he's coming!

She looked at Seb's pale face.

She'd never had to face a crisis like this before. And she felt so lonely.

For the first time in years she wanted her mum.

Jacob blew through the doors of his own A&E department, bypassed Reception and, jacket flying, ran into the maze of corridors that had become like a second home. His gaze flicked to the admissions board but he couldn't see Seb's name.

So he wasn't in cubicles. Nor in Minors.

He had to be in Majors.

Or Resus.

Oh, my God.

He tried to swallow, but his mouth had gone dry. People he worked with tried to say, 'Hi, Merry Christmas!' But he brushed past them and rushed into Resus—where he found Eva by their son's bed. Her eyes were swollen and she held Seb's limp hand in her own.

'Where have you *been*?' she demanded.

Jacob looked shocked. 'I couldn't find a place to park. What's going on? What have they said?'

'They don't know.' She turned back to her son and

clasped his hand again. 'They've run tests, done a CT. We're awaiting results.'

'How is he?'

'The same. They want to move him to Paediatric ICU.'

'When?'

She shook her head. 'I don't know. When they can.'

She had no energy for Jacob now that he was here. All her focus was on her boy.

It wasn't good enough. How many times had he impotently stood by, waiting for a bed space to become available? How many times had he had to console a relative because the beds manager couldn't sort out a bed backlog? Too many times. He'd not been working here for long and he was already fed up with the bureaucracy of the hospital and the stupid red tape that stopped them being able to discharge patients who didn't need to be there.

Jacob turned and grabbed the wall phone, almost ripping it from its lodging as he punched in the number for the bed manager.

'Rick?'

'Yes?'

'Dr Dolan in A&E. My son is here in Resus, awaiting a paediatric ICU bed. What's the hold-up?'

There was a pause, during which he heard a brief shuffling of papers. 'Paediatric ICU is full at present. I understand there may be a bed free soon—though I believe there's a possibility that your son may need surgery first.'

'Surgery?'

He saw Eva's face blanch.

'That's not good enough, Rick. My son needs the

care of the paediatric team and he needs it *now*. Where's Bilby? Surely he's in today?'

William Bilby was the top paediatric doctor in the entire UK, and he happened to work at their hospital. He'd won awards for the work that he'd carried out in neurological medicine, and families came from across the country to consult him.

'He's not here today. He's on Christmas vacation with his family.'

'Call him.'

'That's not in my remit, Dr Dolan.'

'Then, I'll call him myself!'

There was a sigh. 'Look, I'm sorry about your son being ill, but we all have to stick to what we do best for the efficient running of this hospital. I can't prioritise your son…'

'Well, I will!'

He slammed the phone back onto the wall, almost crushing it beneath his grip, and turned to look at Eva. She was pale and shocked.

What was he thinking? She needed him to be strong—not for him to turn into some angry monster. He'd lost his temper badly once before and look at how *that* had turned out.

'Sorry,' he mumbled. Then he went across to Seb's bed and took his son's other hand, held it to his cheek. 'Come on, champ…' He looked at Eva, determined not to cry.

Her eyes were large and swollen with tears. 'You said surgery?'

'They must have found something on the CT. Why has no one come to see us?'

He hated this. Hated this not knowing. This being left in limbo.

She shook her head and a solitary tear descended her cheek. 'Am I going to lose him? *Am* I? I don't think I could bear it, Jacob.'

'We're not going to lose him.' He squeezed his son's hand, hoping somehow that the force of his will would somehow make it so.

At that moment, the doors to Resus opened and Sarah came in, her face full of concern. She went straight over to Eva and Jacob. 'We've had a good look at the CT and the scan confirms that Seb has a small subdural haematoma. It's probably been bleeding for a while, as these injuries are usually slow leaks—as you know.'

'You think it's from that bus crash a couple of weeks ago? He banged his head then.'

'It's likely.'

Jacob frowned. 'The neurologist said he didn't need a scan. The *idiot*! He *missed* this!'

'We all missed it, Jacob.' Eva laid a hand on his arm.

Sarah looked to her friend. 'We'll be taking Seb in for surgery right away. Once we get in there we'll clip the leak and remove the haematoma. That should relieve the pressure on Seb's brain.'

'And he'll regain consciousness?'

'Hopefully.'

Hopefully...

Eva shrugged. 'What do we do whilst we wait?'

Sarah just looked at her. 'Try to remain calm. We'll look after him, Eva. You know we'll do our best.'

They could only hope the hospital's best was good enough.

* * *

Jacob stood up and began to pace the floor, glaring through the glass at people carrying on with their normal lives whilst his was in turmoil.

Of course they all had jobs to do. He knew that. But he couldn't understand how these other people could be so calm whilst he felt...

He could be losing his family here. His precious family! His *son*! His beloved son! The one he hadn't known he had—the one he'd only just got to know, to love, to cherish. He'd thought a few days before that the worst thing in the world would be to tell Eva the truth about what had happened in his past, but he'd been wrong. You had to tell people you loved them because you never knew when they might be taken from you.

This was what was terrible! This was the worst thing *ever*!

'I'm going to call my parents.'

Eva nodded. 'But they'll be upset. So far away, they won't be able to do anything.'

'They'll want to know.'

She acceded, and then turned back to look at the empty space where her son had been.

Eva had thought she was very familiar with the sensations of pain and grief and loss. She'd also thought she was familiar with waiting. Being patient. But she'd had no clue as to the real agony parents went through whilst they waited to hear if their child had made it through life-saving surgery.

She stared at the doors where the surgeons would emerge, praying, begging, pleading for them to open so that someone would come and tell her that Seb was fine. But the doors stubbornly remained closed. For hours.

When they did finally open—when the surgeon did finally emerge—she almost couldn't bear to hear his words, convinced it had all gone wrong.

The surgeon removed the mask from his face and smiled. 'The surgery went very well. No problems. Seb was stable all the way through. You'll have your little boy back with you in no time.'

Eva sagged with relief at the news. *Thank God!*

The staff in Paediatric ICU had done their best to make it *not* look like a department in a hospital. The walls were painted in a soft cornflower blue, bright and brash with cartoon characters from all kinds of series in a kind of cheery, animated Bayeux Tapestry.

The nurses all wore colourful tabards, with teddy bear name badges edged in tinsel, and there were Christmas trees galore, all surrounded with fake presents—empty boxes wrapped in colourful paper. From the ceilings hung paper chains and the children's snowflakes and snowmen, fat Santas and reindeer.

There was too much effort to make it look jolly.

Fake jolly.

To make the parents as well as the children forget that they were in such a terrible place.

Jacob felt as if he was in hell. The one day he'd hoped would pass without incident and it had turned into the day his nightmares about life came true.

This hurt. He ached. He felt powerless. As both a doctor *and* a father. Now he realised why family was so important. He wanted them here. He wanted their support.

He was glad he'd told Eva the truth.

He still didn't know her reaction. She'd not really

had a chance to say. She hadn't looked horrified…but then they'd heard about Seb. She hadn't had a chance to let it sink in.

She might not want anything to do with him. A man who could be so cruel to someone he'd supposedly loved…

If he'd treated Michelle right in the first place—respected her, not taken her for granted once that ring was on her finger—then his happiness now wouldn't be at such great risk!

Eva was the one who had given him Seb. Eva was the one who had cared for and looked after their little boy so well. And then he'd turned up on the day of Seb's accident, distracting her. They'd both been distracted. Both shocked by seeing the other. And they'd missed what had been happening to Seb.

Eva was going to be the one to choose what happened to them all now.

He stared at her, memorising her face. The soft arch of her eyebrows, the laughter lines at her eyes. The gentle slope of her tear-stained cheek. The deep lines across her brow.

'We still need to talk,' he said.

'I can't—not right now.'

He understood. This was the wrong time. She would probably want to wait until Seb was back with them both before she let him down gently.

Hopefully, she would still let him see Seb…

London at dusk was an ethereal place. The sky above was a strange watercolour mix of blue and pink. Purple undertones highlighted the clouds against the dark grey outlines of the buildings. Bright spots of Christmas lights shone out from various streets and windows, and the traffic on the myriad streets below made the place seem alive.

Jacob looked out across the skyline and unclenched his fists. Fear had caused all of this. Fear of losing a boy he'd only just come to love. Fear of losing something, *someone* so precious…

He was calmer now. More sensible now that he knew Seb was going to be okay.

Reaching into his jacket pocket, he pulled out his phone, scrolling through his contacts until he found the number he wanted. William Bilby. The UK's top paediatrician.

It rang a few times, then was answered, the sound fuzzy.

'Hello?'

'Bill? It's Jacob Dolan—'

'No need to say anything, Jacob. I'm on my way in right now. I'm about five minutes from the hospital.'

He was on his way in? But who'd told him about Seb?

'How did you know?'

'Rick told me. He gave me a call. But I've had to drive in from Surrey and the roads are hell.'

Rick. The beds manager. The man he'd yelled at. Jacob closed his eyes in thanks, knowing he would make sure he apologised to the poor man when he got the chance.

'Kids bounce back, Jacob. Much better than adults do.'

'I hope so.'

He rang off, staring out to the horizon. He knew he ought to go back. Knew he shouldn't have left Eva like that. Alone in that horrible empty room. But he'd had to get out. Had to get some fresh air. Be away from other people. The rooftop offered that solace he craved.

His phone bleeped to life.

How's Seb?

His mother had texted. He could only imagine their panic and pain. Could see in his mind's eye his mother's frantic scurrying to get in the car and head from Netherfield Village to London. A place she didn't really like. Today of all days. Leaving her home at Christmastime…

The cold fresh air had done its job, and the chill was now making him tremble and shiver.

And Bilby was coming in, too. He felt sure they could get all this sorted.

Seb had to be out of Recovery soon… Was he already back?

I ought to check. I ought to be there when they bring Seb back to us.

The fresh air had helped. The space. The crispness.

He headed back down.

As Seb was wheeled back into the room a new doctor arrived. Mr Bilby. Eva wasn't sure, but she thought this was the man that Jacob had asked for when he'd rung the beds manager. Whoever he was, he had a kind face with a wide smile, and he did his best to put Eva at her ease.

'I've read the report. The surgery was a great success. We've got Seb's back here—don't you worry.'

Good. He knew they were doing their best.

They all rushed over to Seb's side when his bed wheels had been locked into position.

Jacob grabbed his son's hand and kissed it, then

turned around, nodding an acknowledgement of Mr
Bilby. 'Bill.'

'Observations are good, Jacob. He should come round
soon.'

'Good.'

'Temp's normal. BP's normal. We've just got to wait
for the sedation to wear off.'

William Bilby slipped away and left them alone together. Silent beside their son's bed.

Jacob stared into space, his face shockingly white
against his dark hair, his once vibrant blue eyes pale
and cold.

Eva stood numb beside him as they both stared at
their son. Each of them praying in their own special way.

Early on Christmas Day Seb slowly woke up.

Eva woke instantly, as if by some sixth sense, and
heard Jacob say his son's name.

She leaped to her feet, blinking rapidly to get the
sleep from her eyes so she could see for herself the marvellous result of her son coming back to her.

'Seb? Sebastian? Oh, thank God! You're back!'

Seb blinked slowly, his eyes unfocused, but he gently
gripped his mother's fingers and then closed his eyes
again.

'He'll be tired. He might sleep more before he wakes
again,' Jacob observed.

Eva glanced at him. 'I'm scared to think that this
might end well. I've hoped that way before.'

'His observations are good. His intercranial pressure
is normal. We *can* hope, Eva.'

She stroked her son's fringe back from his face. 'You
wanted to talk earlier?'

He looked up at her and met her gaze, his heart palpitating in his chest. Of course. He'd promised himself—promised them all—that he would face this. Her judgement of his actions.

It was the only way he could set himself free. If she chose to walk, then so be it. He wouldn't blame her. But he *had* to know he would still have Seb! He couldn't lose him.

I don't want to lose her, either. I love her!

He swallowed and looked back at his sleeping son. He didn't want them to break up in front of their son. He believed that Seb might hear them. He wanted this to be private. He wanted the opportunity to talk to her without any chance of interruptions.

'I know where we can talk.'

Giving one final look of love at Seb, he led Eva outside and up onto the hospital roof.

CHAPTER NINE

Eva BEGAN TO SHIVER. And it wasn't just from the cold. 'What is it?'

'It's Michelle.'

Michelle. I knew it! He still carries a torch for her! He still loves her!

'What about her?'

She needed to hear him say it. If he still loved this woman from his past, then fine. She would walk away. She would do the decent thing. Because if the past twenty-four hours had taught her anything, it was that the most important thing in her life was Seb.

'It's *my* fault she's dead. *I* killed her, Eva.'

Eva looked at him, incredulous. 'No, you didn't!'

'Of course I did. Didn't you hear what I said? I didn't treat her right. I got complacent, got stupid. I should have seen what was going on! But I didn't. And because I didn't, I yelled at her. As if it was *her* fault! I upset her so much she couldn't see where she was going and she crashed.'

'I heard you, Jacob. It was terrible, I grant you— tragic—but you weren't to blame.'

He'd been expecting to hear her agree with him. To

start blaming him, too. But she didn't. The shock of hearing something else startled him.

'I wasn't?'

'*No!* She chose to have an affair, Jacob. She could have told you how she was feeling—but, no, she cheated on you with your best friend! And, whilst we're at it, *he* should have known better, too! No one forced her into her car that day. She was upset—she should never have driven. She has to take responsibility.'

'I feel so guilty…'

'Of course you do. You're human. *I'd* feel guilty. But don't forget everyone else on that day and how they must have felt.'

'What do you mean?'

'The driver of the heavy-goods vehicle. Do you think *he* felt guilty? Do you think the paramedics felt guilty because they couldn't revive her? The doctors in the hospital? We both work in A&E—you know how we feel when we lose someone.'

Jacob stared at her hard, his eyes glassy with held-back tears. 'I was so afraid of telling you… I thought I would lose you.'

Eva shivered slightly in the cold. 'What? You thought I'd say it was over? You think you're not worth staying for?'

'I've caused so much pain, Eva.'

'The only thing that will cause more will be if you tell me that you still love her!'

Jacob looked at her in shock. As if it was the last thing he'd be feeling. 'I don't love her.' He looked confused by her statement. 'I never loved her *enough*.'

What? What was he saying? Eva didn't understand.

'I don't understand. Are you in love with her or not?'

'No. I love *you*.' He looked down at the pitched felt rooftop. 'You deserved the truth from me. But if you want to walk away from me now you know it…I'll understand.'

'Walk away? Don't you *get* it, Jacob? I *need* you! I never thought I'd be able to say that about anyone. *Ever!* Apart from Seb…but he's part of me… I knew I loved you ages ago. But I felt I couldn't tell you because I thought you still loved Michelle and that hurt! As I stood by Seb's bed, watching the doctors work, watching them trying to fix him, I felt so alone! And I'm done with that feeling. I'm *done*! You and I… We're… We could have something really special. I knew it all those years ago, when we first met. There was something special between us then.'

'What are you saying, Eva?'

'I'm saying I want to be with you. Together. As a family.'

'But what happened to Michelle—'

'Was a tragic accident! Nothing more! I need you to let that go.'

Jacob sucked in a breath. 'Without you and Seb I'm nothing. I can't let *you* go.'

She stepped closer, pulling the warmth of him against her. 'You don't have to.'

'You mean it?' He hesitantly risked a smile.

'I mean it.'

She reached up on tiptoes and kissed him, and she forgot how cold she was, pressed against him. Feeling herself against him.

With him.

'I spent so long standing alone, Jacob. It was just easier for me, I thought, to push you away before you left of your own accord. I thought I was protecting myself. Protecting my heart from being crushed.'

'I'll never hurt your heart. I'll always cherish it. I'll always cherish *you*.'

She reached up and stroked his face, and as she did so snowflakes began to fall. A soft flurry of snow, sweeping in across the capital in the morning light.

They looked about them in wonder, and then back at each other.

'It's snowing! On Christmas Day! Seb will love this!'

Eva snuggled into his chest, feeling safe, feeling *home*.

'So we're going to do this? Together?'

She nodded. 'Together.'

They kissed.

As the snow fell all around them on the rooftop of the hospital, alone in their own special little world they kissed. Their cold noses pressed against the cheek of the other, and their hot breath warmed their mouths and lips as they proved their commitment to the other.

When they broke apart Jacob looked her in the eyes. 'I love you, Eva. From the moment we met I haven't been able to get you out of my head. You've always been there for me. Even in the dark times. Even when you didn't know it.'

Eva let out a big grin. He loved her!

'I love you, too, Jacob.'

'You do?'

She nodded, then shivered. 'But could we go back inside? I hate to be the one to spoil a romantic moment, but I'm freezing!'

Jacob wrapped his arm around her as they hurried back to the rooftop door. There was a bang in the stairwell as it closed behind them, and they ran down the steps, laughing and breathing heavily.

Back in Seb's room, they found he was still sleeping, so they sat beside each other, knowing Seb would get better, that this story would have a happy ending for all of them. And soon, hopefully, Seb would be out and about on his new bike.

Jacob raised her hand to his lips and kissed it.

When Seb woke again he would have the best Christmas present he could ever have wished for.

EPILOGUE

'I'D LIKE TO make a toast!'

Jacob stood in the lounge of his parents' home, in front of the vast fireplace. A small fire was crackling away, keeping them all warm and cosy despite the fresh snowfall outside.

A whole year had passed, and this Christmas Eve had thankfully arrived without incident.

Eva and Jacob had been married for three months. Their September wedding had gone without a hitch, despite his nerves about it being to the contrary, and this last year had been the happiest of their lives.

He raised his glass to his family, looking at all their happy, smiling faces. There were still one or two pieces of Christmas wrapping paper on the carpet that had been missed, but that didn't matter. Seb was sitting on the carpet, surrounded by a big pile of toys and wearing the paper hat from a Christmas cracker. Eva sat between his parents on the couch, feeling very full after his mother's most ambitious Christmas yet.

'I'd like to raise a toast to family,' he said, raising his glass once again before letting his gaze come to rest on Eva. 'Family is the heart of everything. You don't have to be blood relatives to be family. You just need to be surrounded by those you love and those who love you back. Love is the greatest thing we can give one other.'

Eva beamed at him and gave a little nod.

'But most of all I'd like to make a toast to my wife, Eva…'

His parents raised their glasses and looked towards her.

Eva felt excited. Nervous. She'd been dreaming about this moment for a long time. About telling them. Seeing how they reacted. Because this time she was going to share the experience. This time, she wouldn't be going through anything alone.

'And to the baby she's carrying.'

Molly almost dropped her glass. She gasped, her hand covering her mouth in genuine surprise and joy. 'You're *pregnant*?'

Eva nodded happily.

'You're pregnant! Oh, Eva!' Molly burst into tears and hugged her daughter-in-law, and Eva hugged her back.

This was what she'd wanted. For a long time.

Family.

To belong.

To be loved.

'To family!' she said.

They all raised their glasses, and they were just about to clink them together before taking a sip when Molly grinned and swiped Eva's champagne flute, swapping it for her own—non-alcoholic—orange juice.

'To *family*.'

* * * * *

MILLS & BOON®

MEDICAL ROMANCE™

THE ULTIMATE IN ROMANTIC MEDICAL DRAMA

A sneak peek at next month's titles...

In stores from 4th December 2015:

- **Playboy Doc's Mistletoe Kiss** – Tina Beckett *and*
  Her Doctor's Christmas Proposal – Louisa George

- **From Christmas to Forever?** – Marion Lennox *and*
  A Mummy to Make Christmas – Susanne Hampton

- **Miracle Under the Mistletoe** – Jennifer Taylor

- **His Christmas Bride-to-Be** – Abigail Gordon

Available at WHSmith, Tesco, Asda, Eason, Amazon and Apple

Just can't wait?
Buy our books online a month before they hit the shops!
visit www.millsandboon.co.uk

These books are also available in eBook format!

1115/03